DICKENS, EUROPE AND THE NEW WORLDS

Dickens, Europe and the New Worlds

Edited by

Anny Sadrin
Professor of English
Université de Bourgogne

Foreword by
John O. Jordan and Murray Baumgarten

First published in Great Britain 1999 by
MACMILLAN PRESS LTD
Houndmills, Basingstoke, Hampshire RG21 6XS and London
Companies and representatives throughout the world

A catalogue record for this book is available from the British Library.

ISBN 0–333–72248–5

 First published in the United States of America 1999 by
ST. MARTIN'S PRESS, INC.,
Scholarly and Reference Division,
175 Fifth Avenue, New York, N.Y. 10010

ISBN 0–312–21646–7

Library of Congress Cataloging-in-Publication Data
Dickens, Europe and the new worlds / edited by Anny Sadrin ; foreword
by John O. Jordan and Murray Baumgarten
p. cm.
Papers originally presented at a conference held in Dijon, France
in June 1996.
Includes bibliographical references and index.
ISBN 0–312–21646–7 (cloth)
1. Dickens, Charles, 1812–1870—Knowledge—Europe—Congresses.
2. Dickens, Charles, 1812–1870—Knowledge—America—Congresses.
3. Dickens, Charles, 1812–1870—Knowledge—Foreign countries–
–Congresses.   4. Dickens, Charles, 1812–1870—Knowledge and
learning—Congresses.   5. Dickens, Charles, 1812–1870—Influence–
–Congresses.   6. English fiction—European influences—Congresses.
7. English fiction—American influences—Congresses.   8. America—In
literature—Congresses.   9. Europe—In literature—Congresses.
I. Sadrin, Anny, 1935– .
PR4592.E85D53   1998
823'.8—dc21   98-28417
                                                                CIP

This book is printed on paper suitable for recycling and made from fully managed and
sustained forest sources.

10   9   8   7   6   5   4   3   2   1
08   07   06   05   04   03   02   01   00   99

Printed and bound in Great Britain by Antony Rowe Ltd, Chippenham, Wiltshire

Contents

v

The Colonies and Elsewhere

Part III Dickens and His World

Otherness

The Uncanny

Science

Foreword

The path by which some sixty or so Dickens scholars from all over the globe found their way to Burgundy in the summer of 1996 to discuss 'Dickens, Europe, and the "New Worlds"' leads, curiously enough, through the redwood forests of Northern California. It is a path first travelled by the eminent French Dickensian, Sylvère Monod, in the course of his 1984 visit to a Dickens gathering held on the campus of the University of California at Santa Cruz.

For the past sixteen years, Dickens has had a summer home in California. Since 1981, the University of California at Santa Cruz has hosted an annual conference on Dickens, organised by the Dickens Project, a research consortium composed of faculty and graduate students from the eight general campuses of the University of California and from other research universities in the United States and overseas. In keeping with its mission to promote and disseminate research findings about the life, times, writings and cultural impact of Charles Dickens, the Dickens Project regularly sponsors institutes and conferences for Dickensians from around the world. Professor Monod was among the first of many distinguished international participants to come to Santa Cruz in connection with these events.

As early as 1985, Dickens Project organisers Murray Baumgarten and John Jordan had begun considering the idea of a conference on 'Dickens and Europe'. The goal of such a conference, as they imagined it, would be twofold: first, to locate Dickens more securely in a European, as opposed to a merely British, literary and cultural context; and, second, to broaden the field of Dickens studies by bringing Anglo-Amerian Dickensians into contact with their European counterparts. To achieve these goals, they agreed, it would be important to hold the conference on the continent rather than in California or in Britain. Doing so would not only reinforce the idea of Dickens as a European writer, but would further the goal of decentring Anglo-American hegemony over Dickens studies.

Like many good ideas, the notion of a European Dickens conference was greeted with general enthusiasm, but little material support. It was not until Professor Anny Sadrin of the Université de Bourgogne took notice of it that the conference idea really began to take shape. In visits to Santa Cruz in 1991 and again in 1995, Professor Sadrin agreed to undertake the responsibility of organising and hosting the event. Drawing on the resources of the Dickens Project as well as on her many contacts with other European scholars, she began publicising the conference internationally. Word soon went out over the internet that Dickensians from all over the world would gather in Dijon in June 1996.

In developing the plan for this gathering, Professor Sadrin made a small but significant adjustment in the conference title. 'Dickens and Europe' became 'Dickens, Europe, and the "New Worlds"'. While preserving the original emphasis on Dickens in a European context, this new title opened the way for participants to consider Dickens in a global as well as a regional perspective. 'New worlds' – the term deliberately left unspecified – suggested not only other geographical locations (Australia, North America, the sea), but also new media (film, television, the internet) and new theoretical frames (feminist, postcolonial) in which Dickens might be seen.

The imaginativeness of Professor Sadrin's conference design was matched not only by her skill in securing funding for the event but by her perseverence in bringing it to completion. Working with little or no staff support, she put together a diverse and smoothly organised programme calculated to satisfy the appetites of both mind and body. For her warm and generous hospitality, the sixty delegates are deeply appreciative.

The new contexts provided by the assembled scholars in their papers and discussions offered a view of Dickens as a writer of consequence for world literature. What they accomplished was to underline Dickens's achievement in terms of Europe and those new worlds, at the same time that they showed how those interests were among the informing presences of Dickens's texts. This volume includes some of the most important of the talks delivered at the conference. In their power to illuminate all three of the terms in the conference title – Dickens, Europe, and the New Worlds – they reveal the value of rethinking even so classic a writer as Dickens.

MURRAY BAUMGARTEN and JOHN O. JORDAN

Preface and Acknowledgements

This book bears the title of a conference that was held in Dijon in June 1996. The conference was indeed a truly international event, where no fewer than 14 countries in Europe and the New Worlds were represented. Three retired luminaries, Philip Collins, Sylvère Monod and K.J. Fielding, gave plenary lectures, respectively on 'Dickens's Englishness', 'Translating Dickens into French' and a sceptical 'Dickens and Science?'; overall, more than 50 papers were read.

Charmian Hearne, Senior commissioning editor at Macmillan, who attended the conference, would have liked to publish the whole proceedings, as indeed I would. But a single volume could not hold them all, and the difficult task of making a selection among excellent papers had to be faced. Fortunately, we agreed on most points and I would like to thank Charmian for her generous cooperation. Murray Baumgarten and John O. Jordan rightly say in their Foreword that the volume includes 'some of the most important of the talks delivered at the conference', but I would like to put emphasis on their 'some'. 'Some' excellent papers were not selected simply because we wanted to give priority to representativeness. To give just one example, we had three good talks on Paris and only one was retained. But, for the benefit and pleasure of both Dickens fans and Dickens specialists (as well as for the appeasement of my guilty conscience), most of the unfairly excluded papers will appear in journals devoted to Dickens, namely *The Dickensian* and *Dickens Quarterly*, and other periodicals. Let me at least acknowledge them here by way of thanking the speakers: Murray Baumgarten (Santa Cruz), 'Moving Spirits: Faust, Scrooge and Film'; Nicola Bradbury (Reading), '"Watching with my eyes closed": The Dream Abroad'; Elizabeth M. Brennan (London), 'Curiosities of "Le Magasin d'Antiquités"'; Laurent Bury (Paris), 'London–Paris–Hollywood: A Tale of Three Cities'; Philip Collins (Leicester), 'Dickens's Englishness'; Clotilde De Stasio (Milano), 'Dickens and the "Invisible Towns" of Northern Italy'; Ekaterina Dianova (Moscow), 'Comparative Study of Images of Childhood in Dickens's Novels of the 1850–60s and Russian Prose'; Horst W. Drescher (Mainz), 'Dickens's Reputation in Germany:

Some Remarks on Early Translations of his Novels'; John Drew (Leon), 'Charles Dickens, Traducteur? A New Article in *All the Year Round*'; Joseph H. Gardner (Lexington), 'Captains courageous: Mark Twain and Dickens at Sea'; Robin Gilmour (Aberdeen), '*The Uncommercial Traveller* and the Later Dickens'; Michal Peled Ginsburg (Evanston), 'On Being Recalled to Life: Dickens and Balzac'; A. D. Hutter (Los Angeles), 'Traducing the Foreign: Dickens and *faux Amis*'; Rob Jacklosky (Riverdale), 'Dangerous Import: "Foreign Nationals" in Dickens'; Juliet John (Liverpool), 'A Tale of Two Authors: The Falseness of Dickens's French Fiends'; Leon Litvack (Belfast), 'Dickens, Australia and Magwitch'; Annegret Maack (Bergische), 'Creative Reception: Dickensian References in Recent Fiction'; Helena Michie (Houston), 'The "Young Person" and the Personification of Englishness: Podsnappery Abroad'; Sue Milner (Denton), 'Charles Dickens's Letters from the Continent and America'; David Parker (London), '*Pictures from Italy*: A Traveller's Coming of Age'; Laura Peters (Stoke-on-Trent), 'Dickens, Orphans and Colonial Discourse: The Perils of Mutiny'; Shale Preston (Sydney), 'The Alps in *David Copperfield*: A Site of Enlightenment or Male Hysteria?'; Andrew Sanders (Durham), 'Dickens and Paris: Novelty and Anomaly'; Michael Slater (London), 'Dickens and "John Bull"'; Grahame Smith (Stirling), 'Dickens and Paris: Idea and Reality'; Garrett Stewart (Fribourg), 'Dealing with *Dombey*'; Leona Toker (Jerusalem), 'Further Reflections on Martin Chuzzlewit's America'; Björn Tysdahl (Oslo), 'Paris is not the Other: On *A Tale of Two Cities*'; Max Véga-Ritter (Clermont-Ferrand), 'Violence and the World of "New Women" in *Bleak House*'; Ella Westland (Exeter), 'Dickens and the Sea'; George J. Worth (Lawrence), 'Three English Visitors to America in 1867: Stephen Buckland, Alexander Macmillan and Charles Dickens'.

There is little need to comment on the essays published in this volume or even to account for the selective criteria. The Contents should speak for itself. I would rather thank all the participants who, with their competence and enthusiasm, made the conference what it was. I am particularly grateful to Murray Baumgarten and John Jordan for their encouragement during the nine months of preparation; to Philip Collins who gave us one of his famous Dickens Readings with Mr Podsnap's 'foreign gentleman' as keynote; to David Parker, the well-known curator of the Dickens Museum in London, for setting up an exhibition in the Town Library and taking the risk of crossing the Channel with original editions, manuscripts, objects that had belonged to the Inimitable and iconographic items; to Horst W. Drescher for lending us early translations of Dickens into German; to Murray Baumgarten for sending translations into Danish and Hebrew; to Laurent Bury for showing us a little known (to use a euphemism) silent film directed by Charles Kent in 1911 on *A Tale of Two Cities*; to Michael Slater and Malcolm Andrews who gave a finishing note to the conference, replacing Barbara Hardy's closing lecture, which, to our disappointment, was cancelled at the last minute, by a wonderful performance, 'A Medley', as they called it.

It seems that my gratitude is not fully illustrated in this volume, an unfortunate paradox, for most of my best supporters are not among the chosen few. But this is for reasons that have nothing to do with quality, as I explained earlier, and because several of them felt reluctant or were too busy to revise their papers for publication.

This volume ought to be an incentive to further reading and to re-reading Dickens, as it illustrates so well the diversity of his work and of critical approaches. Contributors have explored many (often contradictory) aspects of Dickens, his Englishness as well as his fascination with otherness, new countries, new worlds, scientific discoveries of his age, narrative innovations. Some have drawn our attention to contemporary re-thinking of a great Victorian who was also a great precursor of Modernity, and the different approaches cohabit peacefully, fulfilling the wish expressed by Roger Sell in his talk, which I thought would be the best of conclusions.

ANNY SADRIN

Notes on the Contributors

Malcolm Andrews is Professor of Victorian and Visual Studies at the University of Kent at Canterbury. He is the author of *Dickens on England and the English* (Harvester Press, 1979), and *Dickens and the Grown-up Child* (University of Iowa Press, 1994) and is the editor of *The Dickensian*.

Matthias Bauer is a postdoctoral research fellow at the Westfälische Wilhelms-Universität Münster, where he is completing a study on *The Mystical Linguistics of Metaphysical Poetry*. He has published several articles on Dickens as well as *Das Leben als Geschichte: Poetische Reflexion in Dickens' 'David Copperfield'* (Cologne, Boehlau, 1991).

James Buzard is Associate Professor of Literature and holds the Class of 1956 Career Development Chair at MIT. Author of *The Beaten Track: European Tourism, Literature, and the Ways to 'Culture,' 1800–1918* (Oxford University Press, 1993), he is currently writing *Anywhere's Nowhere: Fictions of Autoethnography in the United Kingdom*. In 1997–98 he was a fellow at the National Humanities Center in Research, Triangle Park, NC, and coedited a special issue of *Victorian Studies* on 'Victorian Ethnographies'.

Brian Cheadle is Professor of English at the University of the Witwatersrand, Johannesburg. He has worked and published mainly in Renaissance studies, but he has recently concentrated on Dickens and has published two articles (on *Great Expectations* and *Bleak House*) in *Dickens Studies Annual*.

K. J. Fielding is a University of Edinburgh emeritus professor, has edited Dickens's *Speeches* (Oxford, Clarendon press, 1960) taken part in editing the Pilgrim *Letters*, and written a *Critical Introduction* (Longmans, Green and Co., 1958) and numerous articles about him.

Shu-Fang Lai has completed an M.Litt. thesis on Dickens in relation to science at Edinburgh, and is working on science articles in his periodicals for a PhD at the University of Glasgow.

Neil Forsyth is Professor of English at the University of Lausanne in Switzerland. He is the author of *The Old Enemy: Satan and the Combat Myth* (Princeton University Press, 1987), editor of *Reading Contexts* and currently edits *The European English Messenger*.

Lawrence Frank is Professor of English at the University of Oklahoma. He is the author of *Charles Dickens and the Romantic Self* (University of Nebraska Press, 1984) and of essays involving the response of Dickens, Arthur Conan Doyle and Edgar Allan Poe to nineteenth-century science. He is currently at work on a book-length study, '*Reconstructions: Science and Detection in Poe, Dickens and Doyle*'.

Jennifer Gribble is Associate Professor of English at the University of Sydney. Her publications include *The Lady of Shalott in the Victorian Novel* (Macmillan, 1983), *Christiana Stead* (Oxford University Press, 1993), and, forthcoming Penguin edition of George Eliot, *Scenes of Clerical Life*.

John C. Hawley, Associate Professor of English at Santa Clara University, is editor of six books including *Historicizing Christian Encounters with The Other* (Macmillan, 1998) and *Cross-Addressing* (SUNY, 1996). He has published in *Victorian Literature and Culture, Nineteenth-Century Prose, Victorian Periodicals Review*, and elsewhere.

Michael Hollington is Professor of English at the University of Toulon (France). His Dickens publications include *Dickens and the Grotesque* (Croom Helm, 1984), *Charles Dickens: Critical Assessments* (Helm Information, 1995) and *David Copperfield* (Didier Erudition, 1996).

John O. Jordan is Professor of English at the Santa Cruz campus of the University of California, where he directs the Dickens Project. He is co-editor, with Robert L. Patten, of *Literature in the Marketplace: Nineteenth-Century British Publishing and Reading Practices* (Cambridge, Cambridge University Press, 1995) and, with Carol T. Christ, of *Victorian Literature and the Victorian Visual Imagination* (University of California, California Press, 1995). In addition to studies of Dickens and Victorian fiction, he has published essays on South African literature and on Picasso.

Patrick J. McCarthy, emeritus professor at the University of California, Santa Barbara, is author of *Matthew Arnold and the Three Classes* (Columbia University Press, 1964) and of a wide variety of articles and reviews on Victorian poets, novelists and essayists, notably in *Victorian Studies, The Dickensian, The Dickens Quarterly, Dickens Studies Annual, SEL, University of Toronto Quarterly, Victoria*

Institute Journal. He is currently preparing a study of the language of Dickens.

Nancy Metz has published articles on Dickens and Trollope, and on the historical contexts of nineteenth-century fiction. The essay included in this volume incorporates research recently undertaken as part of the forthcoming Companion to *Martin Chuzzlewit* to be published by Helm.

Sylvère Monod taught at the universities of Caen and Paris. He retired from the Sorbonne Nouvelle in 1982. He published *Dickens romancier* (Hachette) in 1953 and *Dickens the Novelist* (University of Oklahoma Press in 1968), edited *Hard Times* and *Bleak House* with George Ford for Norton, and several other Dickens novels in his French translations for Classiques Garnier and Bibliothèque de la Pléïade. He is a past president of the Dickens Society and the Dickens Fellowship.

Patricia Plummer is lecturer in English at Mainz University. She has an MA in English literature and is currently working on her PhD dissertation. Her research interests and publications focus on contemporary women writers, feminist theory, postcolonial studies and Victorian literature.

Robert M. Polhemus is Howard H. and Jesse T. Watkins University Professor in English at Stanford. He is the author of *The Changing World of Anthony Trollope* (University of California Press, 1968), *Comic Faith: The Great Tradition from Austen to Joyce* (University of Chicago Press, 1980), *Erotic Faith: Being in Love from Jane Austen to D. H. Lawrence* (University of Chicago Press, 1990) and, most recently, an author and co-editor of *Critical Reconstruction: The Relationship of Fiction and Life* (Stanford University Press, 1994). Currently, he is at work on a book called *Lot's Daughters.*

Dominic Rainsford gained his PhD in 1994 at University College, London. He has taught at UCL, Imperial College of Science, Technology and Medicine, the University of Warsaw, Loyola University of Chicago and, most recently, the University of Wales, Aberystwyth. His publications include *Authorship, Ethics and the Reader: Blake, Dickens, Joyce* (Macmillan, 1997), and essays in *Contemporary European History*, the *Victorian Newsletter*, *English Language Notes* and *Imprimatur*. He is currently working on a book on the cultural history of the English Channel/*la Manche* since the French Revolution.

Tore Rem is a Junior Research Fellow in English literature at Christ Church, Oxford. He has a Cand. Philol. degree from the University of Oslo, Norway, and has recently completed his DPhil. thesis on parodic structures in Dickens's works. He has published articles on generic aspects of Dickens's novels and short fiction and on TV adaptation.

Anny Sadrin, emeritus professor at the University of Burgundy, is the author of several books on Dickens, including *Great Expectations* (Unwin Hyman, 1988), *Dickens ou le roman-théâtre* (PUF, 1992) and *Parentage and Inheritance in the Novels of Charles Dickens* (Cambridge University Press, 1994). She has published widely on Victorian subjects, notably the Brontës, Carroll, Darwin, Dickens, Eliot and Wells.

Victor Sage is a Reader in English Literature in the School of English and American Studies at the University of East Anglia. He is the author of several works of fiction and criticism and has edited collections of essays on nineteenth- and twentieth-century literature, the latest of which is *Modern Gothic: A Reader* (1996), ed. with Allan Lloyd-Smith. He is currently working on a study of Sheridan LeFanu.

Paul Schlicke, senior lecturer at the University of Aberdeen, is the author of *Dickens and Popular Entertainment* (Allen and Unwin, 1985, Unwin Hyman 1988) and of *The Old Curiosity Shop: An Annotated Bibliography* (Garland, 1988). He has edited *Hard Times* and *Nicholas Nickleby* for World's Classics and *The Old Curiosity Shop* for Everyman. He has compiled the Dickens entry for the 3rd edition of the *Cambridge Bibliography of English Literature* and is general editor of *The Oxford Companion to Dickens*.

Roger D. Sell is J.O.E. Donner Professor of English Language and Literature at Åbo Akademi University. He has led research projects on literary pragmatics, on the facts and fictions of women's life-experience, and on British studies. His recent publications include *Literary Pragmatics* (Routledge, 1991), *Great Expectations: A New Casebook* (Macmillan, 1994), *Literature and the New Interdisciplinarity: Poetics, Linguistics, History* (with Peter Verdonk) (Rodopi, 1994), and *Literature throughout Foreign Language Education: The Implications of Pragmatics* (Modern English Publications and the British Council, 1995). His *Towards a Mediating Criticism: Literary Pragmatics Humanized* is forthcoming. He is also working on two further volumes: *Beautics from History: Literary Criticism as Mediation* and *The Pleasures and Pains of Literature: the Modernist Emphasis Mediated.*

Ronald Thomas is Associate Professor and Chairman of the English Department at Trinity College in Hartford, Connecticut. He has also taught at Harvard University as a Mellon Faculty Fellow in the Humanities and at the University of Chicago. The author of *Dreams of Authority* (Cornell, 1990) and numerous articles on British novelists (including Dickens, Collins, Stevenson, Joyce and Beckett), Thomas is currently completing a book on nineteenth-century fiction and the rise of forensic science (Cambridge University Press).

Sara Thornton is Maître de Conférences at the University of Picardy. She has published articles and edited collections on Thackeray, Dickens, Wilkie Collins, Bram Stoker, the Gothic tale, on food and digestion, monetary systems and symbolic exchange. These are published by PUF, Macmillan (*Children in Culture*), *Editions du Temps*, *Ellipses*, *Cahiers Victoriens et Edouardiens*, *Tropismes*, and *Q/W/E/R/T/Y*. She is currently working on a book which will examine the metaphoric systems in the early and mid-Victorian novel.

Part I
Dickens and Europe

France
Italy

1
Crossing the Channel with Dickens

Dominic Rainsford

This essay seeks to mediate between two apparently conflicting elements in Dickens's writing: on the one hand, the more than physical sense of trauma and dislocation which Dickens associates with crossing the English Channel (as we British presumptuously call it), and, on the other, the feelings of comfort, normality and balance which tend to supervene as soon as he begins to write about actually being in France.

Dickens crossed the Channel many times. From letters, biographies and chronologies, I arrive at a figure of 60 crossings (30 return journeys), the first in 1837 and the last in 1868,[1] but there may well have been more: in particular, as Claire Tomalin suggests, Dickens may have made additional, furtive cross-Channel visits to Ellen Ternan (if indeed France is where she was) between 1862 and 1865.[2] So, crossing the Channel was clearly one of the most familiar and characteristic travel experiences of Dickens's life. Perhaps because of this familiarity, the crossing does not figure largely in the novels – not even in *A Tale of Two Cities* – but, together with the topography and culture of the ports and resorts of either shore, it keeps reappearing as a fruitful theme in the quasi-autobiographical, quasi-fictional space of Dickens's journalism, and as a colourful point of reference in his letters.

I have said that Dickens associates the crossing with a sense of trauma and dislocation. On the most obvious level, this is a matter of physical seasickness, based on his own experience. For instance, Dickens writes to his wife Catherine in February 1847, having just crossed the Channel north-westward, from Boulogne, 'I never knew anything like the sickness and misery of it. And besides that, I really was alarmed; the waves ran so very high, and the fast boat, going at that speed through the water, shipped such enormous volumes of it.'[3] This was a theme to which Dickens returned again and again in his public writings, too. Thus, 'Our

French Watering-Place', Dickens's 1854 study of Boulogne for *Household Words*, associates Channel-crossing definitively with seasickness in its first paragraph,[4] and, in 'Travelling Abroad', written six years later for *All the Year Round*, the Uncommercial Traveller's departure from Dover has become a dreary, inevitable pain:

> Early in the morning I was on the deck of the steam-packet, and we were aiming at the bar in the usual intolerable manner, and the bar was aiming at us in the usual intolerable manner, and the bar got by far the best of it, and we got by far the worst – all in the usual intolerable manner.[5]

As a rule, however, Dickens is very resourceful in turning this problem to artistic profit. After all, it is clear from any one of his novels that Dickens can do good things with states of disorientation, inconvenience and slightly humiliating stress, whether it be David Copperfield's drunkenness or the view from Todgers's Hotel in *Martin Chuzzlewit*, and the banality of seasickness proves to be no obstacle to imaginative embellishment.

Consider, for example, 'The Calais Night Mail', Dickens's last major Channel study, republished, like 'Travelling Abroad', as part of the *Uncommercial Traveller*, where the French port is a living, scheming enemy, and the traveller its plaything and dupe:

> Malignant Calais! Low-lying alligator, evading the eyesight and discouraging hope! Dodging flat streak, now on this bow, now on that, now anywhere, now everywhere, now nowhere! In vain Cape Grinez, coming frankly forth into the sea, exhorts the failing to be stout of heart and stomach: sneaking Calais, prone behind its bar, invites emetically to despair. Even when it can no longer quite conceal itself in its muddy dock, it has an evil way of falling off, has Calais, which is more hopeless than its invisibility. The pier is all but on the bowsprit, and you think you are there – roll, roar, wash! – Calais has retired miles inland, and Dover has burst out to look for it.[6]

But Dickens's Channel trauma goes far beyond this sort of exuberant queasiness; it is not just a physiological problem. In fact, it is often easy to read Dickens's studies of seasickness as metaphoric of a much deeper challenge to the traveller. Especially, perhaps, to the English traveller, who seems likely to find himself, during and just after a Dickensian Channel-crossing, at several kinds of disadvantage.[7] Thus, writing to

Forster in 1837, after his very first crossing, Dickens delivers a brief cautionary tale: that is, the 'gentleman' who accompanies Dickens and his party from the Hôtel Rignolle, and who 'waltzed with a very smart lady (just to show us, condescendingly, how it ought to be done)', has turned out to be nothing grander than the 'Boots'. 'Isn't this French?' Dickens observes (*L*, 1: 281) He is alluding to French egalitarianism, perhaps – the breaking down of social barriers – but there is also the suggestion that the French, like the alligator Calais, have a tendency to take advantage of their English visitors.

Ten years later, again writing to Forster, Dickens incarnates this English insecurity in what will prove to be an enduring *bête noire*, the Customs House at Boulogne. Though by this time, Dickens has chosen, in a significantly equivocal way, to express his sense of French opportunism in the French language. Thus, on leaving the Customs House, Forster is warned, 'Monsieur se trouve subitement entouré de tous les gamins, agents, commissionaires, porteurs, et polissons, en général, de Boulogne, qui s'élancent sur lui, en poussant des cris épouvantables' (*L*, 5: 5).[8] This lurching mass of the tourist industry seems a continuation by other means of the maritime turbulence of an actual Dickensian crossing.

It would be easy to see this as all rather trivial. Dickens gets seasick, and he finds French immigration, in those pre-European Union days, something of an ordeal. But there is more to it than that. In particular, it is important to relate Dickens's cross-Channel anxieties to the violent realities of European history at a time when the French Revolution was still well within living memory – in fact, Dickens makes such connections frequently himself. In a letter of 1853 to Frank Stone, for example, further serio-comic warnings about the Customs House include an explicit parallel with the Terror: 'you will then be passed out at a little door, like one of the ill-starred prisoners on the bloody September night [that is, 2 September 1792, first night of the massacre in the Prison of the Abbaye in Paris], into a yelling and shrieking crowd, cleaving the air with the names of the different hotels – exactly seven thousand, six hundred, and fiftyfour, in number' (*L*, 7: 100). And it seems appropriate to bear this allusion in mind when, in the following year's 'Our French Watering-Place', after the seasickness has subsided, the Customs House again asserts itself: 'the steamer no sooner touches the port, than all the passengers fall into captivity: being boarded by an overpowering force of Custom-house officers, and marched into a gloomy dungeon' (*RP*, 42).

But in order to see the full force of these associations, and to appreciate how intimately they are connected with the imaginative world of Dickens the novelist, we need to look at a complete essay, such as the best, I think, although the first, that Dickens wrote on the Channel-crossing theme. This is 'A Flight', which was published in *Household Words* in August 1851, and which describes a high-speed, disorienting but exhilarating journey by rail and sea from London to Paris.

Here, on the crossing itself, the routine nausea is explicitly linked to a shifting balance of advantage between the English and the French, where one nationality gains what the other loses in a regular economy of insecurity and self-possession:

> And now I find that all the French people on board begin to grow, and all the English people to shrink. The French are nearing home, and shaking off a disadvantage, whereas we are shaking it on. Zamiel is the same man, and Abd-el-Kader is the same man [these are the narrator's rather improbable names for two French fellow-voyagers], but each seems to come into possession of an indescribable confidence that departs from us – from Monied Interest, for instance, and from me.[9]

It is interesting that the British have become 'us' at this point. The narrator had previously distanced himself from 'Monied Interest', a Francophobic City gent, but now, faced with French competition, they are both, literally and metaphorically, all at sea, and in the same boat. The financial overtones of these troubling fluctuations in personal value suggest that Dickens would have been one of the first to see the point of that supposedly fair, emollient and unifying project – if it ever comes to pass – the common European currency.[10] But, as things stand, for Dickens, one mobile European's gain seems to be another's loss.

A quite different level of sliding disadvantage besets the narrator on the last leg of his journey, on the train from the coast to Paris, when he sees soldiers and fortifications from his window, and falls into a daydream in which the title of the essay, 'A Flight', takes on new connotations of persecution and attempted escape:

> I wonder where England is, and when I was there last – about two years ago, I should say. Flying in and out among these trenches and batteries, skimming the clattering drawbridges, looking down into the stagnant ditches, I become a prisoner of state, escaping. I am confined with a comrade in a fortress. . . . The time is come – a wild and stormy night. We are up the chimney, we are on the guard-house roof, we are

swimming in the murky ditch, when lo! 'Qui v'là?' a bugle, the alarm, a crash! What is it? Death? No, Amiens.

(*RP*, 125)

In other words, the train is coming to a station. There is the suggestion here that, even though he comes across as generally pro-French, the narrator is among the enemy. This is almost Charles Dickens as the returning Charles Darnay, in peril of his life, and one can see that *A Tale of Two Cities*, at the other end of the 1850s, will owe a lot to an established sense of English vulnerability *on approaching* French soil which had long attended Dickens's own travels.

Throughout 'A Flight' we find images of shifted significance or inversion, as though crossing the Channel were like going through a kind of prism or Lewis Carroll looking-glass: 'the grown-up people and the children seem to change places in France', we are told. 'In general, the boys and girls are little old men and women, and the men and women lively boys and girls' (*RP*, 125). Having reached Paris, the traveller describes 'the light and glitter of the houses turned as it were inside out' (*RP*, 127). But the rapidity of the journey in 'A Flight' leaves everything unsettled, for the narrator, in a way that is finally as liberating as it is disturbing:

> When can it have been that I left home? When was it that I paid 'through to Paris' at London Bridge, and discharged myself of all responsibility, except the preservation of a voucher ruled into three divisions, of which the first was snipped off at Folkestone, the second aboard the boat, and the third taken off at my journey's end? It seems to have been ages ago.
>
> (*RP*, 127)[11]

We have already encountered the narrator as fugitive from military/political imprisonment; now we have him as fugitive from 'all responsibility', and it is tempting to look forward not only to the mortal dangers of *A Tale of Two Cities*, but also to the illicit pleasure which may have been entailed, as I have already noted, in Dickens's flights to France in the early 1860s.

Yet another disquieting connotation of cross-Channel travel for Dickens, and another development, as I read it, of the seasickness theme, occurs in 'Travelling Abroad'. Here, having survived the 'usual intolerable' motion of the waves, the speaker seems compelled to seek its echo in a different form of nausea. 'Whenever I am at Paris,' he says, 'I am dragged by invisible force into the Morgue. I never want to go there, but am always pulled there' (*UT*, 76). As a result, he is haunted throughout his stay in Paris by 'the large dark man', a washed-up corpse who sounds like a shapeless incarnation of death in general. And this does not seem merely to be a coincidental linkage: 'The Calais Night Mail' is followed similarly, in *The Uncommercial Traveller*, by 'Some Recollections of Mortality', which describes another episode of eager Morgue-crawling.

So, the discomfort and moral disorientation of travelling to France are things that Dickens can be thought of as finding perversely congenial, as things that, despite their frightening aspects, are to be sought out and enjoyed: the cross-Channel turbulence, on whatever level, is intoxicating as well as sickening, a slightly masochistic kind of fun. The Dickensian cross-Channel traveller is someone who is amusingly not his usual self – at a disadvantage, but also, somehow enhanced. This is particularly so in 'The Calais Night Mail' where, in the middle of the rough sea, while other passengers wilt and suffer conspicuously, the narrator experiences 'a curious compulsion to occupy myself with the Irish melodies', particularly 'Rich and rare were the gems she wore' (*UT*, 196). This leads to a strange stream-of-consciousness passage which mingles the words of the song with the events on the boat, and concludes thus:

> Still, through all this, I must ask her (who *was* she, I wonder!) for the fiftieth time, and without ever stopping, Does she not fear to stray, So lone and lovely through this bleak way, And are Erin's sons so good or so cold, As not to be tempted by more fellow-creatures at the paddle-box or gold? Sir Knight I feel not the least alarm, No son of Erin will offer me harm, For though they love fellow-creature with umbrella down again and golden store, Sir Knight they what a tremendous one [wave, presumably] love honour and virtue more: For though they love Stewards with a bull's eye bright, they'll trouble you for your ticket, sir – rough passage to-night!
>
> (*UT*, 197)

This seems a type of cathartic *reductio ad absurdum* of Dickens's Channel anxiety, and it is followed by another sudden inversion (recalling those in 'A Flight'), which fits the speaker's turbulent state of mind, but which points, too, to a certain fairness and harmony underlying the old economy of shifting self-possession and national jurisdiction. Calais now looms ahead, and the narrator's allegiance suddenly changes. He now loves Calais. He had disparaged it vehemently, 'but I meant Dover' (*UT*, 199). And, indeed, in *A Tale of Two Cities*, Dickens does suggest, in a single paragraph, that Dover is madly sea-bombarded, 'piscatory', quite unsavoury and furtive, as it buries its head, ostrich-like, in the surrounding cliffs.[12] It is as though Dickens views the two sides of the Channel as rival factions to be played off against one another, or as rival deities, each of whom must be lauded and appeased, from time to time, but whose ingrained jealousy of one another must not be provoked too far.

This ongoing project of juggling and finding a balance between these two nations separated by the unbalanced Channel is epitomised by the pair of essays on English and French watering-places published in *Household Words* and later placed side by side in *Reprinted Pieces*. 'Our [English] Watering-Place', published in 1851, on the Channel resort of Broadstairs, makes it sound very quiet, provincial, a bit shabby. There is much about the worthy boatmen and their enormous, seemingly wooden trousers. The essay is written with a slightly wry affection throughout.

'Our French Watering-Place' is a good deal more lively. For example, the narrator is moved to utter a 226-word sentence on the Boulogne 'fisherwomen' – on their prettiness, the trimness of their figures and the smartness of their clothes (*RP*, 47). And then, the landlord who features in the piece, M. Loyal Devasseur (who is based on Dickens's actual Boulogne landlord, the benevolent M. Beaucourt-Mutuel), 'carries one of the gentlest hearts that beat in a nation teeming with gentle people' (*RP*, 51). It is as though Dickens is making an effort to persuade his Anglophone readership, who might take the congeniality of Broadstairs for granted, that Boulogne is at least equally safe, appealing, sunny and hospitable. And this extends to French socio-political ideals, as well. For example, Dickens describes summer fêtes in coastal villages, 'where the people – really *the people* – dance on the green turf in the open air' (*RP*, 53; Dickens's emphasis). He seems to be alluding to a national solidarity (as shown elsewhere in the essay by the popular willingness to provide lodgings for soldiers), which will be novel and surprising, it seems, to a British reader. He implies that some of the best ideals of the French Revolution have been realised. By contrast, the British themselves are represented, in 'Our French Watering Place', by the expatriate 'bores' of the Boulogne boarding houses: 'We have never overheard at street corners such lunatic scraps of political and social discussion as among these dear countrymen of ours' (*RP*, 54).

Moving away from the Channel itself, for a moment, but sticking with the theme of England and France held up as parallel entities which inform on one another in defiance of a topographical and cultural divide, it seems appropriate to mention 'A Monument of French Folly', published in *Household Words* in 1851. This is a comparative study of the English and French meat industries, written in support of a plan to relocate Smithfield Market. Here, Dickens inveighs against the gross un-French insanitariness of slaughterhouses in the heart of London:

> Into the imperfect sewers of this overgrown city, you shall have the immense mass of corruption, engendered by these [butchering] practices, lazily thrown out of sight, to rise, in poisonous gases, into your house at night, when your sleeping children will most readily absorb them, and to find its languid way, at last, into the river that you drink – but the French [and here he mimics Francophobes] are a frog-eating people who wear wooden shoes, and it's O the roast beef of England, my boy, the jolly old English roast beef.[13]

This sadly ineffective early warning of mad cow disease is followed by much praise of clean, well-supervised French abattoirs.

Such preoccupations seem morbid at first, but the case is not as straightforward as that. Dickens seems driven by a sense of public responsibility to examine the grimmest institutions, just as when he tours prisons and asylums in *American Notes*, but the feeling of duty, of need and pragmatism, seems enough to keep him clean. He is professional about it; this is his job, as much – and this gets close to my main point – when he is abroad as when he is in England.

Sometimes Dickens seems to go beyond drawing salutary parallels between England and France, and almost to wish that he was French. In February 1855 he writes to Forster indicating that he is disillusioned with a chaotic and out-of-touch British government, and with its handling of the Crimean War (*L*, 7: 523). A week later, Dickens goes to Paris, and he considers 'emigrating' for the summer to the Pyrenees (*L*, 7: 523). In May, the same year, he writes to another correspondent: '[W]e hope to come to Paris at the end of October, and to stay six months. I am living on that hope at present, or I should die of political discontent' (*L*, 7: 606).

But Dickens does not come to France, once he has escaped from the Customs House, as a pitiful refugee. On the contrary, he makes himself at home, and appropriates his surroundings artistically. Writing to Forster, in 1853, from the Château des Moulineaux, Dickens's grandest lodging in Boulogne, he says, '[t]he House is a doll's house of many rooms' (*L*, 7: 103) – a phrase which he repeats, more or less, in letters to H.K. Browne and Thomas Beard. Of the plan which is displayed in the hall of the Château, he says, 'there is guidance to every room in the house, as if it were a place on that stupendous scale that without such a clue you must infallibly lose your way, and perhaps perish of starvation between bedroom and bedroom' (*L*, 7: 104). There are clear parallels here with the eponymous mansion of *Bleak House*, which Dickens was completing at this time. The foreignness of the Château is no hindrance whatsoever to its silent assimilation into the world of an England-centred narrative – despite the mildly xenophobic stereotyping which seems to emerge from that narrative, sometimes, in the characterisation of Mlle Hortense. Had Hortense appeared in one of Dickens's essays, instead of in the more ethically unstable context of the novel, it seems likely that her treatment would have been more circumspect and diplomatic; Dickens might well have detected his own latent Francophobia, and suppressed it.

'Our French Watering-Place', perhaps the most balanced and diplomatic of these texts, ends with gentle mockery of things French as well as things British, and with a vision of *entente cordiale*:

> But, to us, it is not the least pleasant feature of our French watering-place that a long and constant fusion of the two great nations there has taught each to like the other, and to learn from the other, and to rise superior to the absurd prejudices that have lingered among the weak and ignorant in both countries equally.
>
> (*RP*, 54)

That said, the conclusion could seem a little patronising: 'Few just men, not immoderately bilious, could see them [the inhabitants of Boulogne and its environs] in their recreations without very much respecting the character that is so easily, so harmlessly, and so simply, pleased' (*RP*, 54). But compare this with the opening of David Copperfield's narrative, where he speaks of observant men (like himself) who 'retain a certain freshness, and gentleness, and a capacity of being pleased, which are . . . an inheritance they have preserved from their childhood'.[14] So the French – the *humble* French, anyway – seem to be Copperfieldian for Dickens: mild, harmless and simple in the best possible way, and eminently assimilable to his own system of values.

So, as I suggested at the start of this essay, there seems to be a certain conflict here. Getting to France, for Dickens, is extraordinarily traumatic, but being there is perfectly comfortable. It seems that Dickens plays up the Channel-crossing process, but this only goes to make France, once he gets there, surprising, familiar and unthreatening. Dickens seems to be an Englishman for whom France is not really very foreign – or, perhaps, for whom France is no more foreign than England. There is an anti-xenophobic, even-handed sense of being at ease with the world at work within these texts. Crossing the Channel is a standing joke, a farcical, unnecessary obstacle. By flagrantly exaggerating its significance, Dickens simply emphasises that he considers the societies on either side to be equally accessible to his imaginative powers, and equally fit objects for his social criticism and concern.

As I write, in December 1996, the English Channel – la Manche – as the prime site for contending English and French cultural values, economic needs and prejudices, is again very much in the news, as a result of the Eurotunnel fire and the French lorry drivers' blockade. These are crises which Dickens would have enjoyed commenting upon, and, perhaps, exaggerating. But it seems likely that he would also have taken the chance subtly to affirm, once again, the deeper parallels and shared principles of life from which this geographical rift spectacularly distracts us.

Notes

1. See, for example, Norman Page, *A Dickens Chronology* (Basingstoke: Macmillan, 1988).
2. Claire Tomalin, *The Invisible Woman: The Story of Nelly Ternan and Charles Dickens* (1990) rev. edn (Harmondsworth: Penguin, 1991).
3. *The Letters of Charles Dickens*, ed. Madeline House, Graham Storey et al., The Pilgrim Edition (Oxford: Clarendon, 1965–) 5: 30 (cited hereafter as *L*).
4. 'Our French Watering-Place', *Household Words*, 4 November 1854; *Reprinted Pieces*; Also 'The Lamplighter', 'To be Read at Dusk', and 'Sunday under Three Heads', The Fireside Dickens, 15 (London: Chapman & Hall, n.d.) 42 (cited hereafter as *RP*).
5. 'Travelling Abroad', *All the Year Round*, 7 April 1860; *The Uncommercial Traveller*, The Fireside Dickens, 21 (London: Chapman & Hall, n.d.) 74 (cited hereafter as *UT*).
6. 'The Calais Night Mail', *All the Year Round*; *UT*, 193.
7. As John M.L. Drew has recently remarked, the 'effects of motion on the mental processes, and the fundamental similarity between physical displacement or trajectory and wanderings or flights of the imagination, seem to be concepts underlying many of Dickens's sketches and essays about traveling and travelers';'Voyages Extraordinaires: Dickens's "travelling essays" and *The Uncommercial Traveller (Part One)*', *Dickens Quarterly*, 13 (1996) 76–96 (86–7). The cross-Channel disorientation which I discuss here should thus be seen as a sociopolitically significant special case of a much wider Dickensian problematic.

8.   'Monsieur immediately finds himself surrounded by all the urchins, agents, commissionaires, porters and rogues in general of Boulogne, who hurl themselves upon him, uttering terrifying cries' (my translation).

9.   'A Flight', *Household Words*, 4 November 1854; *RP*, 123.

10.   See, for example, Christopher Johnson, *In With the Euro, Out With the Pound: The Single Currency for Britain* (Harmondsworth: Penguin, 1996). 'Separate exchange rates increase the cost of foreign trade and investment. . .and disrupt trade and prices by unpredictable revaluations and devaluations' (193).

11.   The narrator's reverie here discloses Dickens's sympathetic knowledge of French literature: specifically, Alexandre Dumas, *Le Comte de Monte Cristo* (1844–5). See Andrew Sanders, *The Companion to 'A Tale of Two Cities,'* The Dickens Companions, 4 (London: Unwin, 1988) 155.

12.   *A Tale of Two Cities*, ed. George Woodcock (Harmondsworth: Penguin, 1990) 50–1.

13.   'A Monument of French Folly', *Household Words*, 8 March 1851; *RP*, 237. See also the recent reprint of this essay, with an informative headnote by Michael Slater, in *'The Amusements of the People' and Other Papers: Reports, Essays and Reviews 1834–51*, ed. Michael Slater, The Uniform Edition of Dickens' Journalism, 2 (London: Dent, 1996) 327–38. (The other essays which I discuss here will presumably appear in subsequent volumes of the Uniform Edition.)

14.   *David Copperfield*, ed. Nina Burgis, The Clarendon Dickens (Oxford: Clarendon, 1981) 11.

2

Why D.I.J.O.N.? Crossing Forbidden Boundaries in *Dombey and Son*

Anny Sadrin

Not long after I sent my correspondents the list of the papers that were to be given during the conference, my own title, 'Why D.I.J.O.N.?', because of those suspect full stops between each letter, was taken by some as a joke or a riddle. I had a few phone calls from friends who hazarded guesses, at least on the first letter: 'Of course, it is "D" for Dickens,' one said; 'Of course, it is "D" for Dombey,' asserted another. And, of course, 'D.I.J.O.N.', with this unusual spelling, does sound like a cryptic abbreviation, a message to be decoded. Yet I did not have the slightest intention to hide any formula of my own behind these signs. I was very ingenuously trying to answer a question raised in the novel.

Dombey and Son is, to my knowledge, the only text in Dickens where the name of this town occurs, and the name is indeed presented as something like a riddle when we first hear of it. The scene takes place in 'Good Mrs Brown's' lodgings in the presence of the old hag and her daughter, Alice Marwood, while, unknown to Rob the Grinder, who has been asked to spy on Carker and get to know the name of the hiding-place where 'the Manager' and Edith have planned to elope, Mr Dombey is listening and watching from the door, where he stands concealed in the dark. The name, a precious and remunerative piece of information, is not delivered outright, but through a slow process, a mixture of 'guess what' and ritualised revelation: each letter is 'laboriously' chalked on the table by the informer and repeated on Alice's lips. Then, once spelt out, the word is immediately 'obliterated'. The scene is worth quoting at some length, for, obviously, much emphasis is put on its surreptitious character:

> 'Rob! where did the lady and Master appoint to meet?'
> ... 'How should *I* know, Misses Brown?'

...'Come, lad! It's no use leading me to that and there leaving me. I want to know'....

Rob, after a discomfited pause, suddenly broke out with, 'How can I pronounce the names of foreign places, Mrs Brown? What an unreasonable woman you are!'

'But you have heard it said, Robby,' she retorted firmly, 'and you know what it sounded like. Come!'

'I never heard it said, Misses Brown,' returned the Grinder.

'Then,' retorted the old woman quickly, 'you have seen it written, and you can spell it.'

Rob, with a petulant exclamation between laughing and crying – for he was penetrated with some admiration of Mrs Brown's cunning, even through this persecution – after some fumbling in his waistcoat pocket, produced from it a little piece of chalk. The old woman's eyes sparkled when she saw it between his thumb and finger, and hastily clearing a space on the deal table, that he might write the word there, she once more made her signal with a shaking hand.

'Now I tell you beforehand what it is, Mrs Brown,' said Rob, 'it's no use asking me anything else. I won't answer anything else; I can't.'

(liii, 'Secret Intelligence', 830–1)[1]

Yet, Rob is soon persuaded to explain to the two ladies how he came to learn the word:

'Well then, the way was this. When a certain person left the lady with me, he put a piece of paper with a direction written on it in the lady's hand, saying it was in case she should forget. She wasn't afraid of forgetting, for she tore it up as soon as his back was turned, and when I put the carriage steps, I shook out one of the pieces – she sprinkled the rest out of the window... There was only one word on it, and that was this, if you must and will know. But remember! You're upon your oath, Misses Brown!'

Mrs Brown knew that, she said. Rob, having nothing more to say, began to chalk, slowly and laboriously, on the table.

'D,' the old woman read aloud, when he had formed the letter.

'Will you hold your tongue, Misses Brown?' he exclaimed, covering it with his hand, and turning impatiently upon her. 'I won't have it read out. Be quiet, will you!'

'Then write large, Rob,' she returned, repeating her secret signal; 'for my eyes are not good, even at print.'

Muttering to himself, and returning to his work with an ill will, Rob went on with the word. As he bent his head down, the person for whose information he so conscienciously laboured, moved from the door behind him to within a short stride of his shoulder, and looked eagerly towards the creeping track of his hand upon the table. At the same time, Alice, from the opposite chair, watched it narrowly as it shaped the letters, and repeated each one on her lips as he made it, without articulating it aloud. At the end of every letter her eyes and Mr Dombey's met, as if each of them sought to be confirmed by the other; and thus they both spelt D. I. J. O. N.

'There!' said the Grinder, moistening the palm of his hand hastily, to obliterate the word; and not content with smearing it out, rubbing and planing all trace of it away with his coat-sleeve, until the very colour of the chalk was gone from the table. 'Now, I hope you're contented, Misses Brown!'

(liii, 831–2)

The scene is indeed highly dramatised, but there is no need to dwell on the novelist's motivations for creating so much suspense here. The revelation of a secret by a wicked character, who earns his money by spying for the benefit of even more wicked ones, has always been part of his detection episodes. Any reader of Dickens knows that he liked these Gothic scenes of mystery, suspicion, threat, reward for ill-gotten information, and, conversely, Dickens, who liked to please his readers and had a fairly good knowledge of their tastes and expectations, knew only too well that a passage like this one would delight them.

More puzzling by far is the question: 'Why did Dickens choose Dijon, of all places, for the setting of his two elopers' *rendez-vous?*' It seems that he never visited the place. Even with the help of such useful documents as the detailed index of Edgar Johnson's biography, the indexes of the Pilgrim Letters (especially volumes 4 and 5 which cover the years 1844–7), or the various Dickens encyclopaedias, I have found no mention of Dijon outside the context of this particular novel. Had he merely driven through Dijon on his way to Lausanne or Genoa, Dickens would have 'made a note of' it in some letter to a friend, or in his note-books. Moreover, no detail in *Dombey* gives the slightest evidence of any personal knowledge of the place on the part of the author. We are only told that the cathedral's bells are heard ringing, which is what all bells are made for, but no precise description is offered either of that cathedral, whose patron saint, Saint-Bénigne, is not even mentioned, or of the town itself. Dickens's Dijon is a stereotype rather than a place that ever existed, and even 'The Golden Head', a common name for a hotel, is perfectly fictitious. There was no 'Hôtel de la Tête d'Or' in Dijon at the time; nor today either, most unfortunately, for, supposing there was one, I know for certain that all the conferees would have booked rooms there and dreamed dreams not to be disclosed at breakfast.

It goes without saying that the town chosen for a secret and unlawful appointment between a man and a woman had to be a French town. Adultery, as Mr Podsnap would tell you, is 'not English', but, quite notoriously, part of what Philip Collins calls 'French wickedness'. [2] Dijon, a town unconnected with the novelist's private life, had, moreover, the immense advantage that it would lead to no possible biographical gossip on the part of his readers – familiars or critics – even if at that stage of his life there was no Ellen Ternan.

As a cathedral town, middle-sized, placed almost in the centre of the French 'hexagone', as geography textbooks often call our country, it may well have been chosen as supposedly representative of nineteenth-century France, the sort of place where Balzac, the realist, would set his sordid scenes of provincial life.

Yet, what happens in *Dombey and Son* is poles apart from what Balzac would have made of a similar situation. The melodramatic scene in the hotel suite booked by Carker even spectacularly excludes licentiousness:

> He was coming gaily towards her, when, in an instant, she caught the knife up from the table, and started one pace back.
> 'Stand still!' she said, 'or I shall murder you!'
> The sudden change in her, the towering fury and intense abhorrence sparkling in her eyes and lighting up her brow, made him stop as if a fire had stopped him.
>
> (liv, 854)

Edith then goes on expatiating on her hatred of all men, she, 'a woman' who 'from childhood has been shamed and steeled', 'offered and rejected, put up and appraised' (liv, 856), 'hawk[ed] . . . up and down', suffering herself 'to be sold, as infamously as any woman with a halter round her neck is sold on any market-place' (liv, 857). Shamed by her husband and by his manager who courted her like a woman of easy virtue, she closes her long plea for the rights of women by saying: 'my anger rose almost to distraction against both. I do not know against which it rose higher – the master or the man!' (liv, 857).

Aptly interrupted by Dombey's arrival, the episode ends up with a re-crossing of forbidden boundaries by the two 'fugitives'. But neither is the same on reaching British shores. It is a guilt-ridden Carker whom we accompany on his way back home, it is a chastened Edith whom we smeet again after her unhappy visit to the land of depravity, and both will pay dearly for their elopement abroad. But they will pay dearly for intentions rather than for deeds, for harbouring feelings of revenge rather than for lust or lasciviousness.

Edith, anyway, never intended to commit adultery. Her frigidity, her repugnance for men in general and for the sharp-toothed, cat-like womanizer in particular have been made clear throughout.[3] All she wanted was to pretend having an illicit liaison with the manager of the Dombey Firm in order to put her husband to shame and, had it not been for Florence's unexpected visit to the old London house, she would have died pretending: 'There is nothing else in all the world . . . that would have wrung denial from me. No love, no hatred, no hope, no threat. I said that I would die, and make no sign. I could have done so, and I would, if we had never met', she tells Florence, beseeching forgiveness for the 'stain upon [her] name'. Meanwhile, both judge and judged at her self-appointed trial, she pleads guilty, yet not guilty, 'Guilty of much! . . . Guilty of a blind and passionate resentment, of which I do not, cannot, will not, even now, repent; but not guilty with that dead man. Before God!' (lxi, 965). But this confidential revelation of her innocence is unlikely to disperse the whiff of scandal that surrounds her and makes her presence in London undesirable. By chosing to expatriate her at the end of the novel, Dickens cleverly manages to protect her reputation and to remove sinful shadows from the Dombeys' surroundings, achieving an interesting compromise between censure and absolution. Her retreat to Italy is unquestionably a golden exile compared to Martha's or Little Em'ly's (not to mention Alice Marwood's), but it nonetheless contaminates her through associations and gives her the status of a fallen woman.

As for Carker, it is undeniable that he had eloped to France with other expectations, never suspecting that the night in Dijon would take such a turn. When Edith turns him down, he is sexually frustrated and his male pride is deeply wounded. But, during his flight, his state of mind changes significantly. Even if a 'lurking rage against the woman who had so entrapped him' still suggests 'misshapen schemes of retaliation', his thoughts run mainly on the days that preceded her intrusion into his own and Dombey's life:

> Then, the old days before the second marriage rose up in his remembrance. He thought how jealous he had been of the boy, how

jealous he had been of the girl, how artfully he had kept intruders at a distance, and drawn a circle round his dupe that none but himself should cross.

(lv, 866)

His mind is henceforth obsessed by his pursuer, not his rival in love so much as the master who always trusted him, the father figure whose 'will [was] law' (xlii, 684) and whom he both wished to annihilate and to emulate.[4] Ashamed of himself and consumed by remorse, he is anticipating the judgement of the man 'whose confidence he had outraged, and whom he had so treacherously deceived' (liv, 862), so that when their eyes meet he knows he is facing a well-deserved sentence to death. The red-eyed engine is a mere executioner, the instrument in fact of self-inflicted moral retribution. Back in Victorian England, the world of morality asserts its own rights again.

A simultaneous and, to my mind, more interesting, recrossing of forbidden boundaries is the author's.

Dickens was obviously tempted to deal with the question of adultery. He had indirectly approached the subject as early as *Oliver Twist*, through the illegitimate birth of his hero, and he was to touch upon it again, though in a more subtle way, in his next novel, *David Copperfield*, with Dr Strong's young wife's infatuation with her cousin, as well as David's almost incestuous marriage with Dora, the 'child-wife', who reminds us of his child-mother. The suspicious behaviour of Fanny Dorrit once married to Sparkler, the dubious Lammles, the numerous innuendoes about prostitution or marital infidelity are present throughout the later novels. But Dickens never made adultery the central subject of his plots. The consequences of illegitimate sexual relationships are a constant reminder of his obsession, but no scene that would bring 'a blush on the cheek of the young person' was ever described in his works. My contention is that Dijon is the place where such a scene was on the verge of occurring: the décor in the hotel suite with its 'show of state' (liv, 850), too much gilt, too much paint, too much 'crimson drapery', too many festoons, mirrors, candelabras and glittering candles, too many backdoors, the overdone obsequiousness of the man in waiting, the way he speaks of 'Monsieur', knowing full well that 'Monsieur' is not 'Madame''s husband, are all the ingredients needed for a scene *à la* Balzac. We sense the novelist's relish in creating the atmosphere of scandal and debauchery, indulging in false suspense, trying his hand at a new form of writing.

There is even a brief moment when, in place of an erotic scene, we think we are moving on to the sensationalism of a pulp novel. Infuriated and humiliated by Edith's blunt rejection of his sexual overtures, Carker is on the brink of acting with violence and showing his male superiority:

> He would have sold his soul to root her, in her beauty, to the floor, and made her arms drop at her sides, and have her at his mercy.
>
> (liv, 860)

Will he stab the '[s]trumpet' as Sikes stabbed Nancy? Is he considering murder? Is he not rather contemplating rape? The evocation of the passive female body pinned down to the floor at the mercy of the roused male would seem to suggest no less. Edith has indeed a narrow escape since only her visible determination and insubordination – or so we are told – deter the aggressor and prevent the worst: 'But he could not look at her, and not be afraid of her. He saw a strength within her that was resistless', the narrator says by way of explanation.

But my conviction is that, in any final analysis, Dickens knew where to draw the line between his latent desires as a man and his responsibility as the most famous English novelist of his age: he could toy with perversion, yet remain the innocent harlequin who plays tricks on his audience the better to extol virtue. Or, to put it differently, we might say that Carker's attraction and contempt for a fine woman reflect Dickens's love of the fair sex and male chauvinism, whereas the manager's contrition betrays the novelist's shame for almost transgressing his and his country's ethical (and, therefore, aesthetic) standards.

Dijon, I would claim, happened to be the place in his imagination where Dickens fully realised that his reading public would never forgive him what they were ready to accept from a Thackeray, and where he decided never to be the English Balzac.

Notes

1. All references are to the Penguin edition (Harmondsworth, 1970).
2. This was the title of the humorous paper he gave at a conference held at Boulogne-sur-Mer in 1978, published in *Charles Dickens et la France*, ed. Sylvère Monod (Presses Universitaires de Lille, 1978) pp. 35–46.
3. There is indeed a truly proleptic passage in Chapter 45, 'The Trusty Agent': 'Proud, erect, and dignified, as she stood confronting him; and looking through him as she did, with her bright flashing eye; and smiling, as she was, with scorn and bitterness; she sunk as if the

ground had dropped beneath her, and in an instant would have fallen on the floor, but that he caught her in his arms. As instantaneously she threw him off, the moment that he touched her, and, drawing back, confronted him again, immoveable, with her hand stretched out.

"Please to leave me. Say no more to-night"' (xlv, 720).
4. On Carker and Dombey, see Anny Sadrin, *Parentage and Inheritance* (Cambridge University Press, 1994), pp. 60–2.

3

Dickens, *Household Words* and the Paris Boulevards

Michael Hollington

GUSTAVE

'October 4, 185-. No. 9. A male child; newly born; weakly and very small; ticket round the neck with the name of Gustave; coarse linen; red stain on the left shoulder; no other mark.' This is how Dudley Costello, at the end of his impressive *Household Words* article 'Blank Babies in Paris' (*HW*, VIII, 379–82; 17 December 1853), translates the registry entry for a new arrival at the Foundling Hospital in Paris in the Rue d'Enfer. Costello, responding to Dickens's editorial policy of 'dwelling on the romantic side of familiar things', is able to wring metaphor and symbol from his subject. He starts by interrogating the etymology of that street name: it comes from Via Inferior, but 'a poetical imagination soon made the corruption' that ensures that infant orphans in Paris are brought up in the street of hell. The building on that street may be strikingly plain and anonymous ('it lay before us, grey, blank, and dreary, with nothing to relieve the monotony of its general aspect ...'), but the writer is able to imagine its very absence of significant features as pregnant with significance, for it is a place 'where no witness might see the trembling mother deposit her new-born child.'

Dickens himself, in one of the numerous writings in which orphans play a central role, would later describe a similar psychological moment in his story *No Thoroughfare* (written in collaboration with Wilkie Collins), where a mother passes through the streets of London on her way to Coram Street to deposit her illegitimate child:

> As above her there is the purity of the moonlit sky, and below her there are the defilements of the pavement, so may she, haply, be

22

divided in her mind between two vistas of reflection or experience. As her footprints crossing and recrossing one another have made a labyrinth in the mire, so may her track in life have involved itself in an intricate and unravellable tangle.

(*CS*, 539–40)

Here, in what is unambiguously an imaginative piece of writing, the allegorical tendencies latent in Costello's article come to the fore. In two sentences, the city is imagined as a systematically organised totality of zones of contrasting significance. The first sentence proposes a vertical axis in which high signifies transcendental beauty and purity, and low symbolises physical and moral ugliness and dirt. The second considers the city from a horizontal perspective, and treats the labyrinthine patterns of her hesitant journey through mazy streets to the Foundling Hospital (she is Dick Swiveller in a tragic mode) as an emblem of the complex uncertainty of human destiny.

This essay aims to investigate some aspects of Dickens's critical responses to Paris in the 1850s – that is to say, to the city under Haussmann and Louis Napoleon, in the throes of a painful transition towards *modernity* – as well as those of the writers who worked for him on *Household Words*. But as it does this, it will also examine the important role played by allegory in the articulation of these reactions. We shall be concerned to try to develop some outlines of a Dickensian poetics of the city that has much in common, particularly in its emphasis upon allegory and transcendence, with that of his contemporary Charles Baudelaire. It emphasises visual features of the city, and imagines vertical categories, like high and low, or horizontal ones, like straight and crooked, from the standpoint of an observer who looks up and down and round and about at the sights before him. All the writings we shall examine construct this observer through the imaginary figure of the *flâneur*, who represents a kind of city dilettante of the eye, casually strolling in search of visual experience from which he will remain essentially detached. Paris is essentially imagined as a spectacle which first fixes the observer's gaze, and then lures him on (for the *flâneur* is quintessentially male, and the city regularly female) to pursue and pin down its significance.

SPECTACLE

As tourists on the Champs Elysées in 1855, the Dickens family had front row seats for that spectacle. They may have been responding unconsciously to the new accents of modern consumption in Paris at that time, the drive towards the provision of that accessibility to the eye of everything in the field of vision at one single glance which Benjamin analyses in contemporary panoramas, or in contemporary Parisian department stores, where for the first time ticketed commodities (like Gustave in the Foundling Hospital) were presented simultaneously in broad and unencumbered space for the orgiastic delectation of the consumer's eye.

'All of Europe went to Paris to see the goods on display,' wrote Hippolyte Taine in 1855 (Benjamin, 50). The variety and extent and uninterrupted continuity of the sights to be seen from 49 Champs Elysées provided a veritable 'Parisian Nights Entertainments,' to quote the title of an article by Sala that appeared in *The Train* on 1 January 1856, and is mentioned by Dickens in a letter to Wills of 10 January 1856 (*Letters*, VIII, 20). It is Sala, too, again in 'Dr. Véron's Time', who makes the connection in *Household Words* between such feasts for the eye and the exotic comestibles on display at the Palais Royal to the *flâneur*, who might gaze longingly but not partake, i.e. 'train up his appetite in the way it should go by gazing at glowing panoramas of rare eatables and drinkables displayed in the larders of the great Restaurants, and in the window of the immortal Chevet' (*HW*, XIII, 335; 19 April 1856). As Kracauer suggests, the boulevards offered a kind of drug experience – literally so, perhaps, for invalid opium consumers like Wilkie Collins who in 'Laid up in Two Lodgings' comments on the 'everlasting gaiety and bustle of the Champs Elysées' with its 'confused phantasmagoria of gay colours and rushing forms' (*HW*, XIII, 481–6; 7 June 1856).

Dickens's attitude towards the Parisian spectacle can be seen as ambivalent, or even contradictory. Of course, he revelled in 'the view without, astounding . . . the wonderful life perpetually flowing up and down.' (*Letters*, VII, 724; to W.H. Wills, 21 October 1855). But in his psyche there were sensitivities about what it was like to be, not the voluntary observer, but the involuntarily observed. These might be said to centre on the (for him) negative word 'Exhibition', and a complex of emotions perhaps stemming from having felt himself as a boy to be an exhibit in a display case as he labelled blacking-bottles at a window – it was the reason his father removed him from that employment. He boycotted the Great Exhibition at the Crystal Palace in 1851, encased as it was in see-through glass, and did not want to go to that in Paris in 1855, writing in May that year that he had 'not the faintest idea of adding his personality to the French Exhibition, after flying one hundred miles from the English' (*Letters*, VII, 606; to Lady Olliffe, 3 May 1855). For him it was a splendid thing to look out of windows, but his attitude to being looked at was more complex.

But in the end, Dickens did attend the art section of the Paris exhibition, where he was impressed by what he saw of contemporary French art, and about which he writes interestingly in his *Household Words* piece 'Insularities' (*HW*, XIII, 14; 19 January 1856). One may read in the discriminations he makes here and in the related letter to Forster (*Letters*, VII, 742–4; ?11–12 November 1855) between 'the dramatic' and 'the theatrical' a clue to his responses to Parisian street life. On the one hand, he dismisses formal spectacle, as he finds it in English painting at the exhibition, even that of his friend Clarkson Stanfield – 'too much like a set-scene' (*Letters*, VII, 743). He is equally harsh, in Paris, on formal parades outdoors (such as those organised for political purposes during the Crimean War by Louis Napoleon) and classical theatre indoors. What he admires at the exhibition are narrative genre scenes, capturing spontaneous fleeting moments of contemporary life and manners, and it is worth remembering that, in Loyrette's words, 'the success of the genre scene, which set in with the *Exposition Universelle* of 1855, played an important role in the ever more frequent adoption of subjects drawn from modern life' (Loyrette, 270). In his article Dickens notes the insularity of the English who dismiss French painting as 'theatrical,' to which he retorts:

> Conceiving the difference between a dramatic picture and a theatrical picture, to be, that in the former case a story is strikingly told, without apparent consciousness of a spectator, and that in the latter case the groups are obtrusively conscious of a spectator, and are obviously dressed up, and doing (or not doing) certain things with an eye to the spectator, and not for the sake of the story; we sought in vain for this defect.
>
> (*HW*, XIII, 2)

French painting is dramatic, and therefore true, because French and other continental European styles of self-expression are dramatic: as Forster puts it, summarising Dickens's views, 'the French themselves are a demonstrative and gesticulating people . . . and what thus is rendered by their artists is the truth through an immense part of the world' (*Letters*, VII, 743). The *flâneur*/writer's delight in Parisian spectacle could certainly be justified if it focused on its 'dramatic' qualities rather than its 'theatrical' ones.

CARNIVAL AND SEXUAL DISPLAY

As Monte Carlo would also discover later in the century, gambling and
prostitution go together. Zola remarks of Paris at this time in *La Curée* that
'the city was nothing but a great debauch of millions and of women'
(Marchand, 86) and Sala mentions more obliquely, in 'Dr. Véron's Time'
in *Household Words*, a certain gaming house in the Rue du Temple with
the name 'Maison Paphos'. The journal could and did write discreetly
about prostitution and casual sex in Paris without having to make any
direct reference to them simply by using French code words such as
lorette and *grisette* (the *lorettes* got their innocuous-sounding name because
they first walked the streets in the vicinity of Notre-Dame-de-Lorette).
Thus Blanchard's 'A Ball at The Barriers' urges 'the student of character'
(necessarily male, of course) to 'betake himself . . . to the haunts of the
"common people"' such as one of the *bals* at the Barrière du
Montparnasse without having to mention what went on there.
(Marchand comments: 'the "Venuses of the barrières" ruled there,
mingled amongst the families of workers and artisans' [Marchand, 23]).

Dickens's quite complex attitudes to prostitution in Paris again centre
on the question of public display. 'In a great City, Prostitution *will be
somewhere*' is the principle announced in a letter first published in Volume
VII of the Pilgrim House edition in 1993 (691; to Lord Lyttelton, 16
August 1855). That somewhere should not be as public as the theatre, he
says – as had been the case in London in theatres such as the Theatre
Royal, Haymarket, before 1843. Paris offers a better model – in February
he had seen prostitutes at the theatre, but 'they were of the Audience, and
conducted themselves like the rest of the Audience, and nobody was
obliged to know the truth.' Fortunately, in London too, a 'Dancing
Establishment' (the National Argyll Rooms) had come into existence after
the banning of prostitutes from the Theatre Royal, and, according to
Dickens, 'the Police has shewn a sound discretion in not interfering with
it.'

Thus Dickens seems to have been in favour of the principle of the
Parisian *bals* and *maisons closes* and the whole effort of Haussmann and
Louis Napoleon to drive prostitution indoors: 'The great wedges driven
by Haussmann opened up Paris, lit up the public ways, provided greater
security and moralised the street pavements' (Marchand, 208). There
were nearly 300 brothels during the Second Empire, many of them
lavishly appointed, as prostitutes became luxury commodities like
perfumes or expensive items of fashion. Dickens appears to have known
a few of these establishments on the inside. He writes to Spencer

Lyttelton about his disappointment that 'the model (and moral) establishment *is* suppressed – the big number taken down – a dull honest trade driving under the gateway – a melancholy respectability has fallen on that fascinating mansion. I shed a tear, over the way, every Sunday' (*Letters*, VII, 738; 8 November 1855). The Pilgrim House editors footnote it a little timidly: 'given Lyttelton's scapegrace reputation, perhaps a brothel'. I think we can be a little more definite than that, particularly if we take into account the letter to Collins of 22 April 1856:

> On Saturday night, I paid three francs at the door of that place where we saw the wrestling, and went in, at 11 o-Clock, to a Ball. Much the same as our own National Argyll Rooms. Some pretty faces, but all of two classes – wicked and coldly calculating, or haggard, and wretched in their worn beauty. Among the latter, was a woman of thirty or so, in an Indian shawl, who never stirred from a seat in a corner at the time I was there. Handsome, regardless, brooding, and yet with some nobler qualities in her forehead. I mean to walk about tonight, and look for her. I didn't speak to her there, but I have a fancy I should like to know more about her. Never shall, I suppose.
>
> (*Letters*, VIII, 96)

This is fascinating material. Even if Dickens thought he was simply on a busman's holiday from his philanthropic activities on behalf of Miss Coutts for Urania Cottage, there is Schlör's comment on the prostitute-reformers of the nineteenth century to take into account: 'it may very well be that these missionaries experienced erotic pleasure – repressed, denied, dismissed – during their activities' (Schlör, 250). In his apparent Morgue-watching (we might compare Baudelaire's reply to a friend who asked him what he was up to as he scrutinised the girls at the Casino: 'my dear friend, I'm watching death-heads pass by!' [Pichois and Avice 116]), he singles out a face he intends to stalk a second night – this time outdoors.

The allegorising of space here is full of nuance. As Schlör remarks, the driving of prostitution indoors was part of the politics of the Second Empire, designed to establish greater control over the 'dangerous' outdoors, parallel to the bulldozing of paved streets which might provide materials for the erection of barricades. Dickens approves of it, yet he seems to want to meet this exceptional person alone, outdoors, in the 'masculine' world of thse street where after dark men might hunt, master and 'penetrate' the female night (Schlör, 166–8). On these visits to Paris, it might seem that all the ambiguities of Dickens's sympathy for victims on display came to the fore.

As well as the spatial resonances of these excursions, we may also investigate their temporal peculiarities. As Ashford White remarks, 'The winter visit, with evenings at the leading theatres, [became] almost a habit with the novelist.' In Paris winter meant an increasing fear of crime (Chevalier notes that 'it attains its greatest intensity in certain winters of misery and cold' [Chevalier, 35]), but it also meant Carnival, a time outside time, transcending the everyday horrors of mud and snow.

Dickens was in Paris three times during the 1850s in the Carnival season, in 1851, 1855 and 1856. On the first two occasions he was accompanied by rather *louche* companions: Spencer Lyttelton in 1851, and Wilkie Collins in 1855. Concerning the latter visit he announces his intentions with 'facetious' explicitness: 'I want it to be pleasant and gay, and to throw myself en garçon on the festive diableries de Paris!' (*Letters*, VII, 523; 3 February 1855).

But however 'diabolical' these bachelor activities may have been, the real point about them is that they took place once more under the constraints of the new régime. In the time of Louis-Philippe Carnival was an open-air occasion. Kracauer writes of the popularity of 'Milord l'Arsouille', a masked figure who dispensed largesse generously amongst the crowds on the boulevards (Kracauer, 35–41). But as he had done with prostitution so he did with carnival – the showman Louis Napoleon took it indoors. Jerrold's 'Paris with a mask on' is the appropriate *Household Words* reference (19 April 1854; *HW*, IX, 245–8): its *flâneur*-narrator is forced 'to confess a decided disappointment' as he looks for masks on the boulevards, and doesn't find any. But finally he tracks them down to their new lair:

> The fun of the old carnival, however, has now retired from the open streets. The police still annually issue stringent regulations, prohibiting all manner of indecorum, and restraining the old humourists who used to throw their yearly bag of flour from their window upon the crowd below. Men will not mask in the streets with the police at their heels; but give them free way in a dancing hall, and it soon becomes obvious that the old spirit of masked revelry exists still in great vigour.

Thus carnival in 1855 was celebrated, not by men only, as it might seem from this account, in the *bals* where *lorettes* and *grisettes* and *vénus de barrières* were to be found in abundance. There Dickens, if not Collins, might find himself once again caught up in contradictions that the Paris of the 1850s fostered.

MUD

Dickens spent the next winter in Paris (1855–6) knee-deep in allegorical mud. Its emotional significance for him can be gauged if we reflect that his childhood period of 'forced labour' in a boot blacking factory had been dedicated to producing a commodity to remove the traces of mud. In the intervening years, in part to erase the memory perhaps, he had become a dandy, wearing polished boots instead of preparing polish for them, and cultivated the friendship of Comte d'Orsay, the darling of the boulevards.

In 'French Domesticity' (*HW*, IX, 434–8), Mrs Eliza Lynn Linton gives a sharply focused realisation of this nexus of issues as she praises the Frenchwoman's capacity to negotiate her way through various kinds of physical and moral 'uncleanness': 'she has a marvellous facility of walking clean through the dirty streets of Paris, and as marvellous a knack of holding up her skirts with one hand over her left hip . . . and a bewildering habit of mistaking her friend's husband for her own.'

That Paris should be specifically apt to evoke these associations was intrinsic in its name, or rather names. Hugo, like Costello a connoisseur of etymologies, had commented on this: 'the "urbis" of modern times . . . is called *Lutetia*, which comes from Lutus, *mud*, and is called *Parisis*, which comes from *Isis*, the goddess of truth' (Hugo, I, 1479; Labarthe, 51). Its legendary muddiness centred on the Marais and the Faubourg St Antoine, which Dickens, of course, would vividly render in *A Tale of Two Cities*: 'the filthiest in the city; you still find mud there after a two month drought' (Marchand, 58).

But a war of sorts was being waged upon the mud of Paris in the 1850s by the process of Haussmannisation. One could see it either as a positive thing, an annihilation of the medieval city and eradication through macadamisation of the unpaved streets that had created the legendary 'Lutetia', or, in the short term at least, an orgiastic proliferation of mud, as Paris was turned for the time being into one nightmarish giant construction site. One thing is certain: Dickens was there at this precise moment in time, and experienced both the muddy horror and the hope of eventual salvation. He was witness to a kind of allegorical psychomachia waged between the forces of cleanliness, represented ostensibly by Haussmannisation, and the forces of city filth – Merdle, one is tempted to say.

His response seems to have shifted with the passage of time and prolonged firsthand exposure to the Haussmann process. At first, on his way to Italy in autumn 1853, his response is thoroughly upbeat. He writes of the Haussmann projects: 'Paris is very full, extraordinarily gay, and wonderfully improving. Thousands of houses must have been pulled down for the construction of an immense street now making from the dirty old end of the Rue de Tivoli, past the Palais Royal, away beyond the Hotel de Ville. It will be the finest thing in Europe. The quays by the riverside are Macadamized and as clean as Regent Street. Indeed the general improvement in the essential articles of what is to be seen and what is to be smelt, is highly remarkable' (*Letters*, VII, 163; to Mrs Charles Dickens, 13 October 1853). For a while it seems as if London is the muddier of the two cities for Dickens, as a letter of 26 January 1855 (*Letters*, VII, 512; to Miss Burdett-Coutts) attests: 'the condition of the streets to day, is inconceivable – mud and mire, in many places a foot deep.'

But the winter of 1855–6 seems to have evoked another, more pessimistic response. He writes now about getting covered in mud as if it meant losing one's face, features and identity (one's 'morgue', to borrow one of Costello's suggestive etymologies). Of one of his walks in January 1856 he writes to Mary Boyle: 'came back with top-boots of mud on, and my very eyebrows smeared with mud. Georgina is usually invisible during the walking time of the day. A turned-up nose may be seen in the midst of a heap of splashes – nothing more' (*Letters*, VIII, 15; 8 January 1856).

We can trace the change of mood in the letters of that winter. One may start with the superficially breezy but oddly disconcerting announcement to Wills that the apartment on the Champs Elysées has been licked into shape and is 'exquisitely cheerful and vivacious – clean as anything human can be' (*Letters*, VIII, 725; 21 October 1855). The tone darkens in a letter to Mark Lemon, where the battle against defilement seems a losing one: 'We are up to our knees in mud here. Literally in vehement despair. . . . . Nothing will cleanse the streets. . . . Washing is awful' (*Letters*, VIII, 13; 7 January 1856). There is an apparent return of facetiousness to Wills on 19/20 January, with the announcement that 'MUD' (underlined with short double strokes) 'at Paris is 3 feet and 7/8 deep' (VIII, 32). But on the 20th, he appears to have lost faith in Haussmann: 'It is difficult to picture the change made in this place by the removal of the paving stones (too ready for barricades) and macadamisation. It suits neither the climate nor the soil. We are again in a sea of mud' (VIII, 33; to John Forster, [20 January 1856]).

Baudelaire shared these moods that same winter. In December 1855 he wrote to his mother: 'I am sick to death of colds and migraines and fevers, and above all of snow, mud, and rain.' Unlike Dickens he had no choice at this time but to walk in the mud as a pedestrian, and he hated what Haussmann was doing to Paris. Once again he complained about frequently being covered in muck: 'work in progress doesn't spare the pedestrian from mud and filth.' Only he, when he could, chose not to look down at the street-level, where the mud was to be seen – in his one reasonably settled adult abode, from October 1843 to September 1845, he lived in a flat whose main room was 'lit by a single window whose panes were obscured, right up the penultimate level, "so that he'd only be able to see the sky," he said' (Pichois and Avice, 108, 91, 66).

LEMAITRE AND ALLEGORY

Dickens's imagination, as we have seen, often attempted to express and master the complexity of the modern city by seeing it in allegorical terms. Ashford White perceives this in his writings about the Paris Morgue when he observes that 'in the grim winter of 1846-7 the aged white-haired victim of the river seemed to him an impersonation of the snowy season' (Ashford White, 2). In 1851, in 'A Monument of French Folly', comparing abattoirs in London with their counterparts in Paris, and mocking the kind of blind British jingoism in such matters that still has its echoes a century and a half later, allegory shades into ecological prophecy as it contemplates 'evil,' or inadequate slaughtering facilities, rising as a poisonous vapour to consume us all:

> Hard by Snow Hill and Warwick Lane, you shall see the little children, inured to sights of brutality from their birth, trotting along the alleys, mingled with troops of horribly busy pigs, up to their ankles in blood – but it makes the young rascals hardy. Into the imperfect sewers of this overgrown city, you shall have the immense mass of corruption, engendered by these practices, hastily thrown out of sight, to rise, in poisonous gases, into your house at night, when your sleeping children will most readily absorb them, – and to find its languid way, at last into the river that you drink – but the French are a frog-eating people who wear wooden shoes, and it's 'O the roast beef of England, my boy, the jolly old English roast beef!'
>
> (*HW,* II, 553–8; 8 March 1851)

The 'trotting children' and the 'busy pigs' suggest the tangles of modern cities, where high and low, human and animal have got mixed up: in the same impressive piece Dickens addresses French cities as emblematic upward spirals with kennels at their centre, surrounded by images of modernity: 'I know your narrow, straggling winding streets, with a kennel in the midst, and lamps slung across. I know your picturesque street-corners, winding up-hill Heaven knows where!'

Perhaps this is why Dickens accepted so many Fouricrist contributions to *Household Words* from Dixon, derived from Toussenel (despite commanding him to make it plain that he realised such thinking was pretty bizarre). Here all the animals are allegorical, and they express the vices of modernity. The series of five articles starts with the mole, the 'most complete allegorical expression of the absolute predominance of brutal over intellectual strength' ('The Mind of Brutes', *HW*, VII, 564–69; 13 August 1853). In the same piece we have rats, 'the emblem of those miserable and prolific populations which now cover the face of the globe, and which are driven by hunger'; the spider, 'the emblem of the shopkeeper'; dormice, 'the emblems of industrial parasites who spend three-quarters of their time in doing nothing up for their idleness by living upon the labours of others'; and many more. In 'Equine Analogies' (*HW*, VII, 611–15, 27 August 1853) the mule is the 'sad emblem of the feudalism of money' and horses the image of young girls commodified and consumed in Paris: 'Paris consumes annually nearly fifteen thousand horses. About the same number of young girls are every year sacrificed there before the Minotaur of vice.'

But it is Ashford White's word 'impersonation' that permits us to conclude. It was Dickens's regular Parisian winter evenings at the theatre which, on occasions at least, enabled him to see the 'drama of Parisian life' in terms not dissimilar from those Baudelaire employed to describe his ideal of the modern painter in the *Salon de 1845*: 'the painter who will be able to extract from contemporary life its epic side, and make us see and understand through colour and draughtsmanship how grand and poetic we are in our cruelties and polished boots' (Pichois and Avice, 69). Baudelaire meant Delacroix, and such drawings as that of 'La Douleur,' whereas for Dickens it was Lemaitre's acting, and his cry: 'It wasn't I who murdered him – it was Misery!' (*Letters*, VII, 537; to John Forster [?13–14 sFebruary 1856]).

Note

The translations in this essay are my own.

References

Ashford White: F. Ashford White, 'In France with Charles Dickens', *The Dickensian* IX (1913) 37–41 and 64–8.

Benjamin: Walter Benjamin, *Das Passagen-Werk* (Frankfurt: Suhrkamp Verlag, 1982).

Chevalier: Louis Chevalier, *Classes laborieuses et Classes dangereuses* (Paris: Hachette, 1984) [Librairie Générale Française, 1978].

Collins: Philip Collins, ed., Dickens: *Interviews and Recollections*, 2 volumes (London: Macmillan, 1981).

Hugo: Victor Hugo, *Œ uvres poétiques* (Paris: Gallimard, Bibliothèque de la Pléiade, 1964).

HW: *Household Words*, a weekly journal conducted by Charles Dickens, 19 volumes (London: Chapman & Hall, 1850–9).

Kracauer: Siegfried Kracauer, *Jacques Offenbach und das Paris seiner Zeit* (Frankfurt-am-Main: Suhrkamp Verlag, 1994) [Amsterdam: Allert de Lange, 1937].

Labarthe: Patrick Labarthe, 'Paris comme décor allégorique', *L'Année Baudelaire I: Baudelaire, Paris. l'Allégorie*, ed. Jean-Paul Avice and Claude Pichois (Paris: Editions Klincksieck, 1995), 41–56.

Letters: The Letters of Charles Dickens, 8 volumes to date. (Oxford: Clarendon Press). Here I refer exclusively to Volume VII, ed. Graham Storey, Kathleen Tillotson and Angus Easson, 1993, and Volume VIII, ed. Graham Storey and Kathleen Tillotson, 1995.

Loyrette: Henri Loyrette and Gary Tinterow, *Impressionisme. Les origines 1859–1869* (Paris: Editions de la Réunion des musées nationaux, 1994).

Marchand: Bernard Marchand, *Paris, histoire d'une ville: XIXe-XXe siècles* (Paris: Editions du Seuil, 1993).

Martin, Fugier: Anne Martin-Fugier, *La vie élégante ou la formation du Tout-Paris 1815–1848* (Paris: Editions du Seuil, 1993) [Fayard, 1990].

Pichois and Avice: Claude Pichois and Jean-Paul Avice, *Baudelaire/Paris* (Paris: Editions Paris-Musées/Quai Voltaire, 1993).

Pontavice de Heussey: Robert Pontavice de Heussey, *L'Inimitable Boz: Etude historique et anécdotique* (Paris: Maison Quantin, 1889).

Schlör: Joachim Schlör, *Nachts in der großen Stadt* (München: Artemis und Winkler, 1991).

Surveyer: Edouard F. Surveyer, 'Dickens in France', *The Dickensian* XXVIII (1932) 46–56, 122–9 and 197–201.

UTRP: Charles Dickens, *The Uncommercial Traveller & Reprinted Pieces* (Oxford: The New Oxford Illustrated Dickens, 1951).

4

Spectacle and Speculation: the Victorian Economy of Vision in *Little Dorrit*

Ronald R. Thomas

When Dickens's Amy Dorrit is released from the London debtors' prison where she has lived her entire life and takes up residence with her father in a palazzo in Venice, a strange spectacle looms before her as she gazes down at the ancient canals that flow outside her window: Venice disappears, and London rises into view. Dickens describes how Amy would stand on her balcony and, 'watch the sunset, in its long low lines of purple and red, and its burning flush high up into the sky: so glowing on the buildings, and so lightening their structure, that it made them look as if their strong walls were transparent.' Through the shimmering lens of these reflected Venetian palaces, Little Dorrit begins to see images of the familiar prison gates through which she had so often passed: 'She would watch those glories [of Venice] expire' and 'think of that old gate [at the Marshalsea], and of herself sitting at it in the dead of the night . . . and of other places and of other scenes associated with those different times. And then she would lean upon her balcony, and look over at the water, as though they all lay underneath it' (*Little Dorrit*, 520).

As strange as Amy Dorrit's Venetian visions might seem, they were not unlike those of many nineteenth-century Londoners who visited Venice and saw something disturbingly London-like in the spectacle Dickens himself called 'this strange Dream upon the water' when he travelled to Italy in 1844 and wrote his recollections for publication in London's *Daily News*. That dream, according to Dickens, 'was no sooner visible than, in its turn, it melted into something else' (70). This essay offers an explanation for the way Venice seems to melt into England in the eyes of many Victorians by investigating the relationship between visual spectacle and financial speculation in Dickens's representation of

London and Venice in *Little Dorrit* (1855–7) and *Pictures from Italy* (1846). It demonstrates that the Venetian visions of Amy Dorrit, not unlike Ruskin's famous analysis of that city's architecture, commonly transform themselves into a recognition of the economic and political realities of London, bringing into dramatic relief the parallel claims for England and Venice as (at different moments in history) the world's dominant commercial and maritime empires. In each location, the palaces of economic prosperity seem to vanish into prisons of political and economic oppression.

As Tony Tanner has noted, Venice had taken on a new attraction for the English in the Victorian period: 'Venice had become a tourist city – as opposed to a possible stopping-off point on the Grand Tour', he says, a change conveniently marked by the publication in 1842 of the first popular tourist guide to Venice: John Murray's *Handbook of Northern Italy*.[1] Like the flood of such guidebooks that were published in England in the years following, Murray's *Handbook* treats the city as a 'frozen spectacle . . . of separate consumable items', complete with the kind of starring system that has become a required convention of modern tourist guides (Tanner, 75). Denis Cosgrove has gone so far as to label this nineteenth-century transformation of the fabled city as 'the Disneyfication of Venice', a process that served to strip the place of its specific political relevance, mythologise its historical reality, and serve the city up as a vast visual commodity for consumption by modern tourists hungry for entertainment (quoted in Tanner, 75). Dickens himself recalls his own dreamlike trip to Venice in just these terms – as a 'succession of novelties' and 'a crowd of objects' that would suddenly appear and just as suddenly 'dissolve, like a view in a magic lantern' (*Pictures from Italy*, 69).

The Victorians' virtually obsessive preoccupation with Venice should be seen in the context of this commercialised view of the city they had adopted on the one hand, and their changing evaluation of the Italian Renaissance on the other.[2] This latter shift is reflected both in Ruskin's gradual modulation in tone of the withering critique of the Renaissance he launched in *The Stones of Venice* and in the idealisation of the achievements of the Renaissance by later Victorian cultural historians, including Walter Pater, John Addington Symonds and Vernon Lee. I shall argue that the forces that transformed Victorian attitudes towards the Renaissance as it was embodied in Venice from suspicion into admiration are deeply related to commercial questions, and that they may have more to do with the evolving debate on political economy in nineteenth-century England than with the evolution of English taste. 'Nor is this a question of interesting speculation merely,' Ruskin himself says in his critique of the political and economic ideals that caused him to favour the Gothic style over that of the Renaissance in Venice; 'for the distinction . . . is one which the present tendencies of the English mind have rendered it practically important to ascertain' (Ruskin, 239).[3] Indeed, the spectacle of Venice as it was viewed by the Victorians shows itself to be a matter of 'speculation' in at least two different ways: first, as a practical, even pragmatic expression of English pride in replacing Venice as the centre of a certain kind of world commerce based on financial speculation; and second, as a haunting anxiety about England following its imperial predecessor into the murky seas of political and economic decline.

The subject of *Little Dorrit*, Lionel Trilling famously observed, is borne in upon us by 'the symbol, or emblem, of the book, which is the prison', a symbol that has particular power in the text because it is 'an actuality', a literal place, 'before it is ever a symbol' (Trilling, 149). As central to the plot as the prison undoubtedly is, however, two other sites gradually take on equal importance in the novel's concerns – both symbolically and literally: the palace and the bank. The significance of the palace in the text is best represented by the palazzo in Venice to which the Dorrits repair once they come into their miraculous inheritance and are free to leave the debtors' prison that had long been their home. In this respect, the Dorrit prison is transformed into the Dorrit palace. The bank, on the other hand, is of course Merdle's bank, which returns Little Dorrit to her previous state of penury and effectively transforms the Dorrit palace into the Dorrit prison again. As such, the bank may be seen as the literal and symbolic place where the transformation occurs from prison to palace, and then back to prison again – representing a site of both immense, even legendary wealth and of colossal failure and destruction as well.

During the long Dorrit sojourn at the Marshalsea, Mr Dorrit had routinely transformed his familiar cell into a kind of fantasy palace whenever he was honoured as 'the Father of the Marshalsea' with some tribute or 'Testimonial' from the inmates and visitors who treated him as a kind of resident Doge. But after he comes into his fortune, Dorrit transforms his cell into a palace quite literally when he takes his family 'to live in Venice for some few months in a palace (itself six times as big as the whole Marshalsea) on the Grand Canal', as Dickens describes it (519). For Amy Dorrit, however, this change in residence is more symbolic than real. She cannot look at her father in his new palatial setting without seeing the shadows of the old Marshalsea all around him: 'In the brilliant light of a bright Italian day, the wonderful city without and the splendours of an old palace within, she saw him at the moment in the long-familiar gloom of his Marshalsea lodging' (531). Not only does Amy see Mr Dorrit as a prisoner in their new dwelling, but she sees its repressive pretensions as nothing more than an enlarged version of the Marshalsea for all of them – a point of view that enrages her father who is trying desperately to repress the shame of his ignominious past and assume the identity of a wealthy gentleman. 'I am hurt that my daughter, seated in the – hum – lap of fortune should . . . systematically reproduce what the rest of us blot out,' he reproaches her; 'and seem – hum – I had almost said positively anxious – to announce to wealthy and distinguished society that she was born and bred in – ha hum – a place that I myself decline to name' (532–3).

Mr Dorrit's indignant demands that Amy put her past behind her and forget their days in prison are futile, however. Regardless of how hard she tries to cooperate, 'it appeared on the whole, to Little Dorrit herself, that this same society in which they lived [in Venice], greatly resembled a superior sort of Marshalsea' (565). This recurring visual and psychological trick played upon Little Dorrit by the events of her life becomes a motif in the novel. Why does the palazzo constantly turn into the prison in *Little Dorrit*, and vice versa? Whenever Amy would 'lean upon her balcony, and look over at the water' in the Grand Canal 'she would musingly watch its running, as if, in the general vision, it might run dry, and show her the prison again, and herself, and the old room, and the old inmates, and the old visitors: all lasting realities that never changed' (520). In the hallucinatory logic of the text, the Venetian palazzo offers itself as the mirror-image for a London debtors' prison and a fitting alternative home for the Dorrit family. The foundation for this logic, it may properly be said, is in the bank.

In tracing the Italian journey of this individual whose life was so deeply influenced by her youthful experience in a debtors' prison, it should be noted here, Dickens drew upon his own traumatic and humiliating childhood experience when he visited his father in prison. He also drew on his travels in Italy and the account he gave of them in *Pictures from Italy*. This journal of the author's year-long excursion between 1844 and 1845 was originally published in a serialised version in the *Daily News* from January to March 1846 under the title 'Travelling Letters written on the Road'. When it appeared in book form later in the same year, however, Dickens retitled the work *Pictures from Italy*. Apparently, the visual aspects of this material grew essential to Dickens's conception of it as these 'letters' became more accurately designated as 'pictures' in his mind.

The second important feature of the text for our purposes is that it displays two basic kinds of 'pictures' from Italy: on the one hand, vibrant

and energetic spectacles of the marketplace alternating with, on the other,
very different scenes of the most desolate ruins.[4] Dickens begins by
portraying a marketplace that 'looks as if it were the stage of some great
theatre, and the curtain had just run up, for a picturesque ballet' (10). He
then juxtaposes this image of commerce with a view of the crumbling
Genoan palazzo where he resides – a structure which, he maintains,
resembles 'a pink jail' stranded 'in a rank, dull, weedy court-yard' more
than it does a palace (24). A few pages later he offers an even more
eloquent image of his double impression of Italy in his description of the
'English Bank' he visits, a bank that was located 'in a good-sized Palazzo
in the Strada Nuova' (34). Banking was one of the 'characteristic uses' to
which vacant and deteriorating Italian palaces were put, he says, noting
how 'every inch' of the bank's elaborately painted walls was 'as dirty as a
police-station in London' (34–5). Even in Dickens's own journey to Italy, it
would seem, the prison, the palaces and the bank express themselves as
different manifestations of the same place.

Poised between these two contradictory images of Italy in *Pictures from
Italy* is the chapter on Venice. Titled 'An Italian Dream', it describes the
city as nothing less than a fantastic 'view in a magic lantern' (69). The
Venice section shifts in tone dramatically from the rest of the text,
shedding the edge of satire and humour that characterises the rest of the
book, replacing it with a dazzling, rhapsodic vision. Among the first
images of amazement the narrative voice describes in this section is that
of 'a Palace' on a grand Piazza that is linked to a prison:

> It was a great Piazza, as I thought; anchored, like all the rest, in the
> deep ocean. On its broad bosom, was a Palace more majestic and
> magnificent in its old age, than all the buildings of the earth, in the
> high prime and fulness of their youth. Cloisters and galleries: so light,
> they might have been the work of fairy hands: so strong that centuries
> have battered them in vain: wound round and round this palace, and
> enfolded it with a Cathedral, gorgeous in the wild luxuriant fancies of
> the East . . . I dreamed that I was led on, then, into some jealous rooms,
> communicating with a prison near the palace; separated from it by a
> lofty bridge crossing a narrow street; and called, I dreamed, the Bridge
> of Sighs.
>
> (72–7)

This vision of the Ducal Palace and the prison *linked together* by the Bridge
of Sighs, becomes the focal point for the entire text of *Pictures*, combining
its opposing sights of energy and enervation, of prosperity and ruin, and
uniting its contradictory images into some potent historical object lesson

for the English audience of the nineteenth-century. 'Let us not remember Italy the less regardfully,' Dickens warns in the last sentence of the book as if to reinvoke this very image, 'because, in every fragment of her fallen temples, and every stone of her deserted palaces and prisons, she helps to inculcate the lesson that the wheel of Time is rolling for an end . . . ' (176).[5] In *The Stones of Venice*, Ruskin would also admire the Ducal Palace and its prison, joined by the famous bridge, equating them with 'Buckingham Palace, the Tower of olden days, the Houses of Parliament, and Downing Street, all in one' (210). Like Dickens, he recognised something distinctively English about these structures, and saw in them a lesson to be heeded by his contemporaries.[6]

The task of identifying and theorising the reasons for seeing this resemblance between Renaissance Venice and Victorian England brings me to the second important term in my title – *speculation* – and to the work of the economic historian Giovanni Arrighi. In his analysis of late capitalism, *The Long Twentieth Century: Money, Power, and the Origins of Our Times* (1994), Arrighi points to Venice as the imperial model most directly emulated by the British Empire in making itself into the particular kind of global commercial economy it became in the nineteenth century.[7] Much like Venice of the fifteenth and sixteenth centuries, nineteenth-century England was a powerful island nation with a dominating navy, poised at the intersection of the two major trade routes of its time. In the nineteenth century, as Britain looked east to control the trade routes to the Orient (where Arthur Clennam had spent his youth in the import business), it began to 'look like an enlarged replica of the Venetian Republic', as Arrighi puts it (Arrighi, 57). The crossroads of world commerce had by this time shifted to favour England's location, from the eastern Mediterranean to the English Channel, where American and Asian products and materials could encounter European and Baltic markets and supplies. But England's resemblance to Venice was not just a geographical and historical accident. It was a conscious aspiration built on the widespread conviction in England that the British Empire was replacing Venice in this role: 'To be the Venice of the nineteenth century was still the objective advocated for Britain by leading members of the business community at the end of the Napoleonic Wars,' as Arrighi explains. 'The same analogy was invoked again – albeit with negative connotations – when the nineteenth-century expansion of British wealth and power began reaching its limits' late in the century (57).[8]

Venice served, then, as both a model of success to emulate and an example of decline to avoid at different moments in the development of the British Empire. While the city may be seen to function in both ways in

Dickens's images of it in *Pictures from Italy*, the latter seems to dominate in *Little Dorrit*, written a decade later. As Arrighi makes clear, the British Empire of the nineteenth century resembled Venice, not simply because both happened to be strategically placed island republics with powerful navies, but because of the structure of their imperial economies. Both defeated their rivals by making wealth and power dependent upon successful speculation about the price of goods rather than on the acquisition and domination of land and people. Venice emerged as the most powerful state in the subsystem of northern Italian city-states during the Renaissance by establishing itself as the true prototype of the capitalist state – identifying power with the extent of its command over scarce resources and their circulation, that is, *rather than* its control over populations or territories in the manner of its competitors.

England would follow much the same pattern in the development of its global commercial empire among competing European states in the nineteenth century. As in Venice, a 'merchant capitalist' class in England firmly held state power in its grip so that 'territorial acquisitions were subjected to careful cost-benefit analyses and, as a rule, were undertaken only as the means to the end of increasing the profitability of the traffics of the capitalist oligarchy that exercised power' (Arrighi, 37). The 'industrialism' and 'imperialism' peculiar to nineteenth-century Britain, Arrighi concludes, were nothing less than 'integral aspects of its *enlarged* strategies and structures of Venetian' entrepôt capitalism (176). Over the span of three centuries, England essentially changed places with Venice as the world's principal commercial and financial empire, and went on to 'redraw the map of the world and become simultaneously the most powerful territorialist *and* capitalist state the world had ever seen, while Venice lost all its residual power and influence until it was wiped off the map of Europe' (183). It should come as no surprise, then, that when he addressed the House of Commons on world affairs in 1871, Disraeli would call attention to the 'many parallels between Venice and England'.[9]

Such a relationship is amply figured in Dickens's return to Venice in *Little Dorrit*, and his use of the Italian city as a kind of objective correlative for the parable of economic failure in England which the novel documents. There is a reason that Amy Dorrit sees the shadow of the debtors' prison reflected in the canals and palaces of Venice. It is here that Mr Dorrit becomes acquainted with the paradigmatic merchant capitalist Mr Merdle, and is even allied with him when Dorrit's elder daughter becomes engaged to Merdle's son-in-law – that rising star of the Circumlocution Office. Here in Venice, Dorrit is caught up in the general enthusiasm surrounding the mysterious brilliance of Mr Merdle's genius in commercial speculation, declaring to his gathered family in their Venetian palazzo that 'Mr Merdle's is a name of – ha – world-wide repute.' His 'undertakings are immense,' Dorrit continues. 'They bring him in such fast sums of money that they are regarded as – hum – national benefits. Mr Merdle is the man of this time. The name of Merdle is the name of the age' (537). On the basis of this confidence, here, in Venice, Mr Dorrit resolves to invest all his money in Merdle enterprises, a speculation that proves as disastrous for him as it does for everyone else in England. It is as if the 'dilapidated palaces' of Venice serve as a visual spectacle in the novel, to predict the economic ruin of an England that became captivated by the irresponsible speculations of this financial 'man of this time' (517).[10]

Like the prison and the palace in *Little Dorrit*, Merdle is both fact and symbol in the text. Not only is he an international capitalist by profession, he comes to stand for the entire phenomenon of the centralised and mystified control of global markets by financial speculation. The trust invested in him is given credence merely by its repetition and dissemination: 'Mr Merdle's right hand was filled with the evening paper, and the evening paper was full of Mr Merdle,' as Dickens says of him. 'His wonderful enterprise, his wonderful wealth, his wonderful Bank, were the fattening food of the evening paper that night. The wonderful Bank, of which he was the chief projector, establisher, and manager, was the latest of the many Merdle wonders' (613–14).[11] Merdle functions as a kind of spectacle of speculation himself in the novel – an 'illustrious man and great national ornament', a thing to be beheld and admired (756). He *is* all the news that is fit to print.[12] Symbolised most efficiently in the popular imagination by his 'wonderful Bank', he never has to go to Venice because he reincarnates it back home in that London Bank. He is represented in Venice, architecturally at least, by the palazzo in which the Gowans take up residence, the first floor of which, we are told, has been made into a bank.[13] It is only fitting, then, that Dorrit should decide to risk his fortune at Merdle's bank in the confines of the Venetian palazzo, a structure that appears in Amy's eyes to be nothing more than a visual manifestation of a debtors' prison.[14]

There is another commercial man of his time in the novel, of course, who offers an alternative economic model for the nation: the unassuming and disappointed merchant, Arthur Clennam, whose return to London from more than twenty years in the China trade begins the events that set the plot of *Little Dorrit* in motion. The report Clennam delivers to his mother at the outset of the text on the failure of the family venture in

China may be read either as sounding an ominous note for the far-flung commercial empire of his nation, or as a warning that its methods must be modernized in the ways of Merdle. 'Mother,' he says in explaining his resolution to give up the family business located at the far reaches of the empire, 'our House has done less and less for some years past, and our dealings have been progressively on the decline. We have never shown much confidence, or invited much; we have attached no people to us; the track we have kept is not the track of time; and we have been left far behind' (85). In either reading of this scene – as a call for more agressive speculation or as a warning of its dangers – Clennam's repudiation of the family enterprise and his resolution to become a partner with Doyce manufacturing suggest that Clennam's economic role in the novel is to signal a withdrawal from the global to the domestic, from the activity of merchandising and speculation to that of production and hard work.

At the time that *Little Dorrit* was appearing in print, the second Opium War between England and China had already broken out, and England would be faced with the ever more complex challenge of maintaining control of its unstable markets in the Far East. At a moment when pressures for territorial expansion in the Orient were mounting for the British Empire, Clennam´s actions implicitly call for the kind of careful cost-benefit analysis of territorial expansion that Arrighi indicates was a key to the success of Venice.[15] In addition, his support of the Doyce manufacturing enterprise at home aligns him with those who called for increased domestic industrialisation to complement Britain´s growing role in the area of international finance capitalism and thereby avoid the fate of Venice. Arthur´s unending tangle with the Circumlocution Office over the Doyce invention makes clear that such issues reflect institutionalised national policies that stand in need of reform, just as Merdle´s easy alliance with that same office does. While Merdle may have been the ´national ornament´ of the global British economy, Clennam offers an opposing image for the nation emphasising a domestic economy that retains production rather than speculation at its core. Like the famous Venetian traveller five centuries earlier who returned from China after his history-making twenty-year journey, Clennam returns to England a nineteenth-century Marco Polo with a message just as timely and just as controversial as his predecessor´s.[16]

Between the writing of *Pictures from Italy* and *Little Dorrit*, Venice had suffered a humiliating surrender to Napoleon, had witnessed Europe´s most successful republican uprising in 1848, and in 1849 had endured conquest and occupation once more by the Austrian Empire. What appeared as a romantically haunting ´Italian Dream´ in Dickens´s earlier representation of Venice justly became a more haunting nightmare of corruption in *Little Dorrit*, therefore. The precipitous rise and fall of the independent island state that had reigned so long as the world's premier maritime empire offered itself as a particularly powerful object lesson to Victorian England, its imperial – and capitalist – heir-apparent. Ruskin would spend his final days preaching against these policies, regretting, perhaps, the words with which he ended *The Stones of Venice* when he expressed the wish shared by a generation of Victorians: that 'the London of the nineteenth century might yet become as Venice without her despotism' (247). Even Byron's dream-like vision of Venice from the Bridge of Sighs, 'A palace and a prison on each hand', acknowledged what Little Dorrit recognised in the canals of Venice. Like Dickens, Amy seemed to realise as she gazed at the splendid and ruinous spectacle of Venice that, in the capitalist system of speculation, one man's palace – or bank – is always another man's prison.

Notes

1. Jeanne Clegg claims that between the seventeenth and the nineteenth centuries, the English view of Italy underwent a transformation from admiration to hatred, to contempt, to pity, to (in the nineteenth century) a kind of romantic fascination that took different forms in different purposes. See Clegg, *Ruskin and Venice* (London: Junction Books, 1981).

2. As Hilary Fraser notes, 'it has frequently been remarked by historians that the Renaissance was an invention of the nineteenth century' and that Victorian painters, writers and historians 'fabricated the Renaissance in their own image' to the extent that our inherited idea of Renaissance Italy is, ideologically, politically, and culturally, quintessentially a nineteenth-century one (1–2). See Hilary Fraser, *The Victorians and Renaissance Italy* (Oxford and Cambridge, MA: Blackwell, 1992).

3. Ruskin's withering critique of the Renaissance should be seen in relation to the idealisation of it by later Victorian cultural historians such as Walter Pater, John Addington Symonds and Vernon Lee (see Hilary Fraser, 213–34).

4. In *Venice Rediscovered*, John Pemble sees Venice in the nineteenth century as the embodiment of nineteenth-century historicism: as both the ideal project for restoring or 'resuscitating' the past and a symbol that must be conserved in its current condition of decay as a fragile icon of the passing of time.

5. The phrasing seems to anticipate Ruskin's when he describes the 'warning' that is 'uttered by every one of the fast-gaining waves,

that beat like passing bells, against the STONES OF VENICE' (see *The Stones of Venice*, 13).

6. Later in *The Stones*, Ruskin will say that the Bridge of Sighs and its canal 'occupy, in the mind of the Venetian, very much the position of Fleet Street and Temple Bar in that of a Londoner' (*The Stones of Venice*, 195).

7. Others have drawn the analogy, but Arrighi most exhaustively establishes the direct and systematic emulation of the Venetian imperial economy by the British. As John Pemble has shown, the similarities between modern Britain and the old Republic of Venice had also become a recurring theme in writing about Venice during the nineteenth century. Balzac would even call Venice 'the London of the Middle Ages' (See Pemble, *Venice Rediscovered*, 100).

8. In the famous opening of *The Stones of Venice*, Ruskin also makes explicit the connection between Venice and England, announcing that history records only three great 'thrones' to have held 'dominion' over the sea – Tyre, Venice and England (*The Stones of Venice*, 13).

9. Quoted by John Pemble in *Venice Rediscovered* (Oxford: Clarendon Press, 1995), 119.

10. Nancy Aycock Metz argues that the Italian episodes in *Little Dorrit* 'redefine the context of the London scenes', and suggest 'that England's capital is firmly set on a path that can only lead to a fate like ruined Rome's' (478). As Metz shows, '*Little Dorrit* sometimes reads like a museum guide to "lost" London' as it 'lingers over the traces of a London that seems at times more ruin than real' (465–6). I agree, but would argue that Venice is the more powerful model of ruin and decay for London. See Nancy Aycock Metz, '*Little Dorrit*'s London: Babylon Revisited', *Victorian Studies* 33:3 (Spring 1990) 465–86.

11. As Humphry House explains, while the imaginary date of *Little Dorrit* associates the Merdle crash as part of the financial collapse of 1825–6, the extent of Merdle's operations, the number of investors he attracted and the prestige in society he commanded belong entirely to the 1850s. See House, *The Dickens World*, 166.

12. Jeff Nunokawa shows how many characters mystify the source of their property in the novel (Casby, Mr Dorrit, Mrs Clennam, etc.). Even Arthur shares a sense of capitalist guilt, convinced as he is that his business activities abroad have deprived someone of their rightful property. Merdle simply embodies all these mystifications of the origin of capital. See Nunokawa, *The Afterlife of Property*, 19–39.

13. This image of the bank occupying the palazzo seems to have come directly from the passage in *Pictures from Italy* on the 'characteristic uses' to which Italy's deteriorating, unoccupied palaces were put (*Pictures*, 34–5).

14. Timothy Alborn has shown that the phenomenon of failed banks in the mid-nineteenth century was interpreted in at least two ways: economists were inclined to view it as an exceptional example of

how not to manage a financial institution, while novelists such as Dickens and Thackeray saw it as a symptom of something more generally wrong with the money market – 'an early augury of institutional decay brought on by generations of commercialism' (199). Alborn argues that 'anti-corporate fables' like *Little Dorrit* 'offered the institution of the domestic household in an attempt to reintroduce a sense of personal responsibility into modern life' as 'an alternative to the capitalist institutions as they presently stood (and occasionally fell)'. See Timothy L. Alborn, 'The Moral of the Failed Bank: Professional Plots in the Victorian Money Market', *Victorian Studies* 38:2 (Winter 1995) 199–226.

15. With the increasing dominance of Western influence in India and China in the latter half of the century, the authority of existing local regimes began to break down and the British were forced to take over more and more administrative control. See E. J. Hobsbawm, *The Age of Capital*, 136–46.

16. It was not until the nineteenth century that the first scholarly edition of Marco Polo's travels was published (by W. Marsden); the classic English edition by Sir Henry Yule was published in 1871.

References

Alborn, Timothy L., 'The Moral of the Failed Bank: Professional Plots in the Victorian Money Market', *Victorian Studies* 38:2 (Winter 1995) 199–226.

Arrighi, Giovanni, *The Long Twentieth Century: Money, Power, and the Origins of Our Times* (London: Verso, 1994).

Byron, George Gordon, *Byron: Poetical Works* (London, Oxford, New York: Oxford University Press, 1970).

Canepa, Andrew M., 'From Degenerate Scoundrel to Noble Savage: The Italian Stereotype in 18th Century British Travel Literature', *English Miscellany* 22 (1971).

Clegg, Jeanne, *Ruskin and Venice* (London: Junction Books, 1981).

Cosgrove, Denis, 'The Myth and the Stones of Venice', *Journal of Historical Geography* 8:2 (1987) 145–69.

Dickens, Charles, *Little Dorrit* (Harmondsworth: Penguin Books, 1967; first published 1857).

Dickens, Charles, *Pictures from Italy* (New York: The Ecco Press, 1988; first published 1846).

Fraser, Hilary, *The Victorians and Renaissance Italy* (Oxford and Cambridge, MA: Blackwell, 1992).

Hobsbawm, E. J., *The Age of Capital: 1848–75* (New York: Meridian, 1984; first published 1975).

House, Humphry, *The Dickens World* (Oxford: Oxford University Press, 1960; first published 1940).

James, Henry, *Travels in Italy with Henry James: Essays*, ed. Fred Kaplan (New York: William Morrow and Company, 1994).

Metz, Nancy Aycock, '*Little Dorrit's* London: Babylon Revisited', *Victorian Studies* 33:3 (Spring 1990) 465–86.

Nunokawa, Jeff, *The Afterlife of Property: Domestic Security and the Victorian Novel* (Princeton: Princeton University Press, 1994).

Pemble, John, *Venice Rediscovered* (Oxford: Clarendon Press, 1995).

Ruskin, John, *The Complete Works of John Ruskin* (Library Edition), ed. E. T. Cook and Alexander Wedderburn (London: George Allen, 1903–12).

Ruskin, John, *The Stones of Venice*, ed. J. G. Links (New York: DaCapo Press, 1960). Unless otherwise noted, page numbers for quotations correspond to this edition.

Redford, Bruce, 'Venice Mythologized: A Seductive Maritime Playground', *Apollo* (September 1994) 13–16.

Ross, Michael L., *Storied Cities: Literary Imaginings of Florence, Venice, and Rome* (Westport, CT and London: Greenwood Press, 1994).

Tanner, Tony, *Venice Desired* (Cambridge: Harvard University Press, 1992).

Trilling, Lionel, 'Little Dorrit', in *Dickens: A Collection of Critical Essays*, ed. Martin Price (Englewood Cliffs, NJ: Prentice Hall, 1962) 147–57. Essay first published in 1953.

Yeazell, Ruth Bernard, 'Do it or Dorrit', *Novel* 25:1 (Fall 1991) 33–49.

5

Pictures from Italy: Dickens, Rome, and the Eternal City of the Mind

Lawrence Frank

Imagine that an explorer arrives in a little-known region where his interest is aroused by an expanse of ruins, with remains of walls, fragments of columns, and tablets with half-effaced and unreadable inscriptions. He may content himself with inspecting what lies exposed to view, with questioning the inhabitants – perhaps semi-barbaric people – who live in the vicinity, about what tradition tells them of the history and meaning of these archaeological remains, and with noting down what they tell him – and he may then proceed on his journey. But he may act differently. He may have brought picks, shovels and spades with him, and he may set the inhabitants to work with these implements. Together with them he may start upon the ruins, clear away the rubbish, and, beginning from the visible remains, uncover what is buried. If his work is crowned with success, the discoveries are self-explanatory: the ruined walls are part of the ramparts of a palace or a treasure-house; the fragments of columns can be filled out into a temple; the numerous inscriptions, which, by good luck, may be bilingual, reveal an alphabet and a language, and, when they have been deciphered and translated, yield undreamed-of information about the events of the remote past, to commemorate which the monuments were built. *Saxa loquuntur!*

Sigmund Freud, 'The Aetiology of Hysteria' (1896)

On 28 May 1899 Sigmund Freud wrote to his friend Wilhelm Fliess in Berlin, that 'the dream [book] will be': 'No other work of mine has been so completely my own, my own dung heap, my seedling

47

and a *nova species mihi* on top of it.' He goes on to tell Fliess, 'I gave myself a present, Schliemann's *Ilios*, and greatly enjoyed the account of his childhood. The man was happy when he found Priam's treasure, because happiness comes only with the fulfillment of a childhood wish. This reminds me that I shall not go to Italy this year. Until next time!'[1] Freud's letter suggests a context relevant to the whole of the nineteenth century and to those investigations of the human mind that were to become associated with a process of excavation, both geological and archaeological; with the figurative dung heap and graveyard of time; and with Rome, the fabled Eternal City that was to provide an apt metaphor for the mind in Freud's *Civilization and its Discontents* (1930). Within this context it becomes possible to argue that, long before the publication of *Civilization and its Discontents*, Dickens anticipated Freud in his *Pictures from Italy* (1846), imaginatively transforming Rome into a metaphor for the romantic mind.

Both Dickens and Freud participated in an intellectual tradition extending from the first decades of the nineteenth century to the *fin de siècle*: from John Playfair's observation in 1802 about the fossil 'characters', the 'remains of ancient seas or continents' that 'have still their memory preserved in those archives, where nature has recorded the revolutions of the globe' (8) to the moment in 'The Aetiology of Hysteria' (1896) when Freud offered an extended archaeological metaphor for the mind that ended with the exclamation, '*Saxa loquuntur!*' (*Standard Edition*, 3:192): stones speak! Even in the first decades of the nineteenth century, before the publication of *Origin of Species* (1859), mesmerism, phrenology and the emerging discipline that John Elliotson called cerebral physiology (*Zoist*, 1: 1–4) encouraged increasingly naturalistic and materialist discussions of the human mind.[2]

Early on, Dickens had access to a coherent naturalistic tradition in the writings of George Combe, the phrenologist, and of Elliotson, through whom Dickens was exposed to mesmeric experiments; in fact, he and Elliotson were to become friends and for a time Elliotson acted as physician to the Dickens family.[3]

In his *Constitution of Man* (1828), Combe rejected any recourse to metaphysical speculations on the nature of consciousness. Although his readers might reject phrenology as the 'true philosophy of mind', Combe argued that 'we are physical, organic, and moral beings, acting under the sanction of general laws' (*Constitution*, xi). His credo could become both Elliotson's and Dickens's, echoed in Elliotson's *Zoist*, where he sought to bring together cerebral physiology, phrenology and mesmerism: 'Let us not cloak our ignorance by the assumption of an air of mystery and the parade of unintelligible theories' (*Zoist*, 1: 16–17).

It was mesmerism that led to the hypothesis about the existence of 'double states of consciousness independent of mesmerism'. In his 1846 article on this phenomenon, John Elliotson observed, 'Mesmerism is simply an artificial method of producing certain phenomena' (*Zoist*, 4: 157) that reveal the existence of distinct mental states, two discontinuous streams of consciousness, one associated with waking consciousness, the other with a state akin to sleeping and dreaming. From discussions of so-called diseased states of consciousness, it became possible to argue that in every man and woman there is 'a double consciousness . . . a sort of twofold existence' (*Zoist*, 4: 187). The hypothesis of a second state of consciousness not always available to a subject would have its appeal for someone like a Thomas De Quincey or a Thomas Carlyle, each of whom was in the process of suggesting a romantic vision of the mind. In the *Confessions of an English Opium-Eater* (1821–2), De Quincey had claimed that 'there is no such thing as *forgetting* possible to the mind' (328). In 'Characteristics' (1831), Carlyle observed that the 'curious relations of the Voluntary and Conscious to the Involuntary and Unconscious . . . might lead us into deep questions of Psychology and Physiology' (46).[4]

Already the double states of consciousness of mesmerism could be associated with deep questions involving the Conscious and the Unconscious. But such questions defy purely empirical investigation. Anyone who has read *A Treatise of Human Nature* (1739–40) and David Hume's discussion of personal identity can see in his critique of the concept of the self a potentially sceptical analysis of the romantic unconscious whose existence, like that of the self, cannot be demonstrated. Within a Humean perspective, the unconscious, like the notion of the self, is necessarily only a fiction: it exists only through the power of language, through the force of certain figures of speech central to nineteenth-century intellectual life, both in Great Britain and on the Continent. So, it can be argued that Dickens and Freud participated not in the discovery of the unconscious, but in its creation through an archaeological figure of speech that transforms Rome into the Eternal City of the romantic mind.[5]

II

As a man of his time Dickens followed the emergence in the 1830s and 1840s of the historical disciplines, the palaetiological sciences described by William Whewell in his *History of the Inductive Sciences* (1837) that sought 'to ascend from the present state of things to a more ancient condition, from which the present is derived by intelligible causes' (3:481). Dickens was himself interested in, perhaps fascinated by, the palaetiological sciences. In an 1848 review of Robert Hunt's *The Poetry of Science* (1848) in *The Examiner*, he could write on behalf of lay men and women 'capable of making, and reasonably sustaining [speculations], on a knowledge of certain geological facts; albeit they are neither practical chemists nor palaeontologists' (*Miscellaneous Papers*, 1: 67). His words suggest that Dickens could be expected to have read Charles Lyell, Hugh Miller, the Scottish stonemason turned geologist, and, later, Austen Henry Layard, excavator of Nineveh and Nimrud. Dickens owned Lyell's *Elements of Geology* (1838) and referred to it fleetingly in *Martin Chuzzlewit* (1843–4) when Martin is invited by La Fayette Kettle to discourse in public upon Lyell's 'Elements of Geology, or (if more convenient) upon the Writings of your talented and witty countryman, the honorable Mr. Miller' (363): apparently, Kettle can see no distinction between a serious introduction to geology and a book of jokes and anecdotes attributed to the Drury Lane performer, Joe Miller.[6] There is no evidence that Dickens owned Hugh Miller's *Old Red Sandstone*, the most widely read popularisation of geology in Victorian Britain. But he responded to a complimentary copy of the posthumously published *Testimony of the Rocks* (1857) by writing thoughtfully to Mrs Miller. Of course, Dickens was addressing the widow of a man who had committed suicide only a few months earlier. Yet, his letter to Mrs Miller implies a genuine knowledge and appreciation of a writer praised by both Carlyle and John Ruskin.[7] In the case of Austen Henry Layard, there is no doubt; Dickens became the friend of the man who was made famous in 1849 with the publication of *Nineveh and its Remains*; at his death Dickens owned Layard's *Discoveries in the Ruins of Nineveh and Babylon* (1853) and, more significantly, his condensation of *Nineveh and its Remains*, the *Popular Account of Discoveries at Nineveh* (1851).[8]

It is not surprising to see Dickens as someone more than passingly acquainted with geology, palaeontology and archaeology, all of which were seen by William Whewell, along with philology, as different applications of archaeology. In his *History*, Whewell refers to Charles Lyell's discussion of the Temple of Jupiter Serapis, on the Bay of Baiae, Italy, in his *Principles of Geology* (1830–3), the geological work whose figurative language and elegiac tone would have been far more suggestive to Dickens the artist than the more prosaic *Elements*. In volume one of the *Principles* (1830), Lyell reconstructs the history of the temple from its surviving ruins, marked by literal and figurative inscriptions; he engages in an epistemological and narrative *tour-de-force* that Whewell implicitly offers as a methodological model to the nineteenth-century geologist, philologist and archaeologist (1: 449–59).[9]

In discussing a structure once partially submerged beneath the waters of the Mediterranean, Lyell also provided a potential metaphor for those who sought to understand the phenomena associated with the double consciousness of mesmerism and with those Carlylean depths of the Involuntary and the Unconscious. William Whewell's discussions of the palaetiological disciplines in 1837 had already revealed that they might drift, inexorably, to considerations of the human mind: 'In the class of sciences now under notice, we are, at a different point, carried from the world of matter to the world of thought and feeling, – from things to men' (*History*, 3: 487). If John Playfair's fossils can be seen as constituting the earth's memory, then archaeological ruins may become the preserved memories of entire civilisations now lost to human awareness.

In such a way the subterranean depths of geology and archaeology were to become associated with the second consciousness of mesmerism and with the Carlylean Unconscious. In a letter dated 20 February 1836, John Herschel, the astronomer, wrote from the Cape of Good Hope to Charles Lyell; in meditating upon the *Principles of Geology*, Herschel turned from observations on geology to a discussion of philology: 'Words are to the Anthropologist what rolled pebbles are to the Geologist – Battered relics of past ages often containing within them indelible records capable of intelligible interpretation' (as quoted in Cannon, *Proceedings*, 105: 308). Only a few paragraphs later Herschel observed, 'Well. I really *must* hold my hand – at least for the present – but your book has stirred up my brains – & every page I turn brings up some fresh *ooze* from their dark deposits' (as quoted in Cannon, *Proceedings*, 105: 310).

Herschel's letter to Lyell was circulated amongst friends and colleagues.[10] But the drift of thought in it, the self-conscious appropriation of geological, philological and archaeological ideas for an allusion to the dark deposits of the human mind, could make its way into a work of popular science like Hugh Miller's *The Old Red Sandstone* (1841). At one point in his book, Miller observes, 'Physiognomy is no idle or doubtful science in connection with Geology. The physiognomy of a country indicates almost invariably its geological character' (197). In a phrenological moment Miller puns upon the word character, paralleling the existence of geological formations invisible to the eye, yet hinted at by surface features, to the depths of human character that can be inferred from human physiognomy. As he continues, Miller turns from a discussion of the spatial characteristics of geological formations to their temporal dimensions. He considers the history of such formations in order to trace all the various changes recorded in fossil remains, those monuments to the past he compares to 'the involved sculpturings of some Runic obelisk, weathered by the storms of a thousand winters' (222–3). Miller is introducing his readers to periods of time beyond the reach of common sense. In doing so, he uses language that confers on the human mind temporal dimensions difficult to imagine, to be rendered perhaps in a figurative language provided by the disciplines promoted by Herschel, Lyell and Miller himself.

III

The final number of *Martin Chuzzlewit* appeared on 30 June 1844. On 2 July Dickens departed with his family for the Continent, embarking on the journey that would take him to Genoa and, later, to Rome. It was in Genoa that Dickens met Emile and Augusta de la Rue and where he conducted mesmeric experiments on Madame de la Rue in order to relieve symptoms that we, today, would see as those of the classic nineteenth-century hysteric. Even after leaving Genoa on 19 January 1845 for a trip to Rome, Dickens continued to write to Emile de la Rue about his wife and her condition. As he toured Italy, Dickens even engaged in attempts to induce a mesmeric trance in Augusta de la Rue from afar.[11]

In his journey southward, Dickens was clearly preoccupied with Augusta de la Rue's mental state, even as he made the obligatory visits to memorable places and cities. Given the influence of the palaetiological sciences of the day, he was well prepared to transform the Italian landscape, with its geological and antiquarian attractions, into a metaphor for the mind. It is in *Pictures from Italy* (1846), his account of his travels in France and Italy, that Dickens's transformation of the landscape can be seen. On the way to Rome Dickens stopped to visit the stone quarries outside Carrara so that he might see for himself evidence of the geological phenomena described by Lyell, Miller and others. Dickens moved on to Pisa, Leghorn and Siena, finally pausing before a volcanic lake, perhaps reminded of a passage in the *Principles of Geology* which immediately precedes Lyell's discussion of the Temple of Jupiter Serapis: 'Buildings and cities submerged for a time beneath seas or lakes, and covered with sedimentary deposits, must, in some places, have been re-elevated to considerable heights above the level of the ocean' (*Principles*, 1: 448). Dickens's observations in *Pictures from Italy* echo Lyell's as he reflects on the legend of a city 'swallowed up one day' by the lake before him: 'There are ancient traditions (common to many parts of the world) of the ruined city having been seen below, when the water was clear; but however that may be, from this spot of earth it vanished.' Yet, the ground and water above the legendary city 'seem to be waiting the course of ages, for the next earthquake in that place', when they will plunge into the earth's depths to join 'the unhappy city below' (363).

The next day Dickens travels across the Campagna Romana, 'an undulating flat ... where few people can live; and where, for miles and miles, there is nothing to relieve the terrible monotony and gloom.' He goes on to observe, 'Of all kinds of country that could, by possibility, lie outside the gates of Rome, this is the aptest and fittest burial-ground for the Dead City' (364). The legendary city of the lake and Rome merge in Dickens's imagination: he awaits the first glimpse of Rome as if it were a buried city figuratively risen out of the depths of the Campagna. He strains to see the city that finally appears in the distance: 'It looked like – I am half afraid to write the word – like *LONDON!!!* There it lay, under a thick cloud, with innumerable towers, and steeples, and roofs of houses, rising up into the sky, and high above them all, one Dome . . . . It was so like London, at that distance, that if you could have shown it me, in a glass, I should have taken it for nothing else' (364).

Dickens's transformation of Rome – and the London with which he identifies it – into a metaphor for the mind has begun. He responds uneasily to the Roman Carnival, recognising in it vestiges of the pagan Saturnalia enduring into the present, like living fossils of the past. In the catacombs he comes upon a city beneath Rome, with 'great subterranean vaulted roads, diverging in all directions, and choked up with heaps of stone' (386). He emerges from this figurative underworld to continue his investigation of Rome, with its palaces and churches, its obelisks, columns, porticoes and temples: 'It is strange to see, how every fragment, whenever it is possible, has been blended into some modern structure, and made to serve some modern purpose. . . . It is stranger still, to see how many ruins of the old mythology: how many fragments of obsolete legend and observance: have been incorporated into the worship of Christian altars here' (398).

The culminating episode in his experience of the Eternal City occurs as Dickens returns from an outing upon the Campagna, now a sea of ruins, 'to come again on Rome, by moonlight' (397). The moment is no less dream-like than his previous experience of Venice or the later visit to the buried and drowned city of Herculaneum (417), rediscovered along with Pompeii only in the early decades of the eighteenth century. It can be seen to be informed by the *Old Red Sandstone* in which Hugh Miller turns to architectural and antiquarian analogies to clarify the nature of geological formations. In writing of the Ross-shire hills, Miller characteristically compares 'the lines of their horizontal strata' to 'courses of masonry in a pyramid' (24). With fossils embedded in the different strata of a formation, the figurative pyramid can be seen as 'inscribed from bottom to top, like an Egyptian obelisk', an historical record, providing 'wonderful narratives of animal life' (33). But, according to Miller, such figurative narratives are incomplete. The fossil record is fragmentary, akin to 'the broken and half-defaced characters . . . in those obelisks of Egypt round which the sands of the desert have been accumulating for ages' (136–7).[12]

In the scene that Dickens is to describe, there will be no historical gaps. In the moonlight, in the midst of 'narrow streets, devoid of footways, and choked . . . by heaps of dung-hill-rubbish', Dickens finds himself in a square before a church,

> in the centre of which, a hieroglyphic-covered obelisk, brought from Egypt in the days of the Emperors, looks strangely on the foreign scene about it; or perhaps an ancient pillar, with its honoured statue overthrown, supports a Christian saint: Marcus Aurelius giving place to Paul, and Trajan to St. Peter. Then, there are the ponderous buildings reared from the spoliation of the Coliseum, shutting out the moon, like mountains: white here and there, are broken arches and rent walls, through which it gushes freely, as the life comes pouring from a wound.
>
> (397)

In this moment ancient Egypt, imperial and Christian Rome, and the teeming Italian metropolis of the present, with the adjacent Jewish quarter, 'where the people are industrious and money-getting', become a single whole, a complex unity characteristic of the living mind as constituted by nineteenth-century Romanticism: the mind whose true nature is to be glimpsed only when the obscuring 'common light' that is conventional consciousness 'shall have withdrawn' to reveal the stars that are always shining, night and day (*Confessions*, 328–9).

Rome has suggested realms of the mind in which there are no gaps, no strata barren of fossils, no edifices with erased inscriptions. For there is, in De Quincey's words, 'no such thing as *forgetting* possible to the mind; a thousand accidents may, and will interpose a veil between our present consciousness and the secret inscriptions on the mind . . . but alike, whether veiled or unveiled the inscription remains for ever' (*Confessions*, 328). And, as Dickens is to do in *Pictures from Italy*, De Quincey associates such a vision of the mind with things architectural. Under the influence of opium, 'the sense of space, and in the end, the sense of time, [are] both powerfully affected. Buildings, landscapes &c. [are] exhibited in proportions so vast as the bodily eye is not fitted to receive.' Space swells to 'an extent of unutterable infinity'; time expands 'far beyond the limits of any human experience' (328). Within the Eternal City of the mind, a new and enduring permanence has been established.[13]

IV

In perceiving Rome as a buried city rising from the depths of the Campagna, Dickens conferred upon it, in 1845, qualities that Austen Henry Layard was to attribute to the lost city he identified as Nimrud. Layard began the excavations described in *Nineveh and its Remains* in November 1845. Just as Dickens was prepared to see Rome, and later Herculaneum and Pompeii, in a characteristic way, Layard experienced the excavated Nimrud through the prisms of British Romanticism and William Whewell's palaetiological sciences.[14] In his introduction to the first American edition of Layard's book, Edward Robinson was to capture the aura surrounding the rediscovery of buried cities almost lost to human memory. In the cases of Nineveh and Nimrud 'we have to do, not with hoary ruins that have borne the brunt of centuries in the presence of the world, but with a resurrection of the monuments themselves. It is the disentombing of temple-palaces from the sepulchre of ages; the recovery of the metropolis of a powerful nation from the long night of oblivion' (1: ii). Before the Eternal City of Rome, there existed another city, a walled metropolis of palaces and temples, sculptures of immense winged bulls and lions, with human faces, and alabaster slabs decorated with bas-reliefs and cuneiform inscriptions. In their midst there stood a black marble obelisk reminiscent of Hugh Miller's figurative obelisks and the very real Egyptian obelisk that Dickens had come upon in the moonlight in Rome. Layard describes it: 'The whole was in the best preservation; scarcely a character of the inscription was wanting; and the figures were as sharp and well defined as if they had been carved but a few days before' (1: 282).[15] The obelisk testifies to the resilience of human artifacts and the persistence of memory: it suggests those other inscriptions of which De Quincey had written in his *Confessions*, those 'secret inscriptions on the mind' that remain 'for ever' (328).

But, it is in the words attributed to a Bedouin chief to whom Layard turned for labourers to work the excavation that the potential

implications of a Nimrud for a romantic psychology emerge: Sheikh
Abd-ur-rahman says,

> Here are stones which have been buried ever since the time of the
> holy Noah . . . Perhaps they were under ground before the deluge
> . . . My father, and the father of my father, pitched their tents here
> before me; but they never heard of these figures . . . But lo! here
> comes a Frank from many days' journey off, and he walks up to
> the very place, and he takes a stick . . . and makes a line here, and
> makes a line there. Here, says he, is the palace; there, says he, is the
> gate; and he shows us what has been all our lives beneath our feet,
> without our having known any thing about it. Wonderful!
> wonderful!
>
> (2: 71)

There is something disconcerting about the Sheikh's deference to
Layard: the speech may, in fact, be apocryphal.[16] But the revelation of
that which has been unknown to the Sheikh and his ancestors stirs in
him a wonder like that others will experience in the excavation of an
underworld of consciousness.

Nowhere is this more clear than in one of the memorable episodes
in *Nineveh and its Remains* as Layard describes his departure from
Nimrud in June of 1847. He was to leave many of the artefacts in the
ruins of the city, using earth and rubbish to rebury them. Layard
invites us to descend with him 'by a flight of steps rudely cut into the
earth' (2: 89). In the halls of an excavated building, we 'suddenly find
ourselves between a pair of colossal lions, winged and human-
headed, forming a portal' that leads to a 'subterraneous labyrinth'
where – amidst the dust, the frenetic workers, and wild Kurdish
music – there appear 'sculptured gigantic, winged figures; some with
the heads of eagles, others entirely human, and carrying mysterious
symbols in their hand' (2: 90). In this phantasmagoric realm Layard
passes among the various edifices of Nimrud: 'Without an
acquaintance with the intricacies of the place, we should soon lose
ourselves in this labyrinth' (2: 92). Finally, Layard leads us out of the
'buried edifice' to return to the surface from which we have
descended: 'We look around in vain for any traces of the wonderful
remains we have just seen, and are half inclined to believe that we
have dreamed a dream, or have been listening to some tale of Eastern
romance' (2: 92–3).

V

In Dickens's description of a moonlit Rome and in Layard's imaginary walk through the excavated Nimrud, a vision of the buried city as a metropolis of the mind had been suggested decades before Freud was to use an archaeological analogy to introduce the psychoanalytic unconscious in 1896 in his 'Aetiology of Hysteria'. Freud concludes his excavation of a figurative archaeological site by proclaiming, '*Saxa loquuntur!*' (*Standard Edition* 3: 192). But the stones had already spoken in *Pictures from Italy* and in *Nineveh and its Remains*. It was only fitting that Dickens and Layard were to become friends and that, on his visit to Italy in the autumn and early winter of 1853 (in the company of Wilkie Collins and Augustus Egg), Dickens would see Emile and Augusta de la Rue in Genoa and come upon Layard in Naples, where the two climbed Vesuvius, and then again in Rome.[17]

The return to Italy, to Genoa and to the Eternal City was to stir ambiguous memories that served Dickens in good stead, if not in *Hard Times* (1854), then in *Little Dorrit* (1855–7). In the novel, Rome and London become mirror images of each other, each an Eternal City of the mind. On the Sunday after his return from Egypt, Arthur Clennam turns homeward to a reunion with the woman he believes to be his mother. He crosses by St. Paul's and goes down, 'almost to the water's edge, through some of the crooked and descending streets . . . passing, now the mouldy hall of some obsolete Worshipful Company, now the illuminated windows of a Congregationless Church that [seems] to be waiting for some adventurous Belzoni to dig it out and discover its history' (31). In his popular *Narrative* (1820), Giovanni Battista Belzoni, the Italian strongman turned gravecrobber and collector of antiquities for the British Museum, offered an account of his exploits in Egypt, including the rediscovery in 1817 of the temple of Abu-Simbel: the moment was to become a talismanic one for archaeologists and antiquarians of every sort.[18]

In his allusion to Belzoni Dickens has suggested that *Little Dorrit* will involve a figurative excavation, an unearthing of Arthur Clennam's buried past. As the Eternal City of the mind, London retains in its architectural structures a secret that has been buried but not effaced from the memories of those involved in the history of the Clennam family. The old brick house of Arthur Clennam's childhood will finally collapse, bearing with it Rigaud, the blackmailer in possession of the truth about Clennam's birth. The collapse of the house leads to a frantic excavation of the ruins in a search for the corpses of Rigaud and Jeremiah Flintwinch.

The 'dirty heap of rubbish that [has] been' (772) Rigaud is unearthed. But the search for Flintwinch proves futile. Yet, if rumour is to be trusted, 'the depths of the earth' would seem to have yielded up Jeremiah Flintwinch in the guise of 'an old man, who [wears] the tie of his neckcloth under one ear' (773), and consorts with Dutchmen in the Hague and Amsterdam, bearing with him the secrets of the Clennam family: in this way, the past may well speak after all.

In *Little Dorrit*, as later in *Our Mutual Friend* (1864–5) and in *The Mystery of Edwin Drood* (1870), Dickens self-consciously explored the archaeological perspective so central to *Pictures from Italy*. It was a perspective waiting to be appropriated by others interested in the figurative depths of the mind, depths whose existence cannot be demonstrated, but only suggested through the practices and characteristic language of the historical disciplines. Like John Herschel and Dickens, Freud's brain was to be stirred by the writings of antiquarians, geologists and archaeologists: every page he turned was to bring up 'some fresh *ooze* from [the] dark deposits' of his imagination. There is, of course, only fragmentary evidence attesting to Freud's own sense of the way in which his speculations constituted a culminating moment in nineteenth-century thought. We know that in writing to his fiancée, Martha Bernays, in 1884 Freud mentioned Dickens's *Little Dorrit*.[19] In 1899 he gave himself the present of Schliemann's *Ilios*, a book dedicated, appropriately, to Austen Henry Layard.[20] In Freud's personal library, which is now maintained in the Freud Museum in Hampstead, a visitor can examine copies of Layard's *Nineveh and its Remains* and *Discoveries in the Remains of Nineveh and Babylon*. Freud acknowledged his awareness of the larger significance of Abu-Simbel – the site to which Schliemann made the requisite pilgrimage in 1886 – by hanging over the couch on which his patients reclined at 19 Berggasse a print of the temple, an iconographic allusion to the excavation of the human mind.[21]

That excavation was to receive one of its most memorable illustrations in *Civilization and its Discontents*. Here, Freud invokes the archaeological perspective central to the historical disciplines, including psychoanalysis, to suggest that 'in mental life nothing which has once been formed can perish – that everything is somehow preserved and that in suitable circumstances ... it can once more be brought to light' (*Standard Edition*, 21: 69). After offering a brief history of Rome, Freud says, 'Now let us, by a flight of the imagination, suppose that Rome is not a human habitation but a psychical entity with a similarly long and copious past – an entity, that is to say, in which nothing that has once come into existence will have passed away and all the earlier phases of development continue to exist alongside the latest one' (21: 70). Freud acknowledges that Rome is not an altogether apt metaphor for the mind: 'A city is *a priori* unsuitable for a comparison of this sort' (21: 71). But he turns to such a metaphor, always remembering 'how far we are from mastering the characteristics of mental life by representing them in pictorial terms' (21: 71).[22]

That which remains implicit in Dickens's rendering of Rome in *Pictures from Italy* and of London in *Little Dorrit*, and elsewhere, has become explicit in *Civilization and its Discontents*, demonstrating the power of an archaeological perspective to influence the depiction of various phenomena: the historical disciplines exercise their power over the human imagination, leading, if not to the discovery of the unconscious, to its creation through an act of the imagination that confers upon 'the forms of things unknown' – perhaps on 'airy nothing' – 'a local habitation and a name' (*Midsummer Night's Dream*, V. i. 15–17).

Notes

1. Freud to Wilhelm Fliess, Vienna, 28 May 1899. *The Complete Letters of Sigmund Freud to Wilhelm Fliess. 1887–1904*, trans. and ed. Jeffrey Moussaieff Masson (Cambridge, MA: Belknap Press, 1985) 353.
2. For discussions of these issues, see Edwin Clarke and L. S. Jacyna, *Nineteenth-Century Origins of Neuroscientific Concepts* (Berkeley: University of California Press, 1987); Anne Harrington, *Medicine, Mind, and the Double Brain: A Study in Nineteenth-Century Thought* (Princeton: Princeton University Press, 1987); and Robert M. Young, *Mind, Brain and Adaptation in the Nineteenth Century: Cerebral Localization and its Context from Gall to Ferrier* (Oxford: Clarendon Press, 1970).
3. For an account of mesmerism in general, see Adam Crabtree, *From Mesmer to Freud: Magnetic Sleep and the Roots of Psychological Healing* (New Haven: Yale University Press, 1993); for the classic study of Dickens and mesmerism, see Fred Kaplan, *Dickens and Mesmerism: The Hidden Springs of Fiction* (Princeton: Princeton University Press, 1975).
4. For discussion of these issues, see Crabtree, *From Mesmer to Freud*, 109–68; and Kaplan, *Dickens and Mesmerism*, 3–73.
5. For the classic work about the discovery of 'the unconscious', see Henri F. Ellenberger, *The Discovery of the Unconscious: The History and Evolution of Dynamic Psychiatry* (New York: Basic Books, 1970). Also see Ilza Veith, *Hysteria: The History of a Disease* (Chicago: University of Chicago Press, 1965). For the implicit *telos* in any such histories – and in *this* essay – see the warnings of Mark S. Micale's *Approaching Hysteria: Disease and its Interpretations* (Princeton: Princeton University Press, 1995) 19–29.

6. See *The Dickens Index*, ed. Nicholas Bentley, Michael Slater and Nina Burgis (Oxford: Oxford University Press, 1988) 166.
7. For a concise biography of Hugh Miller, see George Rosie, *Hugh Miller: Outrage and Order. A Biography and Selected Writings* (Edinburgh: Mainstream Publishing, 1981) 15–87. For essays on various dimensions of Hugh Miller's career, see *Hugh Miller and the Controversies of Victorian Science*, ed. Michael Shortland (Oxford: Clarendon Press, 1996).
8. See J. H. Stonehouse, ed., *Catalogue of the Libraries of Charles Dickens and W.M. Thackeray* (London: Picadilly Fountain Press, 1935) 71.
9. For a discussion of how the archaeological metaphor was used to instill an historical perspective in geology, and perhaps in psychology, see Paolo Rossi, *The Dark Abyss of Time: The History of the Earth and the History of Nations from Hooke to Vico*, trans. Lydia G. Cochrane (Chicago: University of Chicago Press, 1984) 12–17.
10. See Walter F. Cannon, 'The Impact of Uniformitarianism: Two Letters from John Herschel to Charles Lyell, 1836–1837', *Proceedings of the American Philosophical Society* 105, 3 (1961): 301–4.
11. For the fullest discussion of this episode in Dickens's life, see Kaplan, *Dickens and Mesmerism*, 74–105.
12. For discussions of Miller's theological position and his attitude to the fossil record, see Rosie, *Hugh Miller*, 15–87, and the essays in *Hugh Miller and the Controversies of Victorian Science*, ed. Michael Shortland.
13. For a discussion of nineteenth-century preoccupations with memory, see Gillian Beer, 'Origins and Oblivion in Victorian Narrative', in *Sex, Politics, and Science in the Nineteenth-Century Novel*, ed. Ruth Bernard Yeazell, 63–87, Selected Papers from the English Institute, 1983–4 (Baltimore: Johns Hopkins University Press, 1986).
14. For the life of Austen Henry Layard, see Gordon Waterfield, *Layard of Nineveh* (London: John Murray, 1963).
15. Throughout my discussion of Layard and Nimrud, I quote from the 1849 American edition. The same passages appear, however, in Layard's *A Popular Account of Discoveries at Nineveh* (London: John Murray, 1851), the edition Dickens owned.
16. For discussions of European attitudes to the 'Orient' of the European imagination, see Edward W. Said, *Culture and Imperialism* (New York: Alfred A. Knopf, 1993) and *Orientalism* (New York: Pantheon Books, 1978).
17. For discussions of the relationship between Dickens and Layard and their meeting in Italy in 1853, see Michael Cotsell, 'Politics and Peeling Frescoes: Layard of Nineveh and *Little Dorrit*', *Dickens Studies Annual*. ed. Michael Timko, Fred Kaplan and Edward Guiliano, 15 (1986) 181–200; Fred Kaplan, *Dickens: A Biography* (New York: William Morrow, 1988) 290–300; and Nancy Aycock Metz, 'Little Dorrit's London: Babylon Revisited', *Victorian Studies* 33 (1990) 465 86.
18. See G[iovanni Battista] Belzoni, *Narrative of the Operations and Recent Discoveries within the Pyramids, Temples, Tombs, and Excavations in*

Egypt and Nubia: and of a Journey to the Coast of the Red Sea, in Search of the Ancient Berenice: and Another to the Oasis of Jupiter Ammon, 2nd edition (London: John Murray, 1821). For a life of Belzoni, see Stanley Mayes, *The Great Belzoni* (London: Putnam, 1959).

19. See Ernest Jones, *The Formative Years and the Great Discoveries: 1856–1900*, vol. 1, *The Life and Work of Sigmund Freud* (New York: Basic Books, 1953) 161.

20. For a life of Heinrich Schliemann, see David A. Traill, *Schliemann of Troy: Treasure and Deceit* (New York: St. Martin's Press, 1995).

21. I wish to thank Erica Davies, Director of the Freud Museum, for her thoughtfulness when I examined the Layard books in Freud's library and for her information about Franz Hanfstaengel's print after an original by Ernst Koerner. Also, see *Berggasse 19, Sigmund Freud's Home and Offices, Vienna 1938: The Photographs of Edmund Engleman* (New York: Basic Books, 1976).

22. For a discussion of these issues, see Donald P. Spence, *The Freudian Metaphor: Toward Paradigm Change in Psychoanalysis* (New York: W.W. Norton, 1987).

References

Beer, Gillian, 'Origins and Oblivion in Victorian Narrative', in *Sex, Politics and Science in the Nineteenth-Century Novel*, ed. Ruth Bernard Yeazell. Selected Papers from the English Institute, 1983–4 (Baltimore: Johns Hopkins University Press, 1986) 63–87.

Belzoni, G[iovanni Battista], *Narrative of the Operations and Recent Discoveries within tshe Pyramids, Temples, Tombs, and Excavations in Egypt and Nubia; and of a Journey to the Coast of the Red Sea, in Search of the Ancient Berenice; and Another to the Oasis of Jupiter Ammon*, 2nd edition (London: John Murray, 1821).

Berggasse 19. Sigmund Freud's Home and Offices. Vienna 1938: The Photographs of Edmund Engelman (New York: Basic Books, 1976).

Cannon, Walter F., 'The Impact of Uniformitarianism: Two Letters from John Herschel to Charles Lyell, 1836–1837'. *Proceedings of the American Philosophical Society* 105, 3 (1961) 301–14.

Carlyle, Thomas, 'Characteristics', in *The Emergence of Victorian Consciousness: The Spirit of the Age*, ed. George Levine (New York: Free Press, 1967) 39–68.

Clarke, Edwin and L. S. Jacyna, *Nineteenth-Century Origins of Neuroscientific Concepts* (Berkeley: University of California Press, 1987).

Combe, George, *The Constitution of Man Considered in Relation to External Objects*, 6th edition (Edinburgh: John Anderson, Jr, 1836).

Cotsell, Michael, 'Politics and Peeling Frescoes: Layard of Nineveh and *Little Dorrit*'. *Dickens Studies Annual*, ed. Michael Timko, Fred Kaplan and Edward Guiliano, 15 (1986) 181–200.

Crabtree, Adam, *From Mesmer to Freud: Magnetic Sleep and the Roots of Psychological Healing* (New Haven: Yale University Press, 1993).

Darwin, Charles, *On the Origin of Species by the Means of Natural Selection, or the Preservation of Favoured Races in the Struggle for Life*, 1859. Reprint, with an introduction by Ernst Mayr (Cambridge, MA: Harvard University Press, 1964).

De Quincey, Thomas, *Confessions of an English Opium-Eater together with Selections from the Autobiography of Thomas De Quincey*, ed. Edward Sackville-West (London: Cresset Press, 1950).

Dickens, Charles, *American Notes and Pictures from Italy*. Oxford Illustrated Dickens (Oxford: Oxford University Press, 1987).

—— *Hard Times*, Oxford Illustrated Dickens (Oxford: Oxford University Press, 1987).

—— *Little Dorrit*, ed. Harvey Peter Sucksmith. Clarendon Dickens (Oxford: Clarendon Press, 1979).

—— *Martin Chuzzlewit*, ed. Margaret Cardwell. Clarendon Dickens (Oxford: Clarendon Press, 1982).

—— *The Mystery of Edwin Drood*, ed. Margaret Cardwell. Clarendon Dickens (Oxford: Clarendon Press, 1972).

—— *Our Mutual Friend*, Oxford Illustrated Dickens (Oxford: Oxford University Press, 1987).

—— 'The Poetry of Science', *Miscellaneous Papers, Plays and Poems*. vol. 1, ed. B. W. Matz (New York: Hearst's International Library, n.d.) 64–8.

The Dickens Index, ed. Nicholas Bentley, Michael Slater and Nina Burgis (Oxford: Oxford University Press, 1988).

Ellenberger, Henri F., *The Discovery of the Unconscious: The History and Evolution of Dynamic Psychiatry* (New York: Basic Books, 1970).

Elliotson, John, 'Instances of Double States of Consciousness Independent of Mesmerism', *The Zoist: A Journal of Cerebral Physiology and Mesmerism* 4 (1846) 157–87.

[Elliotson, John], 'Prospectus', *The Zoist: A Journal of Cerebral Physiology and Mesmerism* 1 (1843–4) 1-4.

Freud, Sigmund, 'The Aetiology of Hysteria', in *The Standard Edition of the Complete Psychological Works of Sigmund Freud*, vol. 3, general ed. James Strachey (London: Hogarth Press, 1962) 189-221.

—— *Civilization and its Discontents*, in *The Standard Edition of the Complete Psychological Works of Sigmund Freud*, vol. 21, general ed. James Strachey (London: Hogarth Press, 1961) 59–145.

—— Letter to Wilhelm Fliess. Vienna 28 May 1899, in *The Complete Letters of Sigmund Freud to Wilhelm Fliess*, trans. and ed. Jeffrey Moussaieff Masson (Cambridge, MA: Belknap Press, 1985).

Harrington, Anne, *Medicine, Mind, and the Double Brain: A Study in Nineteenth-Century Thought* (Princeton: Princeton University Press, 1987).

Hugh Miller and the Controversies of Victorian Science, ed. Michael Shortland (Oxford: Clarendon Press, 1996).

Hume, David, *A Treatise of Human Nature*, ed. L.A. Selby-Bigge (Oxford: Clarendon Press, 1964).

Hunt, Robert, *The Poetry of Science, or, Studies of the Physical Phenomena of Nature* (London. Reeve, Benham, and Reeve, 1848).

Jones, Ernest, *The Formative Years and the Great Discoveries: 1856–1900*. Vol. 1, *The Life and Work of Sigmund Freud* (New York: Basic Books, 1953).

Kaplan, Fred, *Dickens: A Biography* (New York: William Morrow, 1988).

—— *Dickens and Mesmerism: The Hidden Springs of Fiction* (Princeton: Princeton University Press, 1975).

Layard, Austen H[enry], *Discoveries among the Ruins of Nineveh and Babylon: with Travels in Armenia, Kurdistan, and the Desert: Being the Result of a Second Expedition undertaken for the Trustees of the British Museum* (New York: Harper and Brothers, 1853).

—— *Nineveh and its Remains: With an Account of a Visit to the Chaldaean Christians of Kurdistan, and the Yezidis, or Devil-Worshippers; and an Inquiry into the Manners and Arts of the Ancient Assyrians*, 2 vols (New York: George P. Putnam, 1849).

—— *A Popular Account of Discoveries at Nineveh* (London: John Murray, 1851).

Lyell, Charles. *Elements of Geology* (London: John Murray, 1838).

—— *Principles of Geology, being an Attempt to Explain the Former Changes of the Earth's Surface, by References to Causes now in Operation.* 3 vols, 1830–3 (Reprint, Chicago: University of Chicago Press, 1990–1).

Mayes, Stanley, *The Great Belzoni* (London: Putnam, 1959).

Metz, Nancy Aycock, 'Little Dorrit's London: Babylon Revisited', *Victorian Studies* 33 (1990) 465–86.

Micale, Mark S., *Approaching Hysteria: Disease and its Interpretations* (Princeton: Princeton University Press, 1995).

Miller, Hugh, *The Old Red Sandstone: or New Walks in an Old Field* (Edinburgh: John Johnstone, 1841).

—— *The Testimony of the Rocks: or, Geology in its Bearings on the Two Theologies, Natural and Revealed* (Edinburgh: Thomas Constable, 1857).

Playfair, John, *Illustrations of the Huttonian Theory of the Earth* (Edinburgh: William Creech, 1802).

Robinson, Edward, Introduction to *Nineveh and its Remains: With an Account of a Visit to the Chaldaean Christians of Kurdistan, and the Yezidis, or Devil-Worshippers; and an Inquiry into the Manners and Arts of the Ancient Assyrians*, by Austen Henry Layard. 2 vols (New York: George P. Putnam, 1849).

Rosie, George, *Hugh Miller: Outrage and Order. A Biography and Selected Writings* (Edinburgh: Mainstream Publishing, 1981).

Rossi, Paolo, *The Dark Abyss of Time: The History of the Earth and the History of Nations from Hooke to Vico*, trans. Lydia G. Cochrane (Chicago: University of Chicago Press, 1984).

Said, Edward W., *Culture and Imperialism* (New York: Alfred A. Knopf, 1993).

—— *Orientalism* (New York: Pantheon Books, 1978).

Schliemann, Heinrich, *Ilios: The City and Country of the Trojans: The Results of Researches and Discoveries on the Site of Troy and throughout the Troad in the Years 1871–72–73–78–79* (London: John Murray, 1880).

Shakespeare, William, *A Midsummer Night's Dream*, ed. Harold F. Brooks, Arden Shakespeare (New York: Metheun, 1979).

Spence, Donald P., *The Freudian Metaphor: Toward Paradigm Change in Psychoanalysis* (New York: W.W. Norton, 1987).

Stonehouse, J. H., ed., *Catalogue of the Libraries of Charles Dickens and W. M. Thackeray* (London: Picadilly Fountain Press, 1935).

Traill, David A., *Schliemann of Troy: Treasure and Deceit* (New York: St. Martin's Press, 1995).

Vcith, Ilza, *Hysteria: The History of a Disease* (Chicago: University of Chicago Press, 1965).

Waterfield, Gordon, *Layard of Nineveh* (London: John Murray, 1963).

Whewell, William, *History of the Inductive Sciences, from the Earliest to the Present Times*, 3 vols (London: John W. Parker, 1837).

Young, Robert M., *Mind, Brain and Adaptation in the Nineteenth Century: Cerebral Localization and its Context from Gall to Ferrier* (Oxford: Clarendon Press, 1970).

Part II
Dickens and the
New Worlds

America

The Colonies and Elsewhere

6
Truth in *American Notes*

Patrick McCarthy

We recall from our schooldays Bacon's essay 'Of Truth' and especially its arresting beginning: 'What is Truth; said jesting Pilate; And would not stay for an answer.' Victorians rarely jested about such matters, Charles Dickens among them. When the accuracy of what he had written was questioned, he was wont to insist that it was the truth. Today in dealing with large matters, we sense that the truth, the whole truth, and nothing but the truth rarely stops to be caught. Even our friends spot this whenever we generalise, and how our 'truths' will look in another century we are blessed in not knowing.

Dickens made insistent claims that *American Notes* was true. He had written the travel book after his first visit to America in 1842 and expected rough handling. British travel writers on America had been called liars and slanderers, and he had discovered that American newspapers could engage in lying slanders themselves. It was the American way, and Dickens was concerned. Even so, why are the claims so sweeping, and why does Dickens protest his 'truth' so often? Such claims are easily adduced and well-nigh impregnable to refutation, but they make moderns uneasy (perhaps Americans in particular?). We find ourselves asking what has impinged on Dickens's 'truth' to concern him so much about it? Or what, we may ask more broadly, are the contingencies and pressures affecting and inflecting Dickens's 'truth' as he presents it to us?[1]

American Notes was a new departure for the youthful Boz, at 30 years of age a gloriously famous writer of fiction. It took many of its first American readers by surprise. Boz would have had some unfavourable impressions, but readers expected that his geniality and humour would gloss over them. Even today, when the rawness and crudity of early American life is no secret to anybody, the surprise lingers in American readers that Dickens would conclude so decidedly, 'I do not like the country.'[2]

From the beginning and as it went on, the story of Dickens's 1842 visit to America and the rapid writing of his account *'for General Circulation'* is a patchwork of anomalies. He had made an agreement 'for publication of such notes as might occur to him on the journey'.[3] As he travelled he kept a detailed account, but he was less than candid about whether he intended to write a book, mostly saying nothing about it, and three months into the visit telling an American friend he had not yet decided to write 'anything about America'.[4] He had gone knowing that conflicting reports had been written about America and American democracy by earlier British travellers. He had read those by Harriet Martineau and Captain Marryat, and at least dipped into Fidler's, Mrs Trollope's and Captain Hall's.[5] Yet he set out with extravagantly high expectations of what he would find. Very quickly disabused of such illusions, he then all but flouted an American public famously thin-skinned whenever it was criticised. He made some efforts to balance his judgements but very little to mollify them. For an established writer to act in this way astounded Edgar Allan Poe. *American Notes*, he said, was 'one of the most suicidal productions, ever deliberately published by an author, who had the least reputation to lose'.[6]

But Dickens had not stripped himself of defenders. America shocked and disappointed him, certainly, but the professional writer in him saw the experience as one he could manage. He divided his subject. The East Coast gentry impressed him as within the social and socially responsible orbit he represented. He liked them, acted accordingly and won their admiration. He anticipated their sympathy for what he would write, dedicated his book to them and when he left, said how much he regretted leaving them.[7] As for his English friends, he not only had them very much in mind, but made sure they knew his thinking as it developed. He did this by writing long letters to John Forster which were to be shown to 'everybody' in their wide circle – to Count D'Orsay, Macready, Fonblanque, Rogers and so on – and were read aloud to a gathering on at least one occasion. Dickens drew confidence from their suffrages, knowing that theirs would be a generally affirmative response.

He then felt free to deal with the second part of his subject: the raw, inarticulate, uncivilised rest of America. If he did not dismiss that world with a Pecksniffian wave of his arm, he considered it from a satirist's distance, with wide-eyed amazement, offended dignity and brilliant humour. His text would be readable, he knew, and would ensure a sale for the publishers and address another problem: his shortage of time.

Dickens had only 4½ months for the entire trip, including the month he spent in Canada. For much of this period he was *en route*; he travelled over 4,000 miles. His mid-America is the world of hotels, canal and river boats, coaches, and fellow passengers, the sharpers and self-promoters as well as new settlers and small businessmen. Time spent in cities was brief, often only a day or two. At each stop he and Catherine rested, shook hands with great numbers of people and saw all that his prodigious energy permitted. So hurried, writing his impressions at every spare moment, he had little opportunity as he went along for developing sympathy or understanding. Nor did he have time to see beyond the surfaces of things, to see what the raw Americans were making of their 'mighty world of eye and ear'. Much of what he beheld was outside his usual ken, outside for example the ordered social world and tamed natural world of his favourite poets, Wordsworth and Tennyson.

The great majority of the East Coast social and intellectual gentry he had cultivated accepted his proffered hand of friendship. But some viewed him with a critical eye. Among them were Richard Henry Dana, who put him down as lacking the 'well-balanced mind' and 'delicate perceptions of a gentleman', and Emerson, who was affronted by the book's obviously commercial purposes and its claims to be true. 'Truth is not his object for a single instant . . .,' he wrote. 'As an account of America it is not [to] be considered for a moment. We can hear throughout every page the dialogue between the author and his publisher, "Mr. Dickens the book must be entertaining – that is the essential point. Truth! damn truth." '[8]

We know that claims of truth were to become a life-long habit with Dickens. Prefaces to his novels from *Pickwick* onwards, bristle with the words 'fact', 'true', 'truly', 'truth' and 'real'. To criticisms of *Oliver Twist*, that the characterisation of Nancy was not natural, he responded in capital letters: 'IT IS TRUE.' And in *Bleak House*, famously, who forgets his bull-dogged defence of spontaneous combustion as based on 'notable facts'? At such times he is Samuel Johnson *redivivus*, kicking his rock to refute yet another Berkeley.

American Notes reaches for such terms in its dedication, prefaces and final pages. The dedication is offered to 'those friends of mine in America' who 'can bear the truth', and the first preface asks readers to find the 'fact' that will prove him right or wrong (46, 48). In the preface to the cheap edition, he says rather more assertively that he has 'nothing to defend' and then pounds out, 'The truth is the truth.' Worried that he will be charged with prejudice, he braces up his truthfulness with assertions of good will and denies he has written with 'ill-nature, coldness, or animosity' (47). In the last pages he seeks to spike the unfavourable reception he expects, again with a bow to his New England friends: 'I have written the Truth in relation to the mass of those who form [American] judgments and express their opinions' (292). His letters to both American and English friends are just as insistent in claiming that his book is 'true', 'honest' and 'honourable' (III, 270, 315, 345).

Only in a preface that was suppressed at the advice of Forster does Dickens admit any limitation to his claims to truthfulness. He has been bound, he says, 'to do justice to what, according to [his] best means of judgment, [he] found to be the truth' (300). His 'best means of judgment' is the phrase that catches our eye, for it was those 'means' that were hedged round with circumstance – with his purposes, his timing, the people he met, the genre in which he was writing.

First of all, *American Notes* is a job of professional work, done under the pressure of time and money and the need to be entertaining, as the angry Mr Emerson saw. Just then particularly, the failure of Sir Walter Scott haunted Dickens, he worried about his own expenses, and knew the obligations he had incurred. And so he went his young, difficult, impetuous way, the very antithesis of a later travel writer, Henry James.

Nor did he travel or write unaccompanied. One cannot not be quite alone who travels and writes as others have before him. It is amusing to think of his gaze directed and his prose inflected by Miss Martineau and Mrs Trollope, but as they had learned from the several British writers of American travel books before them, so he from them. His route, what he chose to see and comment upon in various places, and his modes of getting about were strongly influenced by what others had done before him.[9] As a radical following conservative writers (with the exception of Harriet Martineau), he could expect to play off their attitudes in forming his own, the playing off itself a form of influence.

Dickens's famous fall from hopeful dream of America into stunned reality deeply affected what he remarked upon, especially as his journey went on and he became increasingly disaffected. His disappointment, one may say, bears almost a reciprocal relationship to his 'truth'. One is modified by the other; the more disappointed he is, the more he notices a certain kind of 'truth'. This is not to say that he does not find much to admire and praise; it is also not to deny that the awfulness he found was not sickeningly awful – the spitting, the ill manners, the self-satisfied posturing. On the point Chesterton observes that, with his disappointment 'sharpened and defined', Dickens marks faults that are not especially American.[10] After Dickens leaves New York, turns south and then west, the disagreeables, the oddities and the disgusting never fail to catch his eye.

The *Letters* provide interesting evidence that at certain times Dickens rather more enjoyed himself than his book allows, so disappointed was he on his return. To read in letters that he and Catherine 'enjoyed Washington very much' comes as a surprise to readers of his altogether depressing account in the *Notes*. To read his telling Macready that their boat was 'skimming down the beautiful Ohio' accords little with the wilderness river that flows through the *Notes*. Dickens calls it a 'fine broad river', but it is the dreariest of waters, shadowed by death, empty of life, and eaten by erosion and primaeval waste.

What Dickens was used to seeing and valuing in his world stood as norms of judgement for his reactions to the American scene. Rawness and newness made him impatient for his own established world. He misses snugness; he misses the old and familiar. A Connecticut house in the distance, its blazing fire shining through its windows, cannot be snug. A Sunday morning scene with 'a Sabbath peacefulness on everything' 'would have been the better for an old church; better still for some old graves' (120).

He will not allow that what he sees may change for the better. The present is sacrificed, as Arnold observed, and Dickens will not look beyond it. In Washington DC the unfinished, sparsely settled expanse laid out in accordance with Major L'Enfant's grand design repels him. 'Such as it is, it is likely to remain,' he decides. Such newness and rawness are made insufferable for Dickens by people's incessant boasts of what they are doing. Of Girard College in Pennsylvania he says that 'like many other great undertakings in America, even this is rather going to be done one of these days, than doing now' (146). In the event it grew to be a large, successful school for orphan boys.

In Canada, where he spent almost a month, the tone of the *Notes* radically changes. In a sense he is closer to Britain. Of the roads and inns other travellers complained about, and of the 'wild and rabid Toryism' his letters mention, we hear nothing.[11] His visit to Niagara Falls is especially indicative of how much he disliked mid-America. As soon as he could, he crossed the river to the Canadian side. At the Falls, he had the canonical, quasi-religious experience other nineteenth-century travellers had prepared him to have. He stayed there ten days, relieved to be out of the United States. Here is his comment: 'I never stirred in all that time from the Canadian side, whither I had gone at first. I never crossed the river again; for there were people on the other shore, and it is natural in such a place to shun strange company' (243).

While he is in Montreal, spring bursts out in sudden glory, and the release from the dreary, wearing months spent traversing the American mid-west brightens Dickens's pen. He is also making his turn for home, and at his last stop, in the Hudson River valley at West Point, the country of Washington Irving, his pen touches its beauty into verbal gold. In these travels he had rarely been so fortunate in place and season and beauty.

By contrast his visit to Looking-Glass Prairie, north-east of St Louis, had been as badly timed as could be. The excursion took place during the miserable, muddy winter months which were the nadir of his experience of the American landscape. His day's trip there through 'one unbroken slough of mud and water' reads like a replay of Childe Roland's descent to the dark tower. He arrives at sunset, and in his tired confusion misapprehends the direction in which the sun is setting. About him, the short, ugly grass is checkered with black patches. The vegetation is 'poor and scanty'. He had been told the sight would be 'a landmark in [his] existence', and it was, he conceded, 'a great picture'. But it was a disappointment, yet another one, and he says he will take no pleasure in remembering it (225–6).

Two British naval men had written their impressions of the Looking-Glass Prairie in American travel books. Captain Basil Hall had seen it in the spring of 1830, and Captain Frederick Marryat from another approach in the summer of 1839. Hall thought it 'particularly beautiful of its kind' (III, 395) and, as Marryat was to do after him, spoke of its striking resemblance to the sea. Dickens knew both books; perhaps their accounts had induced him to make the difficult winter journey. Writing to Forster about the prairie, Dickens recalls that 'Hall was quite right in depreciating the general character of the scenery.' The editors of the letters suggest that Hall may have said this to Dickens 'on some occasion when Forster was present' (III, 199–200n). But Dickens's repeating Hall's negative assessment of American scenery by and large, while talking of a place Hall particularly admired, is both an index of Dickens's disappointment and a defence of his own impression.

The experience provides no fair test of how Dickens was able to respond to unfamiliar scenery. Yet his seeing frequently appears to be controlled by generalizing, mythopoetic perceptions. He had tried to prepare himself to see accurately what would be before him, getting books on ornithology and accounts of American life besides the travel books, and reading multiple guide books. But to read Dickens on American landscapes after having read Mrs Trollope on the subject is to note how different were the eyes of these beholders.

Her journey on the Mississippi accords very little with his. True, she travelled up river from New Orleans, her port of entry to the United States, while Dickens joined the river at its confluence with the Missouri.

As Dickens did, Mrs Trollope saw the dismal river, the flat banks, and the 'detestable' and 'eternal forests' of America . . . , their 'fallen trees in every possible stage of decay',[12] but she also could see and name, as Dickens apparently could not, individual trees, shrubs, herbs and flowers: the beech, the chestnut, the tulip tree, the palmetto, paw-paw, the pennyroyal, even the millepore. And she knew birds and named them. Dickens saw birds now and again but names only one, a blue-jay. Amid the varieties of nature the child of the Marshalsea and Camden Town came differently prepared than the child of the quiet rural vicarage.

What he saw of the varieties of America's people was also limited and in ways he could not altogether control. Everywhere feted, lionised out of his privacy, forced to shake hands with hundreds of people who thought he must do so because they had read his books, he had not left the East Coast before the people he saw began to look alike (289). As he moved west from Baltimore, on the long-distance swing that took him as far west as St Louis and then north-north-east to Niagara Falls, he stopped briefly at urban communities large and small. There he met whatever local dignitaries there were, but most of the time he was simply *en route*. His mid-America became a world of hotels, canal and river boats, coaches and fellow passengers. And a levelling, canting, ill-mannered, intrusive, self-satisfied and raw lot they were, or (as Dickens often complained) too rude or inarticulate to speak at all. He was moving among the small businessmen, the sharpers, predators and self-promoters – models for Chadder, Chollop and Scaggers of *Martin Chuzzlewit*.

He speaks little of the settlers and their families, moving west to homestead and farm, to wrest a living from the wild, undeveloped land. They are not talkers nor are they idiosyncratic enough to get more than a mention. One group he pictures being landed on a river bank and then standing motionless while the boat draws away. From a distance he sees others, living in miserable huts by river's side, one woodsman looking wistfully toward the boat, 'at the people from the world' (204–6). His imagination goes no further; he does not know enough about them.

The mythology of the Western settler had not yet been created. We who have read Fenimore Cooper, Willa Cather and A.E. Guthrie are familiar with a type of frontier people set in heroic mould unknown and invisible to Dickens. Even so, some travellers before him viewed the settler farmers more closely than he – Frances Trollope and Harriet Martineau among them. Mrs Trollope compares their independence

(and their loneliness) to Robinson Crusoe's – a Dickens favourite (49) –
while Miss Martineau speaks of them as belonging to 'the real aristocracy
of the country, not only in ball-rooms and bank-parlours, but also in
fishing boats, in stores, in college chambers, and behind the plough'.[13]

Comparisons of this kind may satisfy our critical habit of marking
limitation but what bore upon Dickens and what he brought to his seeing
of the newer world are not easily identified and set out. What one can say
about such complexities misses or understates the point. How can any
'truth' be simple and straightforward that has passed through Dickens's
imaginative eye? His world is a unique – one inclines to say 'inimitable' –
imaginative construct, an amalgam of what and how Dickens saw and
his transformational powers. We can postulate two stages in the process.
First came the physical act of 'seeing' which in Dickens was of an
unmatchable quickness, range and decisiveness. Something, that is to say,
was no sooner observed than placed within an order. By order I mean a
certain range of experiences or convictions: personal, for example, or
moral, social or aesthetic.

The seeing, judging and transforming of what was seen into his full
vision, his 'truth' again, was all but instantaneous. Here indeed is the
compounding of myriad elements drawn from that complicated multi-
sided entity we call Dickens and particularly that part of him we dub for
convenience his imagination. But it is not independent. It works through
and draws on every element in his life. His is a mind haunted by myth
and enchanted by romance. It is dramatic and self-dramatising. In
American Notes he acknowledges his debt to popular entertainments and
to the heritage of great imaginists he had made his own. In his pages Le
Sage, Swift, Goldsmith, Crabbe, Scott and the creator of the *Arabian Nights*
make their presence felt.

And where is the 'truth' that existed before his brilliant animating
power is drawn on? Who but Dickens has seen his 'corpulent' and
'dropsical' coach (186), his failed bank building looking 'rather dull and
out of spirits' (145), his oyster eaters 'copying the coyness of the thing
they eat' (135)? Or his rapid river, seen through the chinks of a bridge,
'gleam[ing], far down below, like a legion of eyes' (188)? In his wilderness
rivers, stately trees fallen into the river become 'grizzly skeletons'. Others
'are bathing their green heads' in the waters, and some are 'drowned so
long ago, that their bleached arms start out from the middle of the
current, and seem to grasp the boat, and drag it under water' (205).

Certainly not least in our experience of *American Notes* is its powerful
authorial presence. On reflection we know Dickens has chosen and
shaped and presented this version of 1842 America, his 'truth'. On

examination we see how often the text depends on other texts, the authors mentioned above, and accounts of slavery and education reports in particular. We may *feel* ourselves urged along by a commanding voice, though (and this may be particularly true of Americans then and now) we very soon sense our cultural distances and varying focal lengths. But we are struck nevertheless by the extraordinary assurance and air of authority that informs almost every page. It matters very little to our reaction to the text that we are aware its voice is self-dramatising, knowingly putting itself forward in every scene, almost stunningly confident.

There may be some but no complete accounting for this presence. It is infused with a sense of its own powers; it glows with a success hailed and validated by popular and critical acclaim. It has the suffrage of a body of notable British writers, the admiration and attention of British aristocracy, the support of literary and theatrical friends. But more surely it derives from its being a representative of old-established traditions, with its proud sense of British order, of right thinking, of political freedom and social decorum.

There may be some but no complete accounting for his emphases on the raw, the rude and the repulsive. What had he gone to the New World to see? Nothing less than a renewed version of the Old World with its best features retained, others improved, and its corruptions eradicated. Even with such hopes chastened by his experiences on the East Coast, as he turned westward from Washington, he began 'to dream again of cities growing up, like palaces in fairy tales, among the wilds and forests' (174). Before such sanguine expectations what experiences could fail to disappoint? And for Dickens the disappointment had few modifying restraints, little sense of context, insufficient qualifications from his own past.

What lay before Dickens as he set sail for America on the Cunard line's *Britannia* that cold January afternoon? Laudation, surely, and disenchantment, just as surely. What did he bring with him? A job of writing that had to be done since he already had an advance against publication.[14] For the task he brought his splendid curiosity, vigour, idealism, courage, astonishing confidence and genius. None of these failed him: creative, readable and humorous Dickens is here in good measure. But his powers are goaded into exasperation and his patience wears out. The confidence over-reaches itself, the curiosity does not or cannot go as far as it might, his sympathies, though deeply touched for the slaves, do not develop for the white settlers. Offended by vulgarity and rawness, praised beyond mortal due and alternately crushed and insulted, rushed and rushing along, he had no time to see the broader horizons of America or to see his limited self seeing America.

Notes

1. While this essay was being written, I was asked to edit a special issue of *Nineteenth-Century Prose* on *American Notes*. The four papers I selected for the journal, and for which mine became a long preface, considerably influenced and broadened my views. I wish to express my obligations to their authors: William Sharpe, Laurie Carlson, Patricia Ard and David Stephens.
2. This conclusion, written to John Forster from Washington, DC, did not change during his tour. See the Pilgrim Edition of *The Letters of Charles Dickens*, ed. Madeline House and Graham Storey (Oxford: Clarendon Press, 1965–) III, 135.
3. John Forster, *The Life of Charles Dickens* (1871; London: Chapman & Hall, Gadshill Edition, n.d.) I, iii, 195–6.
4. *Letters*, III, 185.
5. Edgar Johnson, *Charles Dickens: His Tragedy and Triumph* (New York: Simon and Schuster) I, 360.
6. *Letters*, III, 348n2.
7. The best modern edition is that edited by John S. Whiteley and Arnold Goldman, *American Notes for General Circulation* (New York: Penguin, 1972). See 46, 144. Page references in the text are to this edition.
8. *Letters*, 271n.
9. Jerome Meckier compares these influences fruitfully in his perceptive and genial assessment, *Innocent Abroad: Charles Dickens's American Engagements* (Lexington, University Press of Kentucky, 1990) ch. 3.
10. G.K. Chesterton, *Charles Dickens, the Last of the Great Men* (1906; New York: Readers Club, 1942) 101, 106.
11. *Letters*, III, 38n7, 348n1, 270n4.
12. Frances Trollope, *Domestic Manners of the American*, ed. Donald Smalley (Gloucester, MA: Peter Smith, 1974) 41–2.
13. Harriet Martineau, *Society in America* (London: Saunders & Otley, 1837) III, 29–30. In *Transatlantic Manners: Social Patterns in Nineteenth-century Anglo-American Travel Literature* (Cambridge: Cambridge University Press, 1990), Christopher Mulvey quotes this passage as part of an insightful comparison between early nineteenth and later views of the American settlers. See especially 59–60.
14. *Letters*, III, 1.

7

The Life and Adventures of Martin Chuzzlewit: Or, America Revised[1]

Nancy Metz

Several decades ago, in an influential *PMLA* article, Harry Stone examined for the first time the specific ways in which Dickens transformed the raw material of his American travels into art. Stone emphasised the importance of observation, experience and memory in Dickens's composing process – the relationship between 'fact and fiction' (464–78). The view of the novel which has become dominant in recent years, while it acknowledges the influence on Dickens of canonical travellers' accounts, similarly emphasises the determining role of Dickens's disillusioning experiences. According to this reading, a useful summary of which can be found in Robert Lougy's introduction to his valuable *Martin Chuzzlewit* bibliography, Dickens may have gone to America with the explicit intention of being a better traveller than Martineau and Trollope had been – and perhaps, as a result, writing a more sympathetic book, but he was soon focused on his own wrongs. Violations of decorum and privacy offended him, as did his shabby treatment by the American press with respect to the copyright issue, and it is these personal events, together with the very personal anger they aroused in Dickens, that largely account for the way the New World gets represented in *Martin Chuzzlewit* (Lougy, xiv–xv).

I want to suggest some ways in which this view of Dickens's process in composing the American episodes of *Martin Chuzzlewit* might be revised – primarily by focusing on Dickens's writing in these chapters as itself a process of revision. In doing so, I follow the lead of Jerome Meckier, whose chapter, 'The Battle of the Travel Books', in *Innocent Abroad* has thoroughly informed my own research.[2] Meckier's close reading of the steamboat dinner scene in Chapter 34 demonstrates in particular the degree to which Dickens continued to work very closely

with the issues raised by Fanny Trollope and Harriet Martineau, even
as he fictionalised his own experiences (97–132). I want to argue that in
many similar instances, Dickens constructed dialogue, description and
even entire scenes implicitly as 'conversations' with other travel writers.
This happens more often than we recognise in *Martin Chuzzlewit*, partly
because we do not have easy access to the primary texts through which
Dickens first encountered the New World. Thus we tend to hear
Dickens's voice very loudly – but only hints and whispers of the
sometimes ephemeral writers with whom he engages between the lines.

Dickens, it is clear from biographical evidence, had read widely on
America. He had certainly read the standard accounts – Martineau and
Trollope, Marryat and, very likely, Tocqueville. He had read as well a
whole set of travel writers less well known today: like Franz Lieber,
Captain Thomas Hamilton and Basil Hall. He read guidebooks
intended for tourists and manuals for emigrants. He read travel books
about England written from the American perspective and intended to
answer English criticism – such as Henry Colman's *European Life and
Manners*, which Dickens reviewed for the *Examiner* in 1838. He read
accounts of frontier life, including Catherine Kirkland's *A New Home;
Who'll Follow* (Cardwell, xxxii). He was thoroughly familiar with the
work of the French naturalist George-Louis Leclerc Buffon, whose
counter-myth of the New World as a false paradise – a continent only
lately emerged from the ocean waters – influences the portrayal of Eden
(Gerbi, 3–32). As a reader of *The Times*, the major journals and the
Annual Register, he breathed an atmosphere of international news and
controversy, embracing such issues as the Maine–Canadian boundary
dispute, the British attack on the American ship *Caroline*, the
involvement of American organisations in the Irish Repeal movement,
and most prominently the repudiation by one after another of the
American states of debts incurred to British investors. The lanky,
lounging figure of Brother Jonathan was familiar to him from *Punch*
cartoons, and he had studied closely the arguments and documentary
evidence in W.W. Weld's powerful *American Slavery as It Is: Testimony of
a Thousand Voices* (1839). A generally well-read man, Dickens carried
with him as so much mental baggage representations of the New World
popularised by writers as various as Shakespeare, Goldsmith, Rousseau
and Thomas Moore. Although some of Dickens's reading about the
New World was undertaken at short notice specifically in preparation
for his trip, a great deal more of it was absorbed in a diffused way and
over a much longer period, framing both ends of his comparatively
brief visit to America.

Dickens's reading was thus less a preparation for experience than a process concurrent with it, thoroughly infusing perceptions and influencing the interpretation of events. Textual encounters with the New World were often, in fact, determinants of experience, shaping what Dickens *could* see and what remained in the end invisible to him. As he composed *Martin Chuzzlewit*, Dickens continued to struggle with and against these texts – texts which included (as Stone and others have demonstrated) his own letters home and *American Notes*.

In puzzling over *Martin Chuzzlewit*, it seems to me that we have paid insufficient attention to the ways in which Dickens's 'real' experiences are reinserted in the travel narratives he had read, so that every act of writing about America becomes, in effect, a form of negotiation and debate. A closer look at the main lines of the contemporary debate over the New World as they are refracted in the opening episodes of the American chapters reveals much about Dickens's writing process in the American section as a whole and helps to explain as well why readers have typically found these chapters somewhat anomalous and problematic.

To say anything new at all about the New World was the first challenge Dickens faced. In writing about America, it is clear, Dickens inherited from other travel writers not just a set of issues, but a highly specific agenda. He clearly felt some pressure to cover those multiplicitous details of dress, language and custom which previous writers had definitively associated with American culture. But travel narratives are by convention a leisurely form of discourse, whereas Dickens worked within the tight constraints of the monthly issue, restricted still further by the necessarily limited space available for a subplot. Thus it is that on 'the very brink and margin of the land of Liberty' a compressed, highly allusive prose style takes over a narrative which had until then unfolded discursively and descriptively, more in the picturesque and pastoral tradition (255).[3] Opening the English scenes, Dickens had devoted a full chapter to the Chuzzlewit pedigree, then lingered over an extensive description of the wind which played about the Wiltshire landscape. America, on the other hand, comes at the reader in an overwhelming rush of details, allusions and sensory impressions.

Within the space of a single chapter Dickens packs in an encyclopaedic range of satirical references, many of them laden with multiple literary associations from the extensive discourse of travel. The pages bristle with topical allusions – to American party names, gouging, duelling and violence, politically inspired criminal accusations, lounging, blunt questions, attitudes to immigrants, American English, moneyed aristocracy, American drinking habits, democratic journalism, 'smartness', forgery, Broadway, pigs, master–servant relations, spitting and spittoons, stoves, rocking chairs, repudiation of debts, the prevalence of fires in New York City, dining at a table d'hôte, greedy feeding, the faded beauty of American women, the profusion of meaningless military honours, the pursuit of dollars, the absence of culture and reading habits, American ineptitude for social pleasure and censorship of unpopular ideas. Every satirical detail in Chapter 16 conceals an allusion to others who have similarly singled out this same cultural artefact for critique. The concentrated essence of Marryat, Tocqueville, Hamilton, Trollope, Lieber and others who had written on these same topics is distilled into Chapter 16 – and the whole effect is superimposed on what these writers had taught Dickens to observe at 'first hand'. Of course, Dickens really did observe some pigs – and plenty of piggish manners; and he certainly needed no one to tell him that American newspapers could be libellous. But in representing these things in Chapter 16 – indeed in 'seeing' them in the first place, Dickens often revisits obligatory sites on which others have already left their mark.

Dickens's most important debt to the literature of New World travel lay in his acceptance of its most fundamental premise. Despite his explicit protest to the contrary before he left for America that 'In going to a New World one must utterly forget, and put out of sight the Old one and bring none of its customs and observations into comparison', in practice Dickens embraced the assumption of nearly every British traveller before him that the best way to understand the New World was to compare it with the Old, with a view to determining which culture was better (*Letters*, 2.402). If the characters of *Martin Chuzzlewit* converse on the most casual occasions as if they were figures in a public debate, this is partly because Dickens wanted to satirise American garrulousness, defensiveness and national pride, but partly also because through them Dickens himself was constantly and compulsively casting up accounts in the cultural balance sheet that dominated the nineteenth-century discourse of travel.

And it is clear, if we examine the ways in which this work gets done, that Dickens conceived of his task as a revision process. By interrogating, correcting and sometimes ventriloquising those texts silently in the background of most contemporary readers' engagement with the British/American culture wars, Dickens laboured to acquire and articulate a voice and viewpoint of his own. The work of 'revising America' required rhetorical finesse, a simplifying and focusing of the issues, a strategic displacement of claims and counterclaims, and a deployment of metaphor, wit and dramatic structure as persuasive tools.

We can see this process at work if we glance at how Dickens handled those characteristics of American culture most consistently praised by travellers.

Allowing for variation in emphasis and degree, most travellers agreed that Americans exhibited much enterprise and energy, that they provided better for the education of the common man, and that they could boast a superior record where social problems and human rights (slavery excepted) were concerned. Each of these issues is addressed in *Martin Chuzzlewit*, but in a way that directly undermines the authority of the claims. A typical rhetorical move is to convert into spurious and complacent self-praise the few traits conceded by English writers (often in otherwise critical accounts) as American strengths. Look at Marryat's whimsical tribute to the 'very remarkable energy in the American disposition'. 'If they fail, they bound up again.' 'The New York merchants', he says, 'are of that *elastic* nature that when fit for nothing else, they might be converted into *coach springs*' (17). This same claim is made in *Martin Chuzzlewit*, in the very metaphor of Marryat's pun, but both tone and context are entirely altered when the Rowdy Journal pompously boasts to Martin, 'We are an elastic country . . . We have revivifying and vigorous principles within ourselves' (269).

When Martin proposes education as an exception to Bevan's wholesale denigration of his country's accomplishments, the text positions the Englishman as the fair-minded observer, hopefully seeking to confirm a favourable preconception about America. At the same time, it displaces the role of culture-critic to the only American for whom credibility has been established. Bevan's response to Martin's tentative compliment not only characterises America's educational achievements as 'no mighty matter' after all, but implies that praise for these reform efforts amounted to so much 'noise' and 'boasting' on the part of the country's numerous Colonel Divers, Jefferson Bricks and Major Pawkinses (279). This rhetorical move permits Dickens to offer up for disparagement the one domain of American achievement about which there was near consensus. Even Sydney Smith, who memorably excoriated the Americans for their repudiation of debt, conceded in an *Edinburgh Review* article:

> Too much praise cannot be given to [them] for their great attention to the subject of education. . . . They quite put into the background everything which has been done in the Old World for the improvement of the lower orders, and confer deservedly upon the Americans the character of a wise, a reflecting, and a virtuous people.
>
> (204)

Dickens almost certainly knew this article. Smith was a personal friend and a signatory of Dickens's 1842 copyright petition, and his writings on America were widely reprinted. Martin's tentativeness in proposing to Mr Bevan even this universally acknowledged area of excellence, and Bevan's decidedly lukewarm response, represent a hardening of Dickens's own earlier expressed position. He had written to Macready on 22 March 1842 explicitly excepting education from his overall disappointment with American society (*Letters*, 3.165).

A related strategy for dealing with American claims of superiority was to deny the grounds for any comparison that might prove unfavourable. Americans were reputed to have less poverty, crime and social unrest. But when Bevan addresses these issues indirectly in his dialogue with Martin, he moves quickly to explain away the obvious conclusion: 'We began our life with two inestimable advantages,' Bevan tells Martin. 'Our history commenced at so late a period as to escape the ages of bloodshed and cruelty through which other nations have passed . . . we have a vast territory, and not – as yet – too many people on it' (279). These were precisely the arguments made by Sydney Smith in the *Edinburgh Review* article just mentioned. 'America is exempted, by its very newness as a nation, from many of the evils of the old governments of Europe. It has no mischievous remains of feudal institutions, and no violations of political economy sanctioned by time, and older than the age of reason.' As for its comparatively peaceful populace, Smith wrote, in language that explains Bevan's 'as yet' –

> When they have peopled themselves up . . . until they are stopped by the Western Ocean; and then, when there are a number of persons who have nothing to do, and nothing to gain, and no hope for lawful industry . . . we may consider their situation as somewhat similar to our own, and their example as touching us more nearly.
>
> (204, 207)

Dickens's probable use of the *Edinburgh Review* article as a pivot against which to position himself is thus revealing. The elaborate rhetorical strategies he employed to 'write down' Smith's quite restricted praise of American education – coupled with his unqualified appropriation of ideas where they would support the ends of satire – suggests the degree to which the sharply drawn scenes of *Martin Chuzzlewit* evolve from a process of reduction and simplification.

The same rhetorical process is at work when Dickens turns his attention to American reading habits, a subject treated by many travel writers, but most extensively by Fanny Trollope. According to

Mrs Trollope: '[Americans] are all too actively employed to read, except at such broken moments as may suffice for a peep at a newspaper' (268). In *Martin Chuzzlewit*, it is a nameless lounger at Pawkins' boarding house who expresses these sentiments, in very much the same terms, but with a vastly different inflection: 'We are a busy people, sir . . . and have no time for reading mere notions. We don't mind 'em if they come to us in newspapers along with almighty strong stuff . . . but darn your books' (274). Lost in the translation is Mrs Trollope's concession to circumstantial and cultural differences: Dickens discounts her whole explanation, preferring instead to focus on the scurrilous character of the newspapers which had repeatedly abused his own trust.

So far, I have attempted to illustrate the ways in which Dickens's arguments about America took shape within a much larger and more pervasive context of discussion and debate. I have illustrated Dickens's characteristic ways of working with the texts of other travellers to sharpen his satire and to gain immediate rhetorical advantage for the view of America he had come gradually to hold. I have shown how this process often involved a sacrifice of subtlety and qualification in the interest of efficiency and impact. There is a good deal of more or less overt debate in the exchanges I have cited, which often take the form Hannibal Chollop will later call 'disputating . . . between the Old World and the New' (522). But even in the descriptive and dramatic scenes, where one might expect Dickens to rely primarily on his personal observations and experiences, a closer reading of the context almost always reveals the extent to which these experiences are mediated through published accounts. Indeed, this is true from the moment young Martin gains his first impressions of the New World.

Readers of the novel will remember that Martin's steamer has scarcely pulled up at the dock when the attention of passengers is drawn to an altercation on shore:

> an alderman had been elected the day before; and Party Feeling naturally running rather high on such an exciting occasion, the friends of the disappointed candidate had found it necessary to assert the great principles of Purity of Election and Freedom of Opinion by breaking a few legs and arms . . . These good-humoured little outbursts of the popular fancy . . . found fresh life and notoriety in the breath of the news-boys . . . . 'Here's this morning's New York Sewer!' cried one. 'Here's this morning's New York Stabber! Here's the New York Family Spy! Here's the New York Private Listener! Here's the New York Peeper! Here's the New York Plunderer! Here's the New

York Keyhole Reporter! Here's the New York Rowdy Journal! Here's all the New York papers! Here's full particulars of the patriotic locofoco movement yesterday, in which the whigs was so chawed up; and the last Alabama gouging case; and the interestin Arkansas dooel with bowie knives; and all the Political, Commercial, and Fashionable News. Here they are! Here they are! Here's the papers, here's the papers!'

(256)

In this, Martin's defining first encounter with American culture, Dickens exaggerates behaviours he had ample opportunity to observe at firsthand, as a prominent victim of American newspaper scurrility. The publication of private and even forged letters, and especially the opposition of the press to his cherished schemes for international copyright, had outraged him and wounded his pride. On 11 August 1842, the *New York Tatler* published a letter allegedly written by Dickens to the *Morning Chronicle* in July, full of contempt for his American hosts and for the hospitality he had received. Dickens had, in fact, written a letter to the *Chronicle* on 7 July, blasting American newspaper editors for their flagrant piracies, and the concurrence of the real and forged letter injured his image for a time with the American public (*Letters*, 3.311 and nn.).

He was angry, too, at the ungenerous construction the press placed on his motives for coming to America. Most galling was the accusation that his '*business* in visiting the United States at this season of the year – a season not usually chosen by travellers for pleasure – is to procure, or to assist in procuring, the passage, by Congress, of an International Copyright Law.' Dickens resented the American press's insistence that his sponsorship of the copyright issue constituted unsolicited advice, tendered in poor taste, and with exclusively self-interested motives. And he chafed to find his novels republished without permission alongside 'the coarsest and most obscene companions, with which they *must* become connected in course of time, in people's minds' in newspapers 'so filthy and so bestial that no honest man would admit one into his house for a water-closet door-mat' (*Letters*, 3.83, n.4; 3.60, n.1; 3.230).

These experiences form the angry subtext to Martin's dockside encounter with the American penny press. But there is good reason to believe that the scene owes its dramatic structure to a literary source quite different in tone and atmosphere from the description Dickens came ultimately to write in Chapter 16. Dickens owned and very likely read Francis Lieber's *Stranger in America* (1838), a largely sympathetic account of the author's travels in America. Here are excerpts from Lieber's description of the scene on board a steamboat preparing to leave New York for Albany:

> 'Sir, the Courier and Inquirer! Latest news from Europe, Sir,' says a little fellow, approaching you with a bundle of that paper, in some street not far from the steamboat-landing. 'The Standard, sir! A Jackson paper; the latest news from Washington,' calls another, concluding, from your refusal of the Courier, that you are a friend to the administration, 'Le Blanc's trial and conviction for murder, sir,' calls another; 'A revolution in Paris,' says his opponent; and the nearer you approach, the more these officious messengers of the events and gossip of two hemispheres thicken around you. – . . . . 'The total loss of the ship Raleigh,' utters another news-pedlar, 'The Temperance Recorder!' and a quarto paper is held out to you; 'The Anti-Masonic, –' what? 'Orange Sir?' asks a man, pushing through the crowd of urchins and lads. 'I want nothing but to be left alone.' – 'Very well, sir' – .
>
> (1835, 1.259–60)

Comparing Dickens's scene with Lieber's account, one is struck by the contrasts. Lieber's description occurs nearly halfway through his two-volume narrative. The quoted passage is nested within a chapter which more prominently foregrounds the author's discussions of steamboat travel, his meeting with Washington Irving and his opinions on the issue of literary originality in America. The chapter subheadings reveal Lieber's primary interest in the material. He will recreate 'An Animated Scene', a sort of *Sketches By Boz* close-up, full of motion and colour, drawn from the point of view of a bemused and tolerant spectator. Lieber aims for a rough, portrait-like verisimilitude, quoting headlines and names of newspapers from memory. If his newsboys are 'officious messengers', they are finally harmless enough, trading as much in 'events' as in 'gossip'.

For Dickens, the newsboys' exertions are central; his caricatured description of the scene on the dock becomes the focal point of the chapter and the gateway episode to the whole American subplot. Although Dickens follows Lieber's practice of organising the scene around a series of 'cries', he conveys a very different atmosphere in his description. Both in their actions (like rats, Dickens's 'legions' of newsboys invade the 'highways and bye-ways of the town' and 'overrun' the ship) and in their sleazy wares, these young salesmen violate British conceptions of personal space and decorum. Radically destabilising the boundaries between public and private, the domestic and the political, they trade in betrayal and exposure. Guests reveal the 'particulars of the private lives of all the ladies' at Mrs White's Ball; the Secretary of State's 'own nurse' peddles an exclusive story of his juvenile dishonesty. One could argue, indeed, that all the important issues Dickens will subsequently deal with in the American episodes are encapsulated here – the claims of the public versus the private life – the limits of freedom, the 'nature' of 'natural man', the conflict between individual self-interest and the collective good, the relationship between 'manners' broadly construed and good citizenship. It seems reasonable to suppose that Dickens's rewriting of Lieber – whether or not this was a conscious process, helped him to focus on these issues more precisely and to see their intimate relationships.

In both Lieber's and Dickens's descriptions, the newsboys' patter is interrupted and the scene abruptly broken off. But whereas Lieber's orange seller accepts dismissal politely, Colonel Diver is not so easily shaken off. His first words, intoned 'almost in Martin's ear', uncomfortably intrude on the young hero's thoughts and pre-empt his own interpretation of the scene. 'It is in such enlightened means', he insists 'that the bubbling passions of my country find a vent' (256). Colonel Diver takes Martin to the office of the *Rowdy Journal* where 'behind a mangy old writing-table . . . sat a figure with the stump of a pen in its mouth and a great pair of scissors in its right hand, clipping and slicing at a file of Rowdy Journals' (260). This 'laughable figure' is Jefferson Brick, 'a small young gentleman of very juvenile appearance . . . unwholesomely pale in the face; partly, perhaps from intense thought, but partly, there is no doubt, from the excessive use of tobacco' (260).

A more extensive and complex negotiation of sources informs the scene immediately following. Here Dickens personifies in one individual – the diminutive, swaggering, verbally florid, and bellicose War Correspondent – the chorus of outraged voices from the American newspaper press assembled in Forster's April 1843 *Foreign Quarterly Review* article, 'The Answer of the American Press'. In October 1843 Forster had published an article entitled 'The Newspaper Literature of America', a vitriolic exposure of democratic journalism, for which Dickens had almost certainly supplied evidence in the form of clippings collected during his American tour (*Letters*, 3.xiii). The response this article elicited from angry editors on the other side of the Atlantic prompted a sequel. In 'The Answer of the American Press', Forster quotes excerpts from these responses and extends the arguments made in the original article. The pair of essays, but particularly the latter one, set the terms of the satire in this scene and contribute to some of its more memorable details.

Brick's size, youth and pale, tobacco-wasted appearance aptly represent the British view of America as untried and unformed, 'the unwholesome growth of a young and prematurely forced society' (145). 'The existing constitution of America has not yet outlived the test of fifty years,' the *Foreign Quarterly Review* had urged, and thus 'the government and society of America cannot be assumed to have as yet taken a permanent shape' (135). Calling up Britain's greater wisdom, experience and sheer longevity, Forster's editorial persona adopts a posture of stern rebuke towards this presumptuous, ill-mannered child. And for its part, the American press flaunts the position of bold upstart. 'We are, beyond the possibility of doubt, *the Napoleon of the press in both hemispheres*,' boasted the *New York Herald* in one of the excerpts Forster quoted (148). 'The London Newspaper Press *have endeavoured to stop our career as they did Napoleon's* . . . . They have stormed, and fumed, and raved, and lied, and puffed, and sworn and abused us in all manner of ways', but (as in the case of the *New York Sewer*, 'now in its twelfth thousand, and still a printing off') swelling circulation figures tell the story of their defeat. The one 'astounding and curious result' has been an increase in circulation requiring 'a large additional order to our paper manufactures!' (148).

Brick's editorial position as 'War Correspondent' during a time of peace compounds Martin's initial astonishment at the premature dignity of this little man. Of course, military posturing characterised much American newspaper reporting during this period, and war was regularly predicted. 'The Answer of the American Press' quotes a string of strident and bellicose responses to Forster's charges that American journalism traded in falsehood and scurrility. One American newspaper quoted by Forster even predicted that 'It is very unlikely that the press . . . will be left to fight out the battle. This war of opinion will one day end in a trial of physical strength' (148). Jefferson Brick expresses the same opinion in more grandiose language, 'The libation of freedom . . . must sometimes be quaffed in blood' (262).

Forster's quoted excerpts provide excellent prototypes for these 'flowery components' in Brick's language – his mixed metaphors and ludicrous appropriations of animal and mythological associations. In one passage, for example, the writer proclaims: 'We are a live lion, and it is dangerous for any long-eared animal to protrude his posteriors towards us in a hostile manner.' Another newspaper declared itself 'the Socrates of New York', poised to repel persecution. But excesses of this sort were of course a common feature of American journalism and oratory, and would have been widely available from a variety of sources.

Brick and Colonel Diver assume that their published words strike 'the aristocratic circles of your country' – and more grandly still, 'the cabinets of Eu-rope' (262) – with deadly fear. Just so, an American newspaper quoted by Forster had preened itself on the power of the press to 'carry alarm to the noblesse of Europe'. If 'liberty must be attacked not by the sword but by the pen', they insisted, Americans would be found ready to defeat all aggressors in this war of words. 'Very well, come on. This will cause a sensation throughout the United States. *Don't burst. Keep cool. Be quiet!*' (148) When Dickens composed the *Rowdy Journal* scene, the very language of this aggressive boastfulness must have lingered in his mind, for the words are closely echoed by Colonel Diver, who tells his indignant War Correspondent to 'Keep cool, Jefferson . . . Don't bust!' (262).

More than the sum of these verbal echoes and allusions, Forster's articles on the American newspaper press model the form of the *Rowdy Journal* scene, its extended play with dialogue and debate, question and response. Dickens, of course, works by irony and understatement, misprision and correction, with Martin's questions framed as naive to heighten the impact of Colonel Diver's revelations. Forster's method is more direct. But no less than Dickens, he sets up the terms of the debate rhetorically so that England gets the last word. His second article could more accurately be described as 'The Answer of England to the Answer of the American Press'.

To a greater extent than has been previously recognised, Dickens's representation of America is constructed out of conversations like these with voices twentieth-century readers for the most part no longer recognise or even hear. Much valuable work remains to be done in recovering the full context out of which Dickens wrote. To do so is to gain a more complete understanding of his composing process and a more accurate reading of the ideological ground on which he constructed his view of America – a world of words as much as of experiences, a world which, in revising, Dickens laboured to make 'New'.

Notes

1.   I have taken my subtitle from Frances Fitzgerald's study of the way America has been represented over the decades in twentieth-century school texts.

2..   I wish to record a debt of gratitude to Jerome Meckier for carefully reading a draft of the manuscript from which this essay was constructed.

3.   Page referensces are to the Clarendon edition of *Martin Chuzzlewit*, ed. by Margaret Cardwell.

References

Cardwell, Margaret, Introduction, *Martin Chuzzlewit* (Oxford: Clarendon Press, 1982) xv–lx.

Fitzgerald, Francis, *America Revised: History Schoolbooks in the Twentieth Century* (Boston: Little, Brown, 1979).

[Forster, John], 'The Newspaper Literature of America', *Foreign Quarterly Review* (October 1842, 103-17).

[Forster, John], 'The Answer of the American Press', *Foreign Quarterly Review.* (October 1842) 135–54.

Gerbi, Antonello, *The Dispute of the New World; the History of a Polemic, 1750–1900*, trans. Jeremy Moyle (Pittsburgh: University of Pittsburgh Press, 1973).

House, Madeline and Graham Storey, *The Pilgrim Edition of the Letters of Charles Dickens*, vol. 2 (Oxford: Clarendon Press, 1969).

House, Madeline, Graham Storey and Kathleen Tillotson, *The Pilgrim Edition of the Letters of Charles Dickens*, vol. 3 (Oxford: Clarendon Press, 1974).

Lieber, Francis, *The Stranger in America*, 2 vols (London: R. Bentley, 1835).

Lougy, Robert E., *'Martin Chuzzlewit': An Annotated Bibliography* (New York & London: Garland, 1990).

Marryat, Captain Frederick, *Diary in America with Remarks on its Institutions* (New York: D. Appleton & Co., 1839).

Meckier, Jerome, *Innocent Abroad: Charles Dickens's American Engagements* (Lexington: The University Press of Kentucky, 1990).

Smith, Sydney, *Wit and Wisdom of the Rev. Sydney Smith* (New York: Armstrong and Son, 1880).

Stone, Harry, 'Dickens' Use of his American Experiences in *Martin Chuzzlewit*', *PMLA* 72 (1957) 464–78.

Trollope, Frances, *Domestic Manners of the Americans* (New York: Dodd, Mead & Co., 1927), rptd from the 1839 edition, with an Introduction by Michael Sadleir.

8
Borrioboola-Gha: Dickens, John Jarndyce and the Heart of Darkness

Jennifer Gribble

We first hear of Mrs Jellyby's plans for 'the great African Continent' in Chapter IV of *Bleak House*, entitled 'Telescopic Philanthropy':

> The African project at present employs my whole time: it involves me in correspondence with public bodies, and with private individuals anxious for the welfare of their species all over the country. I am happy to say it is advancing. We hope by this time next year to have from a hundred and fifty to two hundred healthy families cultivating coffee and educating the natives of Borrioboola-Gha on the left bank of the Niger.[1]

Edward Said's *Culture and Imperialism* conspicuously fails to notice Dickens's indictment of mid-Victorian imperialism in this novel. Said's comments on the Jellybys' 'eccentric ties to Africa' do not engage with Dickens's far-reaching analysis of those ties, and he is content to reiterate generalisations about Dickens reproducing the imperialist ideology of his time and using new worlds chiefly as a way of enriching favoured characters and disposing of unwanted ones.[2]

Certainly Mrs Jellyby here voices imperialism's characteristic mixture of motivations and justifications. The passage satirically juxtaposes a missionary fervour with the grab for land it elides. In the process of imposing British culture on the indigenous population and the opening up of new markets, 'our superabundant home population' (30), in Mrs Jellyby's Malthusian phrase, will be unloaded. The word 'cultivation' shifts rapidly between its etymologically related meanings (derived from the Latin *colere*, to cultivate: *cultura* comes to represent both the tilling of the soil and the refinements of education)[3] as references to the project continue: 'the general cultivation of the coffee berry – *and* the natives' (30); 'the merits of the cultivation of coffee, conjointly with the natives' (152). The chief target of Dickens's criticism of philanthropy in *Bleak House* is generally perceived to be Mrs Jellyby's representative myopia: with her telescopic gaze perpetually fixed on Africa she is unable to scrutinise her own self-serving busy-ness, nor indeed to set in order the household whose disorder provides so rich a vein of sardonic comedy, as she devotes her attention to housing 150 of the families of others in a far distant place. Mrs Jellyby's airy way with geography is caught in the syntactic ambiguity of her sentence about 'private individuals anxious for the welfare of their species all over the country'. Which country and which species is indeed the question.

John Jarndyce is one such private individual. The curious quality of his involvement with Mrs Jellyby is signalled in this very episode. These are among Mrs Jellyby's first words to her house guests, Esther, Ada and Richard, who have been sent there overnight *en route* to their new home. Mr Jarndyce, who is 'desirous to aid any work that is likely to be a good work and . . . is much sought after by philanthropists, has, I believe, a very high opinion of Mrs Jellyby,' Conversation Kenge has told them (30). It is an opinion based not so much on culpable ignorance as on a kind of double-thinking we are to see most clearly in Jarndyce's benevolence to the parasitic Skimpole. His motive in foisting three genteel young adults on a household already overcrowded, undernourished and strained to breaking point seems to be the confirmation of suspicions he is unable to face. All does not seem to be well with this woman of whom he entertains such a high opinion. '"I may have sent you there on purpose"' (54) he tells his wards, as his questions elicit their unspoken reservations. '"You all think something else, I see!"' (54). Here, for the first time, they encounter, and learn to collude with, his way of evading the evidence of his own and others' weaknesses: '"She means well", said Mr Jarndyce hastily, " the wind's in the east"' (55).

Not only is Dickens not offering the kind of distinction Said finds in the 1840s Victorian novel between 'home' and 'away',[4] he is not, I think, making the kind of distinction critics often made between John Jarndyce's Bleak House and Mrs Jellyby's neglected household. While Jarndyce's rehousing of the three orphans in his *ad hoc* family does offer a model against which Mrs Jellyby's household, among others, is measured and found wanting, the similarities are as interesting as the differences. These in turn reflect on Dickens's own philanthropic involvements. His dislike of 'organized charity' did not get in the way of a generous investment of energy in educational and housing projects, as Philip Collins has amply shown.[5] That he shares John Jarndyce's divided feelings about the Mrs Jellybys of his world is evident in his private but well-known comments on her real-life model Caroline Chisholm, whose 'Family Colonization Loan Society' he had supported ('I dream of Mrs Chisholm and her housekeeping. The dirty faces of her children are my continual companions').[6] More curious still is his claim, in response to Lord Denman's attack on the novel's apparent indictment of The Society for the Propagation of the Gospel, that the Borrioboola-Gha episode was 'invented'.[7] Well yes, of course, but drawing, we know, on an actual event, the 1841 Niger Expedition. As *Bleak House* makes clear, Victorian philanthropy is blinkered by its inability to confront what we might call 'home truths'. Dickens's impulse to evade what he knew to be the case about African projects underlines his personal identification with mid-Victorian England's failure to look into its own dark heart.

Dickens's view of the Niger Expedition, in his 1848 *Examiner* review of its narrative, amounts to what must be one of the most trenchant contemporary satires of the burgeoning of British imperialism. His summary of the expedition's aims sets the tone:

> the main ends to be attained by the Expedition were these: the abolition, in great part, of the Slave Trade, by means of treaties with native chiefs, to whom were to be explained the immense advantages of general unrestricted commerce with Great Britain in lieu thereof; the substitution of free for Slave labour in the dominions of those chiefs; the introduction into Africa of an improved system of agricultural cultivation; the abolition of human sacrifices; the diffusion among those Pagans of the true doctrine of Christianity; and a few other trifling points, no less easy of attainment. A glance at the short list, and a retrospective glance at the great numbers of generations during which they have all been comfortably settled in our own civilized land, never more to be the subject of dispute, will tend to remove any aspect of slight difficulty they may present.[8]

We are reminded, throughout this review, of Dickens's sharp ear for verbal humbug. Smug assumptions of moral superiority are exposed not only by such apparently bland summaries as this, but also by quotations that allow Her Majesty's Commissioners to condemn themselves in their own words. (Dickens seizes with glee on a phrase of Thomas Buxton, the moving spirit behind the Expedition, that 'the people of Africa were to be awakened to a proper sense of their own degradation' [53]). Judicious quotation also exposes the carrot-and-stick tactics by which King Obi is persuaded of his interests: 'the vessels he saw were not trading ships, but belonging to our Queen, and were sent, at great expense, expressly to convey the Commissioners appointed by Her Majesty, for the purpose of carrying out her benevolent intentions, for the benefit of Africa' (55); 'the more you persuade your people to exchange native products for British goods, the richer you will become' (55); 'you cannot sell your slaves if you wish, for our queen has many warships at the mouth of the river' (58); 'our countrymen will be happy to teach our religion, without which blessing we should not be prosperous, as a nation, as we are' (59); 'the Commissioners requested Mr Schon, the respected missionary to state to King Obi, in a concise manner, the differences between the Christian religion and heathenism:

Mr S.: There is but one God.
King Obi: I always understood there were two.

(59)

Dickens is large. He contains multitudes. Following the Indian Mutiny, he can be heard to cry 'exterminate the brutes'. He notoriously supported the actions of Governor Eyre.[9] But not only is the colonised given voice in the Niger *Review*, he is observed to be enjoying the last laugh (indeed, he is observed to be enjoying private jokes throughout the interview, perhaps, Dickens surmises, because he knows that slaves will continue to be shipped off at parts of the coast where Her Majesty's warships never dreamed of going, and because he clearly intends to break the treaty at the first opportunity. Furthermore, King Obi proves quite as adept a practitioner of moral pragmatism as his teachers, and is given to unsettling their comfortable assumptions: 'in agreeing to the additional article, binding the Chief and his people to the discontinuance of the horrid custom of sacrificing human beings, Obi very reasonably enquired what should be done with those who might deserve death as punishment for the commission of great crimes.' 'Something like this question of Obi's had been asked, once or twice', Dickens comments, 'by the very government which had sent out these "devil ships" or steamers, to remodel his affairs for him; and the point has not been settled yet' (61). The bizarre dress of King Obi, in a harlequinade of cast-off clothing from an earlier expedition, the voyage of the steamers up river through 'dull dead mangrove trees, the slimy earth, the rotting vegetation', the dénouement in which human sacrifices continue unabated as King Obi sells his people for rum and the expedition and its model farm are ravaged by fever, anticipate various aspects of Conrad's *Heart of Darkness* and provide an imaginative seed-bed for the novel Dickens is about to write.

Reviewing the Niger Narrative, he is clearly struck by the sharp questions it addresses to the liberal conscience of Victorian England. What to make of the fact that a man like Buxton, motivated by the most worthy of aims, the abolition of the slave trade (a cause in which Mrs Dickens herself was involved), should find those aims corrupted by the financial and political backing needed to expedite them? Must ethical and territorial imperatives pull in different directions? Is a concern for the welfare of the species inevitably entangled in self-interest? The actual geographical possession of land, as Said points out, is what imperialism is all about: 'to think about distant places, to populate or depopulate them'.[10] Mrs Jellyby's African project extends into the new world that mesmeric fixation on property that makes the Jarndyce and Jarndyce suit so potent an image of mid-Victorian capitalism. The supposed barbarism of the natives sheds a continuing ironic light on the so-called civilisation of the would-be colonisers. Even the most benign of colonisers makes objects of property out of the recipients of his charity.[11] Born into the suit, as John Jarndyce remarks, no one escapes its taint. This is the dark heart into which *Bleak House* looks.

The case of Mrs Jellyby is more interesting than is often recognised. If we reflect further than Ada and Esther are able to do on the sources of Mrs Jellyby's obsession with Africa we notice that she combines a hatred of domesticity with a fecundity for which the marginalised Mr Jellyby ('he might have been a native, but for his complexion') (36) seems indispensable. The sycophantic Mr Quale is equally indispensable, bolstering the queen bee with his adulation. Mrs Jellyby's plan to marry him to Caddy and retain them both as slaves hints at subterranean emotional currents of the kind often found within the apparently more domestically regular Victorian families. Esther and Ada cannot help noticing the impropriety of her dress, which 'didn't nearly meet up the back . . . the open space was railed across with a lattice-work of stay-lace' (33). This steadily widening area of imperfectly controlled naked flesh suggests in a way quite characteristic of Dickens the intimate connection between Mrs Jellyby's looking to Africa as the repository for surplus population and her own sexual and domestic entrapment.

What is deftly and satirically touched on in Mrs Jellyby is given more penetrating exploration in John Jarndyce, whose household shows some similar displacements and sublimations. If the history of the suit may be read in the labyrinthine structure and growlery of Bleak House, John Jarndyce's chapter of it rests on the spoils of empire: 'a Native-Hindoo chair . . . brought back from India nobody knew by whom' (56); pictures that variously depict the death of Captain Cook, 'the whole process of making tea in China' (56) and the usual trophies of the gentry's more local exploits in the shape of dead fish and birds. It is home to Skimpole, in whom Mrs Jellyby's annexation of Africa takes on a would-be charming whimsy: 'I can sympathize with the objects. I can dream of them. I can lie down on the grass – in fine weather – and float along an African river, embracing all the natives I meet, as sensible of the deep silence, and sketching the dense overhanging tropical growth as accurately as if I were there' (60).

Dickens suggests the conquistador in the benevolent Jarndyce right from the start. Heavily muffled in furs, angrily muttering at the signs of Esther's distress, he is a disguised and threatening fellow traveller for the young Esther as she takes the coach to school: more nearly resembling the wolf than the benign grandmother of 'Little Red Riding Hood', the story Esther will later tell to the Jellyby children. At the handing over of the wards in Chancery, the Lord Chancellor gives particular emphasis to Jarndyce's being 'not married'. A certain restless energy (not entirely subdued by his habit of taking cold baths and sleeping through the English winter with his window open) suggest the physical basis of his repressive habits. He is still handsome, as Esther often notes, despite being nearer 60 than 50 (54), and in our enlightened times, not to mention those of Dickens, one would feel inclined to disagree with David Holbrook's recent pronouncement that he is too old to be considered as a husband for Esther.[12]

Dickens was clearly well aware that generous paternal feeling may have a strong admixture of sexual need and desire. In Jarndyce he shows a man whose sexual interests are at odds with, but enabled by, his role as surrogate father (a word that makes his kind face cloud over when Esther uses it). While he attempts to fix her in the daughterly role by affectionate nicknames of the 'Dame Durden' variety, he establishes an emotional bond with his 'little woman' as they keep house together that emerges the more clearly through Esther's unwillingness to see it for what it is. It is a bond that slowly enables Jarndyce to flower out of initial caricature into a more freely feeling and expressive being. It later emerges that his plan to make her his wife began when she was 'very young' (705), so that his constant unseen watching over her growing up is uneasily poised, like his marriage proposal, between benevolence and desire. The physical possession which is his ultimate goal remains to the end entangled in property issues of one kind or another.

His proposal to her is often read as a generous rescue from the threatened social disgrace of her illegitimacy and the physical disfigurement left by fever. Indeed, this is how the letter of proposal presents itself, and how Esther herself chooses to see it. 'Not a love letter, although it expresses so much love', its terms, relate primarily to household arrangements prompted by the loss of Ada as chaperone: 'it asked me, would I be the mistress of Bleak House?' (502) If Esther's diminished value in the marriage market enables Jarndyce to pursue his innermost desires, those desires remain occluded by his insistence on the old guardian role. Also occluded is Esther's love for Allan Woodcourt. Esther is placed, once again, under the obligation to repay her continuing sense of indebtedness.

The critical rehabilitation of Esther as a study of debilitating guilty anxiety and consequent self-policings has recently helped to suggest why she should be particularly vulnerable to emotional and sexual transactions that specify themselves in the language of debt and reparation.[13] The tardiness of her reply to the question 'would she be the mistress of Bleak House?' makes her real response to it abundantly clear. The form of the question allows her to honour her promise, however, while breaking it, when she at last becomes the mistress of a new Bleak House closely modelled on the old.

Esther's rehousing is not only a model of colonising behaviour. It is a reminder of Dickens's intense interest at this time in the lives of fallen women. Housed in Urania Cottage, they were to be redeemed by resettlement in the colonies and eventual marriage there – a plan Dickens describes as giving him 'a wonderful power over them'.[14] Dickens's study of John Jarndyce discovers the ways in which morally admirable intentions prove deeply founded in the desires of a complex self, linking Jarndyce with the novel's more blatant self-deceivers and double-thinkers, and with the political unconscious of the Victorian civilising mission.

Is there, as Grahame Smith many years ago suggested, an 'unconscious element of revenge' in Jarndyce's final act of benevolence?[15] It is a question surely raised as the genuine delicacy of Jarndyce's recognition and renunciation of his own self-interest is belied by the exultant and compensatory power with which he tantalizes both Esther and Woodcourt with his plans to replicate the Victorian middle-class household in far-flung Yorkshire:

> we would make him as rich as a Jew, if we knew how . . . rich enough to live, I suppose? Rich enough to work with tolerable peace of mind? Rich enough to have his own happy home, and his own household gods – and goddesses too, perhaps? . . . He seems half inclined for another voyage. But that appears like casting such a man away.

'It might open up a new world to him,' said I. 'So it might, little woman,' my guardian assented. 'I doubt if he expects much of the old world. Do you know I have fancied that he sometimes feels some particular disappointment, or misfortune, encountered in it. You never heard of anything of that sort?'

I shook my head.

'Humph,' said my guardian. 'I am mistaken. I dare say.'

As there was a little pause here, which I thought, for my dear girl's satisfaction, had better be filled up, I hummed an air as I worked which was a favourite with my guardian.

'And do you think Mr Woodcourt will make another voyage?' I asked, when I had hummed it through.

(565)

Nothing could be more horrifying than Esther's determined humming. Yet Jarndyce tightens the screw still further. Summoned to Yorkshire to see how carefully her own tastes and preferences have been consulted in shaping this home for Woodcourt and his household goddess, Esther is made to feel an overwhelming sense of loss: 'And here she is,' said my guardian, 'laughing and crying together! . . . Why, how you sob, Dame Durden, how you sob' (703). Woodcourt, whom Jarndyce has persuaded to confide his love for Esther, is similarly required to believe that he loves in vain: '"I gave him no encouragement, not I, for these surprises were my great reward, and I was too miserly to part with a scrap of it"' (706). Generous feeling expresses itself to the last in terms of property: '"Allan"', said my guardian, "take from me a willing gift, the best wife that man ever had"' (706). This way of putting it underlines the retention of Jarndyce's control in Esther's life, and a vicarious possession of her through the replication of the life they have shared. If repression and social power are intimately connected in John Jarndyce, however, the same is true of Esther, as John Kucich argues.[16] The power-play elaborated in recent revisionary studies of Victorian repression, however, seems beside the point in the face of the raw feeling exposed in an ending Kucich sees as 'the greatest successful action in *Bleak House* . . . an unqualified good release.[17] Esther's anguished response to Jarndyce's heroic self-abnegation and self-gratification shows how impossible it must ever be for her to enjoy the blessings of Bleak House without a continual reminder of its costs: a prolongation, in fact, of her belief that, as in the case of her mother, she is responsible for the unhappiness of the person to whom she owes most.

The second Bleak House, like the first, is enabled by offshore exploits. The friends Woodcourt has made through his valiant service to the survivors of the shipwreck in the East Indies help to procure his Yorkshire practice, though it is Jarndyce 's money that buys his house. The apparent pastoral of the happy ending shows the new world founded on the unacknowledged and irresolvable feelings of the old, and driven by the essential selfishness of libidinal energies. '"Jarndyce", proclaims Skimpole, "in common with most other men I have known, is the incarnation of Selfishness"' (831). The intense feelings that run through Esther's narrative recognize that our common selfishness is what makes us human: notably contradictory and liable to self-deception. Given that individual philanthropy was firmly located at the centre of contemporary political theory as the most appropriate response to the social problems created by industrialism, as Kitson Clark points out,[18] Dickens's recognition of how benevolent mission will project its own dark heart is timely, astute and, I think, personal in its application.

Notes

1. *Bleak House* (Herts: Wordsworth, 1995) 33. All subsequent references are to this edition.
2. (London: Vintage, 1994).91, 126.
3. David Spurr, *The Rhetoric of Empire* (Duke, Durham and London, 1993) 5.
4. Said, 69ff.
5. Philip Collins, *Dickens and Education* (London: Mamillan, 1963): *Dickens and Crime* (Basingstoke: Macmillan, 1994).
6. John Butt and Kathleen Tillotson, *Dickens at Work* (London and New York: Methuen, 1982) 194.
7. Ibid., 195.
8. Review of 'Narrative of the Expedition sent by Her Majesty's Government to the River Niger in 1841, under the command of Captain H. D. Trotter R.N. 'by Captain William Allen R. N., Commander of the H.M.S. Wilberforce, and T.R.H. Thomson M.D., one of the medical officers of the Expedition', in F.G. Kitson, ed., Charles Dickens, *To be Read at Dusk and Other Stories, Sketches and Essays* (London: George Redway, 1898).
9. Brahma Chaudhuri, 'Dickens and the Question of Slavery', *Dickens Quarterly* VI, 1 (1989) 3–10.
10. Said, 91.
11. As James M. Brown, *Dickens: Novelist in the Market Place* (London: Macmillan, 1982) puts it.
12. David Holbrook, *Charles Dickens and the Image of Women* (New York and London: New York University Press, 1993) 44: 'it is surely inconceivable that they could ever marry.' The proposal is seen as part of the fantasy mode Holbrook finds in Jarndyce's 'Prospero role'.
13. See e.g., Q.D. Leavis, 'A Chancery World', in F. R. Leavis and Q.D. Leavis, *Dickens the Novelist* (London: Chatto and Windus, 1970); Alex Zwerdling, 'Esther Summerson Rehabilitated', *PMLA*, 88, 3 (May 1973);

Timothy Peltason, 'Esther's Will', *ELH* 59, 3 (1992); Judith Wilt, 'Confusion and Consciousness in Dickens's Esther', *NCF* 32, 3 (1977); Barbara Gottfried, 'Fathers and Suitors in *Bleak House*', *Dickens Studies Annual* 3 (1990); Jasmine Yong Hull, 'What's Troubling About Esther', *Dickens Studies Annual* (1993); Peter Thomas, 'The Narrow Track of Blood', *NCL* 50, 2 (1995).

14. Quoted in Peter Ackroyd, *Dickens* (London: Minerva, 1990) 564.
15. Grahame Smith, *Charles Dickens: Bleak House* (London: Edward Arnold, 1974) 31: 'there is a quality here which, under the guise of benevolence, looks very close to cruelty....it does seem possible that there is an unconscious element of revenge at work in the whole episode.'
16. John Kucich, *Repression in Victorian Fiction* (Berkeley: University of California Press, 1987) 258.
17. John Kucich, *Excess and Restraint in the Novels of Charles Dickens* (Athens, GA: University of Georgia Press, 1981) 151.
18. Brown, 75, cites *The Making of Victorian England*.

9
Despatched to the Periphery: the Changing Play of Centre and Periphery in Dickens's Work

Brian Cheadle

The 'world system' of Empire and informal Empire impinges continually on Dickens's works. An exquisitely droll vignette is that of Herbert Pocket in such despondency with the results of his looking about him 'as to talk of buying a rifle and going to America with a general purpose of compelling buffaloes to make his fortune' (34.293).[1] The moment one's smile fades at the absurd notion of Pocket as the great white hunter, smudgy implications surface. The middle-class fantasy of achieving wealth without real work depends upon displacing the actual making of the fortune onto the buffalo (a structure of thought which could equally accommodate slaves or natives); exploitation is disguised as a test of manhood; and the violence of the envisaged 'compelling' is naturalised by the humour, and by the convenient assumption that the periphery is empty of all but natural resources. For, as Micawber says grandly of the 'fatal shore' to which he is bound, unwittingly pronouncing on the 20,000 aborigines killed in clashes, 'The denizens of the forest cannot . . . expect to participate in the refinements of the land of the Free' (57.876).[2]

In the post-colonial wake it is impossible not to recognise that even the genial and hapless Herbert is heir to the arrogant centrism pervading nineteenth-century culture, and crystallised in such lines as:

> The earth was made for Dombey and Son to trade in, and the sun and moon were made to give them light . . . to preserve inviolate a system of which they were the centre.

> (1.50)

Post-colonial criticism does not, however, always avoid its own foreshortening in dealing with the centre. It tends to forget that the 'system', like all symbolic economies (including the Dickensian novel), was constitutively unstable and full of discrepancies – such as the gap between Dickens's disenchantment with Dombey and the gentle relish with which he indulges Herbert's fantasy.

The opposition between centre and periphery in Dickens's work engaged not only contradictory structures of feeling but a range of discrete phenomena. Though a sense of imperial convenience governed Victorian attitudes very broadly, the periphery was figured in quite different ways: it tended to be imagined as a receptacle if transportation and emigration were at issue, or as a cornucopia if the focus was on fortune seeking and free trade. In Dickens's work one finds both these figurings, as well as swervings from them because of complex self-division within his alignment to the centre. In this essay I shall use *Oliver Twist* to sketch the initial dispositions of centre and periphery in Dickens's symbolic economy; I shall explore the dislocations so simple a binary scheme encountered, even in *Oliver Twist*, to the extent that a model of agitated exchanges and slippages would seem more appropriate; and I shall with an irresponsible impressionism and a shameless use of obvious examples indicate some of the more important subsequent developments of the initial binary scheme.

In *Oliver Twist* a whole set of characters is very deliberately despatched to the periphery. David Miller has argued that the ideological scheme of the book entails a cordoning off, whereby the delinquent world of Fagin and his gang, along with the structures such as workhouse and apprenticeship which are supposed to reform the delinquent, is enclosed and separated from the world of middle-class security.[3] Beyond this containment, there is equally a pattern of ritual dispersal aimed at purging the centre. Fagin is despatched on the gallows; Sikes despatches himself in a gruesome parody of that event; Monks is despatched to the New World to die in ignominy; and the chief remaining members of the gang are sent packing, to die 'as far from home' (53.475) as Monks, doubtless after going at the Queen's pleasure to Australia.

As the inclusion of Monks suggests, the process of purging the centre extends well beyond transportation. Not just the criminals, but all who have been contaminated by the book's initiating transgression – Oliver's illegitimate birth – are systematically despatched. Oliver's father dies in Rome. There his intentions of providing for the girl he had wronged are thwarted by his estranged wife, and his son Monks, who had been living in novelistic exile in Paris (prefiguring a long line of those cast away in ignominy in the pit of France, down to the Veneerings and Lammles in *Our Mutual Friend*). Having returned from the continent, Monks is despatched again to the West Indies, and to complete the pattern, Oliver's maternal grandfather flees from the family shame into 'a remote corner of Wales' (51.458), which is probably as peripheral as you can get within the British Isles.

Dickens continued to the end to figure the periphery as a receptacle for the unwanted. Long after Wackford Squeers, Uriah Heep and Littimer have been transported, Jenny Wren still holds this bogey before her recalcitrant child. And though the notion of emigration is temporarily indulged as a promising possibility in *David Copperfield*, it remains an option really only for the ineffectual, the inoffensive lower orders, and those such as Little Em'ly, Martha Endell and Tom Gradgrind, who cannot be ideologically accommodated at the centre.

Dispersal and cordoning off are aspects of the effort to maintain the ideological purity of the centre by neutralising that which would threaten or weaken it. But the naive binarism is soon ruffled by complications and reversals. Oliver's movement is *in* to the central city to be absorbed as rightfully middle-class, but it is ominously shadowed in two ways. First, Dickens's conviction that poverty and crime are the product of the system opens the threat that Oliver's fate will be the contamination, rather than the rescuing, of what is properly central; and secondly, Oliver's movement in from the provinces is doubled in that of Noah Claypole, who is not ejected but enlisted as an establishment spy – a disturbing reminder that containment of the delinquent requires the murkiest forms of surveillance.

The ambivalent cost of maintaining the purity of the centre is brought out even more disturbingly in the presentation of Brownlow, for clearly the benevolent 'uncle' is a disciplinary figure, in this case virtually a prototype of the detective. Brownlow's efforts of surveillance extend beyond going to the West Indies in search of Monks, to taking evidence from Nancy, from Bumble and from the workhouse crones; and to a final interrogation of Monks which involves kidnapping him and putting him under duress in a way David Miller describes as 'vigilantism' (*The Novel and the Police*, 7).

When, however, the furious Brownlow finally teams up with Henry Maylie and joins the London mob in the hunt for Sikes, his authority is eroded: he suffers a nameless anonymity, and the mob is oblivious to his offer of an extra reward for taking Sikes alive, its anger threatening to spill over into something alarmingly close to lynching. The authority of the centre is thus not only ensured by the most dubious means, but most precariously ensured. This is emphasised by a set of disturbing incursions and returns. The Maylies' country haven is not secure against burglary; Fagin and Monks irrupt disconcertingly into Oliver's rural dream; Kags, a member or contact of the criminal gang, is a transportee who far from being securely despatched has illegally returned. And though, after the murder of Nancy, Sikes sets out blindly from the centre and blunders as far as Hatfield, he is drawn back inexorably to what would seem to be the city's very heart, the *terra incognita* of Jacob's Island which vividly figures London in terms of pollution and decay, and which acts as an appropriate locus for the hunger of the rapidly gathering crowd.

The notion that *Oliver Twist* is single-mindedly dedicated to cultural cleansing thus needs to be qualified. Even at this early stage of Dickens's career the novel reflects a centre divided against itself. Lionel Trilling long since argued that a decisive feature of nineteenth-century imagining was that the major writers increasingly sited themselves in an adversarial relationship to the assumptions of the centre.[4] The claim grossly oversimplifies the problems of achieving a critical stance towards the culture of which one is a subject, and after Foucault it is dangerous to talk glibly of literature as working subversively. But as Foucault himself pointed out, power cannot be thought of apart from the presence of a plurality of 'mobile and transitory points of resistance. . . fracturing unities and effecting regroupings'.[5] It is part of Dickens's strength that he was, as Orwell put it, 'generously angry'[6] at injustice in any form. He was anything but a radical reformer, and in standing up for fellow-feeling and common humanity he looked to promote social change very much on middle-class terms. It is equally clear that he strove, more than his predecessors and contemporaries in the English novel, to give a voice to the silent oppressed. Oliver's 'Please, sir, I want some more' (2.56) became an icon of social injustice, disseminated on the stage and in keepsakes as much as by the text. Even the Prime Minister, Lord Melbourne, had to descend with Whiggish suavity to weaning the Queen from her partiality towards the deprived waif, declaring of the workhouses, pickpockets and coffinmakers the book depicted, 'I do not like those things; I wish to avoid them'.[7] It is to Dickens's credit that he made it harder to do so.

Frederic Jameson rightly insists, however, that within the asymmetrical world system of nineteenth-century mercantile and industrial capitalism, any resistance could be only partial, in that the racist inequities of the colonial periphery were inaccessible to metropolitan experience.[8] Major Bagstock's nameless and speechless black servant in *Dombey and Son* is the embodiment of this truth, though the reality of colonial exploitation and violence surfaces vividly enough, as when, to revert to *Oliver Twist*, Charley Bates boasts of having bought sugar so fine the 'niggers' (39.349) must really have slaved to produce it, or when Mr Grimwig alludes to a man in Jamaica hanged for murdering his master despite having had the fever six times (14.149). Dickens himself never entirely evaded the condescending simplification he patronised in Mr Willet in *Barnaby Rudge*, for whom all remote lands were 'inhabited by savage nations, who were perpetually burying pipes of peace, flourishing tomahawks, and puncturing strange patterns in their bodies' (78.700); and his tendency towards racism became blatant after the Indian Mutiny and the Governor Eyre fiasco. It is necessary to point such things out; but it is unproductive to stop at pointing them out. What is more pertinent to insist on for Victorian studies is first that within the culture's constructed system of imaginative space the periphery, and the slippages *it* evinces, deserves much more attention; and secondly, that the radical impingement of the periphery must be complexly understood in terms of its class and gender no less than of its racial and colonial implications. The periphery began, after all, at Field Lane, and extended to Norfolk Island and the New World by way of the workhouse and the whorehouse. In Dickens's view all those painted savages were not so much irredeemably beyond the pale of civilisation as simply a lesser priority than the savages at home.

The symbolic economy of centre and periphery was continuous with the opposition of high and low; and in an age which was heir to the romantic belief that the energies of the self were the final sanction for being there was an obsessive fascination with extreme conditions which went deeper than an ideological desire to neutralise or contain the otherness at the social margins. If the culturally sanctioned self is constructed against the differences of an excluded other, metropolitan culture has an obsessive need to present its peripheries and its others continually to itself in the attempt to define its own psychic limits; and such presentations produced much more profound challenges to the centrist assumptions than Oliver with his bowl.

Rose Maylie shows instinctive sympathy for Nancy; but Brownlow, the representative of patriarchal authority, can encounter her only liminally on London Bridge at midnight. It is his cleansing instinct to despatch her to 'some foreign country' (46.414), but she is not so easily to be expunged from the middle-class consciousness. The prostitute perversely chooses to go back to her pimp and be murdered; and the murder of Nancy obsessed the Victorians with all the 'fascination of repulsion'.[9] The horror of the scene challenged the assurance of elitist insulation from human brutality; but the scene was more insidiously disturbing. Dickens laboured to invest the murder with pathos and with the 'moral intensity' Peter Brooks sees as marking the attempt of nineteenth-century melodrama to deliver a 'clear nomination of the moral universe'.[10] Hence the stagy palaver whereby Rose's handkerchief is exalted by allusions to *Othello*, and wielded by Nancy before Sikes as a talisman of grace and compassion. One side of Dickens would have applauded the contemporary reaction of J. Hain Friswell who observed that the murder 'teaches us . . . to pity the guilty while we hate the guilt'.[11] But Friswell's insistence on Nancy's sexual guilt makes the encounter in effect the climax to a line of illicit liaisons; and his defensiveness highlights the erotic implications in the image of the male clubbing down on the contaminated body of the half-dressed and drowsy woman. Nancy's continuing loyalty to Sikes muddies the waters further with the disturbing reminder that there are girls who choose to go to the bad. Dickens tries to key Nancy's death to the reassuring image of the female martyr with upturned eyes, but that itself is a motif whose ecstatic erotic charge Bernini has sculpted in our consciousness. It is not, however, only the horror and the eroticism that is so disquieting. Nancy's choice of victimhood suggests the intricacies of need and desire inherent in female submissiveness, but she has previously dared to show physical aggression towards the male, crossing gender barriers by deploying a masculine strength in her protection of Oliver. The book begins and ends by disciplining female transgressiveness, its last words recalling Agnes Fleming as 'weak and erring' (53.480); and the valencies of Sikes's aggression seem to offer the grotesque mirroring of a displaced disciplining, whereby a hatred of 'the guilt' might be acted out by a patriarchal moral authority. If Nancy is disturbing because in her the female body resists moralisation, Sikes is disturbing because his male aggression is too extreme to allow for moral identification: the scene thus has the most disconcerting ability to suggest the patrolling of defensive boundaries, only to breach them and confound the hierarchies of morality and feeling.

Melodrama forces its way across social boundaries, and contrary to Peter Brooks's indications its excesses have far more capacity than modes of greater refinement to disrupt the economy of high and low. There is always a danger in crossing cultural boundaries. Steerforth says arrogantly before visiting the Peggotys, 'Let us see the natives in their aboriginal condition' (21.360), and his assurance has an ominously proleptic irony; but his contemptuous imagery also suggests the continuity of attitudes towards the *disparate* aspects of the periphery. Imagining the intimacy of Nancy and Sikes, of Steerforth and Em'ly, of

Eugene and Lizzie, was thus a necessary step towards coming to terms with much else that was seemingly unimaginable in a century whose asymmetries were of class and gender as well as of race.

If Dickens's sentimental melodrama was an essential strategy for opening the centre to its challenging psychic extremities, his anarchic humour was equally disruptive. The current tendency to recoil from the very idea of social cleansing would seem inseparable from a tacit sociopolitical utopianism – for, sadly, societies can hardly do without *some* form of disciplining and cleansing. Dickens understood this well, but his own ultimate resistance to disciplining took an anti-utopian rather than a utopian form. *Oliver Twist* works, in at least one often remarked upon case, in a way that is openly anarchic and disruptive of all symbolic economies. The Artful Dodger at his trial jauntily sums up what the book has consistently demonstrated, that 'this ain't the shop for justice' (43.396). He is one of those 'booked for a passage out' (43.390); and though his fate is presumably comprehended in the formulaic death far from the centre, such an end is inconsistent with the resilient, streetwise capacity for survival he embodies. He is ignored in the tying up of loose ends, the silence confirming the sense that in the Dodger, Dickens's imaginative vitality presses beyond any disciplinary scheme. To say this is not to sentimentalise the Dodger as though he represented some utopian 'jolly life' (18.183) open to those beyond social restraint, for Dickens's tart comment that beer and tobacco have 'tinctured [the Dodger] for the nonce, with a spice of romance and enthusiasm, foreign to his general nature' (18.181) clearly implies that what impels him is not jollity but a darker and more selfish energy, akin to the passion for survival that marks Oliver's first moments and makes him at Mr Sowerberry's tear asunder 'the dainty viands that the dog had neglected ... with all the ferocity of famine' (4.74).

That this harder and darker anarchic pressure is endemic to Dickens's imagination becomes clear if one considers a few trivial yet discommoding impingements of the periphery. After the plan of indenturing Oliver to the sweep falls through, the board threatens to ship him as a cabin boy 'in some small trading vessel bound to a good unhealthy port ... the probability being, that the skipper would flog him to death, in a playful mood' (4.68); in his flight to London, Oliver is saved from starvation by 'a benevolent old lady . . . who had a shipwrecked grandson wandering barefoot in some distant part of the earth' (8.99); and Noah Claypole's father is a drunken ex-soldier 'discharged with a wooden leg and a diurnal pension of twopence-halfpenny and an unstateable fraction' (5.78). In such details the viewpoint is shifted onto the victims of imperial schemes, and the ordinary instances of cruelty, estrangement, and loss make starkly clear the unregarded injuries of class that are incident to 'shovelling out paupers' and the policing of the periphery. The understanding has a hard-eyed quality which is quite as potent in the novel as the structural scheme, and which weaves into the fabric a lack of illusions about *both* the dominant, centrist assumptions, *and* the fate of the victims (including Oliver himself in the first half of the book). The effect is not so much subversive as suggestive of a casual heartlessness. The dimensions of this stance become clearer, however, from the more spectacular moment in which Mr Gamfield proffers the secrets of his trade:

> Boys is wery obstinit, and wery lazy, gen'lmen, and there's nothink like a good hot blaze to make 'em come down vith a run. It's humane too, gen'lmen, acause, even if they've stuck in the chimbley, roasting their feet makes 'em struggle to hextricate theirselves.
>
> (3:61)

Faced with Gamfield and the misery he inflicts, earnest protest and even anger seem innocently inept; for he represents a cast of mind with which moral and spiritual controls will never cope. Dickens refuses pity, lest any consolatory gesture divert him from precisely defining the sweep's callousness, its knife-edge teetering between sly ingratiation and a boastful sadism. But if only the detachment of comedy can adequately register Gamfield, it is the nature of the absolute comic to develop an anarchic relish for what it registers. In a Gamfield world, which would seem to justify the Malthusian pessimism Dickens had set himself against, it was as though the novelist's only way to sanity was by developing an appetite for what S.J. Newman nicely calls 'the fabulous monstrosity of man' (25).[12]

Given the distance between this anarchic hardness of vision and the moral project of keeping Oliver unsullied, it is hardly surprising that the final mark of self-division in the novel is that genteel society finds itself at the conclusion not so much ideologically secured, as set uneasily apart from the central social nexus – one in which institutionalised authority and the seamy underworld unite in a brutal concern for number one. In recoil from the pervading self-interest, Brownlow ends up 'removing' with Oliver as his adopted son to the Maylie village. This dubious final shift is clearly an attempt to establish green and rural England as a charismatic locus, but it achieves only the fragile vulnerability of 'a *little* society, whose condition approached *as nearly* to one of perfect happiness *as can ever be known* in *this changing world*' (53.476, my emphasis).

This decentring of the 'true' centre anticipates correspondingly idealising changes whereby, from the time of *Dombey and Son* (preoccupied as it is with trying to balance the accounts of mercantile capitalism and free trade), Dickens begins to figure the colonial periphery more consistently as a cornucopia rather than a receptacle.

Early in *Dombey and Son*, Walter Gay indulges the naive fantasy of running away to sea and returning decked out in an Admiral's dolphin-like array of colours, or with a Post Captain's 'epaulettes of insupportable brightness', to win Florence as a bride – this despite the forbidding present image he has of Mr Dombey's 'teeth, cravat, and watch-chain' (9.174). The reification of Dombey epitomises the aggression, arrogant display and ultimate constriction of bourgeois materialism at which Dickens was looking increasingly askance. The containment which in *Oliver Twist* had seemingly cleared a space for the culturally sanctioned self has by now revealed itself as the self-enclosure of a sterile social order. Dickens sets against it Walter's dream of a romantic heroism validated by patriotic Englishness, though the implication of the dream is that true selfhood is now to be won by a restless movement away from the centre.

The dichotomy proposed between Walter's way and Dombey's is, however, a false one, for all the heroism of all the Post Captains serves only to keep open Dombey's trade routes. When Walter accepts Dombey's mission to Barbados, he prefigures Herbert Pocket by imagining the periphery as an unpeopled cornucopia ripe for pillaging, full of 'lively turtles, limes for Captain Cuttle's punch, and preserves' which he will send home in ship-loads (19.331). Walter's final voyage to the periphery is given even the highest sanction of domesticity by his taking Florence on honeymoon to China, from whence they return with a new little Paul. Not just selfhood but community itself would seem to need to be created afresh at a remove from the corrupted centre. But the notion is undercut by the revelation that all the voyaging has been no more than the prelude to Walter's taking up a post 'at home' within the family firm, where he is assisted by a repentant Dombey to mount up the ladder 'with the greatest expedition' (62.974). Valorous expeditions are no more than the most expeditious way of realising the fruits of a single imperial economy; and, for all the critique of materialism which the book has mounted, it has taken little more than Carker's death and the banishment of Edith to Italy to secure the centre. Suvendrini Perera sums up the contradictions in Dickens's attitudes by remarking that he proceeds to 'romanticize colonial expansion even as he decries its material agent, the expansion of capital, for its metropolitan consequences'.[13]

Once again this is an insight that needs to be handled without foreshortening. One of the revealing continuities of *Dombey and Son* is the easy way in which the presentation of Sol's shop proceeds by way of an initial glance at the offices of Dombey and a lingering description of the rich East India House 'teeming with suggestions of precious stuffs and stones, tigers, elephants, howdahs, hookahs, umbrellas, palm-trees, palanquins, and gorgeous princes of a brown complexion sitting on carpets, with their slippers very much turned up at the toes' (4.88). The continuity is a clear indication that Walter's dream of adventuring his way into selfhood is commercially contaminated. The description of the East India House opens by eyeing 'precious stuffs and stones' as the objects most attractive for colonial appropriation, and it might seem to show a lordly condescension towards those exotic others whose slippers turn up at the toes. But when the wearers of those slippers are gorgeous princes, they are allowed to be brown, and wonderful imaginings have such a generous quality that Bella Wilfer can even dream of marrying an Indian prince; and the passage swells with an intoxicated response to the otherness of strange cultures, which must be offset against the demeaning tendency to see them as curious and subordinate. It is too easy to demonise the whole colonial enterprise, as though history had never before, or concurrently beyond the West, entailed conquests and plunder and exploitation; and as though the notion of moral responsibility towards other cultures had not evolved gradually (and mostly within a western ambit). Dickens's relish for the beckoning variousness of things is not innocent, but it would be an impoverishing Puritanism to write it off imperiously as bad faith.

Then too, *Dombey and Son* evinces essential contradictions and dubieties within its upbeat celebration of colonial expansion. There is for a long interval lack of news about Walter and fear that he has drowned. The fantasy of brave success abroad opens the threat of engulfment and loss, making it unclear whether the rich periphery figures redemption or death – for empires are sources of deep anxieties as well as of plunder. Nor do all those who return with rich pickings seem capable of renewing the centre. The simple wedding of Walter and Florence is set off against the pretentious nuptials of 'a yellow-faced old gentleman from India' who could 'pave the road to church with diamonds and hardly miss them' (57.900), but whose union with a young wife does nothing to gratify the heart of Mrs Miff the pew-opener. The son whom Bill Blitherstone sends home to be educated is, on Major Bagstock's recognizances, 'a born fool' (10.189); and Major Bagstock himself, though monstrously entertaining, is, in Chesterton's words, 'simply the perfect prophecy of that decadent jingoism which corrupted England'.[14]

Such dubieties open the way for the two features (latent even in *Oliver Twist*) which will be crucial in Dickens's subsequent treatment of the periphery. First, he consistently attempts (as with Walter Gay though without any further facile pretence of mythically resolving irreconcilables) to separate his heroes from the contaminated centre, as a prelude to having them return to achieve what precarious identity they can within its necessary ambit. They thus come from abroad (John Harmon, Arthur Clennam), act bravely at the periphery (Alan Woodcourt), or rehabilitate themselves abroad (Pip in Egypt, and David Copperfield in the Alpine wastes). Secondly, he becomes fascinated by characters who return unbidden from the periphery to challenge the centre, as, even in *Dombey and Son*, Alice Marwood to an extent does. The most disturbing of these figures is Magwitch who returns with all the power of the repressed, and with all the smouldering resentment of the excluded. There is of course a superficial sense in which Magwitch is doing homage to the centre in his obsessive desire to 'own' a 'London gentleman' (39.339) more authentic than the arrogant colonial upstarts who spurned him in their dust. But the corrosive subversiveness of his return is well brought out by a decisive image in which he reverses the assumptions of those countless Victorian exhibitions which encouraged complacent centrists to 'think of the Bushmen'[15] or other savage exotica: Magwitch, by contrast, conceives of himself as the 'Exhibitor' (40.353) of that freakish creation; a man who neither toils nor spins. Others who return to challenge and disturb the centre include Captain Hawdon who brings back from the periphery only the opium habit, which speaks ominously to the bourgeois fear of the exhausted will and the fall from selfhood. And finally there are the significantly named Landless brother and sister from Ceylon.

Drood opens with a hallucinatory opium vision 'spiking' the cosiness of the cathedral town, and the menace of an undermining savagery from the eastern periphery is ubiquitous; but the Landless siblings are a particularly disturbing intimation of reverse colonisation, prime examples of what Homi Bhaba calls mimicry in being 'almost the same but not quite'.[16] They are in consequence both more tigerish and more vital than the home-grown Rosa whose coy timidity extends to a last tenuously ambivalent attempt to purge the centre by 'putting her little pink fingers to her rosy lips, to cleanse them from the Dust of Delight that comes off the Lumps' of Turkish sweetmeat (3.58).

By this stage the boundaries which David Miller sees as firmly policed in *Oliver Twist* are dissolving in the most disconcerting ways. An exemplary image of this dissolution may come, however, not from *Drood* but from the finale to its predecessor, *Our Mutual Friend*. Mortimer Lightwood assures Lady Tippins, who is prone to gobble up reputations with every mouthful and who is not the least of the book's birds of prey, that at his last acquaintance the 'savages' of Juan Fernandez, 'were becoming civilized . . . at least they were eating one another, which looked like it' (4.17.888) – a retort which makes cannibalism the defining mark of her kind of civilisation. But as the 'savages' in question are Eugene and Lizzie, who have put themselves beyond the pale by ignoring social boundaries, and as Mortimer's bitter riposte takes a side glance at the maiming consequences of their relationship, we have by this stage reached a point where civilisation and savagery, centre and periphery are becoming hardly distinguishable, though the tensions of the agitated exchanges remain as strong as ever.

Notes

1. All quotations from novels by Dickens are from the Penguin editions, with a chapter and page reference in parenthesis.
2. See Robert Hughes, *The Fatal Shore* (New York: Knopf, 1986).
3. See the title essay in D.A. Miller's *The Novel and the Police* (Berkeley: University of California Press, 1988).
4. See *Beyond Culture* (New York: Harcourt, 1965).
5. See the 'Method' section of *The History of Sexuality* (New York: Vintage Books, 1980) especially p. 96.
6. George Orwell, 'Charles Dickens', in *Inside the Whale* (London: Gollancz, 1940) 85.
7. From *The Girlhood of Queen Victoria: a Selection from her Diaries 1832–40*, ed. Viscount Esther (1912), quoted in Philip Collins, *Dickens: The Critical Heritage* (London: Routledge, 1971) 44.
8. Frederic Jameson, 'Cognitive Mapping', in Cary Nelson, ed., *Marxism and the Interpretation of Culture* (Urbana: University of Illinois Press, 1988).
9. Dickens's famous phrase, given currency in John Forster's *The Life of Charles Dickens* (London: Chapman and Hall, 1874) 11.
10. *The Melodramatic Imagination* (New Haven: Yale University Press, 1976) 17.
11. From 'Mr. Charles Dickens', in *Modern Men of Letters 'Honestly Criticised'* (London, 1870), quoted by David Paroissien, *Oliver Twist: An Annotated Bibliography* (New York: Garland, 1986) 127.
12. S.J. Newman, *Dickens at Play* (London: Macmillan, 1981) 25.

13.   Suvendrini Perera, 'Wholesale, Retail and for Exportation: Empire and the Family Business in *Dombey and Son*', *Victorian Studies* 33, summer 1990, 607.

14.   G.K. Chesterton, *Charles Dickens* (New York: Schocken Books, 1965) 186.

15.   The phrase is from Dickens's essay 'The Noble Savage', *Household Words* VII, (11 June 1853), collected in *The Uncommercial Traveller and Reprinted Pieces* (Oxford: Oxford University Press, 1958) 468.

16.   Homi Bhaba, 'Of Mimicry and Man', *October* 28 (Spring 1984) 126.

10

'Anywhere's Nowhere': Dickens on the Move

James Buzard

'Where would you wish to go?' she asked.
'Anywhere, my dear,' I replied.
'Anywhere's nowhere,' said Miss Jellyby, stopping preversely.
'Let us go somewhere at any rate.' said I.

Dickens, Bleak House[1]

Omnia determinatio est negatio – the very demarcation of a social totality places it under the sign of contingency.

Perry Anderson, 'Components of the National Culture'[2]

ETHNOGRAPHY INSIDE OUT

With the exception of D.A. Miller's brilliant but exceptionable chapter in *The Novel and the Police* (1988), nearly all important accounts of *Bleak House* have given some sustained attention to the novel's dual narration, that famous experiment which Steven Marcus called (with much justice) 'the most audacious and significant act of the novelistic imagination in England in the nineteenth century'.[3] Miller's having so little to say about the matter, already remarkable in a chapter entitled 'Discipline in Two Voices', becomes more remarkable still when we remember that Miller interrupts his argument with some theoretical reflections on how '[p]henomenologically, the novel form includes the interruptions that fracture the process of reading', yet pays almost no attention to the factor that makes this particular novel into a veritable self-interrupting machine: the dual narration.[4] Regarding the relationship between Dickens's impersonal narrator and Esther Summerson as a kind of hypertrophied specimen of the novel's intrinsic relationship between narrator and character, third-person and first-, and thus as a nineteenth-century

113

representation of novelistic form, this essay will argue that *Bleak House* defines the novel for its era as the self-interrupting genre *par excellence*, and that it does so as part of what I consider its 'proto-ethnographic' labour. This argument is part of a larger one that attempts to redescribe the nineteenth-century British novel as a crucial link between late eighteenth-century theories of cultural pluralism and the early twentieth-century social science of 'ethnography', which took the plural and relativistic concept of 'culture' as its bailiwick.[5] I believe that the novel was pre-eminent among several allied genres in anticipating formal modern ethnography *negatively* or dialectically – that is, by furnishing the elements of ethnography in reverse, in inverted form, or in the form of something we could call 'anticipatory travesty'.[6] The form best suited to represent the life of modern Western societies mirrored and prefigured the social scientific form for representing the life of 'primitive', 'traditional', 'integrated' cultures. The novel functioned, in other words, as the leading mode of what I call 'metropolitan autoethnography': it 'ethnographised' the Western imperial metropolis (and environs) in the century *before* a theoretically explicit social science expatriated the ethnographic gaze to the far-flung corners of the globe.

It is not simply the recognition, basic to Dickens criticism, that *Bleak House* attempts to provide what Edgar Johnson called a total 'anatomy of society' and J. Hillis Miller 'a model in little of English society'[7] that encourages me to make this connection, but rather the unexplored link *between* the totalising representational effort and the dual narration. For the same linkage was basic to twentieth-century ethnographic science, which founded itself upon reciprocally reinforcing conceptions of its object – a culture – and its authorised practitioner – a 'participant observer'. As Christopher Herbert has noted, once we define 'each "culture" [as ethnography did] as a discrete, self-contained whole . . . [then] there can be no substitute for a system of concentrated fieldwork designed to generate something resembling an insider's view of it.[8] Yet though the 'participant' side of the label has received most of the press, the 'observer' side was no less crucial, for it was addressed to the (often implicit) requirement that the fieldworking ethnographer get back 'outside' again, or that enough of him *remain* outside, even while some part of him passed 'in', to permit him to retain his bearings as a scientist and be capable of producing ethnographic knowledge. In his epochal *Argonauts of the Western Pacific* (1922), Malinowski insisted that the ethnographer attain the perspective of a member of the culture he or she studied, the aim being 'to grasp the native's point of view, his relation to life, to realise *his* vision of *his* world'; but every professional exigency demanded that the perspective actually amount to one of (in Bernard McGrane's phrases) 'simulated membership' or 'membership without commitment to membership'.[9] A practitioner's authority hinged upon the demonstration of what we might call an *outsider's insideness*, an achieved passage into alien lifeways that nevertheless held 'going native' to be an abdication of authority and identity alike. To exhibit a culture ethnographically was also to exhibit *oneself* as both psychically flexible enough to undergo 'immersion' in the alien *and* proof against any erosion of identity threatened by that 'destructive element' into which one had plunged. In ethnographic texts, this could require not only the narration of the ethnographer's passage 'inside', but the continual *interruption* of that narrative by portions of the text issuing from that other, steadfastly detached perspective retained by the truly worthy claimant to ethnographic authority.

Malinowski's *Argonauts* sets out to narrate one typical cycle of the Kula gift-exchange system, linking this attempt (which occupies much of the central portions of the book) to the ethnographer's quest for the 'insider's' view. The narrative is marked by such reflections as 'As I sat there, looking towards the Southern mountains, so clearly visible, yet so inaccessible, I realised what must be the feelings of the Trobrianders, desirous to reach the Koya, to meet the strange people, and to *kula* with them, a desire made perhaps even more acute by a mixture of fear.' He relates various stages of the Kula journey as they would appear to a Trobriand participant, sometimes a novice participant – such as, in a sense, he is himself. In the followings passage, for example, Malinowski puts himself, as first-time Kula traveller, into the consciousness of the young native initiate: 'Of all these marvels the young Trobriander hears tales, and sees samples brought back to his country, and there is no doubt that it is for him a wonderful experience to find himself amongst them for the first time . . .'[10] But the anthropologist breaks off his story in numerous places in order to explain what he is telling, to address the sociological embeddedness and ramifications of various details in his account, thereby showing, for all the 'insideness' he has achieved, that he has not relinquished the scientist's proper distance on his material. What emerges from this dynamic is the possibility that *self-interrupting narration* may function as ethnography's textual analogue for its practitioner's dual role as participant observer.

On behalf of the novel of its time, *Bleak House* envisages its object – Dickens's own nation – much as later ethnographers would envision alien 'cultures', as a system of functional integrity whose total order is imperceptible to ordinary members or 'mere insiders' (these are the 'natives' of ethnographic rhetoric, the 'characters' in the novel) and thus requires the outside–inside combination of the participant observer. Natives, Malinowski wrote, are *'of* [their culture] and *in* it', but have 'no vision of the resulting integral action of the whole . . . [11] Likened to a mystery cult, the Chancery proceedings in *Bleak House*, the substance of which no two parties can agree on, body forth a vision of *anti-culture* negatively foreshadowing those totalising cultural performances of ritual, which Durkheim would describe at the end of the nineteenth century, laying the functionalist foundations for British anthropology as he did so. In representing its authorised perspective, the work of metropolitan auto-ethnography employs the same metaphors of spatial relation as would later structure ethnographic rhetoric, but it uses them, as it were, inside out. Instead of a master-narrative about the achievement of an outsider's insideness in another culture, it tells one about an *insider's outsideness* with respect to its own.

If 'culture' has provided one particularly powerful concept for expressing the constitutive ambivalence of modern societies, it should not be surprising to find it, in embryonic form, involved in the constitution of that genre we consider among the most definitively modern. In ethnography and in novelistic autoethnography alike, 'a culture' is what comes into focus through an interplay of 'dwelling' and 'travelling': its distinctive wholeness may be apprehended only by some mobile self not susceptible to determination by it, though capable of understanding what such determination feels like, and liable to idealise the process.[12] Depending on where one stands, 'travelling' can stand for the autonomy or the dissolution of the self, 'dwelling' can convey security or imprisonment; so each can recompense us for the other. It is to the ambivalent figurations of travelling and dwelling in Dickens that I now turn.

BODIES, REST AND MOTION

Moral beauty in Dickens, typically female and/or pre-pubescent, is essentially stationary. The beauty is made to be looked at, to shine as a beacon to the world, so it had *better* keep still: Oliver Twist and Little Nell make their most forceful impressions when we watch them sleeping – and of course in Nell's case, dead. From this point of view – which is reminiscent of theological perspectives on divine perfection and change – to move is to be defiled: consider the wayward Alice Marwood of *Dombey and Son*. Plainly, such inert moral presences as Oliver and Nell put a strain on the narrative's own movement; one way to incorporate them in narrative is to presuppose a fall, prior to the story's commencement, which has created a gap between actual and proper settings for the beauty which it is the narrative's task to cross. Rather than being the volitional source of movement, the moving beauty *is moved* through this narrative by some force outside itself – much as, in *The Old Curiosity Shop*, the flesh-and-blood Nell is carted through the streets alongside a waxen Brigand, to advertise the opening of Mrs Jarley's exclusive waxworks exhibition.[13] This narrative pattern, reserved for those characters marked as beyond or outside desire, is significantly extended in *Martin Chuzzlewit*, in which the inertly good Mark Tapley is dragged along on young Martin's ill-fated quest towards that Dickensian heart of darkness, Eden, USA.

On the other hand, there is *Pickwick Papers*, in which perhaps the most powerful source of comic pleasure is to be found in the figure of the man self-invented on the move, free of determination by place and culture. Whatever the passing attractions of Dingley Dell or of the fine new house at Dulwich (a telling name) which Mr Pickwick builds himself in the end, a vision not unlike that of Tennyson's 'Ulysses' propels this work, the vision of an elastic self potentially equal to the world whose wealth of experience it seeks to incorporate. Bearing the surname of an actual coach proprietor, Pickwick signifies that he is less a 'character' than an embodied commitment to keep moving; Jingle gives his address as 'No Hall, Nowhere' (*PP*, 584). Tennyson's figure proclaims, 'I am become a name', and the name of the man who turns his back on his one particular domain in favour of vast and vague 'experience' is, in the Homeric joke, *outis*, nobody: a generic self (nobody in particular, 'just anybody'), ranging free of definition by any single role. In a famous set-piece on a dying Fleet prisoner, Dickens identifies such an anonymous humanity with ceaseless motion, as a 'restless whirling mass of cares and anxieties, affections, hopes, and griefs' whose tragedy it is to fall into the hands of confining legal and other institutions (*PP*, 734–5).[14] *Pickwick Papers* places Dickens in company with the entire tradition of philosophical accounts of liberty for which, as Elaine Scarry points out, 'the image of unimpeded physical movement' constitutes the nearly unavoidable model. For Jingle and Bob Sawyer no less than for Epictetus, freedom may be summed up in the adage, 'I go wherever I wish; I come from whence I wish.'[15] Dickens's footloose males are always on the run from those man-traps of marriage, family, property, vocations, institutions, respectability and responsibility, all overseen by women seeking mates. The hero himself falls prey to Miss Witherfield, a sort of female minotaur at the centre of the labyrinthine White Horse Inn, and he falls foul of the marriage-minded Mrs Bardell and winds up in the Fleet. It is no coincidence that with his liberation from jail comes the reappearance of the uncontainable Sawyer and a delirious return to the road. Phiz's illustration of 'Mr. Bob Sawyer's mode of travelling' brilliantly captures the radical devotion to restlessness animating *Pickwick*, that Sawyeresque appetite for which even the moving vehicle is too confining: Sawyer sits spread-legged atop the moving coach, a sandwich in one hand and a bottle in the other.[16] Sawyer would concur with Sam Weller's declaration that 'I feel that I ain't safe anyveres but on the box' (*PP*, 832).[17] The perfunctory punishment which this book metes out to Jingle pales in comparison with its animus toward the Law, represented by Dodson and Fogg, among others, but set in motion *only* at the behest of female characters. In sum, the novel's ultimate aim of safeguarding the inalienable mobility of men even while acknowledging the minimal claims of social order makes it a veritable panegyric on that proverbial cornerstone of English liberty, the right of *habeas corpus*: as Sam Weller memorably puts it, '[t]he have-his-carcase, next to the perpetual motion, is vun of the blessedest things as wos ever made' (*PP*, 701).

On still *another* hand (we need more than two), male figures in Dickens may require prodding into movement and may even be chastised, as Marley's Ghost chastises Scrooge, for refusing to 'walk abroad among [their] fellow men, and travel far and wide'[18] – for hoarding and refusing to 'spend' themselves in society. In this instance, mobility appears a style of philanthropy sharply distinguishable from Mrs Jellyby's desk-bound shuffling of papers, and it signals the reconnection of the stagnant soul with its community. Some such commitment underpins the labours of the urban rambler who wrote *Sketches by Boz*, and it is to be seen in the nocturnal perambulations of Master Humphrey as well – slow and serious researches into 'the characters and occupations of those who fill the streets', forays which are explicitly contrasted to the erosive 'pacing to and fro, [the] never-ending restlessness, [the] incessant tread of feet wearing the rough stones smooth' that constitutes normal daily life (*OCS*, 43).

Yet on still a further hand (one may, if convenient, envisage a statue of Siva), constant motion erodes the defining boundaries of the self: we may recall how Jingle's self-creating staccato bursts of language wind up mere disconsolate sputterings in the Fleet; or how the little crossing-sweeper of *Bleak House* starts the novel clinging to the wreckage of a proper name – the two letters of 'Jo' – but loses even these in his continual 'moving on'; or how the fugitive Magwitch of *Great Expectations* is encountered in the cold, 'clasping himself, as if to hold himself together'.[19] Viewed this way, motion is inimical not only to personal identity, but to the social order that is its ground and guarantor. The anti-social characters of Dickens's imagination seem ceaselessly and unpredictably on the move, driven by some evil perpetual-motion machine somewhere deep within themselves: Fagin, Monks and Quilp share the alarming tendency suddenly to materialise wherever one happens to be, and to vanish just as inexplicably (as in the case of the missing footprints in *Oliver Twist*).[20] Stoked to constant readiness for action, Quilp's misshapen body jerks and capers its way through every scene, 'arms a-kimbo,' impelled by 'that taste for doing something fantastic and monkey-like, which on all occasions had strong possession of him' (*OCS*, 124). Such propensity to constant, ultimately aimless and *self-cancelling* movement is a symptom of a barbarous and even bestial condition of existence 'beyond culture', existence by appetite alone. Quilp drives himself to an accidental drowning; Sikes, who after his murder of Nancy roams Cain-like against the purposeful flow of traffic, beats the hangman only by usurping his office (*OT*, 423-32, 453); Rigaud/Blandois of *Little Dorrit* brings the Clennam house down upon his own head.[21] In such Dickensian villains, Iago's 'motiveless malignancy' becomes malignant and seemingly aimless mobility. Multiplied, it manifests itself in 'mobs', like the 'bands of unemployed labourers parad[ing] in the roads' in *The Old Curiosity Shop* – 'maddened men, armed with sword and firebrand, spurning the tears and prayers of women who would restrain them, [who rush] forth on errands of terror and destruction' (*OCS*, 424). Its terminus is that vision of cultural meltdown in *Barnaby Rudge*, of selves literally dissolving in the 'liquid fire' of burning liquor in the street, consumed by their own rage to consume: 'the wretched victims of a senseless outcry, became themselves the dust and ashes of the flames they had kindled, and strewed the public streets of London.'[22]

The variously conflicting drives towards motion and stasis cohabit in the implicitly male and explicitly female narrators of *Bleak House*. Running contrary to this gendered division of labour is Lady Dedlock, whose wanderings towards the close of the novel, a literalising comment upon her past sexual 'errancy', make her the rule-proving exception *par excellence*, and whose difference from her daughter is never more pointedly illustrated than when in pursuit of her, Esther rides as the passenger of Mr Bucket, who acts as something like an 'emissary of the third-person narrator'.[23] In the logic of *Bleak House*'s dual narration, the final expulsion of the self-propelled woman must be authored, and authorised, by the woman who is driven by an eternally restless man, the Mr Bucket whom, the novel says, '[t]ime and place cannot bind'.[24] Bucket represents but the most prominent of Dickens's gestures in *Bleak House* towards what Audrey Jaffe has called the nineteenth-century novel's 'project of omniscience', the 'fantasy of unlimited knowledge and mobility' produced by a culture that felt such a perspective to be irrevocably lost.[25] Another might be the original name for the Jarndyce house, 'the Peaks', from which eminence we have fallen into a pitiable embroilment 'in Chancery', and other of Dickens's works furnish numerous examples, such as the Ghosts of *A Christmas Carol*, the famous 'Good Spirit' who flies above our rooftops in *Dombey and Son*, and the 'Shadow' whom Dickens presents as the presiding spirit of *Household Words* – this last a creature who can "go into any place, by sunlight, moonlight, starlight, firelight, candlelight and be in all homes, and all nooks and corners, and be supposed to be cognisant of everything and go everywhere, without the least difficulty."[26] Implicit in all these is something like that 'lust to be a viewpoint and nothing more' which Michel de Certeau has described in 'Walking in the City'; all employ the spatial metaphors of 'getting outside' or 'getting above' the level of practice.[27] But in Dickens, I think, we must recognize this lust in a more particular way, as a lust to be a viewpoint *on a culture that remains one's own* – or rather, that comes into view *as* 'a culture' at the moment one claims to have got outside or above it. Elevation and mobility are the tropes for an authority that figures identity and culture in tropes of confinement and depth – as matters of being 'inside' or 'down in' a place.

From the opening page of *Bleak House*, two things are implicit in the fact that it is the impersonal narrator who introduces us to the intolerable condition of being '*in* Chancery', of being 'in' culture as such. The first is that being in Chancery *means* longing to get out, to attain a position 'beyond culture'. This recognition is powerfully encoded in the arrangement of Krook's house, the travesty Chancery court. Anonymous humanity – Nemo, or 'just anybody' – occupies the middle floor, beneath Miss Flite and above 'the Lord Chancellor', as if torn between the desire to soar free and the weight of social being. The parallel identification of Krook with the human body (ineluctible until death) and of Miss Flite with the soul (imprisoned, as are Miss Flite's birds, until death) contributes to that conflation of ideas about culture in general and ideas about one particular culture (mid-Victorian Britain's) which is so basic a part of *Bleak House*'s meaning. It takes a perspective that sees social environments as integrated and determining 'super-organic' forces to so forcefully associate embodied being with social being, crediting one particular form of the latter with the inescapability of the former.[28] The second point implied from the very outset of *Bleak House* is that the voice which first addresses us issues from the perspective of one who has by means of grit or luck or magic made the journey out from Chancery. As has been noted, this voice ranges from the mere insider's topical present ('London. Michaelmas term lately over') to the dawn and end of time (through its references to primaeval mud and megalosaurus on the one hand, and to the 'death of the sun' on the other [*BH*, 49]). Moving from 'In Chancery' to 'In Fashion', it portrays itself as that perspective capable of moving 'as the crow flies' between segments of the culture whose inhabitants cannot perceive their connection. This voice flaunts its putative privilege over mere insiders by posing pointedly rhetorical questions: 'what connexion can there be, between the place in Lincolnshire, the house in town, the Mercury in powder, and the whereabout of Jo the outlaw with the broom . . . ?' (*BH*, 272). More than this (much of which J. Hillis Miller perceived years ago, though in different terms),[29] this narrator goes on to present himself as capable of almost unlimited *crossings-back* into the story-space and cultural order from which he has absconded – of re-entries without the risk of entrapment. The two holes in the shutters of Nemo's room, looking like a pair of 'sad, gaunt eyes' upon the nameless dead, testify not to the narrator's simple detachment, but to his intimate and sympathetic watchfulness over English life (*BH*, 187–8). More remarkable is the passage in Chapter 10 in which Mr Snagsby watches a crow fly into Lincoln's Inn Fields, where Tulkinghorn lives, upon which the narrative shifts its attention *to* Tulkinghorn – flying with the crow, as it were – and follows him as he makes his way back to Snagsby's, moving 'as the crow came' and exhibiting other crow-like features (the glossy black clothes, the 'scavenging' for information). The bird that began its life in this novel as part of the figure of speech for describing the narrator's freedom of movement has temporarily become a creature visible to characters in the novel, and has even 'become' a character, Tulkinghorn – who, as someone bent on making the connections, is after all one of the novel's more prominent partial objectifications of its narrator. Taking Tulkinghorn along with other degraded or defeated interpreters like Guppy, Krook, Mrs Snagsby or Bucket, we may concur with Audrey Jaffe's claim that nineteenth-century omniscience constructs itself 'in relation to and at the expense of what it constructs as characters',[30] and we may go further, in likening it to the ethnographer's authority (as Claude Lévi-Strauss described it): as consisting in 'the subject's capacity for indefinite self-objectification (without ever abolishing itself as subject), for projecting outside itself ever-diminishing fragments of itself'.[31] Buss's famous image *Dickens' Dream*, showing the novelist in his study, surrounded by the tiny forms of his own novelistic characters, acquires new resonance in this connection.

CIRCLE OF DUTY

But in *Bleak House*, of course, the voice that tries to convince us it has travelled from the claustral inside of its culture *out* is paired with one that speaks of a journey from the bleak *outside* of culture *in*. Esther's life story recounts a passage from 'barbarian' – she is raised by the aptly named Miss Barbary in almost total seclusion – to 'mistress of Bleak House'. Together, the two narrators' itineraries describe a *chiasmus* that is perhaps the master-trope for the nineteenth-century mode I am calling metropolitan autoethnography.[32] Esther's voyage *in* defines a self that is rewarded for differing from her mother's brand of wandering womanhood;[33] in turn, the shadowy male voice of *Bleak House*'s other chapters takes Esther as the model of a defined selfhood it rejects for itself. Purporting to exceed any socially situated identity, this grand unplaceable self nevertheless defines *itself* by the same contrastive mechanisms that operate within culture's order of signification. It is to answer the apparent need for a contrasting self which can be seen as fully 'houseable' in its role that, in Chapter 3, the character who names herself by reference to her dependence on the recognition of others – 'they called me Esther Summerson' (*BH*, 63) – receives her commission to narrate, promising to bear away from her counterpart the onus of contingent identity.

But if the third-person narrator of *Bleak House* is animated by the spirit of Tennyson's Ulysses and shares that figure's condescension towards situated social being, it is also animated by the spirit of Tennyson's Tithonus, looking back nostalgically at the condition it has wished to escape. Esther's first words treat her task as if it were an onerous assignment – 'I have a great deal of difficulty in beginning to write my portion of these pages' (*BH*, 62) – yet the narrative she contributes is a report on her providential rescue and acculturation, her process of acquiring a local habitation and a name – in fact, a good number of names, a surfeit of signification as if in recompense for her early lack. *Bleak House* cannot wholeheartedly share Hillis Miller's tragic sense of the gap between names and being, cannot simply lament the fact of identity's thoroughly relational character.[34] (Indeed, the reflection that no name names its subject truly or finally must be a rather cheering one if your name is, say, 'Prince Turveydrop'.) Basic to the novel's logic is the acknowledgement that being somebody, and being of consequence, means being seen to occupy a social slot: the fates of Nemo, Jo and even the hapless Mr Jellyby illustrate the lesson that non–recognition is tantamount to nonentity. Esther's childhood recollection of her doll's 'staring at me – or not so much at me, I think, as at nothing' bespeaks the powerful desire to be included in culture's circle of recognition, which, however arbitrary it may be, is the self's one source of identity and value. If culture is that 'complex whole' of which E.B. Tylor wrote in 1871, if it consists, as E.E. Evans-Pritchard later claimed, only of 'relations . . . and relations between these relations', then it must most rigorously be seen as a 'self-referential system "without [so-called] positive terms"'.[35] The 'emptiness', the 'lack of a convincing inner life', the evacuation of 'ego' and 'will' that critics have long complained of in Esther may be the marks of that ethnographic sensibility for which the self is the bearer of its culture or it is nothing, nowhere.[36]

So imagined, being somebody means having a place – in other words, *not* having *everyplace*; it means standing in determinate relation to a limited number of people – in other words, standing in *no* relation to 'the world' or to 'humankind'. To Skimpole's praise of Ada, 'she is the child of the universe', John Jarndyce replies, 'The universe . . . makes rather an indifferent parent, I am afraid' (*BH*, 122). Faced with the negative examples of Mrs Jellyby's telescopic philanthropy and its vague commitment to the 'brotherhood of Humanity' (*BH*, 90), Esther resolves, 'I thought it best to be as useful as I could . . . to those immediately about me; and to try to let that circle of duty gradually and naturally expand itself' (*BH*, 154). Complementing that male dream of omniscience which finds its apogee in the 'Our Father' of Jo's dying prayer[37] is the ideal of a mappable *female* authority coextensive with a specific, limited domain: in charge of sweeping out a particular Bleak House, acting as somebody's wife, somebody's child, somebody's mother. The novel's formula for *this* vision, in so far as it has one, might be Caddy Jellyby's remark 'Anywhere's nowhere', or to cast it in terms more clearly related to personal identity, 'Everyone's no one' – *or*, to bring it fully within the world of *Bleak House*, 'Everyone's *Nemo*'.

It is the sense that half of *Bleak House* is invested in *this* vision of the relationship between self and culture that encourages me to think that among those partial objectifications of the impersonal narrator must be Allan Woodcourt, a man who departs from his culture to return later on bearing a new authority and commitment to its service. In the marriage of Esther and Woodcourt, the novel bids, with considerable strain, to square the circle of duty and freedom, place and mobility, dwelling and travelling. It is not a marriage that 'works', as many readers have felt and as the novel, with its elaborately self-conscious 'second Bleak House' business, seems to acknowledge. But it is a union that bears out what the novel was always suggesting, that the greatest extent to which the circle of duty could expand and remain meaningful – remain a 'place' – was to the borders of the nation. Esther, like Jo and Nemo, is a figure of essentially *English* no-one-ness. Offspring of a Nemo and a Barbary, a nobody and a barbarian, she embodies a veritable formula for meritocracy and for the hybrid vigour of what Defoe called that 'heterogeneous thing', the English subject. Raised in Windsor, she weds a man half Welsh and half Highland Scot. Their union has before it some cautionary counter-examples, such as: the marriage of a Prince (Turveydrop) and a Caroline (Caddy Jellyby); the conflict between a George (Rouncewell) and his enemies (the Smallweeds), one of whom habitually calls out for 'Charley over the water' (*BH*, 345); and, most notably, a marriage (the Dedlocks') that recapitulates the strife between Cavaliers and Roundheads (*BH*, 140–1). All the threats to the nation from without and within that are evoked by these references are to be laid to rest by the marriage of Esther and Allan. So is Jarndyce and Jarndyce itself, that embodiment of anti-culture that defines the very nation it is destroying: as Kenge says, it 'is a cause that could not exist, out of this free and great country' (*BH*, 68). So too are those other English no ones (Nemo, Jo) whose deaths were rebukes specifically addressed *to* the nation, not to anything so general and Jacobin-sounding as 'the brotherhood of Humanity.' Jo's death, presented as an event occurring 'thus around us every day' (*BH*, 705), invokes and delimits the English 'us' in the very gesture of indicting it. Benedict Anderson's suggestion that the 'sociological solidity' of the nation may be felt in what he calls the novel's '*general* detail[s]', 'none in itself of any unique importance, but all representative [of the national life]' could hardly find better support than this episode affords.[38]

In *Bleak House*, then, for culture no less than for the selves it constructs, *Anywhere's nowhere.* This was a vision of the single culture's dependence upon limitation and relation for *its* identity later to be promulgated by such theorists as Ruth Benedict; at the Victorian mid-century it might have seemed appealing for several reasons. The dismal outcome of the Oxford Movement, initially aimed at revitalising the English Church, combined with the 'Papal aggression' of 1850 (the reinstitution of the Catholic hierarchy in Britain) may have encouraged assertions of Englishness to counteract creeping 'Catholicity'. Then again, the inescapable event of 1851 England, 'the Great Exhibition of the Works of Industry of All Nations' (which Dickens managed to escape mentioning in *Bleak House*) may have given momentum to recuperative, holistic imaginings of one nation, laying stress on the 'works of industry' – the human by-products like Nemo and Jo – omitted from the Crystal

Palace.[39] Such imaginings might also have appealed to an expanding imperial power, its very success occasioning anxiety about what 'Englishness' might mean, if it could be, theoretically, *anywhere*. The backdrop and defining contrast for the vision of England-*as*-a-culture might be named, for example, after the object of Mrs Jellyby's telescopic philanthropy: 'Borrioboola-Gha' – as good a name as any for the vague and boundariless 'rest of the world' on which the single culture turns its back.

Notes

1. *Bleak House* (1853; Harmondsworth: Penguin, 1985) 96.
2. In Alexander Cockburn and Robin Blackburn, eds., *Student Power: Problems, Diagnosis, Action* (Harmondsworth: Penguin, 1969) 214–84; quotation on 264.
3. Marcus, 'Literature and Social Theory: Starting in with George Eliot', in *Representations: Essays on Literature and Society* (New York: Random House, 1975) 194.
4. D.A. Miller, 'Discipline in Two Voices: Bureaucracy, Police, Family, and *Bleak House*', in *The Novel and the Police* (Berkeley: University of California Press, 1988) 83.
5. My work derives considerable inspiration from Christopher Herbert's excellent book *Culture and Anomie: Ethnographic Imagination in the Nineteenth Century* (Chicago: University of Chicago Press, 1991), even though Herbert tends not to make generically applicable claims.
6. The perspective I am using here can be compared, but also contrasted, to Lukács's 'necessary anachronism' in *The Historical Novel*, trans. Hannah and Stanley Mitchell (1962; rpt. Lincoln, Nebraska: University of Nebraska Press, 1983) 61.
7. 'Anatomy of society': Edgar Johnson, *Charles Dickens: His Tragedy and Triumph* (New York: Simon & Schuster, 1952) II, 762–82; J. Hillis Miller, introduction to Dickens, *Bleak House*, 11.
8. Herbert, 150-1.
9. Bronislaw Malinowski, *Argonauts of the Western Pacific* (1922; rpt. Prospect .Heights, Ill.: Waveland Press, 1984) 25; McGrane, *Beyond Anthropology: Society and the Other* (New York: Columbia University Press, 1989) 125.
10. Malinowski, *Argonauts*, 220–1.
11. *Argonauts*, 11–12.
12. Cf. James Clifford, 'Traveling Cultures', in Lawrence Grossberg et al., eds., *Cultural Studies* (New York: Routledge, 1992) 96–116; esp. 99, 114–15.
13. *The Old Curiosity Shop* (Harmondsworth: Penguin, 1985) 286. Subsequent references cited in the text as *OCS*.
14. Readers of *Bleak House* will want to recall that this prisoner has been beggared by Chancery.

15. Scarry, 'The Railway Emergency Brake: The Use of Analogy in Legal and Political Argument', unpublished typescript, 4–5.

16. The illustration appears in Chapter 50. Not coincidentally perhaps, the coach is pursued by a family of Irish beggars, figures who represented to English imaginations a rather more alarming version of vagrancy.

17. Weller considers himself 'a privileged indiwidual', for 'a coachman may be on the wery amicablest terms with eighty miles o'females, and yet nobody think that he ever means to marry any vun among 'em' (*PP*, 832).

18. *A Christmas Carol*, in *The Christmas Books*, Vol. I (Harmondsworth: Penguin, 1971) 61.

19. *Great Expectations* (Harmondsworth: Penguin, 1985) 38.

20. *Oliver Twist* (Harmondsworth: Penguin, 1985) 309–13. Subsequent references cited in the text as *OT*.

21. *Little Dorrit* (Harmondsworth: Penguin, 1985) 862–3. One is tempted to include Merdle, always taking himself into custody, and to regard financial speculation as one more form of errancy in the Dickensian catalogue.

22. *Barnaby Rudge* (Harmondsworth: Penguin, 1986) 618.

23. The phrase is Richard T. Gaughan's, in '"Their Places are a Blank": The Two Narrators in *Bleak House*', *Dickens Studies Annual* (New York: Arno Press, 1992) 79–96; cf. 86.

24. *Bleak House* 76. Subsequent references to the novel will be cited in the text as *BH*.

25. Jaffe, *Vanishing Points: Dickens, Narrative, and the Subject of Omniscience* (Berkeley: University of California Press, 1991), 6.

26. Quoted in Robert Newsom, *Dickens on the Romantic Side of Familiar Things: Bleak House and the Novel Tradition* (New York: Columbia University Press, 1977) 8. As Christopher Herbert has observed, 'Almost more than any other single function, the double narration in *Bleak House* serves to bring to the surface the inherently fantastic property of omniscient narration – fantastic especially in the context of an occluded world like this one, where omniscience is scarcely conceivable.' Cf. 'The Occult in *Bleak House*', *Novel: A Forum on Fiction* 17/2 (Winter 1984); rpt. in Harold Bloom, ed., *Charles Dickens's Bleak House* (New York: Chelsea House, 1987) 123.

27. *The Practice of Everyday Life*, trans. Steven Rendall (Berkeley: University of .California Press, 1984) 92.

28. Cf. Alfred Kroeber, 'The Superorganic', *American Anthropologist* 19/2 (1917), 163–213.

29. J. Hillis Miller, *Charles Dickens: The World of his Novels* (orig. 1958; rpt. Cambridge, MA: Harvard University Press, 1965) 160–204.

30. Jaffe, 13.

31. Lévi-Strauss, *Introduction to the Work of Marcel Mauss*, trans. Felicity Baker (London: Routledge, 1987) 21-44; quoted in Homi Bhabha, 'DissemiNation: Time, Narrative, and the Margins of the Modern Nation', in Bhabha ed., *Nation and Narration* (London: Routledge, 1990) 301.

32. Indeed, it seems that the constitutive ambivalence of *Bleak House* manifests itself not only through the dual narration but also within each narrator's account: the anonymous 'escapee' who begins the novel cannot resist the impulse to 'return' (as Bucket, Tulkinghorn, etc.), and the successfully acculturated Esther eventually gets liberated by her disfigurement – that is,

her release from the order of signification or *figuring* which had doomed her to represent her fallen mother. Both within and between the two narratives, each movement doubles back on itself.

33. I draw here upon Virginia Blain, 'Double Vision and the Double Standard in *Bleak House*: A Feminist Perspective', in Bloom, ed., *Charles Dickens's Bleak House*, 139–56.

34. Miller, introduction to *Bleak House*, 22–4.

35. Herbert, *Culture and Anomie*, 11.

36. For a survey of reactions, cf. Jeremy Hawthorn, *Bleak House: The Critics Debate* (Houndmills, Basingstoke: Macmillan, 1987) esp. 27.

37. Blain, 141.

38. Anderson, *Imagined Communities: Reflections on the Origins and Spread of Nationalism* (London: Verso, 1983) 36, 35. Consider how pertinent to *Bleak House* is Anderson's remark about a particular moment in the experience of the hero of *Semarang Hitam*, a 1924 Indonesian novel: 'Nor does he care the slightest who the dead vagrant individually was: he thinks of the representative body, not the personal life' (37).

39. Cf. John Butt and Kathleen Tillotson, *Dickens at Work* (London: Methuen, 1957): 'In a novel where the life of England in 1851 is otherwise fully represented, the Great Exhibition is deliberately, even conspicuously, excluded' (182). I am indebted to Tatiana Holway's *Speculation and Representation: Charles Dickens and the Victorian Economic Imagination* (dissertation in progress, Columbia University), for the fullest treatment of *Bleak House*'s relationship to the Great Exhibition.

Part III
Dickens and His World

Otherness

The Uncanny

Science

11
Little Dorrit, *Pictures from Italy* and John Bull

Tore Rem

Our sense of geographical and ethnic identity has many different facets, and the result of an investigation of it depends on the microscopes and telescopes we use. About that great other, America, Dickens stated: 'I do not find in America one form of religion with which we in Europe, or even in England, are unacquainted'.[1] This statement is not quoted here because of its discussion of Dissenters but because of the 'we in Europe' and Dickens's European identity. Even an Englishman might, of course, be inclined to stop referring to Europe as distinct from his own country when so far away from home, but it is my thesis that Dickens had both a critical attitude towards his own people regarding national identity and – for an Englishman at the time – a rather unusual openness to what Europe represented. This essay attempts to illuminate aspects of Dickens's relationship to Italy as it is reflected in his letters, *Pictures from Italy* and *Little Dorrit*.

There is no denying that the great cockney on his journeys had an eye for the familiar. When approaching Rome Dickens even reveals a certain wariness of this fact: 'The Eternal City appeared, at length, in the distance; it looked like – I am half afraid to write the word – like LONDON!!!'[2] Dickens was, of course, as English as the English come. Chesterton is perhaps the critic who has argued this point most forcefully, if indeed arguing ever was Chesterton's project. To him Dickens was 'the Englishman abroad; [and] the Englishman abroad is for all serious purposes, simply the Englishman at home.'[3] This enunciation is part and parcel of Chesterton's view that Dickens was blissfully shut off from anything 'other', from anything truly European. But to the extent that it is true, I believe this 'homey' attitude in Dickens also has positive consequences. Chesterton rightly observes about *Pictures from Italy* that '[Dickens] sees amusing things; he describes them amusingly. But he would have seen things just as good in a street in Pimlico, and described them just as well.'[4] What Chesterton does not perceive is that, being critical of the state of his own nation and sharing little of the Englishman's xenophobia, Dickens approached the man in the Italian *strada* as he would the man in the street back home. Peter Ackroyd even suggests that he 'recognised some of the great theatrical strengths of the Italians, their vivacity and their humour, also within himself'.[5]

The strikingly new element in *Pictures from Italy* is the concern with the common, contemporaneous, living people of Italy. Although he can be construed as patronising, Dickens thoroughly enjoyed 'the beautiful Italian manners, the sweet language, the quick recognition of a pleasant look or cheerful word; the captivating expression of a desire to oblige in everything'.[6] The concern with art and the picturesque evinced by the Grand Tourists – most often scornful of the barbarous Italians, sometimes wholeheartedly ignoring their existence – plays only a peripheral part in Dickens's descriptions.[7] With rare exceptions, nature was not his thing – in his novels it too easily becomes the cardboard stage-setting of a London theatre – and art he approached in what was at best an idiosyncratic manner.

Although often deeply ambivalent about aspects of Italian life, Dickens loved the land and many of the places he visited. Of more significance in this context, however, is his statement in a letter to Miss Burdett Coutts: 'I like the common people of Italy, very much'.[8] The people of Genoa, whom he got to know best, are described in *Pictures from Italy* as 'very good-tempered, obliging, and industrious'.[9] Could one ask for a greater eulogy from a Victorian Englishman? His love for the people, unshared by the Grand Tourists, distinguishes his travel writing, and a true interaction between people from his own country and the Italians remains an ideal. When Littimer condescendingly reports on Emily's whereabouts in Italy in *David Copperfield*, his remarks should be interpreted as something positive, as Little Em'ly's idyll:

> She may have had assistance from the boatmen, and the boatmen's wives and children. Being given to low company, she was very much in the habit of talking to them on the beach, Miss Dartle, and sitting by their boats. . . . Mr James was far from pleased to find out, once, that she had told the children she was a boatman's daughter, and that in her own country, long ago, she had roamed about the beach, like them.[10]

A character in Walter Savage Landor's *High and Low Life in Italy* from 1831 exclaims: 'A man to leave Italy and not to write a book about it! Was ever such a thing heard of?',[11] and Dickens is not above this tradition of literary exploitation of the South. But he also shows a fascination with the idiosyncrasies of the Italians which rarely drowns in customary generalisations. The poor cicerone showing Dickens the plot of grass where five of his children are buried appears as a dignified presence in *Pictures from Italy*, and his final characterisation of the Italians as 'a people, naturally well-disposed, and patient, and sweet-tempered' is another example which illustrates the eccentricity of this Victorian Englishman's attitude towards Italy.[12] Holding Thackeray up as a contrast, with his 'typical English boasting' and feeling of racial superiority, George Orwell observes that 'one very striking thing about Dickens, especially considering the time he lived in, is his lack of vulgar chauvinism'.[13] The xenophobia *Punch* exhibited even while run by Dickens's radical friends also forms an interesting backdrop to his attitudes. In his involvement with Italy Dickens sympathised with the revolutionary leader Mazzini (whom he had met), and David Paroissien notes that he joined two groups in London working for the Italian cause.[14] To be so committed to the liberty of the citizens of another state was indeed 'not English'. Dickens is scathing about the condescending recipes for travel English tourists were presented with in guidebooks such as Murray's. He admits that 'I have such a perverse disposition in respect of sights that are cut, and dried, and dictated – that I fear I sin against similar authorities in every place I visit.'[15] The only travel book that receives positive mention is the *Tour in Italy and Sicily* (1828) written by Simonds, a Frenchman who had left his country for America during the early stages of the Revolution.[16] Judging from their reputation with guidebooks and English tourists, Italian inns were the epitome of all that was shabby, filthy and un-English.[17] Dickens, in a letter to Forster, notes the prejudice of his countrymen: 'it is a great thing – quite a matter of course – with English travellers, to decry the Italian inns.'[18] But to him the inns are 'immeasurably better than you would suppose', and he rehabilitates them in *Pictures from Italy*; the attendants receive high praise both in this letter and in *Pictures*.[19] Dickens was not content with the traditional English stereotype of Italy, he had to experience the country for himself. It was only then that he was able to create, as he always did, what seem his own idiosyncratic 'stereotypes'.

On his second trip with Wilkie Collins and Augustus Egg in 1853, Dickens was impressed by the thriving development that had taken place in the country since his first stay. About Genoa he declared in a letter to Miss Burdett Coutts: 'If it goes on in the same way, long, its old commercial greatness will be renewed.'[20] The criticism of Italy expressed in *Pictures from Italy* has certainly not been erased, but Dickens's attitude is more positive. Indeed, a typical trend in the descriptions in *Pictures from Italy* is initial hostility followed by delight as the new becomes familiar.[21] After a few months in the country, Dickens wrote to the Countess of Blessington, 'We like Italy more and more, every day.'[22] On first entering Genoa, Dickens records a mass of negative evidence against the place, only to observe: 'I little thought, that day, that I should ever come to have an attachment for the very stones in the streets of Genoa, with many hours of happiness and quiet! But these are my first impressions honestly set down; and how they changed, I will set down too.'[23] This is hardly the voice of a man simply entering a Dickensland wherever he goes. In his letters he often starts out in a negative tone, only to find that he is delighting in and enjoying what he experiences.[24] It is as if he has to remind himself that he has made a deliberate choice to be open. Dickens's encounter with Italy is not static, it develops both throughout his first stay and his life. Nor does it become all-harmonious; his descriptions remain mixed, but there is an involvement in the state of the country – which was, we must remember, far from its former glory – and a sympathy for the people which deepens the more Dickens is exposed to this part of Europe.[25] Perhaps the cockney in him helped in bringing Italy close. Andrew Sanders claims that 'If Dickens abroad remains a cockney Dickens, it is because his imaginative and his critical faculties went hand in hand'.[26] Personally, I do not think the cockney in Dickens always had the upper hand when he was abroad (some of his somewhat superior observations, e.g. on America, are more representative of a middle-class, Whiggish and narrow-minded English Protestant), but, in relation to Italy, some of the most sympathetic of his reactions might be attributed to the unceremonious and naive cockney in him. As travel literature goes, it was perhaps an advantage for *Pictures from Italy* that Dickens was not an expert on art or had a passionate relationship to nature. His strong antipathy against the many connoisseurs helped him dwell less on what so many English travel writers had been masticating for so many decades.

Although it is easy to point to some of Dickens's criticisms of his countrymen and show his own rootedness in similar insularities, I believe that his conscious criticism of what he saw as unfortunate English attitudes is a vital factor that sets him apart from the mass of English writers.[27] His comic treatment of John Bullist prejudice becomes the more effective because it shows his own struggle against the trap of nationalism.[28] It is telling that before him only George Sand, a French woman, had satirised English boorishness in Italy to a similar extent.[29] Without losing his Englishness, Dickens emerges as a European in his comic treatment of his own countrymen; John Bull never had anything even faintly approaching self-awareness. Speaking of himself and his own people in his 1856 *Household Words* article 'Insularities', Dickens asserts: 'One of our most remarkable Insularities is a tendency to be firmly persuaded that what is not English is not natural.'[30] In a letter to Forster from Paris, he pronounced the judgement that 'it is extraordinary what nonsense English people talk, write, and believe, about foreign countries'.[31] These sentiments are profoundly radical as they strike at the root of English self-complacency. To George Bernard Shaw, *Little Dorrit* was more seditious than *Das Kapital* because of its attack on society: 'All over Europe men and women are in prison for pamphlets and speeches which are to *Little Dorrit* as red pepper to dynamite.'[32] But Dickens's radicalism is particularly daring in that he satirises English attitudes towards foreigners at a time when the Empire was beginning to take itself very seriously indeed. When Dickens, in the letter to Forster, moves on to some savage generalisations about the French, as if he was completely free from prejudice, the comedy, partly aimed at himself, redeems him. Even if he was not free from John Bullishness, he was fiercely critical of the insularity of his countrymen.

The ability to see his own people from the outside, in a European perspective as it were, also leads to a demand for mutual respect. Insularity can, as Dickens sees it, also exist on the mainland. The article 'Foreigners' Portraits of Englishmen' in *Household Words* (1850) contains many examples of how Englishmen are portrayed in Europe, particularly in theatres across the continent. The last mention is of a new piece in the Carl Theatre, Vienna, called 'Lord Pudding, ein reisender Englander' [*sic*]. The author of the article hopes that 'our Continental neighbours' will have a chance to improve their knowledge of the English when they come to the Great Exhibition and 'have the advantage of seeing us at home, and in a mass; and will henceforth cease to judge us by those follies which they observe in a few idle tourists from these islands'.[33] These same tourists are evidently a major embarrassment to Dickens abroad. Writing to Kate from Lausanne in 1853, he exultantly exclaims: 'We have as yet, marvellous to say, met no English people whom we have known.'[34] In *Pictures from Italy* there are English tourists like the omnipresent Mrs Davies about whom Dickens writes that, in spite of her having been to every sight possible, 'I don't think she ever saw anything or ever looked at anything'.[35] Others are busy being insensible to every impression that does not fit their guidebook. During a re-enactment of the Last Supper as part of the celebrations of the Holy Week in Rome, an English gentleman who keeps croaking about whether there is a mustard pot on the table or not causes Dickens great aggravation.[36]

Dickens was also able to see both himself and the foreigner from the outside during a transition between countries. In 'A Flight' (*Reprinted Pieces*), he observes: 'And now I find that all the French people on board begin to grow, and all the English people to shrink. The French are nearing home, and shaking off a disadvantage, whereas we are shaking it on.'[37] It is the complete lack of humility, the ignoring of the need to adapt, and the refusal to come to terms with a new situation which Dickens reacts most strongly against in some of his countrymen abroad.

However fascinating his letters, journalism and travel books may be, they are not the main reason for studying Dickens. To discover the lasting significance of his attitude towards Italy, and towards Europe, we must turn to his fiction. In this part of the argument I would like to examine how a ridicule of John Bull tends to erase the boundaries between England and Europe in Dickens's works. Mr Sapsea in *The Mystery of Edwin Drood* is the last in a line of world-wise Englishmen in Dickens. Sapsea, who believes he knows something of the world, expresses himself on the subject with 'unspeakable complacency': 'If I have not gone to foreign countries, . . . foreign countries have come to me.'[38] In this extreme case, knowing everything before you go simply makes the going unnecessary. At the other end of Dickens's canon, in *Nicholas Nickleby*, a commensurately open-minded Mr Lillyvick asks: '"What's the water in French, sir?" "L'Eau," replied Nicholas. "Ah!" said Mr Lillyvick, shaking his head mournfully, "I thought as much. Lo, eh? I don't think anything of that language – nothing at all."'[39] Comic treatments of the insularity of his countrymen were part of his novels from the first phase of his career, but it is Mr Podsnap who has come to represent the epitome of English middle-class parochialism. However, the fictional handling of English attitudes is more interesting in *Little Dorrit* than in *Our Mutual Friend* because the novel is set partly on the continent and features several foreigners. Besides, Dickens's portrayal of some of his own countrymen anticipates his celebrated satire on Podsnappery.[40]

Mr Meagles, for all his positive and genial characteristics, is a portrait of the petty bourgeois Podsnappian Englishman with his admiration for the upper rungs of society and his complacent sense of superiority towards foreigners. Podsnap, in that triumphal tautology of nationalism, will declare: 'We know what Russia means . . ., we know what France wants;

we see what America is up to; but we know what England is. That's enough for us.'[41] Meagles, for his part, merely claims that 'we know what Marseilles is' (53). But the approach is the same: generalisations as broad as the channel place foreigners in neat little boxes. Meagles furthermore exposes a vulgar superiority through his lack of interest in learning any of the languages of the countries in which he travels. He naturally expects the foreigner somehow to 'be bound to understand' straightforward English (61), and in a narratorial comment he is explicitly and appropriately given the label John Bull.[42]

Mrs General, representative of the English middle-class society the Dorrits frequent in Italy, is a complementary figure to Mr Meagles. Her chief characteristics are her blinkered respectability and her dislike and easy dismissal of impropriety (the way to get 'rid of it was to put it out of sight, and make believe that there was no such thing' (503),[43] which prefigures the famous 'I don't want to know about it; I don't choose to discuss it; I don't admit it!' uttered by Podsnap and accompanied with 'that flourish of his arm which added more expressively than any words, And I remove it from the face of the earth'[44] Mrs General is, quite appropriately, the Victorian feminine version of this opinionated gentleman in that she 'had no opinions. Her way of forming a mind was to prevent it from forming opinions. She had a little circular set of mental grooves or rails on which she started little trains of other people's opinions' (503). The basic flaw in the Englishman abroad is this lack of openness to another country and to other people, partly a result of the traditions surrounding these tours, partly as a result of insecurity.[45] The narrator clinches the point when referring to Mrs General's former tour of Europe to see those treasures which it is 'essential that all persons of polite cultivation should see with other people's eyes, and never with their own' (501). In Dickens's literary vision, English eyes are closed at home, never to be opened abroad. Mrs General simply reiterates what she has read in Murray's guidebook and picked up from various Podsnaps whose minds are rigidly closed to anything 'Not English'.

Moving back from the continent to an England unknown to Podsnap or Mrs General, we find that in Bleeding Heart Yard prejudice is exercised in a more friendly, but nevertheless similar manner. The foreigner who attends Mr Podsnap's dinner party in *Our Mutual Friend* is treated 'as if he was a child who was hard of hearing',[46] whereas the fragmented Podsnaps of the earlier novel speak to Cavalletto 'as if he were stone deaf' and treat him 'like a baby' (351).[47] Even if the Bleeding Hearts are less solid than Podsnap and his plate, they are not particularly welcoming to foreigners. The narrator in *Little Dorrit* gives a whole list of traditional English ideas about foreigners, i.e. continental Europeans, which are held in reverence by the Plornishes and their neighbours. The first two and perhaps most fundamental are the axioms that 'every foreigner had a knife about him' and 'that he ought to go home to his own country' (350). Apart from struggling with these two preconceived notions, the foreigner will come up against challenges near identical to those from Podsnap and his circle, e.g., 'that it was a sort of Divine visitation upon a foreigner that he was not an Englishman' and 'that foreigners were always immoral' (350–1). In attitudes to foreigners there seems to be little class division in Dickens's world. The prejudice found in Bleeding Heart, the City, and among the Grand Tourists is a glue in the social fabric. Even the view of language, abstracted from the tribal differences so characteristic of English society, is identical. Mrs Plornish has a peculiar power of 'penetrating [Cavalletto] with a sense of the appalling difficulties of the Anglo-Saxon tongue' (351) which anticipates Podsnap's 'Our Language . . . is Difficult. Ours is a Copious Language, and Trying to Strangers'.[48] The harsh and pointed satires on English attitudes towards the rest of Europe in *Little Dorrit* manifest a narratorial centre sympathetic towards Europe, towards 'the other'. Dickens typically works by counterassertion rather than by assertion; he is often more fond of dismantling assertive conduct than of presenting a positive alternative.[49] By criticising his countrymen's blinkered views, Dickens implicitly emerges as a European as well as an Englishman.

Little Dorrit is a radical reworking of the traditional depictions of Italy in English fiction. The route is the same, and following a group of Grand Tourists rather than the new middle-class travellers triggers associations with the eighteenth rather than the nineteenth century, but Dickens uses the old images for new fictional purposes. Italy is seen through Little Dorrit's eyes and the country is primarily a background for her inner landscapes, rather than a picturesque setting. It is used in a new and subtle way which works against customary and predictable reactions. Rather than being the stupendous reality Dickens had experienced, Venice, invaded as it is by English tourists, is no better to Little Dorrit than, 'a superior sort of Marshalsea' (565).[50] The only reality for her is an analogy from home.

The universalism of the prison imagery, or shall we say its Europeanism, is perhaps a result of what Chesterton calls 'travels in Dickensland',[51] and Chesterton would say that to the cockney Dickens every place in the world is England anyway, and England is a prison. But it would be unfair to maintain that Dickens, like the tourists he satirises, never really ventured into another country. His negative and positive reactions towards Italy were in the spirit of a fellow European. Italy's heritage was *his* heritage. Indeed, he adopted a far more inclusive and generous approach towards this European country than he ever did towards America. The contrast is immense if we compare the movement in fictional approach from *American Notes* (1842) to *Martin Chuzzlewit* (1843–4) with that from *Pictures from Italy* (1846) to *Little Dorrit* (1855–7). In the latter novel the social criticism of Italy has completely gone, and Italy simply brings out the vices of the author's own countrymen who become travesties once placed in a new and sympathetically portrayed context.

A telling instance of Dickens's positive view of the Continent as opposed to his own country is Doyce's eventual, and involuntary, defection to 'a certain barbaric power' with a ridiculous notion of 'How to do it' (735). At home he has been 'The Great English Public Offender' because of his ingenuity, but at the end of the novel he returns from abroad 'medalled and ribboned, and starred and crossed' (891) for his services. When all this is said, Dickens does of course, like Doyce, prefer home. His Anglophilia has been well documented, perhaps most solidly in Malcolm Andrews's *Dickens on England and the English*.[52] But it is a patriotism free from the jingoism characterising so many of his contemporaries when Europe was in question, that is not to say that he was unbiased, only to emphasise the point that he consciously tried to express his fellow-feeling with continental Europeans. Dickens's Englishness had its limits.[53]

Seen in the context of his disillusionment with his own country, even the social criticism in *Pictures from Italy* becomes mild and hopeful. No judgement on Italy ever was as grim as this one on England:

> I do reluctantly believe that the English people are habitually consenting parties to the miserable imbecility into which we have fallen, *and will never help themselves out of it.* Who is to do it, if anybody is, God knows. But at present we are on the down-hill road to being conquered, and the people WILL be content to bear it, sing 'Rule Britannia', and WILL NOT be saved.[54]

Complacent nationalism is here seen at the root of England's problems. In a letter to Bulwer Lytton in 1851 Dickens even writes: 'London is a vile place, I sincerely believe. I have never taken kindly to it, since I lived abroad.'[55] London's 'special correspondent for posterity', in Bagehot's famous phrase, having tasted the Continent, seems already willing to pass the city on.[56] The effect travelling in France, Switzerland and Italy had on him should not be underestimated. *Pictures from Italy* is full of declarations of love for the country. Venice made an impression on Dickens beyond anything else he had experienced. The man who controlled everything in such confident imaginative ways with his pen had to admit: 'Venice is a bit of my brain from this time . . . But the reality itself, beyond pen and pencil. I never saw the thing before that I should be afraid to describe. But to tell what Venice is, I feel to be an impossibility.'[57] In *Pictures from Italy* he chose not to attempt a description of the reality of the city but approached it as a dream, and in *Little Dorrit* the only reality is the Marshalsea. Contrary to the social pessimism which he developed with regard to the state of England in the later part of his life, on his return to Italy in 1853 he noticed 'an extraordinary increase everywhere . . . of "life, growth and enterprise"' in Genoa.[58] If Venice was a dream on his first visit, it seems as if the rest of Italy had now become the dream. Dickens's old American dream has been substituted with an Italian dream. The American dream was lost on arrival, while the Italian lived on after several visits.

Notes

1. 'American Notes', in *American Notes and Pictures from Italy* [1842] (Oxford: Oxford University Press, 1991) 249. In *Martin Chuzzlewit*, the narrator clearly prides himself on the cultural tradition of Europe when he exposes American ignorance in a report of General Fladdock's conversation: '[The general] lowered his voice and was very impressive here: " . . . oh the conventionalities of the a-mazing Eu-rope!"', *Martin Chuzzlewit* [1843–4] (Harmondsworth: Penguin, 1986) 353.
2. 'Pictures from Italy', in *American Notes and Pictures from Italy*, 364.
3. G.K. Chesterton, *Charles Dickens* [1906] (London: Methuen, 1936) 112.
4. Ibid., 111. We tend to think of Dickens's characters as glued to the streets of London, but this is, if we are to believe his Preface of 1867 to *Dombey and Son*, not the way he conceived them. 'I began this book by the Lake of Geneva, and went on with it for some months in France, before pursuing it in England. The association between the writing and the place of writing is so curiously strong in my mind, that at this day, although I know, in my fancy, every stair in the little midshipman's house, and could swear to every pew in the church in which Florence was married, or to every young gentleman's bedstead in Doctor Blimber's establishment, I yet confusedly imagine Captain Cuttle as secluding himself from Mrs MacStinger among the mountains of Switzerland. Similarly, when I am reminded by any chance of what it was that the waves were always saying, my remembrance wanders for a whole winter night

about the streets of Paris', *Dombey and Son* [1846–48] (Harmondsworth: Penguin, 1985) 43. It is not as if a foreign place did not make an impression on Dickens's mind, nor is it always London to him.

5. Peter Ackroyd, *Dickens* [1990] (London: Minerva, 1991) 484. In his *Household Words* article 'Insularities' Dickens – renowned for his flash, un-English waistcoats – seems to find Englishmen's insularities when it comes to clothing to be of great import.

6. Charles Dickens, *Travelling Letters Written on the Road*, 2 vols, New York, 1846, I, 683 (quoted in Paroissien's introduction to *Pictures from Italy* [London: Deutsch, 1973] 19).

7. David Paroissien, in his introduction, modifies the general impression of eighteenth-century descriptions of Italy: 'it is worth remembering that the eighteenth-century experience of Italy was not so monolithic that one can rest with Addison. Travel writers such as Samuel Sharp, Smollett, Lady Anna Miller, the Earl of Cork, and Mrs Piozzi all had a keen eye for social conditions and none were so deeply immersed in humanistic pursuits as to ignore the Italians of the present day' (13). Paroissien also mentions that in 1826 Mary Shelley refers to 'a new generation' of travellers labelled 'Anglo-Italians'. They have 'an understanding of the language, fewer complaints about being starved, upset, and robbed, more independence from guide books, and a deeper interest in the Italian people', ibid., p. 10. Dickens obviously partakes of this new trend.

8. *Pilgrim Letters*, ed. by Kathleen Tillotson (Oxford: Oxford University Press, 1977), 4, 280.

9. *Pictures from Italy*, 299.

10. *David Copperfield* [1849–50] (Harmondsworth: Penguin, 1985) 738.

11. Quoted in Churchill, 66.

12. *Pictures from Italy*, 322 and 433.

13. George Orwell, 'Charles Dickens', in *The Collected Essays, Journalism and Letters of George Orwell*, vol. 1, ed. Sonia Orwell and Ian Angus [1940] (London: Secker & Warburg, 1968) 413–60 (431–3).

14. Paroissien's introduction to *Pictures from Italy*, 14–15. Susan Schoenbauer Thurin interestingly refers to Ugo Piscopo who, reviewing Italian criticism of Dickens, 'supports Dickens's indictment of religion in the oppression of the people and says that *Pictures from Italy* gives a lively and passionate account without rhetoric of the causes of the Italian nationalist movement'. Thus, with very different backgrounds and partly varying aims, Dickens resembles certain Italian revolutionaries and anarchists even in his attitudes to Roman Catholicism, 'Pictures from Italy: Pickwick and Podsnap Abroad', *Dickensian*, vol. 83 (Summer 1987) 66–78 (71–3).

15. *Pictures from Italy*, 321. In a letter to Count Alfred D'Orsay he complains that 'The Holy Week is in full force at this time; and hundreds of English people with hundreds of Murray's Guide Books and a corresponding number of Mrs. Starkes' in their hands are chattering in all silent places, worrying the professional Ciceroni

to death', *Pilgrim*, 4, 282. The parodist in *Mephystopheles* seems not to have noticed this aversion, or tries, by ignoring it, to tease his object of attack. He refers to how 'the proud young porter has "Murray" by heart', *Mephystopheles*, xiv, 170.

16.   *Pictures from Italy*, 301 and 357. Dickens, in a letter to Forster, states about the *Tour of Italy and Sicily*: 'it is a most charming book, and eminently remarkable for its excellent sense, and determination not to give in to conventional lies', [3 August 1844], *Pilgrim*, 4, 164.

17.   See Churchill, 138.

18.   *Pilgrim*, 4, 221–2.

19.   Ibid.; *Pictures from Italy*, 361–2; and 326. The Dorrit family is, of course, also treated in a very civil manner, but theirs is the position of Grand Tourists, and they can afford to pay for a higher level of service than the average English tourist of the nineteenth century could.

20.   *Pilgrim*, ed. by Graham Storey and others (Oxford: Oxford University Press, 1993) 7, 190. See also letter to Forster, [? 29–30 October 1853], *Pilgrim*, 7, 181.

21.   In *Pictures from Italy* he observes that 'in the course of two months, the flitting shapes and shadows of my dismal entering reverie gradually resolved themselves into familiar forms and substances; and I already began to think that when the time should come, a year hence, for closing the long holiday and turning back to England, I might part from Genoa with anything but a glad heart. It is a place that "grows upon you" every day', 290–1.

22.   *Pilgrim*, 4, 227.

23.   *Pictures from Italy*, 283.

24.   In a letter to Count D'Orsay, 7 August 1844, there is first a paragraph on 'what a sad place Italy is!', but then Dickens adds: 'I have [a gre]at interest in it now; and walk about, or ride about, the [town] when I go there, in a dreamy sort of way, which is very comfortable. I seem [to be] thinking, but I don't know what about – I haven't the least idea. I can sit down in a church, or stand at the end of a narrow Vico, zig-zagging uphill like a dirty snake: and not feel the least desire for any further entertainment', *Pilgrim*, 4, 169.

25.   The erudite narrator of *Middlemarch*, seeing Rome through Dorothea's eyes, focuses on the same alloy: 'all this vast wreck of ambitious ideals, sensuous and spiritual, mixed confusedly with the signs of breathing forgetfulness and degradation', *Middlemarch* [1871–2] (Harmondsworth: Penguin, 1994) 193.

26.   Andrew Sanders, 'The Dickens World', in *Creditable Warriors: 1830–1876*, ed. Michael Cotsell, in the series *English Literature and the Wider World*, vol. 3 (London: Ashfield, 1990) 131–42 (134).

27.   His conscious detachment from typical English attitudes to foreigners is enough to disqualify him from Humphry House's characterisation of him as 'an elementary John Bull', even in his anti-Catholicism, Humphry House, *The Dickens World* (London: Oxford University Press, 1941) 128.

28. According to the *Oxford English Dictionary*, a John Bullist is 'one who favours the English'. Five years after *Pictures from Italy* appeared, in 1851, John Henry Newman referred to 'Anglo-maniacs or John Bullists, as they are popularly termed' (Oxford: Oxford University Press, 1989) vol. viii, 258.

29. George Sand was a pioneer in the way Italy was portrayed abroad. She combined a focus on its great works of art with an interest in contemporary life. Kenneth Churchill claims about *Pictures from Italy* that 'To an extent one can plot its position on the chart of developing attitudes to Italy, in so far as its responses to the common life of the Italian people build on the work of George Sand, and are in total contrast to the interests of the Grand Tourists' (137).

30. Charles Dickens (ed.), 'Insularities', *Household Words*, Saturday, 19 January 1856, vol. 13, 1–4 (2).

31. Letter to John Forster, [6 December 1846], *Pilgrim*, 4, 676.

32. Quoted in Malcolm Andrews, 131. Michael Cotsell links the issue of the system with national pride: 'The July Revolution of 1830 in France sparked off risings throughout Europe and accelerated the passage of the Reform Act of 1832. Yet in so far as reform was a child of foreign influences, it was an ungrateful one. Its very success in England led, in the following years, to a diminishment of sympathy with foreign radical nationalism, though fear of further democracy was equally a factor. The unwritten British constitution had again proved itself to be the triumph of the race. To satirize it, as Charles Dickens or Matthew Arnold were to do, was to risk being judged "not English"', Introduction to *Creditable Warriors*, 1–51 (3).

33. *The Uncollected Writings of Charles Dickens*, ed. by Harry Stone. vol. 1 [1968] (London: Allen Lane, 1969) 149–50.

34. *Pilgrim*, ed. by Graham Storey and others (Oxford: Oxford University Press, 1988) 6, 166.

35. *Pictures from Italy*, 378.

36. *Pictures from Italy*, 402. In a letter to Thomas Beard, 21 October 1846, Dickens at length describes the arrogance of an English tourist who, being completely dependent on a fellow French traveller for communication with the locals, is nevertheless extremely patronising when the same Frenchman communicates back to him in imperfect English, *Pilgrim*, 4, 639–40. The Grand Tourists in *Little Dorrit* exhibit a similar insensitivity to the locals and are, if possible, even more aloof than the English gentleman in *Pictures from Italy*.

37. 'A Flight', in *The Uncommercial Traveller and Reprinted Pieces* (Oxford: Oxford University Press, 1994) 474–84 (479).

38. *The Mystery of Edwin Drood* [1870] (Harmondsworth: Penguin, 1985) 64–5.

39. *Nicholas Nickleby* [1838–9] (Harmondsworth: Penguin, 1988) 274.

40. It is worth remembering the generally unsympathetic reception *Little Dorrit* had among English reviewers. Sir James Fitzjames Stephen's article in the *Edinburgh Review*, 'The License of Modern Novelists', is extremely hostile to the idea of inexpert novelists meddling in the affairs of the country. The negative comparisons

with other countries in *Little Dorrit* makes Sir James smart: 'we should doubt whether we were much worse governed than our neighbours', and he claims that the corruption and blackmail involved in the running of other countries are 'utterly and absolutely unknown in our own country'. 'The Licence of Modern Novelists', *The Edinburgh Review*, July 1857, no. 215, 124–56 (134–5). The article was published anonymously. When popular novelists started satirising the system in such fundamental ways, the ignorant masses could apparently be led dangerously astray. By attacking his country and his countrymen in *Little Dorrit*, the always market-conscious Dickens was willing to risk critical hostility and to endanger his sales.

41. *Our Mutual Friend* [1864–5] (Harmondsworth: Penguin, 1985) 887.

42. As the Barnacles are about to leave the wedding celebrations of Pet and Henry Gowan, the narrator comments on '[the chief Barnacles] with all affability conveying to Mr and Mrs Meagles that general assurance that what they had been doing there, they had been doing at a sacrifice for Mr and Mrs Meagles's good, which they always conveyed to Mr John Bull in their official condescension to that most unfortunate creature', *Little Dorrit*, 459.

43. Vereen M. Bell calls Podsnap one of Mrs General's descendants and convincingly argues that Mrs General is middle-class England, 'Mrs General's Victorian England: Dickens's Image of His Times', *Nineteenth-Century Fiction*, 20 (September 1965) 177–84 (179).

44. *Our Mutual Friend*, 174 and 188.

45. In his preliminary word to the first issue of *Household Words*, Dickens made a point of the desirability of an open attitude to other countries: 'Our Household Words will not be echoes of the present time alone, but of the past too. Neither will they treat of the hopes, the enterprises, triumphs, joys, and sorrows, of this country only, but, in some degree, of those of every nation upon earth. For nothing can be a source of real interest in one of them, without concerning all the rest', *Household Words*, Saturday, 30 March 1850, vol. 1, 1.

46. *Our Mutual Friend*, 177.

47. Dickens seems to have caught on to this idea from his own servants: 'We have a couple of Italian work-people in our establishment; and to hear one or other of them talking away to our servants with the utmost violence and volubility in Genoese, and our servants answering with great fluency in English (very loud: as if the others were only deaf, not Italian), is one of the most ridiculous things possible', Letter to John Forster [? 20 July 1844]. Pilgrim, 4, 156–7.

48. *Our Mutual Friend*, 179.

49. John Kucich discusses this aspect of Dickens's comic technique in *Excess and Restraint in the Novels of Charles Dickens* (Athens, GA: University of Georgia Press, 1981) 7.

50. Churchill argues that 'Dickens brilliantly combines the relation of the girl's feelings with the dominant prison image of the novel and a

biting satire on the purposelessness of what George Eliot later (in Chapter 20 of *Middlemarch*) called "the brilliant picnic of Anglo-foreign society"', *Italy and English Literature*, 139.

51. Chesterton, 111.
52. *Dickens on England and the English* (Brighton: Harvester Press, 1979).
53. Dickens's love of Italy even extends to language. In a letter written in 1853 he exclaims that 'The language has a pleasant sound in my ears, however spoken almost, which no other has except my own'. One suspects that the great novelist regarded American English, which he so often ridiculed, with less fondness than Genoese. Letter to Miss Burdett Coutts, 13 November 1858, *Pilgrim*, 7, 190.
54. Letter to W.C. Macready, 4 October 1855, *Pilgrim*, 7, 715–16.
55. Letter to Sir Edward Bulwer Lytton, 10 February 1851, *Pilgrim*, 6, 287.
56. Walter Bagehot in 'Charles Dickens', *National Review*, vol. 7, October 1858. Extract in *Charles Dickens* (Penguin Critical Anthologies), ed. by Stephen Wall (Harmondsworth: Penguin, 1970) 123–43 (127).
57. Letter to John Forster, [17 and 18 November 1844], *Pilgrim*, 4, 217.
58. John Forster, *The Life of Charles Dickens*, ed. by J.W.T. Ley (London: Palmer, 1928) Book 7, Ch. 3, 580.

12

Charles Dickens and his Performing Selves

Malcolm Andrews

Charles Dickens was both novelist and actor. This combination helped to form the distinctive character of his fiction and also to make him an anomalous presence in the culture of middle-class Victorian England. Within that culture these two activities were seen as, in many ways, incompatible careers. The one private and creative; the other public and interpretative. The one a gentlemanly intellectual employment; the other exhibitionist role-playing in a bohemian subculture. I want to consider the implications of Dickens's histrionic gifts for the special character of his art as a writer and public reader. And I want to examine this under two headings: the first is the polyphonic voice that is exercised in his fiction and in his reading performances, and the second (related to this) has to do with attitudes within Victorian culture towards the constitution of the self.

Dickens's powers of mimicry were well developed by the age of 20 when he applied for an audition at Covent Garden. He was to perform a virtuoso piece from Charles Mathews's repertoire which would demonstrate his prodigious gift for impersonating a range of social types. Mathews's speciality was the 'monopolylogue', in which the soloist would take all the parts in a short play, with a different voice for each character. Illness prevented Dickens from keeping that appointment, and his literary career began to displace his ambitions to become a professional actor. However, as Forster remarked, 'He took to a higher calling, but it included the lower.'[1]

Dickens's gift of mimicry has a compulsive element: it is not just an occasional playful self-indulgence, but an essential part of his act of creation – the trying out of voices. What was a boyhood gift – much cultivated – became a professional practice in his 'higher calling'. The trying out of voices takes place, not only as it were phonetically in the proliferation of speech styles in his cast of characters, but also in the polyphonic mode of his own narration and description. This multi-vocal character of his fiction has long been recognised. It was most notably explored in Bakhtin's classic study *Discourse in the Novel* (1935). Bakhtin sees a variety of languages or discourses competing for cultural authority within any given society, especially within more complex, mixed societies. In his essay he explores the tensions between the unitary, centralising discourse and the subversive, centrifugal play of dialogised heteroglossia – that is, the engagement of a medley of alternative discourses. This theoretical model has intriguing implications both for the mixed culture of Victorian England and for the particular art practised by Dickens in his fiction and readings.

The early Victorian period was one particularly rich in contending discourses and speech styles. It was a period of acute professional specialisation and social mobility. Professional specialisation required a strengthening of the distinctions between the professions, and this could be greatly assisted by the development of specialised discourses: a medical discourse, a legal discourse, a parliamentary discourse. Social mobility generated an anxiety about language and pronunciation as treacherous markers of social origins. Late in the century, the pressures towards received pronunciation threw into sharp relief divergent vernaculars and promoted widespread diglossia in England, for the first time in history.[2] The young Dickens – Boz – relished the variety of such discourses, both as recorder of dialects and as narrator-cum-cicerone to the world of the *Sketches by Boz*. He enjoyed as a writer trying them out just as he had enjoyed, as an aspiring actor, trying out different voices. There is the grandiloquent fastidious editorial discourse, the smart, arch, man-about-town observer discourse, the earnest investigative journalist discourse, and so on. The aspiring writer has to confront heteroglossia and make a selection, as Bakhtin argues:

> Consciousness finds itself inevitably facing the necessity of *having to choose a language*. With each literary-verbal performance, consciousness must actively orient itself amidst heteroglossia, it must move in and occupy a position for itself within it, it chooses, in other words, a 'language'.[3]

Dickens's authorial voice is polyphonic, ventriloquous, now sentimental-elegiac, now mock court-circular, now moral-didactic. The point of particular interest here is that the heteroglossia is not simply objectified as a medley of speech-styles of different fictional characters in the novel, signalled by quotation marks to separate them from the narrator's consistent, uniform discourse: the heteroglossia is inherent in the narrator's own language. Dickens cannot resist the histrionic impulse to speak in different voices, some ironised and some not, even when he has no cast of characters to whom he might appropriately distribute those voices. In fact the only controlled homogeneity of narrative discourse in Dickens occurs when he has formally adopted another character as the narrator of his story: David Copperfield, or Toby Magsman in 'Going into Society'. These consistently monologic narrations are great sustained acts of impersonation. Heteroglossia and the monopolylogue both luxuriate in these disconcerting performances. Compulsive and prolific impersonation is the hallmark of Dickens's fiction, and its source is deep in his actor-novelist character. I shall come back to the issue of polyphony later, but want now to turn to the theatre and Victorian culture.

When Dickens started his public readings there were various prejudices against his going on stage. Forster, his friend and biographer, urged him not to take this step: 'It was a substitution of lower for higher aims; a change to commonplace from more elevated pursuits; and it had so much the character of a public exhibition for money as to raise, in the question of respect for his calling as a writer, a question also of respect for himself as a gentleman.'[4]

The Victorian prejudice against the theatre had to do both with its bohemianism and with the mutability inherent in the acting profession itself – the very art of role-playing. The socially competitive, upwardly mobile, Victorian middle classes – the parvenus culture, as they have been called – were keen to distance themselves from bohemianism. On Charles Mathews's death, several respectful obituaries made a point of reassuring readers that the actor's gentlemanly status had never been contaminated by the theatrical milieu in which he had passed his life. Arguably, a society that is as preoccupied as this about its own identity and is doing some fairly earnest role-playing in its ordinary social life will have ambivalent feelings towards the theatrical spectacle of role-playing.

Nina Auerbach, in *Private Theatricals*, has developed a fascinating study of the way in which the Victorians perceived theatricality as both recreation and threat. In this perception 'theatricality' is directly opposed to the valued concept of 'sincerity':

Reverent Victorians shunned theatricality as the ultimate, deceitful mobility. It connotes not only lies, but a fluidity of character that decomposes the uniform integrity of the self. [It encourages] the idea that character might be inherently unstable ... The theatre, that alluring pariah within Victorian culture, came to stand for all the dangerous potential of theatricality to invade the authenticity of the best self.[5]

The theatre is the place where this instability, this fluidity, this kaleidoscopic mobility is not only licensed, but positively celebrated. Viewed in this light, as a violation of approved norms of behaviour, the theatre resembles Bakhtin's concept of the 'carnivalesque':

> As opposed to the official feast, one might say that carnival celebrates temporary liberation from the prevailing truth of the established order; it marks the suspension of all hierarchical rank, privileges, norms and prohibitions. Carnival was the true feast of time, the feast of becoming, change and renewal. It was hostile to all that was immortalized and complete.[6]

Think how often Dickens introduces such iconoclastic presences into his novel, in the form of groups or individuals who, in Bakhtin's words, are 'opposed to all that is finished and polished, to all pomposity, to every ready-made solution in the sphere of thought and world outlook'. Dickens's first fictional villain was an actor, Alfred Jingle, a nimble practised rogue who duped the unworldly, staid, monologic middle-class Pickwickians by a variety of impersonations. Theatre, particularly popular theatre of the kind on which Dickens was nurtured, is a place on the margins of civilised society, like the Circus in *Hard Times* which occupies a piece of 'neutral' ground on the outskirts of Coketown. Here is a brief glimpse of the circus folk, from near the opening of Chapter 6, Book the First:

> [The man's] legs were very robust, but shorter than legs of good proportion should have been. His chest and back were as much too broad, as his legs were too short. He was dressed in a Newmarket coat and tight-fitting trousers; wore a shawl round his neck; smelt of lamp-oil, straw, orange-peel, horses' provender, and sawdust; and looked a most remarkable sort of Centaur, compounded of the stable and the play-house. Where the one began, and the other ended, nobody could have told with any precision. This gentleman was mentioned in the bills of the day as Mr E.W.B. Childers, so justly celebrated for his daring vaulting act as the Wild Huntsman of the North American

Prairies; in which popular performance, a diminutive boy with an old face, who now accompanied him, assisted as his infant son . . . Made up with curls, wreaths, wings, white bismuth, and carmine, this hopeful young person soared into so pleasing a Cupid as to constitute the chief delight of the maternal part of the spectators; but, in private, where his characteristics were a precocious cutaway coat and an extremely gruff voice, he became of the Turf, turfy.

It is very difficult to keep a steady focus on identities here. The capacity for exotic metamorphosis is the most arresting aspect of these folk. Mr Childers is an oddly assembled human being: everything is out of proportion, as if he has been fitted together from the wrong component limbs. And does he belong in the stable or in the playhouse? Like a Centaur, there is something indeterminate about his species identity. His stage son is another mass of physical contradictions: a charming diminutive ethereal Cupid, whose off-stage character is forbiddingly gruff and earthy. The fluidity of identity of these circus folk, their polymorphous, carnivalesque being, is their chief attraction, and the most conspicuous symptom of their opposition to the monolithic inflexibility of Gradgrind and Bounderby.

There is another example of this elemental opposition in *A Christmas Carol*. Scrooge and his drab, fog-bound, cramped world is invaded by one of these embodiments of fluidity and mobility, the Ghost of Christmas Past, in Stave Two:

> a strange figure – like a child: yet not so like a child as like an old man . . . the figure . . . fluctuated in its distinctness: being now a thing with one arm, now with one leg, now with twenty legs, now a pair of legs, without a head, now a head without a body: of which dissolving parts, no outline would be visible in the dense gloom wherein they melted away.

This protean figure, a surreal version of the circus folk, is the agent of Scrooge's redemption. Itself constantly metamorphosing, the Ghost has come to disturb Scrooge into a recognition – first painful then joyous – of his true multifaceted self (surrogate father, uncle, child, businessman, pledged to live in the Past, the Present and the Future).

Polymorphousness is cousin to heteroglossia and monopolylogue: all represent teasing threats to the buttoned-up, respectable, monologic identity. All three highlight the potential diversity of selves of which the single identity might be composed. Let me add a fourth agent, one that became very voguish in this period and one that fascinated Dickens: mesmerism. Mesmerism, rather like the monopolylogue, could be another formalised occasion where a single self can, under public observation, seem to be releasing different and normally suppressed facets of the personality. The case studies issuing from this practice seemed to confirm suspicions that the unitary self is less the essential fact of our nature than the result of suppression under cultural influences. Its imaginative suggestiveness was very potent. 'With every day, and from both sides my intelligence, the moral and the intellectual, I thus drew steadily nearer to that truth . . . that man is not truly one, but truly two. . . . I hazard the guess that man will be ultimately known for a mere polity of multifarious, incongruous, and independent denizens.'[7] Such was Henry Jekyll's last testament. In *The Picture of Dorian Gray* Oscar Wilde reflected on the ideas of the unitary self:

> He used to wonder at that shallow psychology of those who conceived the Ego in man as a thing, simple, permanent, reliable, and of one essence. To him, man was a being with myriad lives and myriad sensations, a complex multiform creature that bore within itself strange legacies of thought and passion.[8]

The true fluidity of identity is suppressed to enable the human to function within a culture that views the multiform character as unstable, bohemian or diseased. Illness, physical or mental, alcohol, opium or the theatre can breach what Stevenson called 'the fortress of identity'. Often in Dickens, as Miriam Bailin has shown, fevered illness is associated with the near dissolution of identity.[9] In *Great Expectations*, for example, Pip falls ill and becomes delirious: 'I often lost my reason [and] I confounded impossible existences with my own identity.' Dickens, like Stevenson and other writers of the later nineteenth century, became very interested in the implications of such phenomena, as he was in mesmerism and monopolylogue. In his last novel he was, as we know, exploring the idea of a divided personality in which one self presents a coherent single identity, gentlemanly, at the cost of a great effort of self-control, whereas the other self escapes from such controls, dissolves into incoherence and inhabits a world teeming with phantasmagoric inconsistencies. Which is the 'real' personality?

The Victorians then developed an anxious fascination with the idea of the multiple personality and it is in this context that I want to position Dickens's readings.

The solo dramatic reading of the kind Dickens practised, was, as I have said, strongly influenced by his childhood idol Charles Mathews and the tradition of the monopolylogue. It is a strange hybrid form of entertainment, neither a play, nor a straight story-telling, but an amalgam of both. In a play you have a stage full of characters but no narrator (usually). In a reading you have the solitary narrator, but no separate actors, except those you can persuade the audience's imagination to create. Some of Dickens's readings are great narrator vehicles: some are great opportunities for a variety of character parts. Usually they are a blend of the two. Dickens loved the role of story-teller almost as much as he loved acting out the parts. The problems for the soloist come not so much from the narration or the impersonation of the character parts, but in controlling the transition between them. It is easier to do a straightforward comic cockney monologue, unframed by a narrator, than it is to have the narrator describing, introducing and then making way for the character into whose voice he then has to jump. There is a tension between the narration and the dramatisation. An interesting contemporary review of Dickens's readings developed a theory about the art of reading:

> The true theory of the performance is not that it is acting in which the actor, as much as possible, forgets himself into the very likeness of what he personates, but is rather that a gentleman dramatically tells a story among friends, indicating rather than perfectly assuming the characters of the personages brought before us; never wholly, indeed, never nearly, losing sight of his hearers and himself; never wholly, never, at any rate, for very long, getting away from the gentlemanly drawing-room, with its limiting conventionalities, into the wider and freer atmosphere of the stage.[10]

The critic is concerned to distinguish two kinds of performance, and to emphasise that they belong in two very different worlds. In a public reading performance, the reader should *indicate* the characters of the people in his story, but should not *assume* them. Once you *become* your characters, you lose that control over them which the gentlemanly narrator-reader ought always to maintain. The emphasis is on the lapse from middle-class propriety when the public reader wholly assumes the personalities of the characters in his story. In doing so he disturbs two conventional hierarchical relationships, one artistic and the other class status: the former is that relationship which exists between the narrator and the objects and characters of his narrative, where the narrator must, as the young Henry James insisted in his review of *Our Mutual Friend*, maintain intellectual superiority over the passions which are the substance of his story. The latter is the spectacle of the gentleman degenerating into the actor and the drawing-room degenerating into the theatre. Like Bakhtin's 'carnivalesque', such an occasion 'suspends all hierarchical rank'. We may recall Forster's warning that for Dickens to undertake professional public readings was to raise the question of 'respect for himself as a gentleman'. Those 'limiting conventionalities' become perilously fragile. Gentlemanliness in a public reading is evidently measured by the extent to which the performer retains control; observes the overarching monologic controls, which is the histrionic manifestation of the securely unitary self. Self-control is paramount – never 'losing sight of . . . himself'. You cannot be said to control a self that is continually fracturing into a variety of personalities. Such fissility jeopardises social status in that culture.

Mimicry of the kind practised by Dickens and Mathews is an act of the sympathetic imagination. Byron praised Mathews as one who went beyond mere mimicry and who was gifted with the rare talent of intuitively identifying himself with the minds of others. 'Impersonation' has this sense of inhabiting the personality of an-*other*, and thereby they become no longer quite so 'other'. Whereas the staunchly unitary self, manning the 'fortress of identity', needs others to be distinctly 'other'. But as Forster remarked of Dickens: 'What he desired to express he became.' Such repeated acts of imaginative identification involved a temporary suspension of the self: one admiring account of Mathews put it even more strongly: 'The power of self-annihilation possessed by Mr Mathews, gives to all his portraits a separate identity.'

Dickens's willingness to experiment with a kind of self-annihilation and to make a public exhibition of it, is reflected in the language he used when he prepared for or reported on the theatricals and public readings. He repeatedly uses the expression 'tear myself to pieces'. This is, like 'self-annihilation', a vivid literalising of the process I have been exploring. 'I have just come back from Manchester', he writes, after those performances of *The Frozen Deep*, 'where I have been tearing myself to pieces, to the wonderful satisfaction of thousands of people.' He used to stand in the wings just before going onstage to give his readings, pledging, 'I shall tear myself to pieces.' He talked of himself as 'the modern embodiment of the old Enchanters, whose Familiars tore them to pieces'.[11]

This is a writer one of whose greatest ambitions was to restore community, to reunite classes, to repair the web of corroded or broken connexions, to make others less 'other'. In this light, Dickens's nightly self-annihilation, generating the extraordinary dance of proliferating selves, parading in one person the full panorama of English society, may be seen as an extension of his mission as a novelist. And by all accounts he achieved it in the microcosmic setting of the auditorium. Listen to him reporting again on the *Frozen Deep* performances, in the same letter as he mentions the old Enchanters: 'I had a transitory satisfaction in rending the very heart out of my body by doing that Richard Wardour part. It was a good thing to have a couple of thousand people all rigid and frozen together in the palm of one's hand.' Obviously the exercise of power of this kind fascinated Dickens. But notice again the language: disintegration is practised so as to produce integration. After a reading of 'Little Dombey' he reported, 'I never saw a crowd so resolved into one creature before.'

Down around the fringes of a bohemian sub-culture, night after night, luxuriating in heteroglossia and monopolylogue, the Old Enchanter tears himself to pieces, in order to fuse thousands of strangers into one community.

Notes

1. John Forster, *The Life of Charles Dickens* (London: Chapman and Hall, 1872–4) II, 181.
2. See Raymond Chapman, *Forms of Speech in Victorian Fiction* (Harlow: Longman, 1994) especially Chapter 3.
3. M. Bakhtin, 'Discourse in the Novel', trans. Michael Holquist and Caryl Emerson (Austin: University of Texas Press, 1981): repr. in P.Rice and P.Waugh, eds, *Modern Literary Theory: A Reader* (London: Edward Arnold, 1989) 200.
4. Forster, *Life of Charles Dickens*, III, 165.
5. Nina Auerbach, *Private Theatricals: The Lives of the Victorians* (Cambridge: Harvard University Press, 1990) 4.
6. M. Bakhtin, *Rabelais and His World*, trans. H. Islowsky (Indiana University Press, 1984) 10.
7. R.L. Stevenson, *The Strange Case of Dr Jekyll and Mr Hyde* (Wordsworth Classics, Hertfordshire, 1993) 42.
8. Oscar Wilde, *The Picture of Dorian Gray*, in Oscar Wilde, *Plays, Prose Writings & Poems* (London: Dent, 1960) 187.
9. Miriam Bailin, *The Sickroom in Victorian Fiction* (Cambridge University Press, 1994) Chapter 3.
10. Anon., *The Nation* (New York) (12 December 1867) 482.
11. *The Letters of Charles Dickens*, Pilgrim Edition, Volume 8, ed. G. Storey and K. Tillotson (Oxford: Clarendon Press, 1995): Letters of 28 August and 7 December 1857, 421 and 488.

13
Foreign Languages and Original Understanding in *Little Dorrit*[1]

Matthias Bauer

Foreign languages, in Dickens's novels, act as a foil to make us aware of certain qualities and dangers inherent in verbal exchange. They may even function as a paradigm of human communication in general, as they serve to point out that, whether 'foreign' or not, each one speaks differently from anybody else and attaches a meaning of his or her own to what another person says. An example from *Nicholas Nickleby* will show that Dickens, from the first, was attracted to the subject of foreign languages and, more specifically, to the fact that the response to a foreign idiom is not to be separated from thoughts, attitudes and expressions belonging to the listener's own sphere of life. In Mr Lillyvick's and Nicholas Nickleby's discussion about the French language, Dickens seems to point out that understanding means adapting what one hears to one's personal experience and familiar linguistic patterns. Nicholas is asked by Mr Lillyvick whether he considers French a 'cheerful language':

'Yes,' replied Nicholas, 'I should say it was, certainly.'
    'It's very much changed since my time, then,' said the collector, 'very much.'
    'Was it a dismal one in your time?' asked Nicholas, scarcely able to repress a smile.
    'Very,' replied Mr Lillyvick, with some vehemence of manner. 'It's the war time that I speak of; the last war. It may be a cheerful language. I should be sorry to contradict anybody; but I can only say that I've heard the French prisoners, who were natives, and ought to know how to speak it, talking in such a dismal manner, that it made one miserable to hear them. Ay, that I have, fifty times, sir – fifty times!'

After a moment's silence, Mr Lillyvick adds:

> 'What's the water in French, sir?'
> '*L'Eau*,' replied Nicholas.
> 'Ah!' said Mr Lillyvick, shaking his head mournfully, 'I thought as much. Lo, eh? I don't think anything of that language – nothing at all.'[2]

While in this example the personal way of responding to a foreign language mainly presents its comic side, in *Little Dorrit* its more serious implications for the process of understanding become visible as well. A case in point is the restless traveller Mr Meagles, who translates (or transforms) the words *allons* and *marchons* of the *Marseillaise* into his favourite formula 'allonging and marshonging'. (The English suffix quite literally shows that the French words present a special aspect to him.) Mr Meagles's resounding formula not only epitomizes the uproar of life abroad [3] but also seems to express what he will soon be longing for when he has come back to his cherished home so that he and his family will go along again and visit foreign parts.[4]

The question that arises from these examples is how the personal and individual character of language relates to its communicative functions. In *Little Dorrit* it may conduce to deceit or a struggle for power (as when Jeremiah Flintwinch forces Mrs Clennam 'to adopt his phrase', 1.15.174) or it may have a quite different effect. The fact that two characters speak different languages may even contribute to their mutual understanding as it may reveal their original or child-like humanity. The question thus taken up in *Little Dorrit* is how the curse of Babel may be overcome.

At the beginning of the novel, the people who 'come to trade at Marseilles' do not merely represent many different nationalities but are expressly called 'descendants from all the builders of Babel' (I.1.1). The curse of Babel is referred to again in Book I, Chapter 5, when Mrs Clennam's devotion to the revengeful god she has made for herself is called an 'impious tower of stone she built up to scale Heaven' (45). Dickens thus *draws attention to the two main features of the Babel story: human desire for unlimited power (not only over others but also over God) and, as a consequence, the confusion of tongues. (At the end of the novel, when Arthur Clennam and Little Dorrit have come to understand each other, the confused and confusing uproar of voices still rages in the streets into which they go 'down'.) In the opening chapter both features are stressed, the wish for domination as well as the division of languages. The first words that are exchanged between the murderer Rigaud-Blandois and the harmless contraband trader John Baptist Cavalletto, who are locked up together in a prison cell, are 'Get up, pig' and 'It's all one, master' (I.1.5). Rigaud tries to assert his superiority over the little Italian, maintaining that it is his character to govern (I.1.11).

While John Baptist just speaks Italian and some French (cf. I.13.155, 164), Rigaud calls himself a 'citizen of the world', a 'cosmopolitan gentleman' (I.1.10) of mixed Swiss, French, English and Belgian descent who is 'an excellent master in English or French' (I.30.347). But Rigaud, as becomes clear very soon, is the devil of the story and, accordingly, his command of several languages does not seem to be a recommendation in itself. Moreover, moving from one language to another, he alters the meaning of words. When he proudly calls himself a 'Knight of Industry' (II.30.747), for example, he apparently feels sure that his listeners do not exactly know what this literal translation of *chevalier d'industrie* ('swindler') means, or he himself does not know its meaning.[5] A similarly questionable case is Mr Dorrit, whose reputation of being skilled in foreign languages contributes to his almost mythical position in the Marshalsea: 'As to languages – speaks anything. We've had a Frenchman here in his time, and it's my opinion he knowed more French than the Frenchman did. We've had an Italian here in his time, and he shut *him* up in about half a minute' (I.6.64). This is only hearsay, however, and, moreover, to shut somebody up in half a minute is not exactly a mark of proficiency in speaking the language. The doubtful nature of foreign language skills seems confirmed in the person of Mr Meagles who 'never by any accident acquired any knowledge whatever of the language of any country into which he travelled' (I.2.22).[6] The narrator stresses that Mr Meagles would no longer be himself if he tried to speak somebody else's language, while 'in his own tongue' he is 'a clear, shrewd, persevering man' (II.33.783). These limits do not apply to his daughter Pet, who speaks 'three foreign languages beautifully' (II.9.511) or to Arthur Clennam, a man of 40 who has lived for more than 20 years in China. Clennam not only learns from Flora Finching that he must speak Chinese 'like a Native if not better' (I.13.145) but actually speaks Italian and French fluently and even musically (cf. 156). His command of languages links him with Rigaud (who claims his fellowship with a Latin 'Salve', II.28.721), but in him it is a sign of his power to sympathise, as can be seen when he acts as good Samaritan to Cavalletto after his street accident in London. Rigaud, who is as ubiquitous as he is multilingual, rather fits Defoe's statement in *The History of the Devil* that the Evil One 'learned to speak all the languages' used after Babel.[7]

The material fact, then, that a character speaks several languages, doesn't tell much about his or her communicative skills. Nevertheless, foreign languages are used to point out qualities which are necessary for verbal exchange to become fruitful. This can first be seen in the exchange between Rigaud and Cavalletto in the Marseilles prison cell. Rigaud, trying to assert his status as a gentleman bullies Cavalletto into acknowledging his superiority:

'. . . You knew from the first moment when you saw me here, that I was a gentleman?'

'ALTRO!' returned John Baptist, closing his eyes and giving his head a most vehement toss. The word being, according to its Genoese emphasis, a confirmation, a contradiction, an assertion, a denial, a taunt, a compliment, a joke, and fifty other things, became in the present instance, with a significance beyond all power of written expression, our familiar English 'I believe you!'

(I.1.9–10)

'Altro' is an interjection 'beyond all power of written expression'. Its meaning is ambiguous, making the word quite apt for slave language (or Aesopian, as it was called by communists). The self-absorbed Rigaud of course believes that it means 'I believe you' (or that 'I believe you' means that Cavalletto believes him) while in fact it allows John Baptist to speak his mind.[8] The interjection becomes so much of a *leitmotiv* for Cavalletto that he is even named 'Altro' by Mr Pancks, who calls him 'that lively Altro chap' (II.13.557) and (in a striking parallel to Amy Dorrit's name) 'little Altro' (563). John Baptist's expression often goes together with a gesture also belonging to his native language: 'that particular back-handed shake of the right forefinger which is the most expressive negative in the Italian language' (I.1.9). His 'significant forefinger' is mentioned again several times (II.28.726, 729).

This combination of interjection and sign-language in the figure of Cavalletto alludes to certain linguistic tenets which were much debated in the eighteenth and nineteenth centuries. They concern the perennial question of the origin of language, which was, in Dickens's time, at least as much a matter of belief or ideology as of linguistic and anthropological research.[9] In empiricist concepts concerning the origin of language, as they were put forth by Locke and, to name just two others, Warburton and Condillac, both interjections and the language of gesture assume a prominent place. Warburton, for example, had stressed that 'in the first ages of the world, mutual converse was upheld by a mixed discourse of words and ACTIONS', [10] a view which was taken up by Condillac's concept of primitive language being based on vocal gestures, *'cris naturels'* or interjections which 'gave expression to some inward passion'.[11] At the turn of the nineteenth century, Horne Tooke, in his influential *Diversions of Purley* (1786–1805, reprinted in 1829, 1840, 1857, and 1860)[12] regarded interjections not only as very similar to the sounds made by animals but also as characteristic of men in 'their natural state'; '[w]here speech can be employed', he says, 'they are totally useless', and accordingly are never used for 'laws, or in books of civil institutions' but only in such works as 'poetry . . . novels, plays and romances'.[13] What to Horne Tooke seemed rather negligible had been regarded as essential for the understanding of human society by Giambattista Vico in his *Principles of New Science . . . Concerning the Common Nature of the Nations.*[14] To Vico, 'articulate language began to develop by way of onomatopoeia' followed by 'interjections, which are sounds articulated under the impetus of violent passions'.[15] This imitative as well as emotional origin of speech is indicative of the fact 'that the world in its infancy was composed of poetic nations'[16] and, accordingly, 'all the first people were poets'.[17]

The Giambattista of *Little Dorrit*, John Baptist Cavalletto, seems like a representative of Vico's 'children . . . of the human race' who 'had a natural need to create poetic characters' and in whom, accordingly, imagination was 'excessively vivid'.[18] He is imaginative, cutting his prison food of dry bread like a melon or like an omelette, and so on, in order to make it palatable. Furthermore, he is repeatedly connected with a 'natural state' and presented as a man whose utterances, however ambiguously, betray his inner emotions. We remember that Rigaud calls him 'pig', and while this is mainly a sign of Rigaud's contempt for him, it is the narrator himself who compares him to 'a lower animal' (I.1.14). Of course, this describes his degraded state in the prison cell but his instinctive knowledge 'of what the hour is' (5) and where he is at any given moment, as well as his capacity 'to sleep when he would' (14) also indicate his closeness to nature and a rather 'instinctive' kind of human existence. Cavalletto can be *reduced* to an animal state but he also, in a Platonic or Wordsworthian sense, has *retained* a 'natural' spontaneity.

Later on, in Bleeding Heart Yard, John Baptist soon rids the inhabitants of all the national prejudices in which they have long been trained by the leading families of the country, the Barnacles and Stiltstalkings (I.25.295). They begin 'to accommodate themselves to his level, calling him "Mr. Baptist", but treating him like a baby and laughing immoderately at his lively gestures and his childish English' (296). Again a more 'natural' state of humanity is implied when the verbal exchange between Mr Baptist and the 'Bleeding Hearts' is compared to the communication between the

savages and Captain Cook or Friday and Robinson Crusoe. It is not Mr
Baptist, however, who is compared to Friday or the savages, but the
Bleeding Hearts: 'They constructed sentences, by way of teaching him the
language in its purity, such as were addressed by the savages to Captain
Cook, or by Friday to Robinson Crusoe' (296). It is as if Mr Baptist were
the colonist and representative of civilisation. And in a paradoxical way
this is actually the case. He is being taught but he also teaches; however
ridiculous their sentences may sound, they are the true sign of the best in
these Londoners, their compassionate hearts, brought out by Cavalletto.

The Bleeding Hearts speak indeed the language in its purity, that is to
say, they use it for its true purpose of achieving mutual understanding.
This stands out even more clearly when seen against the background
of the Circumlocution Office, where heaps of 'ungrammatical
correspondence' (I.10.100) are produced for no purpose whatsoever –
except for keeping the Barnacle and Stiltstalking families in control. Their
chief, Lord Decimus, is described as 'trotting, with the complacency of an
idiotic elephant, among howling labyrinths of sentences which he
seemed to take for high roads and never so much as wanted to get out of'
(I.34.397, cf. II.24.672: 'those elephantine trots of his through a jungle of
overgrown sentences'). The image of language as a kind of primaeval
forest in which Lord Decimus gets quite wilfully lost shows that
civilisation may be closer to savagery than its representatives would
admit. Thus, upon one occasion (II.15.589), the civilised Britons are
expressly called 'Island Savages' and those who prostrate themselves
before Mr Merdle's supposed riches do so 'more degradedly and less
excusably than the darkest savage' who propitiates his deity (II.12.539).
The latent savagery of civilisation is confirmed in the person of Mrs
Merdle, who regrets being unable to go back to a 'natural state' (I.20.235)
or 'primitive state of society' (237) only to testify to her refinement by
taking an Opera dancer's corruptibility for granted.[19] The parrot, Mrs
Merdle's constant companion, ironically confirms the imitative instinct of
its kind when it does *not* speak but rather shrieks in a savage manner.[20]

To Dickens, the original human nature which makes possible the
spontaneous communication between people who speak different
languages is not dependent on the development of the human species or
society as a whole. His novels evince neither the belief in a continuous
refinement nor a continuous decline of human civilisation. While the
savagery into which civilisation may collapse appears archaic and
preternatural,[21] the child-like spontaneity of understanding appears
original or archetypal in an ideal sense. Whether there once was a golden
age (to be recaptured in everyone's childhood) or whether ancient

savagery had to be civilised is, in *Little Dorrit*, a question not to be answered generally but individually by looking at the way in which two persons communicate with each other. By becoming like a child,[22] each individual who interacts and communicates with other individuals has the chance to strike upon a natural form of understanding and thus rediscover a state before the division of tongues. According to Wilhelm von Humboldt, successful communication depends on the common humanity of speaker and listener, for the power of speech is an essential part of human nature; conversely, there must be a common human nature since people can understand one another.[23] Cavalletto's 'childish English' strikes a chord in Mrs Plornish's heart and mind; he awakens in her, so to speak, the slumbering genius of a similarly childlike form of 'Italian'.

The suspension of the curse of Babel is not achieved by language skills in a rationalist sense but by means of 'accommodating' oneself to the person one talks to and by being sensitive to extra-semantic levels of speech. 'The language in its purity', as Dickens points out in this scene, is not just English any longer but becomes Italian as well:

> Mrs. Plornish was particularly ingenious in this art; and attained so much celebrity for saying 'Me ope you leg well soon,' that it was considered in the Yard, but a very short remove indeed from speaking Italian.
>
> (I.25.296)

Mrs Plornish's home-bred tendency to drop her aitches felicitously coincides with the muteness of the same sound in the Romance languages and her uninflected grammar is a symbol of unbent, unperverted communication. The poor people in Bleeding Heart Yard can teach a pure language to John Baptist, the servant, because they are puerile in the sense of being childlike. To Giambattista Vico, languages were called vernacular because they were spoken by the *vernae* or *famuli*.[24] Vernacular languages are characterised by natural significations 'because of their natural origins'. Accordingly, as different climates lead to the acquisition of different natures, different languages arose. They only express different points of view, however, upon 'the same utilities or necessaries of human life'.[25] This is what Mrs Plornish and the other ladies of Bleeding Heart Yard seem to know when they teach Mr Baptist English:

> As he became more popular, household objects were brought into requisition for his instruction in a copious vocabulary; and whenever he appeared in the Yard ladies would fly out at their doors crying

'Mr. Baptist – tea-pot!' 'Mr. Baptist – dust-pan!' 'Mr. Baptist – flour-dredger!' 'Mr. Baptist – coffee-biggin!' At the same time exhibiting those articles, and penetrating him with a sense of the appalling difficulties of the Anglo-Saxon tongue.

(296)

The ladies not only employ a language of things reminiscent of *Gulliver's Travels* [26] but instinctively apply a method of language learning which in the mid-nineteenth century became known as the 'direct' or 'natural' method. As it is described in a review article by J.S. Blackie for the *Foreign Quarterly Review* in 1845,[27] one of its characteristic features is the 'direct relation . . . between the sound and the thing signified' (176–7). Just as if the method was expressly designed for a student called 'Mr. Baptist', Blackie recommends the teacher to 'commence by presenting to the pupils a series of distinct and familiar objects and baptising them audibly with their several designations in the language to be acquired' (180). The expression 'baptising' seems quite appropriate to a method that imitates the progress 'of a child learning its mother tongue'.[28]

The language school of Bleeding Heart Yard is characterised by a kind of dialectical movement between the home-rooted natures of its participants and their openness to foreign modes of speech and life. This is similar to Mr Meagles's love for his home, which goes together with his being drawn away from it. The narrator mildly ridicules Mr Meagles's 'unshaken confidence that the English tongue was somehow the mother tongue of the whole world' (II.33.783), but he also has him point out that, accordingly, he 'can't be put to any inconvenience' (II.33.789) by ill-willed interlocutors whom he does not understand. Mr Meagles's proverbial motto, 'Home is Home though it's never so Homely' (with its counterpart, 'Rome is Rome though it's never so Romely') coincides with his 'perfect conviction' that foreigners are 'bound to understand' his idiom somehow (I.2.22). To Vico, the fundamental unity of all nations is evinced by the fact that 'proverbs, which are the maxims of human life' are 'a mental language common to all nations',[29] a view which is confirmed in the person of Mr Meagles: home itself, as expressed in the proverb he uses, is a value shared by all good-willed people who consequently cannot fail to understand one another. This is corroborated throughout the novel. Cavalletto has left his own home far behind but his construction of English becomes not unlike Mrs Plornish's whenever his memory goes 'nearer home' (II.22.656). Rigaud-Blandois, who speaks several languages, is, as he says of himself 'of no country' (I.30.348). To him language is mainly a power game; to be a 'master of languages' is a means of 'success' (II.30.747). While his mother was 'French by blood,

English by birth' he seems proud of the fact that he neither has a home nor a mother tongue. The speechless Mr Merdle is 'never at home' (I, 33, 390). It is people like Mrs Plornish and Cavalletto, 'homely' (rather than 'Romely') persons, who can understand each other. In *Little Dorrit*, it seems, you have to have a home or long for one (like Arthur Clennam, whose home is neither home nor homely)[30] or take it with you (like Little Dorrit) in order to understand foreigners.

The importance of the 'home' for the success of the Italo-English communication in Bleeding Heart Yard leads us back to the question of the personal, home-bound response to a foreign idiom. The Bleeding Heart Yard scenes are marked by an interplay between personal (or local and subjective) features of language and more general (or ubiquitous and objective) ones. On the one hand, 'objective' features seem to be emphasised, not only because of the household 'objects' which are used but also because of the Bleeding Hearts teaching Cavalletto not to speak anyhow but making him aware of 'the appalling difficulties of the Anglo-Saxon tongue' (I.25.296). On the other hand, however, this awe-inspiring structure assumes a highly individual shape in Mrs Plornish's attempts at using it in its pure, unalloyed, objective form.

According to Humboldt, language must be 'Subject und abhängig', dependent on the personality of the speaker, in order to become 'Object und selbständig'.[31] Language cannot be understood by considering it as an abstract system but only by listening to it as a means of expression which is formed anew by every speaker. Humboldt emphasises that the individual use of language is the condition for its becoming an 'objective' means of verbal exchange: 'Language arrives at its final determination only in the individual, and only this makes the notion complete. A nation as a whole of course has the same language, but not every member of it . . . and if one advances further in order to be most precise, every man truly has a language of his own.'[32]

This view of the communicative process is a two-sided one: on the one hand, it makes clear that even within the same language two speakers will never share the same idiom. This may be due to social or regional differences of grammar and vocabulary but it may also be a consequence of individual attitudes and intentions. Even when the form of the words is familiar, their meaning may not be shared. When Frederick Dorrit stands up and protests, in plain English, against the treatment of Little Dorrit by her family, he is as little understood as if 'he had made a proclamation in an unknown tongue' (II.5.469). On the other hand, only a personal form of language (as opposed, for example, to a clichéd one) is truly communicative. Humboldt's case in point is the great writer who creates his or her own language while contributing to the objective side of language and its communicative force.

The more positive aspects of the process are prevalent in the Bleeding Heart Yard scenes. Mrs Plornish, the prototypical mother, who treats Cavalletto 'like a baby', never speaks anything but a mother('s) tongue, be it English or the delightful pidgin with which this 'linguist' (II.27.713) tries to make Mr Baptist feel at home. Hers is a language of emotion, which is the reason why it surmounts linguistic barriers: '. . . Mrs. Plornish, not being philosophical, wept. It further happened that Mrs. Plornish, not being philosophical, was intelligible' (712). Her being 'intelligible' does not preclude such remarkable statements as the one in which she expresses her surprise at Mr Baptist's perseverance, 'winding up in the Italian manner . . . Mooshattonisha padrona' (713). This is indeed a private or 'home' language, not unlike baby talk, which, however un-Italian, is perfectly understood by Cavalletto.[33]

Of course Mrs Plornish's 'Tuscan sentence[s]' (713) are a far cry from being Italian. They are products of her motherly imagination and seem derived from the 'one little golden grain of poetry' (I.12.130) sparkling in Bleeding Heart Yard. This is why they are true in spite of being incorrect. They are a paradigm of the common language of mankind just as the Plornish family's 'Happy Cottage' or Old Nandy's songs are paradigms of the way in which the pastoral world or the Garden of Eden or Vico's age of poets may be (re-) created in the fallen world. We have already seen that John Baptist is a similarly imaginative man. In Bleeding Heart Yard he begins to earn his living by carving flowers. This artistic impulse, I think, can also be seen in the use of 'his' word *altro*. 'Altro' (the word is derived from Latin *alius*, 'other') may have different, even contradictory meanings, but they are, like Mr Baptist himself, *all true*. Mrs Plornish, the self-appointed interpreter, explains:

'What's Altro?' said Pancks.
'Hem! It's a sort of a general kind of a expression, sir,' said Mrs. Plornish.

(298)

As a consequence Mr Pancks and Mr Baptist get along splendidly by exchanging nothing but 'altros':

'Hallo, old chap! Altro!' To which Mr. Baptist would reply, with innumerable bright nods and smiles, 'Altro, signore, altro, altro, altro!' After this highly condensed conversation, Mr. Pancks would go his way; with an appearance of being lightened and refreshed.

(298)

The foreign word becomes a magic word, representative of quite a range of possibilities for verbal exchange. In Cavalletto's reply to Rigaud it has a conciliatory as well as protective function; in Bleeding Heart Yard, on the other hand, it serves to create harmony and mutual understanding. The word is an example of how subjective and objective features of a language depend on each other: it is determined by local usage ('according to its Genoese emphasis', I.1.9) and so characteristic of John Baptist Cavalletto that it becomes like another name. At the same time, it is 'a sort of a general kind of a expression', an excellent tool for conversation between persons from the most different backgrounds. In German, popular etymology derives the word for poet, *Dichter*, from the word for 'to condense,' *dichten* or *verdichten*. John Baptist's 'highly condensed' conversation, then, truly shows him to belong to the real masters of language, who keep it alive as a means of original understanding by putting their own stamp on it.

Notes

1. An earlier version of this essay has been published in *The European English Messenger*, 6.2 (1997). It is supplemented by an article in which I have been concerned with the use of material things as means of communication in this novel: '*Little Dorrit*: Dickens and the Language of Things', *Anglistentag 1996: Dresden Proceedings*, ed. Uwe Böker and Hans Sauer (Trier: Wissenschaftlicher Verlag, 1997). I am grateful to Professor Inge Leimberg for a number of critical suggestions.
2. *Nicholas Nickleby*, intro. Sybil Thorndike (Oxford: Oxford University Press, 1950, 1987) ch. 16, 203–4.
3. 'As to Marseilles . . . It couldn't exist without allonging or marshonging to something or other – victory or death, or blazes, or something' (I.2.15); later on, it becomes clear that the 'Allongers and Marshongers' inhabit at least both France and Italy (II.9.510). *Little Dorrit*, ed. Harvey Peter Sucksmith (Oxford: Clarendon, 1979). Further references to this edition appear in brackets in the text, including book and chapter numbers.
4. Cf. I.16.192: 'This was Mr. Meagles's invariable habit. Always to object to everything when he was travelling, and always to want to

get back to it when he was not travelling . . . . "Something like a look out, *that* was, wasn't it? I don't want a military government, but I shouldn't mind a little allonging and marshonging – just a dash of it – in this neighbourhood sometimes. It's Devilish still."'

5. In fact, the expression is used in a derogatory sense when the narrator informs us that 'the police were called in to receive denunciations of Mr. Meagles as a Knight of Industry, a good-for-nothing, and a thief' (II.33.783). *Little Dorrit* thus postdates the *OED* entry ('knight' *n.* 12.c.) in which it is regarded as obsolete and a phrase from Smollett's *Peregrine Pickle* is given as the last example. In an article for *Household Words* ('Wisdom in Words', 4 [22 November 1851]: 208–9) Henry Morley denounced the expression as characteristically un-English: 'A black-leg is called in France, *chevalier d'industrie*, and the phrase shows that in France vice is too lightly regarded' (209). On Gallicisms in *Little Dorrit*, see G. L. Brook, *The Language of Dickens* (London: Deutsch, 1970) 70–1.

6. Brook remarks that 'Mr Meagles followed the example of Dr Johnson in firmly refusing to speak French when in France' (69). This shows that Mr Meagles's attitude is not necessarily a sign of linguistic incompetence.

7. Daniel Defoe, *The History of the Devil Ancient & Modern*, intro. Richard G. Landon, reprint of the 1818, ed. T. Kelly (East Ardsley: EP Publishing, 1972) 161.

8. I agree with Carlo Pagetti that Cavalletto's 'altro' is opposed to the false language of pretension spoken by many characters in the novel. At the same time, I doubt that Cavalletto can be regarded as imprisoned by language. "*Little Dorrit*: Dickens e il labirinto del linguaggio', *Studi inglesi* 2 (1975) 155–78, see 172–3.

9. See, for instance, the relevant passages in Hans Aarsleff, *The Study of Language in England, 1780–1860* (Princeton: Princeton University Press, 1967), especially ch. 6, and Linda Dowling, *Language and Decadence in the Victorian Fin de Siècle* (Princeton: Princeton University Press, 1986), especially ch. 2. Cf. also Barry Thatcher, 'Dickens' Bow to the Language Theory Debate', *Dickens Studies Annual* 23 (1994) 17–47.

10. William Warburton, *The Divine Legation of Moses Demonstrated* (1765), vol. 3 (New York: Garland, 1978) Book IV, Section 4, 108; the phrase is quoted in Aarsleff, 21.

11. Aarsleff, 22, referring to Condillac's *Essai sur l'origine des connoissances humaines* (II, i, i, par. 6) as reprinted in *Oeuvres philosophiques de Condillac*, ed. Georges Le Roy (Paris: PUF, 1947); examples of 'inward passion' are 'desire, want, hunger, fear', which also characterise the prison scene in ch. 1 of *Little Dorrit*.

12. Aarsleff, 44–5.

13. John Horne Tooke, ΕΠΕΑ ΠΤΕΡΟΕΝΤΑ *or The Diversions of Purley* (1798), 2 vols (Menston: Scolar Press, 1968) 1: 63–4.

14. This is the title of the third edition (1744) translated into English. Cf. *The New Science of Giambattista Vico*, trans. Thomas Goddard Bergin

and Max Harold Fisch (Ithaca: Cornell University Press, 1968, 1984), xv.

15. Vico, sections 447, 448: 150.
16. Section 216: 75. Vico adds, 'for poetry is nothing but imitation'; correspondingly, 'poetic sentences are formed by feelings of passion and emotion' (section 219, 75).
17. Section 470: 158.
18. Sections 209, 211: 75–6.
19. In his essay on 'The Noble Savage', which first appeared in *Household Words* 7 (11 June 1853, repr. in *The Uncommercial Traveller and Reprinted Pieces*, intro. Leslie C. Staples [Oxford: Oxford University Press, 1958] 467–73), Dickens stresses that he has 'not the least belief in the Noble Savage' and attacks him as a humbug (to praise him is as hypocritical as Mrs Merdle's wish for a more primitive state of society); Dickens also makes clear that so-called civilisation is by no means free from ignoble savagery. Cf. his ironical remark that 'we have assuredly nothing of the Zulu Kaffer left' (472).
20. For the shrieking parrot both as an image and a judge of Mrs Merdle, see I.33.390–1 ('the parrot . . . watching her . . . as if he took her for another splendid parrot of a larger species'; 'the parrot . . . presiding over the conference as if he were a Judge').
21. Cf. the 'preternatural darkness' (I.29.337) in Mrs Clennam's house, which collapses with Mrs Clennam and her archaic, savage religion.
22. Cf. the narrator's ironical view in *Nicholas Nickleby*: 'It is a pleasant thing to reflect upon, and furnishes a complete answer to those who contend for the general degeneration of the human species, that every baby born into the world is a finer one than the last' (ch. 36, 460).
23. Wihelm von Humboldt, *Über die Verschiedenheiten des menschlichen Sprachbaus, Werke in fünf Bänden*, ed. Andreas Flitner and Klaus Giel, vol. 3 (Darmstadt: Wissenschaftliche Buchgesellschaft, 1963, 1988) 220: 'Was für mich am überzeugendsten für die Einheit der menschlichen Natur in der Verschiedenheit der Individuen spricht, ist . . . : dass auch das Verstehen ganz auf der innern Selbstthätigkeit beruht, und das Sprechen mit einander nur ein gegenseitiges Wecken des Vermögens des Hörenden ist' [To me the most persuasive argument for the unity of human nature is . . . that understanding also wholly rests on the inner activity of the self, and speaking with one another only means awakening the listener's capacity] (220). Humboldt's treatise (written between 1827 and 1829) could not have been known to Dickens; it nevertheless provides a valuable intellectual foil.
24. Vico, section 443: 147.
25. Sections 444–5: 147–8.
26. On Dickens's allusion to the universal language promoted by the academy in Lagado see Bauer, '*Little Dorrit*: Dickens and the Language of Things'.
27. J.S. Blackie, 'On the Teaching of Languages', *Foreign Quarterly Review* 35 (1845) 170–87; on Blackie's article and the context of

contemporary methodology, see the chapter 'Natural Methods of Language Teaching from Montaigne to Berlitz' in A.P.R. Howatt, A *History of English Language Teaching* (Oxford: Oxford University Press, 1984) 192–208. I am grateful to Professor Lienhard Legenhausen for bibliographical information concerning the history of language teaching.

28. Blackie, 176. In fact, Blackie closely links the child's acquisition of a language to the adult's 'learning a foreign language by residence in the country where the language is spoken' (176).

29. Vico, sections 445: 148, and 161: 67.

30. On the absence or negative influence of Arthur's home, see Frances Armstrong, *Dickens and the Concept of Home* (Ann Arbor: UMI Research Press, 1990) 108–13.s

31. Humboldt, 225.

32. Humboldt, 228; my translation ('Erst im Individuum erhält die Sprache ihre letzte Bestimmtheit, und dies erst vollendet den Begriff. Eine Nation hat freilich im Ganzen dieselbe Sprache, allein schon nicht alle Einzelnen in ihr . . . und geht man noch weiter in das Feinste über, so besitzt wirklich jeder Mensch seine eigene').

33. In this respect I do not fully share the views of J.G. Schippers who includes Mrs Plornish in a group of speakers whose language is 'emptied of meaning and made useless for the purposes of communication': 'So Many Characters, So Many Words: Some Aspects of the Language of *Little Dorrit'*, *Dutch Quarterly Review* 8 (1978) 242–56; here 254–5.

14

Foreign Bodies: Acceptance and Rejection of the Alien in the Dickensian Text

Sara Thornton

The study of the notion of foreignness in the Dickensian text seemed to me to require a novel in which references to the foreign are rare and whose effects are isolated and therefore discernible. I was therefore attracted to a text that seems to deny the influence, or even the existence, of the cultural Other, a hermetically sealed universe, closed in upon London with only brief trips to another quintessentially English country house. The bleak circularity and insularity of *Bleak House* was my choice. We see foreign worlds only in controlled spaces and as brief interludes in the otherwise relentless pursuits of the narrow, choked streets of London. London is the first word and sentence of the novel. The jarring full stop immediately after the word indicates a *huis clos*: one word, one world into which we are abruptly pushed but from which we are not released, for movement, let alone travel is difficult, and visibility is poor. We are taken as far as Greenwich and even onto the ships and barges in the Thames estuary, but the fog affords no view of the Channel, let alone the continent, and we are quickly turned back inland to the 'spongey fields',[1] which like everything else in the novel are saturated, overfull, unhealthy.

Secondly, the text itself constitutes a prison-house of language, which is incestuous and turned in upon itself. This occurs not only in relationships between characters (Esther, Jarndyce and the new Bleak House, for example) but in the circulatory economy of the text. It is a board-game, which we as readers are invited to play. We piece together the 'signs and tokens' offered in the text to find a way out of the hellish labyrinth of London by means of a 'judgement' or some hope of salvation. Esther's last, unfinished sentence seems to imply that although we 'connect' we cannot 'collect' but must go back to the start, which is of course back into the heart of London. As Hillis Miller has pointed out, retiring to the second and sinisterly repeated Bleak House does not sweep up the mud produced by the system, a machine which continues to throb away in the city.[2] The unease of unresolved conflict means we cannot safely leave and dismiss the novel, clutching a hard-won moral apothegm. We find ourselves in a literary purgatory which, like Krooks' shop, absorbs more and more data without the possibility of using it or clearing it, however much Esther and Jo sweep.[3] Deferral is the only solution as we cling to the illusion (as Krook does in his attempt to decipher words letter by letter) that if we collect a sufficient number of clues we will, as Jameson says, come face to face once and for all with objects.[4] Hillis Miller has called this a 'circular game of substitution' (26) or an 'inexhaustible set of permutations' (26), which of course is writing, inscribed not on the wall as a revelation or liberation but on Esther's face in the form of scars, which serve only to link her back to London via Jo.

Thirdly, the text of *Bleak House* seems to be crying out for redemption. This is a fallen world, a suffocating world of subterranean gloom, a vision of hell. The hope of Genesis in the first page with the waters retiring from the face of the earth is transformed into an apocalypse of black soot or into an anarchic universe of survival of the fittest which denies the ordering principle of man's and God's centrality by turning to dinosaurs and Darwinian primaeval slime. Like Krook's simmering toxic system, it is a sick body threatening to disintegrate at any moment. The decay of the urban Gothic, the 'solitary and sterile self-indulgence'[5] of characters like Tulkinghorn and Krook, or vampires like Vholes feeding on their own kind, create nasty buried secrets, hidden in the vaults like Poe's Lady Madeline who will provoke the fall of the house. The urban Gothic of *Bleak House* considered by Allan Pritchard underlines the importance of London as a gloomy castle sheltering an obsolete and decrepit regime of moral and social failure. The alternative picturesque Gothic of Bleak House is not a resolution but merely a way of providing 'relief from the grimness of the urban Gothic that is the dark centre of the novel'.[6] If anything can topple or clear away this ruin, then surely a new and refreshing wind from the continent might help to disturb the ancient foundations.

Fourthly, to continue the metaphor of the sick body but to add to it that of the dysfunctional machine, we are faced with the idea of overproduction. The mechanical production of waste by machines gone mad suggests a need for a *deus ex machina* to redefine the parameters of this text-factory. Mud, papers, grease and words multiply, accumulate, 'multiplying at compound interest' like the leaves at Chesney Wold. The novel seems to be full of metaphors for a capitalism gone mad in which increment turns to excrement, surplus value to surplus waste. Repetitions of situations (Bleak House), exertion without purpose, create a wasteland or bowel in which Chadband is an 'Oil Mills' dealing in the ceaseless wholesale production of oil, which fills his 'warehouse' to the brim (319), and Mrs Snagsgy has 'her own dense atmosphere of dust, arising from the ceaseless working of her mill of jealousy' (790). Kucich in *Excess and Restraint* sees the mechanical in Dickens as a metaphor for the experience of excess, by which he means the notion of pure expenditure and loss as opposed to gain and profit. The machines of Dickens's universe, which include people and institutions such as Chancery, are machines gone mad, producing gratuitously, meaninglessly. He sees a conservative ideology working to contain that pure play or movement, a framework of restraint.

We first need to consider any attempts to look for intervention from beyond the system (which is constituted by all England as the lawyer Kenge asserts) to halt the workings of this sick machine. Do foreign cultures function as a window on the world? Is 'Allegory' pointing to another place, another possibility beyond the chartered prison of England? This very un-Victorian barely dressed Latin on the ceiling of Tulkinghorn's chambers, who is 'for ever toppling out of the clouds' (642), is from a classical world where skies are blue and horizons vast. In his constant pointing – for he is always 'at his old work pretty distinctly' (642) – he suggests a somewhere else beyond the fog and grime which might be an answer to the conundrums posed by the woolly heads and 'walls of words' of Chancery. A somewhere or something else involving light and air which might release the inmates of the asylum from their chains.

Dickens does indeed give us glimpses of these possibilities, of light and air. In the choking closeness of England's atmosphere they function as bright oases, which fleetingly evoke other worlds, only to disappear. Others, however, have the potential to alter the course of the system. Taking these references to foreign worlds: the lawyers on holiday, Lady Dedlock in Paris, Borrioboola-Gha, the reference to France and eating at the Slap-Bang dining house and the role of Hortense, we might consider which, if any, have leverage in the novel. Certain of these are, of course, conventional evocations of the Other which have the function of contributing to the identity of the subject (England) and of confirming the latter in its superiority. Mrs Jellyby's Borrioboola-Gha is safely and irrevocably elsewhere and serves as a means of illustrating excessive and blinkered attitudes to charity. Like Jellyby's perverse philanthropy, the Dickensian text telescopes other cultures, using a foreign culture to give itself an identity or meaning but at the same time keeping it at arm's length. Borrioboola-Gha is never allowed to exist in its own right or to steal any of the 'affect' that Dickens so concentratedly pours into other spaces of the text.

The holidays taken by the members of the 'Bar of England', who are 'scattered over the face of the earth' (313), are similarly impotent. This last quotation echoes the tones of Genesis found in the first page in which London emerges as the waters retire. The linking has the effect of affirming the centrality and importance of London, although the tone is altogether less of a slough of despond, and 'the shield and buckler of Britannia' (313), with their connotations of barrier, identity and defence, have been discarded for merry-making in France, Switzerland, Constantinople, Venice and Germany. Britannia, however, defines their behaviour in the very fact of being discarded, acting as a prophylactic to any too promiscuous a mixing with the continent. 'Scattering' may allow for a 'going forth', but the notion of increasing and multiplying is firmly held at bay. Then, as if to affirm the transient and aberrant nature of such behaviour, the last holiday venue to be mentioned is the English coast. As in the first pages of the novel we are escorted to the borders of these foreign worlds only to be pushed quickly back inland at the end of the paragraph. These wanderings out of the labyrinth are a hiatus, not a serious alternative, a carnival *monde-à-l'envers* in which grim barristers may become light and carefree during brief sojourns, which are merely the safety-valve of a conservative economy.[7]

Similarly, the elegant names of the Dedlocks' trip to Paris are listed with the *ennui* of convention. They have no weight or power of their own and are not accompanied by the sensual details of eating and drinking provided by Thackeray, for example, when he writes of Paris. These names have no flesh but wander unfettered and without anchorage in our minds, like a set of table manners which serve only to define the English *beau-monde*.

A more potentially subversive reference is that made to the French language and culture during Guppy's dinner. This could have been used to conjure up a counterpoint to the regulated ugliness of London life, yet although aesthetics has the potential to rival the inexorable logic of the capitalist machine, this potentially powerful force is often smothered or diverted. In the scene of the Slap-Bang restaurant we are as far as might be conceived from the notion of French aesthetics, for it is a mechanical, utilitarian world with an overweening metaphor which is one of slime, grease and unwholesomeness. Dickens describes Guppy, Jobling and Smallweed's dinner as taking place in 'a considerably heated atmosphere in which soiled knives and tablecloths seem to break out spontaneously into eruptions of grease and blotches of beer' (331). The cauliflowers are 'artificially whitened' (329) and the slugs which Jobling warns Polly not to include in the summer cabbage are echoed in the 'glistening nature of his hat which resembles a 'snail promenade' (331). This eating place has no trace of the elegance of French dining, while its textual function is to prepare for Krook's own eruption later in the text when two of the diners will be witness to Krook's last supper, which turns out to be himself. When the spontaneous combustion comes the metaphors are not changed (much like the tablecloths at the Slap-Bang which are endlessly re-used) and the slide from restaurant to dead man, from roasted animal flesh to combusted human flesh is achieved imperceptibly. The 'foetid effluvia' associated with this eating is combined with an automated, pre-prepared production-line efficiency, which is alien to the careful staging and unveiling of the French *service russe*. Ingestion of the food is accompanied by a reckoning of the cost, a list of prices.

Into this comes the evocation of French eating habits in the form of a philosophical reflection on the part of Jobling: 'Ill fo manger' (332). This remark recognises a superiority in foreign attitudes to food, for Jobling insists that it is a French saying and that 'mangering is as necessary to me as it is to a French man' (332). However, the double 'l', of 'il' degrades the French by associating it with illness and the word 'manger' is pronounced, as the narrator tells us, 'as if he meant a necessary fixture in an English stable' (332). This has the effect of playing off the content and the form of the utterance against each other. At the same time as Jobling recognises the superiority and the status of French culture and aesthetics he degrades it and enfolds it back into the English economy of eating. It is also a way of underlining the ignorance of the diners and having a joke at their expense, but the assertion that his brute hunger makes him a more valid diner than a Frenchman reduces food to function, not art.

A far more powerful threat, if not the greatest foreign threat, is of course Hortense. She wanders dangerously at large in the city, a living, breathing piece of foreign culture planted firmly on the shores of Albion. Her lack of measure and startling actions momentarily halt the unhealthy accumulation (of misery and papers in Chancery, of unhealthy secrets in Tulkinghorn). The puncturing or piercing of Tulkinghorn's 'hide' has the power to eradicate his store of 'hidden' secrets and do some serious sweeping up, whereas the explosion of the hoarding Krook only further disseminates the unhealthy accumulation by spreading more mud and slime around the city. If anyone has the power to 'sweep the cobwebs out of the sky', then it is not Esther with her ineffectual jangling keys, but

Hortense with her gun. We might remember that it was not French culture that unnerved the English in mid-century London, but the force of French politics.

Hortense – 'the foreign female', as Snagsby calls her (641) – does not, of course, have revolution of a political nature in mind but something far more personal and localised. However, her hatred takes on irrational proportions quite out of measure with the slight received from Lady Dedlock. Her motivation remains a mystery and only her rage is continually reaffirmed to the reader. She is a 'lowering energy' from which Esther instinctively recoils, likening her to 'some woman of the streets of Paris in the reign of terror' (373). Hortense remains a disruptive element in a far wider sphere than she had imagined and this fact asks us to consider for a moment the nature of her power.

She has a ferocious, unpredictable and sudden energy quite unlike the regular, implacable rhythm of systems like the Slap-Bang or Chancery itself. This gives her the status of an unexploded bomb. Her ferocity is suggested in her rolled 'r's, which complement the many references to her as a tiger or 'feline' creature, ready to bite and 'tear' her adversaries (such as Bucket's wife) limb from limb.

She is also dangerous in her ambiguity and unidentifiable nature. She is heterogeneous and a focus of conflicting forces: her walk through the wet grass barefoot (a signal both of sensuality – like that seen in the barefoot Lucy Westenra in *Dracula* – and extreme of emotion) is a mark of passionate fury, yet executed without discomposure, 'steadfastly and quietly' (312), a 'peaceful figure in the landscape' (312). The serving man observes that she most probably imagines herself walking through the blood of an adversary (312). Her grotesque multiplicity is further suggested in the combination of her 'native gentility' (370) – even at the moment of her arrest she is 'uncommonly genteel' (799) – and her having the aspect of an animal that might, I quote, 'foam at the mouth' (646). The latter is often described as 'tightly shut' (642) ('dry lips closely and firmly together' [795]) or on the contrary, undergoing a 'tigerish expansion' mentioned twice (646 and 794). Her eyes are similarly indecipherable, being 'in one and the same moment very nearly shut, and staringly open' (644), and at the moment of her arrest almost concealed by the 'drooping lids', 'and yet they stare' (798). This oxymoronic quality is present in the 'angry, tight nods of her head' (644), as she passes from catalepsy to violent motion. She is both open and closed, both composed ('arms composedly crossed' [793]) and on the edge of some explosive act. This lack of fixity makes of her a subversive element, a threat to any orthodoxy,[8] if that orthodoxy relies on a steady production, as is the case here.

Added to this there is a pent-up energy translated by the 'spasm' (792) which shoots across her closed, 'concentrated' (793) face or the 'dark cheek beating like a clock' (793) or 'that something in her cheeks [that] beats fast and hard' (793). This boiling cauldron gives vent to the bullet that kills Tulkinghorn, an explosive energy like that which kills Carker in *Dombey and Son*.[9] Unlike Mrs Snagsby or Mr Chadband, whose excesses have the regular monotony of a mill and whose excessive behaviour is therefore part of a certain regulation overproduction, Hortense's excess seems to have no law. Her repetitive hyperbolic speech 'forever . . . again and again . . . forever' stands out as unconstrained, and we only need to compare her with that other potentially subversive figure, Lady Dedlock, to appreciate this. The shame and misery felt by Lady Dedlock act as chaperone to her dangerous and un-English passion for Hawdon and she is thus contained and kept down. Throwing down the coins given by Tulkinghorn, walking barefoot in the rain, which Kucich points out is a form of reckless self-annihilation, places Hortense in a category of textual and moral anarchy quite alien to containing conservatism.

Hortense also puts in jeopardy the mill-like production of Dickens's own text, the very bagginess of his 'baggy monster', or what Maud Ellmann has called 'the fat prolixity' of the novel.[10] She has none of the contributive qualities of, for example, a Guppy or a Micawber, whose verbosity and rhetorical incontinence help to fill the pages of each number of a novel. Instead, she detracts from the accumulation of words by erasing the textually pregnant Tulkinghorn, a chief source of words and documents and carrier of the clandestine speeches of others. She herself is a woman of few words (like Goethe's Faust she denies the sovereignty of the word, exalting action instead), and the words she does contribute are halting and lacking in fluency, for she does not command English fully. Her language is thus barren and cannot proliferate. She is indeed a viper in the Dickensian bosom and it is only the mastery with which she is undone and eliminated that prevents her from remaining dangerously on the loose, like Becky Sharp who, at the end of *Vanity Fair*, will continue to work her spells on the society to which she remains an outsider.[11]

Despite these powers, the ripple created by Hortense is not felt for long. She is neatly defused, like a bomb, by the quintessentially English Bucket, who unravels her with words, fragments her with text. Enfolded, absorbed, this potentially subversive element is perversely used by the text to perpetuate rather than rearrange or destroy the system. The way in which this is effected deserves attention and occurs at the moment of her arrest, although Hortense's assimilation or absorption as a foreign body into the bloodstream begins well before this. It is as if there are preparations for the drawing of her fangs and subsequent reassimilation even before she is fully let loose to wreak havoc. In her confrontation with Tulkinghorn, which prepares for and mirrors the scene of her arrest by Bucket, Tulkinghorn explains her dismissal from the services of Lady Delock by evoking a description of her as 'the most implacable and unmanageable of women' (646). The word 'implacable' returns us once again to the second sentence of the first paragraph of the novel, which is not a sentence but a label which describes London, Chancery, the System of England and even the Lord Chancellor himself in the words 'Implacable November weather' (49). This is a dead metaphor in the sense that implacable is an adjective associated with human behaviour transferred from its original source to one of atmospheric conditions. Hortense in some sense reclaims and revives the metaphor through Tulkinghorn's description of her; yet in doing so Tulkinghorn confers upon her a proximity to the regularity and endless continuation of the fog and mud of London life in a similar way to the linking of the lawyers' foreign holidays with the evocation of London in the same first page. These subliminal associations attenuate any rebellious or subversive activity by evoking the grinding inevitability and implacability of the system.

Chapter 54, 'Springing A Mine', sees the capture of the pent-up tigerish energy which Bucket must dominate in Hortense. From the moment of her entry into the trap set for her by Bucket she pulsates with a tangible fury. Bucket is shown to be able to read her thoughts even though she is silent at first. He immediately advises her not to speak, mocking her with bad French, 'the less you Parlay, the better' (794). We see Bucket underlining her foreignness, her alien nature, the better to strip her of her distinctiveness, her identity, by caricaturing and belittling her language and culture. After one of her outbursts Bucket says, 'I thought the French were a polite nation, I did, really. Yet to hear a female going on like that, before Sir Leicester Dedlock, Baronet!' (794). The reductive epithet 'female' makes of her no more than a gendered body, which contrasts with the social identity conferred upon Sir Leicester by means of his titles and names. The fictitious polite Frenchman is then replaced by the label 'intemperate foreigners', again evoking difference as universal truth and commonplace in order to reduce individuality. Bucket conjures up the mistrust of the French as 'intemperate' and unpredictable, and displays the tactics of xenophobia and colonialism in classification and simplification.[12]

The narrator himself joins in to caricature her further by exaggerating her French accent. Having been quite capable of pronouncing 'th' in all her former speeches, Hortense miraculously uses a 'zz' in 'altogezzer' (794) as if Bucket's brainwashing is having its effect. She responds to each caricature Bucket creates, becoming more intemperate and more French with every sentence, a puppet in his hands, flesh become automaton. She finally loses her ability to speak. This is effected by Bucket's account of a conversation with his wife in which he describes filling the latter's mouth with a sheet to stop her exclaiming. Such a display of his ability to silence women creates a choking fog reminiscent of that seen in the 'implacable November weather':

> Two things are especially observable, as Mr. Bucket proceeds to a conclusion. Firstly, that he seems imperceptibly to establish a dreadful right of property in Mademoiselle. Secondly, that the very atmosphere she breathes seems to narrow and contract about her, as if a close net, or a pall, were being drawn nearer and yet nearer around her breathless figure.
>
> (797)

The pall will stifle her and leave her not a menace, but a timeless fallen woman, one of the many prostitutes for whom Bucket, as he tells us, has acted as nursemaid. This adds to the narrowing of Hortense's field of action, to her increasing anonymity as 'one of a kind'; she cannot speak, her nationality is a source of ridicule, no longer a force of subversion. Bucket, like Jobling, mispronounces French and the word Hortense spoken by an Anglophone with its hard 'H' makes her a whore, if not *the* Whore of Babylon, but who is gradually transformed into a meek if unrepentant Mary Magdalene. Not only does Bucket call her 'dear' and 'darling', while she responds with some vestige of irony with 'my angel' (798–9), but he speaks of her possible earlier arrest as 'taking her' ('I should have taken her' [798]). He refers to the behaviour of her 'sex', as he referred to the behavior of the French, and having divested her of all distinction leads her away. He allows her to admit defeat ('Then do as you please with me' [799]) and to make one last half-hearted tirade against Sir Leicester before the narrator silences her:

> With these last words, she snaps her teeth together, as if her mouth closed with a spring.
>
> (799)

The 'snap' and the 'spring' still have something of her old suddenness and the unpredictability of a trap, yet they also align her with the mechanical world and reveal a marionette-like obedience as she is taken away, a silent lamb to the slaughter. More important still is the description of Bucket's leading her away, for it seems to mirror precisely the way in which the Dickensian text deals with the foreign body once it has served its purpose:

> It is impossible to describe how Mr. Bucket gets her out, but he accomplishes that feat in a manner so peculiar to himself; enfolding and pervading her like a cloud, and hovering away with her as if he were a homely Jupiter, and she the object of his affections.
>
> (799)

How many times have we seen this manner of eliding a nasty truth, an unspeakable system, an uneradicable stain in Dickens? The anger of Hortense is that of many a cast-off of a hierarchy, be it aristocratic or industrial. Her removal, like that of Stephen in *Hard Times* or Little Nell in *The Old Curiosity Shop*, does not sponge away the situation that created her. Instead she is lifted out of harm's way and into a space where the system can control her. Bucket seems to have taken on the guise of the Roman Allegory who descends from his cloud to sweep away any aberration in the landscape. The soft-focus ending provides a marriage, an image instead of a complete explanation. Kucich has noted the use of the fairy-tale ending which anchors the narrative but does not close it, a 'soothing metaphorics of union' (247), here between Jupiter and his lover, a 'terrorless image of loss itself' (254) with an absence of ideological and social content 'exceeding significance by dissolving itself into the pure mechanism of narrative convention' (253–4).[13] Thus is the foreign neatly and painlessly excised from the text. It is usually heroines who undergo such erasure, as Helena Michie has pointed out, yet here it is a villain and not Little Dorrit or Little Nell 'whose body slowly evaporates from the novel ... scarcely to ruffle the surface of the text'.[14] The 'foreign body' – for Hortense was very much a physical and sensual being as well as an alien – is enfolded and eliminated, and her flesh is cut out of the text to leave only a spirit, lighter than air, to be 'hover(ed) away with'.

Finally, to add insult to this very fleshly injury, Hortense unwittingly becomes part of the economy of the world of *Bleak House* and in fact subscribes to Englishness and the continuing of the productions of the System. Removing Tulkinghorn, in fact, has the effect of giving impetus to the machine. The old secrets must be renewed, and as surely as Tulkinghorn took over from his colleague who committed suicide, so will another empty and avid repository of secrets replace him. The crumbling domain of the aristocracy symbolised by the debilitated Sir Leicester and Volumnia, a grotesque relic, is symbolically murdered by Hortense when she kills Tulkinghorn who embodies the archives, the memory, of this dying breed, as the lines of aristocratic coaches at his funeral reveal. Yet, who is to replace the aristocracy as litigators? Sir Leicester's remark that 'the floodgates' are burst open when the Ironmaster enters Parliament may help us to answer this, for the revolutionary Hortense, driven by hatred for her betters, only helps to open the gates to a new 'Steel and Iron' squirearchy which will continue to feed the ovens of Chancery with a new and more ferociously destructive energy. Litigation, as we know, was fuelled by the railways, its entrepreneurs and passengers alike, and it is Rouncewell and his like who will now employ the services of an army of new Tulkinghorns.

If in *Bleak House* we see an England engaged thus in an act of self-perpetuation, it is important to recognize that Britannia has not used her own progeny to effect change, but has brought in an immigrant worker to do the dirty work, so to speak. The change is of course no change at all, but a means of maintaining the status quo with new energy from the world outside. Bleak House, the Gothic ruin of England, does not fall like the House of Usher. Lady Madeline is allowed to rave and shriek, but then allows herself to be led quietly back to her tomb across the Channel.

Notes

1. All references are to *Bleak House* (Harmondsworth: Penguin Classics, 1971).
2. J. Hillis Miller, Introduction to *Bleak House* (Harmondsworth: Penguin, 1971).
3. Jeremy Hawthorne in *An Introduction to the Variety of Criticism: Bleak House* (London: Macmillan, 1987) considers the filth of the opening page as provoking a positive attitude in readers towards those characters who seek to clean up this 'universally mired system' (65), while André Topia in '*Bleak House*: les mots et les choses', *Tropismes – Cartes et Strates*, 7 (1995), 103–28, has explored what he calls the 'circuits bloqués' in *Bleak House*, which include the processes of accumulation and agglomeration of both words and objects.
4. Frederic Jameson, *The Prison-House of Language* (Princeton, NJ: 1972).
5. Allan Pritchard, 'The Urban Gothic of *Bleak House*', *Nineteenth-Century Literature* (1991) 432–52.
6. Ibid., 452.
7. Mikhaïl Bakhtin's discussion of the function of the carnival in *L'oeuvre de François Rabelais et la culture populaire au moyen âge et sous*

la renaissance (Paris: Gallimard, 1970), is a useful one in terms of the novels of Dickens.

8. See in this connection Jean Baudrillard, *De la séduction* (Paris: Denoël – Collection Folio/Essais, 1979).

9. John Kucich, in *Excess and Restraint in the Novels of Charles Dickens* (Athens, GA: University of Georgia Press, 1981) considers the 'surplus violence that transcends purpose' (68) associated with Carker and other Dickensian villains. Carker's 'limitless fantasies of violence' (68) lift him out of an economy of purpose and into 'a world of transcendentally profitless combat' (69). This could be said both of Tulkinghorn and Hortense herself, yet, whereas both male villains are eradicated by sudden and violent means (a bullet and a train), Hortense, as I shall demonstrate, is gently smoothed and cleansed away, or ushered out of the back door, in a more insidious manner, which perhaps demonstrates the superior threat that she poses to the Dickensian system.

10. See Maud Ellmann, *The Hunger Artists* (London: Virago, 1993).

11. Becky too has French origins and is likened to a serpent or viper on many occasions. Her mother was a 'dancer' at the French opera, Becky tells us, while the narrator reveals the prosaic reality that her grandmother is a hideous old box-opener at the theatre in Paris.

12. Edward Said's introduction to Rudyard Kipling's *Kim* (Harmondsworth: Penguin Twentieth-Century Classics, 1987) provides a useful study of such tactics, as does his *Orientalism* (Harmondsworth: Penguin, 1985).

13. John Kucich, *Excess and Restraint in the Novels of Charles Dickens* (Athens, GA: University of Georgia Press, 1981).

14. Helena Michie, '"Who is this in Pain?": Scarring, Disfigurement, and Female Identity in *Bleak House* and *Our Mutual Friend*', *Novel* (Winter 1989).

15

'A Far Better Rest I Go To': Dickens and the Undiscovered Country

John C. Hawley

WHAT THE WAVES WERE ALWAYS SAYING

On 2 November 1867, just a week before Charles Dickens was to embark on his last visit to the United States, his friends in London decided to host what was billed as a 'Farewell Banquet' in his honour. The valedictory nature of the title and of the event were prescient, since the novelist's death followed so soon after his return from America. With more than 450 guests in attendance, and another 100 looking on from the galleries, Charles Kent was surely correct in his estimation that 'a Great Author certainly never had any more magnificent demonstration than that which was afforded Charles Dickens':

> At length the doors were thrown open, and the well-known faces of Dickens and Bulwer appeared at it. They were arm-in-arm. A cry rang through the room, handkerchiefs were waved on the floor and in the galleries . . . and the band struck up a full march. As Dickens passed up the aisle his cheeks were on fire, his eyes flamed. He glanced around the room, on whose walls all around were written in great gold letters the names of his works. Ahead he saw the English flag knit with the Stars and Stripes, and above them the word 'Pickwick.' There was a serious look on the face of Lord Lytton, and it seemed to me to say, 'How gladly would I give up my title and my estates to have this enthusiasm surging up to me from the Anglo-Saxon heart.'
>
> (Fielding, 369)

In his speech later in the evening, making himself heard over the frequent loud applause, Dickens acknowledged the challenge that all in his audience seemed to recognise:

181

Since I was there before, a vast entirely new generation has arisen in the United States. . . . You will readily conceive that I am inspired . . . by a natural desire to see for myself the astonishing change and progress of a quarter of a century over there. . . . Twelve years ago, when, Heaven knows, I little thought I should ever be bound upon the voyage which now lies before me, I wrote, in that form of my writings which obtains by far the most extensive circulation, these words of the American nation:– 'I know full well, whatever little motes my beamy eyes may have descried in theirs, that they are a kind, large-hearted, generous, and great people.' [*Cheers*] In that faith I am going to see them again. In that faith I shall, please God, return from them in the spring; in that same faith to live and to die! [*Loud and continued cheering.*]

(Fielding, 372–3)

As the evening concluded, J.B. Buckstone began a concluding toast by suggesting that 'Mr. Dickens has exhausted the Old World, and is going to the New' (Fielding, 374). The ironies of his remarks reverberated later, when the New seemed, indeed, to have completely exhausted the hero. More immediately, they could not but help underline a tension that all in attendance must have been feeling: lionised though he undoubtedly had been in London, they were sending him off as a Daniel unto his foes, if memory served. Had he not been the one who had written of his fellow travellers on a canal boat heading to Cincinnati:

All night long, and every night, on this canal, there was a perfect storm and a tempest of spitting. . . . Nobody says anything, at any meal, to anybody. All the passengers are very dismal, and seem to have tremendous secrets weighing on their minds. There is no conversation, no laughter, no cheerfulness, no sociality, except in spitting; and that is done in a silent fellowship round the stove, when the meal is over. Every man sits down dull and languid; swallows his fare as if breakfasts, dinners and suppers were necessities of nature never to be coupled with recreation or enjoyment; and having bolted his food in a gloomy silence, bolts himself in the same state. . . . [T]o empty each creature his Yahoo's trough as quickly as he can, and then slink sullenly away; to have these social sacraments stripped of everything but the mere greedy satisfaction of the natural cravings; goes so against the grain with me, that I seriously believe the recollection of these funeral feasts will be a waking nightmare to me all my life.

(*American Notes*, 148, 158, 170)

Such descriptions would not, surely, make the famous author welcome among the citizens of Ohio. Nor could the citizens of the Mid-West easily forgive his classy debunking of any European mythologising of the confluence of the Ohio and Mississippi rivers, with their ludicrously misnamed city:

> At the junction of the two rivers, on ground so flat and low and marshy, that at certain seasons of the year it is inundated to the housetops, lies a breeding-place of fever, ague, and death; vaunted in England as a mine of Golden Hope, and speculated in, on the faith of monstrous representations, to many people's ruin. A dismal swamp, on which the half-built houses rot away: cleared here and there for the space of a few yards; and teeming, then, with rank, unwholesome vegetation, in whose baleful shade the wretched wanderers who are tempted thither droop and die, and lay their bones; the hateful Mississippi circling and eddying before it, and turning off upon its southern course, a slimy monster hideous to behold; a hotbed of disease, an ugly sepulchre, a grave uncheered by any gleam of promise: a place without one single quality, in earth or air or water, to command it: such is this dismal Cairo.
>
> *(American Notes,* 171)

Perhaps the 'new' world would be, indeed, more literally the New Jerusalem than the new Eden it had once appeared to be. After all, if anyone had changed in those brief 12 years, surely it had been the author and not his audience.

The piquancy of that London send-off, therefore, emotionally confirmed in the minds of his well-wishers the admiration that most Victorians felt for their many compatriots who travelled to exotic and dangerous locales and who did them the kindness of safely and vicariously sharing the commodities of 'the Orient'. They knew that America, despite the tales of sudden eruptions of violence in unexpected and supposedly civilised spots, was not especially dangerous to their persons. Yet, English in so many ways, America was insufficiently English to be embraced as familiar. In Dickens his peers saw one very much like themselves, one who faced, through American encounters, the far more formidable threat posed by this challenge to one's dreams of a better place – a place where humanity might begin anew and perfect itself.

In what follows I would like to suggest the outlines of that danger as it appeared to Charles Dickens. His first trip to the new world clearly took shape in emotional terms. As he wrote to John Forster on 13 September,

1841, 'I am still haunted by the visions of America, night and day. To miss the opportunity would be a sad thing. Kate cries dismally if I mention the subject. But, God willing, I think it *must* be managed somehow' (House II, 380). Though the words belie his inevitable future disillusionment ('the vision of America', after all, suggests a projection of dreams), he apparently felt that he entered upon the enterprise with at least a greater objectivity than earlier travellers had done. He had criticised Frances Trollope's typically British disgruntlement at American boorishness, and he wrote to Andrew Bell on 12 October 1841, 'My notion is that in going to a New World one must for the time utterly forget, and put out of sight the Old one and bring none of its customs or observations into the comparison – or if you do compare remember how much brutality you may see (if you choose) in the common street and public places in London' (House II, 402). As others have pointed out, the novelist subsequently made it a point to illuminate the squalor of the Old World, as well as the New – but, he thought, it was not squalor that he had come to America to examine. He just, somehow, had it thrust upon him.

He clearly finds a certain swashbuckling glamour in the rugged individualism of the American West, and in his renditions of this aspect of his journey confirmed Britain's enduring notion of cowboys as the 'real' symbol for America.[1] To David Dolden on 4 April 1842, he wrote: 'I feel something between Robinson Crusoe and Philip Quarll,[2] with a dash of Sinbad the Sailor – and think of leaving off ordinary clothes, and going clad, for the future, in skins and furs, with a gun on each shoulder, and two axes in a belt around my middle' (Houses III, 183-4). But his choice of examples suggests his sense of isolation from other fully civilised companions. Boston had been wonderful, New York a little less so, and the rest, increasingly abysmal. In Boston he could write (to William Macready on 31 January 1842), 'their Institutions I reverence, love and honor' (House III, 44) but by 22 March he would confess to the same correspondent, 'I *am* disappointed. This is not the republic I came to see; this is not the republic of my imagination' (House III, 156).

The romantically overblown fantasy that Dickens, in a rather surprising naiveté, had none the less brought with him to America is suggested by the vehemence of his description of the country's *infelix culpa* in private correspondence. Apparently forgetting his criticism of Trollope's jingoism, he told Macready on 1 April 1842,

> I have not changed – and cannot change, my dear Macready – my secret opinion of this country; its follies vices, grievous disappointment...
>
> I believe the heaviest blow ever dealt at Liberty's Head, will be dealt by this nation in the ultimate failure of its example to the Earth...

the intrusion of the most pitiful, mean, malicious, creeping, crawling, sneaking party spirit, into all transactions of life – even into the appointments of physicians to pauper madhouses. . . . I say nothing of the egotism . . . which is not *English*.

(House III, 175)

Sounding a little like Dorothy in *The Wizard of Oz*, this 30-year-old rather more elegantly concludes that there is no place like home. But the problem went further, as his later and darker novels were to make clear: home itself was no place like home. As Jerome Meckier has summarised the issue, 'the resolute Englishman he became after 1842 continued to abhor the Utilitarian *present* but could not countenance Romantic nonsense about recapturing an idyllic *past*. Least of all could he tolerate visionary projections of society's movement into the *future* as the working out of a slow but unstopping amelioration' (240). The problem, increasingly inescapable, appeared to be not only spatial but also temporal: there was no better place to go, no finer time in which to live – which was an ironic and bitter inversion of Pangloss's optimism.

The failure to find a more hopeful land[3] displays itself in the author's various other travelogues. He did seem to continue to hold out some hope for Australia as an even newer America, a possible garden for new human improvement. But Michael Slater suggests that this was a last outpost that was surely very close in his dreams to the world of Robinson Crusoe:

It is possible that if he had actually gone to Australia, as he later contemplated doing, he would have had the same reaction there. Never having seen it, however, he could continue to imagine it as a thriving, briskly developing country, where the Micawbers, the Peggottys, Mr. Mell, the poor schoolmaster, and even that dejected magdalen, Martha, could all begin a new life and contribute to the building up of a new society. He sent not only fictional characters there but also two of his own sons. The only member of the Dickens family to emigrate to America, on the other hand, was the novelist's scapegrace youngest brother, Augustus, who deserted his English wife and children, made a bigamous marriage in Chicago, and died in 1866, having come to little good.

(Slater, 30–1)

Far closer to home and to the personal experiences of his readers, of course, was Italy, a principal venue for the Grand Tour. Yet Dickens does his best to render the comforting familiarity of its exoticism at once decadent and mundane: all his own illusions, he suggests, are behind him. The glorious past, in which so many of his Victorian peers sought erudite refuge, was both unattainable and tawdry:

> We entered on a very different, and a finer scene of desolation, next night, at sunset. . . . and after climbing up a long hill of eight or ten miles extent, came suddenly upon the margin of a solitary lake . . . . Where this lake flows, there stood, of old, a city. It was swallowed up one day; and in its stead, this water rose. There are ancient traditions (common to many parts of the world) of the ruined city having been seen below, when the water was clear; but however that may be, from this spot of earth it vanished. The ground came bubbling up above it; and the water too; and here they stand, like ghosts on whom the other world closed suddenly, and who have no means of getting back again. . . . We entered on the Campagna Romana. . . . so sad, so quiet, so sullen; so secret in its covering up of great masses of ruin, and hiding them; so like the waste places into which the men possessed with devils used to go and howl, and rend themselves, in the old days of Jerusalem. . . . When we were fairly off again, we began, in a perfect fever, to strain our eyes for Rome; and when, after another mile or two, the Eternal City appeared, at length, in the distance; it looked like – I am half afraid to write the word – like *London!!!*
>
> (*Pictures*, 159–61)

That so unEnglish a city as this Catholic, lethargic, Machiavellian Rome could transform itself, at least in Dickens's imagination, into the very capital of the Victorian empire suggests that the novelist was making a point: the world is the same everywhere. More importantly, humanity is the same as well.

Pictures From Italy was written just four years after Dickens's first trip to America. If the volume offers evidence for an increasing sense of, and even preoccupation with, human corruption, Dickens's personal life and the public's response to it would soon provide him with more reason for this heightened sensitivity. Although his second tour of America did not take place until 1867, he had earlier thought of returning in the late 1850s. What is more, there is reason to suspect that he had hoped that Ellen Ternan would be able to meet him there. As Meckier suggests, 'given the furor that separation from Catherine caused in 1858, six months in America may have seemed ideal as a retreat, not just a business proposition' (135). That Dickens could have entertained such an idea is rather remarkable, considering the experience various Britons had had with the American press. Still, not to have seen such a scheme materialise, coupled with what may have appeared to be society's hypocrisy in such matters, cannot have encouraged the writer to modify his views of human nature – nor, as we shall see, his views of himself.

DRAGGED BY INVISIBLE FORCES

In recent years in the United States federal funding for the National Endowment for the Arts has been seriously curtailed and even threatened with death. Part of the rationale offered for its slow or sudden starvation has been the moralistic outcries of senators over the photographs of artists such as Robert Mapplethorpe and Andres Serrano. Among Mapplethorpe's photos are those of nude and semi-nude children posed provocatively and erotically (though Mapplethorpe claimed he had no intention to eroticise the children). Among Serrano's photographs, those found to be seriously offensive involve what some consider to be the desecration of religious objects – the portrayal of a crucifix, for example, submerged in a beaker of the artist's urine, and entitled 'Piss Christ'. This is part of a series that incorporates various religious symbols with most human bodily fluids. Among his recent studies have been the elaborately staged portraits of various parts of corpses in the morgue. What is objected to in this last case is the objectification of these anonymous victims of generally violent deaths.

These preoccupations of artistic focus, and the objections they raise, are not far distant from what Steven Marcus has called Charles Dickens's 'spiritual necrophilia', in which the deathbed scene takes centre-stage thematically. Much like the protagonist in Alexandre Dumas's immensely popular *Camille* (1852), Dickens's pathetic characters seem to take a painfully long time actually to stop breathing. In fact, the scene itself transmogrifies and finds rebirth in novel after novel. Frequently enough the inevitability of death is given sharper focus by coming 'too soon', as with the death of a child, so that Dickens, like Mapplethorpe and Serrano, might be accused of prostituting his children by objectifying them for our delectation, or of treading close to sacrilege in whatever degree it may be that he calls into question the ultimate meaning of the final, rather than the primal, scene of a child's embrace by the Grim Reaper. By lingering and prolonging the deaths, he dessicates their meaning.

What this may have to do with Dickens and America will become clear in what follows. In a passage from *The Uncommercial Traveller* Dickens was certainly as fascinated by corpses as Serrano ever was, and as photographic in his recording of his reactions:

Whenever I am at Paris, I am dragged by invisible force into the Morgue. I never want to go there, but am always pulled there. One Christmas Day, when I would rather have been anywhere else, I was attracted in, to see an old grey man lying all alone on his cold bed, with a tap of water turned over his grey hair, and running, drip, drip, drip, down his wretched face until it got to the corner of his mouth, where it took a turn, and made him look sly. One New Year's Morning (by the same token, the sun was shining outside, and there was a mountebank balancing a feather on his nose, within a yard of the gate), I was pulled in again to look at a flaxen-haired boy of eighteen, with a heart hanging on his breast – 'from his mother', was engraven on it – who had come into the net across the river, with a bullet wound in his fair forehead and his hands cut with a knife, but whence or how was a blank mystery. This time, I was forced into the same dread place, to see a large dark man whose disfigurement by water was in a frightful manner comic, and whose expression was that of a prize-fighter who had closed his eyelids under a heavy blow, but was going immediately to open them, shake his head, and 'come up smiling.' Oh what this large dark man cost me in that bright city!

(ch. 7, 64–5)

Later in the same passage Dickens projects on other onlookers the sort of criticism that others might direct his way. As, together, he and others look at a corpse he thinks 'there was a much more general, purposeless, vacant staring at it – like looking at a waxwork, without a catalogue, and not knowing what to make of it. But all those expressions concurred in possessing the one underlying expression of *looking at something that could not return a look*' [emphasis in the original] (ch. 19, 192).

Dickens's never wanting to go to a morgue is perfectly understandable. His always being pulled there is what most people would find extraordinary and rather morbid – especially as this was Christmas Day, and then New Year's Day – not quite the celebration the novelist might have wanted us to imagine at Bob Cratchit's home. Nor, in his subsequent laboured effort to find something comic to describe in the large, dark, disfigured corpse of one who had drowned do we hear an especially kind-hearted observer. In fact, his weak effort at gallows humour shows us a much harsher sensibility than that which could write the following infamous lines of Victorian sentiment:

Waving them off with his hand, and calling softly to her as he went, he stole into the room. They who were left behind drew close together, and after a few whispered words – not unbroken by emotion, or easily uttered – followed him. They moved so gently, that their footsteps made no noise; but there were sobs from among the group, and sounds of grief and mourning. For she was dead. There, upon her little bed, she lay at rest. The solemn stillness was no marvel now. She was dead. No sleep so beautiful and calm, so free from trace of pain, so fair to look upon. She seemed a creature fresh from the hand of God, and waiting for the breath of life; not one who had lived and suffered death . . . . 'It is not,' said the schoolmaster, as he bent down to kiss her on the cheek, and gave his tears free vent, 'it is not on earth that Heaven's justice ends. Think what it is compared with the World to which her young spirit has winged its early flight, and say, if one deliberate wish expressed in solemn terms above this bed could call her back to life, which of us would utter it!'

(*The Old Curiosity Shop*, Chapter 71: 652-4)

Typically, Dickens implies that the death of this 13-year-old is a question of injustice – that she was wronged by life and, furthermore, that to call her back into life would be to inflict further injustice upon her. We are taught by him no longer to expect justice for such as Nell. She is too good for us. *We* have somehow had a hand in the death of such as these – probably because we have outlived her into adulthood. We have survived to enter the grey world where innocence can only be preserved by becoming mentally defective, like a Mr Dick. Thus, we can safely scoff at the drowning of this large dark man, since he was clearly able to take care of himself – after all, he had the expression of a prize-fighter – and that must mean that he, in his turn, had somehow allowed the injustice of the premature deaths of many youngsters around him.

There is an odd and untenable logic at work here, which makes us question its emotional base. It is true that there are adults who die in Dickens who are presented in a forgiving rose-tinted light. For all the Carkers, Quilps and Madame Defarges, whose violent deaths cause us vindictive and justice-affirming delight, there is the occasional Alice Brown Marwood, whose deathbed conversion reassures us that her defiler, or Quilp, or Defarge, might likewise have put aside the nasty affairs of adults and regained their Edenic innocence had they so chosen. Alice's recompense is, like Nell's, postponed until the endtime when all manner of thing will be made well:

Harriet complied and read – read the eternal book for all the weary, and the heavy-laden; for all the wretched, fallen, and neglected of this earth – read the blessed history, in which the blind lame palsied beggar, the criminal, the woman stained with shame, the shunned of all our dainty clay, has each a portion, that no human pride, indifference, or sophistry, through all the ages that this world shall last, can take away, or by the thousandth atom of a grain reduce – read the ministry of Him who, through the round of human life, and all its hopes and griefs, from birth to death, from infancy to age, had sweet compassion for, and interest in, its every scene and stage, its every suffering and sorrow?

(*Dombey and Son*, Ch. 58, 923)

Unhappily for Nell and Alice, and for Dickens himself, this ministry lasted through the round of human life, and set an example for those who might be generous enough to minister in a similar way in their own lives. But Alice, of course, had left this life, and the injustices she endured (and perhaps sometimes, as an adult, inflicted) remain unanswered. Where is Chirst *now*?

Is *this* what the waves were always saying? In a death bed scene even more sentimentalised than Nell's, Paul Dombey asks his long-suffering sister, 'And where is my old nurse? Is she dead too? Floy, are we *all* dead, except you?' The orthodox Christian answer might be Yes, until we are reborn through grace. But for Dickens, one often gets the impression, the answer is: 'Unfortunately no, *we* are still living.'

The golden ripple on the wall came back again, and nothing else stirred in the room. The old, old fashion! The fashion that came in with our first garments, and will last unchanged until our race has run its course, and the wide firmament is rolled up like a scroll. The old, old fashion – Death! Oh thank God, all who see it, for that older fashion yet, of Immortality! And look upon us, angels of young children, with regards not quite estranged, when the swift river bears us to the ocean!

(*Dombey and Son*, Ch. 16, 297-8)

Our race will run its course, as did the Apostle Paul's, Dickens suggests – but perhaps Dickens is here more insistently asserting that our *human* race, the race of Adam, must have fully run its course before all this business of Nature, red in tooth and claw, would have worn itself to the bone. As needful as Dickens's readers must have been for some reassurance that the death of children – and, by implication, their own deaths – would, in retrospect, be assembled into a meaningful narrative, there is more evidence that Dickens himself shared the agnostic concern of Hamlet:

> For who would bear the whips and scorns of time,
> The oppressor's wrong, the proud man's contumely,
> The pangs of despised love, the law's delay,
> The insolence of office and the spurns
> That patient merit of the unworthy takes,
> When he himself might his quietus make
> With a bare bodkin? Who would fardels bear,
> To grunt and sweat under a weary life,
> But that the dread of something after death,
> The undiscovered country from whose bourn
> No traveler returns, puzzles the will,
> And makes us rather bear those ills we have
> Than fly to others that we know not of?
>
> (*Hamlet* III, i)

Thus, if Charles Darnay must remain in the city, condemned to life, to marriage, to continuing the cycle of those caught in History, Charles Dickens can imagine it otherwise. He can imagine one who knows himself to be a conflicted, benighted scoundrel who, as Sidney Carton tells Lucie, feels that he is 'like one who died young' (*Tale of Two Cities*, II, Ch. 13, 181). In a Jerry Cruncher, Dickens comes as close as he could in his dissection of the Victorian hope for resurrection in a New World that would be just like this one – only nice.

The end of *A Tale of Two Cities* seems to reverse some of Dickens's reliance on children to lead adults. Instead, Carton leads the gentle maid to her death with traditional words of comfort as if he had a map for her journey into unfamiliar territory:

> 'What I have been thinking as we came along [she says to him], and what I am still thinking now, as I look into your kind strong face which gives me so much support, is this – If the Republic really does good to the poor, and they come to be less hungry, and in all ways to suffer less, [my sister] may live a long time: she may even live to be old.'
>
> 'What then, my gentle sister?'
>
> 'Do you think,' the uncomplaining eyes in which there is so much endurance, fill with tears, and the lips part a little more and tremble: 'that it will seem long to me, while I wait for her in the better land where I trust both you and I will be mercifully sheltered?'
>
> 'It cannot be, my child; there is no Time there, and no trouble there.'
>
> (III, Ch. 15, 463–4)

'Perchance to dream. Aye, there's the rub.' By putting the noble Hamlet's fear in this simple victim's words Dickens implies that even his child saviours – his Nells, Pauls and all the others who were to redeem corrupt adults by dying in innocence – shared his own essential anguish about the next (better) land – and that this nagging uncertainty would continue to be the unkindest cut of all.

The world beyond death remained for Dickens an undiscovered country, intractably uncanny. If this metropolis somewhat obsessively sent his own children out into the world's peripheries, and if he sent his fictive children over the borders into the land of sleep, it is, perhaps, an indication that, like our disturbing contemporaries, he found himself fixated on the naked corpse of a child and on the glare which this reflected back on his own adult image. As he wrote to John Forster on 13 March 1842, about the inmates he observed in the Philadelphia Penitentiary, 'I looked at some of them with the same awe as I should have looked at men who had been buried alive, and dug up again' (House III, 124). Like them, the novelist looked out from a small room in America near the end of his life and saw that he had nowhere left to go.

The Old World had wearied of its internal dissensions. The New World, once coddled by the European imagination of a Dickens, now seemed to outdo its parent in corruption before old enough to outgrow a rather seductive naivete. And 'the [American] Nation', as he wrote to Macready (1 April 1842), 'is a body without a head; and the arms and legs are occupied in quarreling with the trunk and each other, and exchanging bruises at random' (House III: 176). Only in the world of the imagination might one yet find cause for 'a tender and a faltering voice' (*A Tale of Two Cities* III, Ch. 15, 466).

Notes

1. Aldous Huxley, for example, read *American Notes* and *Martin Chuzzlewit* in 1925 to prepare for his trip to the US, and concluded that they confirmed his own experience of Americans. Thus, as Jerome Meckier writes, 'the modern revaluator can proclaim Dickens the ultimate victor in the battle of the Victorian travel books. His was the lasting view of America formed not just by a plenitude of Victorians but by subsequent Englishmen like Huxley who applied that view to America's posterity' (237).
2. Much like Crusoe, Quarll was the hero of the 1727 *The Hermit*, and of Peter Longueville's 1795 account of a man, accompanied by an

ape, who lived alone for 50 years and was ultimately discovered by a Mr Dorrington, a Bristol merchant.

3.   As he wrote to Dolby on his second American tour: 'These people have not in the least changed during the last five and twenty years' (158–9) (cited in Meckier, 238).

References

Dickens, Charles. *American Notes and Pictures from Italy*, intro. Sachevell Sitwell. London: Oxford University Press, 1957.
—— *Dombey and Son*. Harmondsworth: Penguin, 1970.
—— *The Old Curiosity Shop*. Harmondsworth: Penguin, 1972.
—— *The Uncommercial Traveller and Reprinted Pieces*. Oxford: Oxford University Press, 1987 [1860].
—— *Pictures from Italy*, with an introduction by David Parossien. New York: Coward, McCann & Geoghegan, 1974 [1846].
—— *A Tale of Two Cities*. Oxford: University Press, 1988.
Fielding, K.J., ed. *The Speeches of Charles Dickens: Complete Edition*. Hemel Hempstead: Harvester Wheatsheaf, 1988.
House, Madeline and Graham Storey, eds. *The Letters of Charles Dickens*, 8 vols. Oxford, Clarendon Press, 1965–95.
Meckier, Jerome. *Innocent Abroad: Charles Dickens's American Engagements*. Lexington: University Press of Kentucky, 1990.
Slater, Michael, ed. *Dickens on America and the Americans*. Austin: University of Texas Press, 1978.

16

The 'Other World' of 'A Lazy Tour of Two Idle Apprentices'

Paul Schlicke

In September 1857 Dickens and Wilkie Collins undertook a whistlestop tour of the north of Britain, visiting Carlisle, Cumberland, Leeds and Doncaster. The ostensible purpose of the tour was to gather material for an article, written in collaboration by the two authors, to boost flagging sales of *Household Words*. Dickens's biographers are convinced, however, that the real purpose of the expedition was to give Dickens an opportunity to see Ellen Ternan, whom he had first met that summer, and who was acting at the Theatre Royal, Doncaster, with her mother and sister that autumn. The resulting article, 'A Lazy Tour of Two Idle Apprentices', duly appeared in five instalments between 3 and 31 October. It was not reprinted during Dickens's lifetime and has attracted little notice since its first appearance. Such comment as it has attracted has located its primary interest not in its merit as travelogue but in its cryptic revelations of Dickens's unsettled emotions at this period of his life. While I agree that the biographical interest is genuine, in the present essay I would like to suggest that 'A Lazy Tour' is also worth notice for its literary value. In drawing attention to this neglected piece of journalism, I want to argue that travel to unfamiliar places provided Dickens with a vehicle for two fascinating tales of the uncanny, as haunting as the tales of Edgar Allan Poe. Kathleen Tillotson has suggested that, whereas Dickens generally avoided overtly supernatural effects in his novels, he was quite happy to introduce them in his shorter works, such as the Christmas books. 'A Lazy Tour' is a particularly good example of the kind of interior journey into the uncanny at which Dickens is particularly adept, and travel is an integral component of that journey.

Dickens proposed the tour in a letter to Collins dated 29 August 1857:

> Partly in the grim despair and restlessness of this subsidence from excitement, and partly for the sake of Household Words, I want to cast about whether you and I can go anywhere – take any tour – see any thing – whereon we could write something together. Have you any idea, tending to any place in the world? Will you rattle your head and see if there is any pebble in it which we could wander away and play at Marbles with? We want something for Household Words, and I want to escape from myself. For, when I *do* start up and stare myself seedily in the face, as happens to be my case at present, my blankness is inconceivable – indescribable – my misery, amazing.
>
> (P, 8. 423)

As the Pilgrim editors note, Dickens had written only one article for *Household Words* since the preceding June, and sales were flagging. A key purpose of the journey, then, was an opportunity to gather material for a five-part article, to be written jointly by Collins and himself. But as the tone of the letter makes abundantly clear, most of all Dickens wanted an escape from himself. His emotions were in wild turmoil, and he was desperate for relief. As other letters from the time indicate, he had become deeply disillusioned with his marriage – 'Poor Catherine and I are not made for each other', he confided to Forster a few days later (P, 8. 430), and a month later he ordered the door to her bedroom to be sealed off (P, 8. 465). That summer he had flung himself into the amateur theatrical production on Collins's play *The Frozen Deep*, as a result of which he first came into contact with Ellen Ternan. Although letters at the time, including the one to Collins quoted above, and 'A Lazy Tour' itself make a pretence that the destination of the journey was immaterial, in fact Dickens booked rooms before they set off, in Doncaster, where the Ternans were acting at the time. Without doubt, a primary motive of the journey was a desire to see Ellen Ternan again.

Dickens had other sources of unrest. He had completed *Little Dorrit* and by autumn the nervous energy which invariably accompanied his creative invention was starting to return. With his customary all-consuming passion he saw to every detail of the production of *The Frozen Deep* during the summer. In addition, he was deeply distraught over the sudden death on 8 June of his dear friend and fellow author Douglas Jerrold. His son Walter embarked for India that summer, just as the Mutiny broke out, and although hard news did not arrive until later, Dickens's fears for his son were well founded, for Walter was even then taking part in two major battles of the insurrection.

Dickens's restlessness is prominent in the resulting article. The central conceit, taken from Hogarth, portrays Dickens and Collins as idle apprentices, Francis Goodchild and Thomas Idle, respectively, and characterises them as embodiments of contrasting types of idleness. Whereas Thomas Idle is passive and indolent, reluctant to engage in any activity, Francis Goodchild is frenetically energetic, whisking them from London to Carlisle, up Carrock Fell in pouring rain, on to Wigton, Allonby, Lancaster, Leeds and finally Doncaster. Walking, observing, fantasising, demanding new distractions, Dickens as Goodchild is the very picture of uncontrollable nervous energy. The contrast between the two is intensified at the initial stage of their travels, when Collins suffered an accident during the descent from Carrock Fell, badly twisting an ankle, which left him lame for the remainder of the expedition, leaving all the activity to Dickens.

Collins wrote the description in chapter 1 of 'A Lazy Tour' of the ill-fated adventure on Carrock, emphasising his initial reluctance, his depressed spirits as they got lost in the impenetrable mist, his perpetual lagging behind Dickens and their guide, and his utter helplessness after he fell. Dickens, by contrast, sent a letter to Forster describing the same incident more succinctly, vividly and humorously than the published account, and giving a clue of his dominant emotions even then, when he pictured himself carrying Collins 'Melo-dramatically (Wardour to the life!) everywhere' (P, 8. 439–40) – Wardour, of course, being Dickens's role in *The Frozen Deep*, the self-sacrificing hero who dies rescuing his rival in love. The point of the comparison is driven home in a letter he sent to Wills once the travellers had reached Doncaster two weeks later, expressing a wish to be 'a good boy' and admitting, 'But Lord bless you, the strongest parts of your present correspondent's heart are made up of weaknesses. And he just came to be here at all (if you knew it) along of his Richard Wardour! Guess *that* riddle, Mr Wills!' (P, 8. 449).

In fact, the whole article is scattered with references to Dickens's love-lorn state. Before the travellers even set off they argue facetiously about the lover in the Scots ballad 'Annie Laurie', who would 'lay him doon and dee'. Idle complains that he wouldn't have anything to do with love, but Goodchild is contemptuous:

What an ass that fellow was! . . . Lay him doon and dee! Finely he'd show off before the girl doing *that*. A sniveller! Why couldn't he get up, and punch somebody's head? . . . If I fell into that state of mind about a girl, do you think I'd lay me doon and dee? No sir, I'd get me oop a peetch into somebody.

Goodchild, we are told, 'is always in love with somebody, and not infrequently with several objects at once' (*HW*, 16.313). He is eager to visit Allonby largely because the connecting station is at Aspatria, named for the mistress of Pericles, renowned for her beauty, but deflatingly pronounced 'Spatter' by the locals (*HW*, 16. 361). Later, on hearing of an inn where bride-cake is served after every meal, Goodchild lets out 'a lover's sigh' (*HW*, 16. 367), and in Doncaster he falls 'into a dreadful state concerning a pair of little lilac gloves and a little bonnet that he saw there' (*HW*, 16. 411) – almost certainly an allusion to Ellen Ternan.

But it is the two tales that are most directly concerned with aberrant love. According to Forster the first was written by Collins, but it is so integrated into the fabric of the whole that Dickens certainly had a part in its conception. Goodchild is fascinated by the wild eyes and pallid expression of Mr Lorn, assistant to the doctor called to treat Thomas Idle's ankle, and Dr Speddie tells Lorn's tale: found, apparently dead in an inn by a careless young man who turns out to be his half-brother, Lorn disappears when he discovers a love-match between his rescuer and the woman to whom he is betrothed. The focus of the story is the horror of discovering a corpse in a double-bedded room, the greater horror of finding it alive after all, and the pathos of Lorn's subsequent empty life of negation and forgetfulness. It is surely not accidental that the story is set in Doncaster, and the dissipated youth who wins the girl is named 'Holliday'.

The second tale concerns a man who in vengeance and greed orders his wife to die. A youth, who has watched it happen from a tree, is murdered by the husband and buried beneath the tree, which takes on magical powers, metamorphosing into the shape of the youth. Eventually the corpse is discovered and the murderer hanged, whereupon the villain is fated, like the Ancient Mariner, to live forever telling his tale, and to multiply each night into as many ghostly figures as the hours tolled through the night. Again, details are revealing: Ellen is the name of the woman beloved by the youth, and Dick is the name of the auditor's companion, who alone can release the murderous husband from the curse.

Passionate, unfulfilled love thus lies at the heart of both tales, and links with the love-lorn state of the Dickens-figure Francis Goodchild. Both tales are also centrally concerned with lurid and unnatural deaths: the death-in-life of Lorn and the life-in-death of the murderous husband. Again this theme recurs in the main body of the travelogue, where Goodchild describes the faces of race-goers at Doncaster looking identical to those of the notorious murderers Thurtell and Palmer. Indeed, the theme expands and intensifies as the article progresses: on Carrock, discomfort and injury put the travellers in a position of danger, lest they not find their way down from the mountain; in the first tale, the corpse is only apparently dead; in the second, there are two murders and an execution, with the ghost of the murderer multiplying on the hour; and in the final chapter the town is described as being filled entirely with villainous physiognomies.

The tales thus link into details of the travelogue, reinforcing themes of love and death. Where the tales take leave of the mundane realism with which the sights and events of the tour are recorded, the entire article is dominated by an urgent impetus to escape the here and now. The travellers flee London to the northernmost parts of England, sometimes within sight of Scotland. They remove themselves in time as well as space: on Carrock Fell the mist is described as 'pre-Adamite sop' (*HW*, 16.337); Wigton appears to be built of 'Druid stones' (*HW*, 16.338), and comparisons look back to Greek myth (Cadmus – *HW*, 16.410) and to Arabian nights (*HW*, 16.367, 412). Throughout the travelogue references to fantasy, magic and the supernatural pull against the humdrum detail of linen-drapers' shops, men chatting by a town pump, out-of-date copies of the *Illustrated London News* in a shop window. Thus the landlord who guides the travellers up Carrock adds a stone to the cairn 'with the gesture of a magician adding an ingredient to a cauldron in full bubble' (*HW*, 16.317). The stones of Lancaster 'whisper' that the ill-gotten earnings of local slave merchants 'turned to curses, as the Arabian wizard's money turned to leaves, and that no good ever came of it, even unto the third and fourth generations, until it was wasted and gone' (*HW*, 16.367). Most surreal of all is the railway junction where 'wooden razors shaved the air', where converging tracks form 'a Congress of iron vipers', and where at night the air seems filled with 'boughs of Jack's beanstalk', and the walls glow like a 'hippopotamus's eyes' (*HW*, 16.366). In the tale of murder, the ghostly speaker holds Goodchild with a mesmeric eye, just as Goodchild himself ascends Carrock with the defiance of the Wandering Jew (*HW*, 16.317). In Lancaster, Goodchild visits a lunatic asylum, where he observes a madman intently poring over a web of matting (*HW*, 16.385); in Doncaster, the entire town seems a lunatic asylum filled with madmen and their keepers (*HW*, 16.410)

The inventive eye of the observer, in short, repeatedly infuses the journalistic account of a holiday in unfamiliar locations with more than a whiff of surrealism, and prepares the ground for the decidedly uncanny tales they hear along the way. 'A Lazy Tour of Two Idle Apprentices' is thus a fascinating and coherently told journey, not merely into regions remote from Dickens's usual haunts, but into realms of the imagination where his creative powers enjoy free play. 'A Lazy Tour' is assuredly not the best piece of journalism Dickens ever wrote, but I hope I have been able to suggest reasons why it merits more than the nearly total neglect accorded up to now.

References

Dickens, Charles, 'A Lazy Tour of Two Idle Apprentices', *Household Words*, October 1837, Vol. 16, 313–19, 337–49, 361–7, 385–93, 409–16.
Dickens, Charles, *Letters*, The Pilgrim Edition, Vol. 8, eds. Graham Storey and Kathleen Tillotson, Oxford, Clarendon Press, 1995.

17

Dickens's Science, Evolution and 'The Death of the Sun'

K.J. Fielding with Shu Fang Lai

At Dijon I gave a paper called 'Dickens and Science?'[1] which was mainly on problems which seem to come from a wish to make him seem more involved than he was with certain contemporary scientific advances. My conclusions then, as at any time, were not to insist on Gradgrindian facts or relentless accuracy. For the last thing I want is to wag a square forefinger at fellow-Dickensians and demand the suppression of insight and imagination in discussing Dickens's ideas or biography. For without mistakes we would not be given the clues we need to detect the underlying misconceptions that are sometimes advanced as the latest discovery. The great need is to distinguish between fact and fancy. For if a new insight is claimed, let us have the evidence for it; if a piece of writing is assigned to Dickens, let it be his and not someone else's; dates and names should preferably not be confused, and care should be taken not to claim to have seen something in a work which is not there – and so on.

It seems simple. Yet what has happened is that in wanting to show the all-embracing scope of Dickens's art and imagination, especially in the cause of science, some writers have been persuaded that they have enough evidence to convince themselves of conclusions which are untrue. In doing so they set an example of looking for results to fit prior conclusions instead of working the other way round. The best example of this was Ann Wilkinson's essay, '*Bleak House*: From Faraday to Judgment Day' (*ELH* 34 [1967]: 225–47), which I suggested had set us off on a set of false trails.

Even so, it showed one excellent insight: that there was probably an intellectual and imaginative connection between spontaneous combustion in *Bleak House* and an article in *Household Words* on 'The

Chemistry of a Candle', written shortly before (3 August 1850; 1: 439–44) and, even more, that ideas related to it were developed thoughout the novel. All this was eloquently and intelligently explained, and the connection accounted for between the article by Perceval Leigh (known for his *A Comic English Grammar* and *A Comic Latin Grammar*) and the distinguished scientist Michael Faraday, who had provided Dickens with his notes on the subject from his lecture given at the Royal Institution.[2] All this was persuasive, with no more than a forgivable oversight in saying that the author of the piece in *Household Words* was 'of course' Charles Knight.

It was the further specific conclusions that were both disturbing and influential, and which had no demonstrable relation with *Bleak House*. For, from the fact that Faraday obligingly lent his notes to be used by a journalist, there was a leap to the conclusion that Dickens in someway knew and understood Faraday's advanced work on electricity and related fields, and almost that Dickens was ahead of him! From that point, we were then asked to accept that Dickens was aware of the second law of thermodynamics, stated clearly for the first time in the same year that he began the novel, i.e. 1850. Both conclusions apparently require us to believe that we know this because of what is expressed or 'embodied' in his novels – namely in *Bleak House* which is the subject of the essay, and to some extent in *Little Dorrit* – since there is no direct reference to anything of the kind in Dickens's life or writings.

This has now found its way into the current main Dickens biography by Peter Ackroyd, who evidently takes his information directly from Ann Wilkinson's essay, though it is wrong in other ways which are not the present issue. But it leaves open the interesting question of how Dickens learned even the simplest physics. Ann Wilkinson has a suggestion, that no one else cares or dares to mention, that it came from the Jungian 'collective unconscious'. But it is really unnecessary to take this up again.

Yet one might well consider the problem from another angle, and ask ourselves what we could infer about Dickens's knowledge of electricity as shown or implied by his two major periodicals – except that this also tends to take us off in another direction. In fact, it is even rather premature to draw conclusions about Dickens as an editor, if safe to say that his approach to Faraday was exceptional, comparable only with his connection with Sir Richard Owen. In general many of the 'scientific' contributors to *Household Words* appear to have been almost as far below competence in their subjects as Faraday was above it. From once being thought of as almost entirely unconcerned with science, Dickens's interest is now recognised in some aspects such as popular astronomy, geology, evolutionary ideas, possibly natural history, and some of the technical advances of the time. But is it only the fear of being caught out in a mistake of one's own that prevents anyone from saying that there is hardly the slightest sign in his own writings having other than the most general interest in physical science?

Yet there remains that possibly puzzling reference to the 'death of the sun' (*Bleak House*, ch. 1) already referred to in 'Dickens and Science?' and elsewhere. As we all know, it comes in the first paragraph:

> Smoke lowering down from the chimney-pots, making a soft black drizzle, with flakes of soot in it as big as full-grown snow-flakes – gone into mourning, one might imagine, for the death of the sun.

And, though it may just be a Dickensian joke, the phrase has a precise flick at the end of the sentence, as if it were exactly referring to something. It appears in a paragraph laden with allusions (Lincoln's Inn Hall, Genesis, the Megalosaurus, and so on), many of which we immediately recognise as linked with the Biblical story of Creation or more scientific accounts. The *Dickens Companion* series, which lives and breathes through seeing allusions, naturally spots it as having one, referring to the 'nebular hypothesis' of Pierre-Simon Laplace (1749–1827), perhaps echoed in a similar way in *In Memoriam* (1850; but written 1833–4), with its 'murmurs from the dying sun'. We can be reminded of similar rather ambiguous remarks in later novels. In *Hard Times*, for instance, Stephen Blackpool says that he believes that something will never happen, 'will never do't till th' Sun turns t'ice' (Book 2, ch. 5). *The Companion* to *Our Mutual Friend* notes the description of 'a foggy day in London' when gaslights flared as if 'the sun itself . . . showed as if it had gone out and were collapsing flat and cold' (Book 3, ch. 1). Again it sees the possible derivation from Laplace and comparison with Tennyson, plus the fact that, by the date of *Our Mutual Friend* (March 1865 for this monthly number) the work of William Thomson 'and others on the dissipation of energy had established the idea that the sun was cooling and that the solar system would in time be reduced to dead matter rolling in space.'[3]

Perhaps so, with a few reservations we can disregard for the moment; but, so far as *Bleak House* is concerned, we need to bear in mind that the first chapter was written in November 1850, and that we know from the manuscript that the phrase was not slipped in before publication in March 1851. And, of course, if we were to think of it as a recognisable topical allusion (even a popular one, perhaps?) it would have to have been coined and knowable before that. Leaving aside Tennyson and

Laplace, so far as *Bleak House* goes it has to be said that a connection with William Thomson is out of the question. His ideas were not available. His name is pulled out of the air, whereas the popular 'scientific' journalists Dickens usually associated with and relied on at this time were often not far ahead of the general public. To return to Laplace, even he is unlikely to have been Dickens's direct source, though there could have been an intermediate one. The question, therefore, remains where *did* Dickens get the idea if not from the 'collective unconscious' or his fancy?

It may be because of this that another suggestion has recently been put forward, also mentioned in 'Dickens and Science?'. For, as noted there, Professor Gillian Beer has suggested a reference with a suitable date which does not depend on believing that Dickens had almost spontaneous communication with William Thomson and immediately understood the full implications of the 'second law'. As she notes in her essay on 'Origins and Oblivion in Victorian Narrative' (p. 76), which she takes up again in her '"The Death of the Sun": Victorian Solar Physics and Solar Myth', the apparent allusion in *Bleak House* 'calls in still another Victorian anxiety, the new theory current since the physicist Hermann von Helmholtz's 1847 essay *Über die Erhaltung der Kraft*, which argued that the sun is cooling and that the earth will become too cold for life'.[4]

Yet, though the date fits in one sense, the statement that Helmholtz's essay says that the sun is cooling is mistaken, since the essay has no reference to it or anything like it. No doubt it would also have been an extremely improbable direct source for Dickens since, as Helmholtz explains, his essay or lecture was directed to specialists, and there is the difficulty that it was not translated into English until 1853. Even so, a knowledge of what was in the German could only have shown anyone that it does *not* say that the sun is cooling. There has been a confusion between the 1847 lecture or essay and one Helmholtz gave in 1854. But to make a distinction between the two is not a matter of being 'accurate': it lies in initially realising the complete difference between stating the negative truth that Dickens was unaware of the latest theories in physics in 1850 and that he could have been informed about and understood them. He was not that sort of man.

There is also a distinction between understanding that there is a limit to the life of the sun and a grasp of the laws of thermodynamics. For there was no need to wait for the second law to be enunciated by Clausius and William Thomson. What burns, usually burns out; and, in spite of some persistent and curious beliefs about the nature of the sun, it was usually well understood before 1850 that it was burning, hot and incandescent. John Herschel, whose *Outlines of Astronomy* (1850; 1st edition, 1833) was in Dickens's library in 1870, though not in the published library list,[5] wrote in 1833 that it was a 'great mystery . . . to conceive how so enormous a conflagration (if such it be) can be kept up' (p. 212). He was better informed than his father, Sir William Herschel, who supposed that there might be inhabitants on the sun's surface. Further great advances were made in the study of solar thermodynamics; and an awareness of them even penetrated to some of the general public, as the study of sun spots and eclipses was regularly reported in the press during the 1840s.

Our account is limited by compression, and by a lack of anything but general knowledge.[6] Yet, meanwhile, in the 1840s, theories were advanced by Julius Robert Mayer that the sun was stoked (as it were) by the gravitational fall of meteors into it, and by John James Waterston that its heat was maintained by gradual contraction of its mass. Their theories were taken up by William Thomson (who was later Lord Kelvin) who put forward the meteoric theory at the Royal Society of Edinburgh in 1854, after showing his paper to Helmholtz; and it was only then that the German physicist introduced his discussion of solar heat into a popular lecture in the same year, at Königsberg, translated as 'On the Interaction of Natural Forces'. Like Mayer, who had worked 'within the framework of the increasingly popular nebular theory' of the origin of the solar system (Hufbauer, p. 56), he explained 'how gravity had first shaped the solar system and then provided, through the contraction of the sun', the heat on which the history of the Earth depends. He explained how that inevitably had to end, but in the distant future, more remote than recently supposed.[7]

In spite of an overlap, this takes us further than 'Dickens and Science?' and we approach the question of whether something more positive can be said about the apparent 'allusion'. Even so, we may wonder what, on any interpretation, some of Dickens's readers would have made of it, if they caught the phrase in 1851. No doubt, not everyone needs to catch every allusion. Nevertheless, Dickens is remembered as the editor who once advised, 'You write to be read, of course?' (*Letters*, 7: 677). So it is reasonable to ask what he supposed his readers could make of the point. For generally speaking, in scientific matters, he thought that most *Household Words* readers had to be coaxed; and he must have known that there were others a generation or two behind.

For the steady progress in solar physics cannot have reached the understanding or imagination of all his readers. One of them, for example, was so struck by his fanciful essay 'A Child's Dream of a Star' in the second number that he took it literally. Dickens's essay is in fact connected with a work in his Library list which records a curious pamphlet entitled *Inquiry into the United Evidence of Scripture and Nature with Regard to a Future State*, by Andrew Carmichael, of Dublin. It has on it a written inscription:

> For Charles Dickens, Esqre., from the Author, with all those deep sentiments of Respect in which he participates with all the world, but particularly in discharge of a debt of gratitude which he owed him for his beautiful little Tale of 'A Child's Dream of a Star' so coincident in idea with the present work, and so curiously evincing how two independent minds may without connection or correspondence light on and illustrate the same important truth.[8]

Reading the booklet one finds that Carmichael supposed that they both believed that, after the death of someone close to them, the person they loved might be taken either to a nearby star as Dickens fancied, or to live on the surface of the sun as Carmichael swore he actually believed of his brother. He argued at great length that it was on the sun's surface that Christ took up a temporary stay at times, when absent from the Earth between his crucifixion and ascension. It is obviously eccentric, though no different in its solar geography from Sir William Herschel, nor from the fantasy or science-fiction of Sydney Whiting, whose strange novel *Heliondé: or Adventures in the Sun* (Chapman & Hall), was reviewed at length in *The Times*, 1 November 1855. This is about a visit to its English-speaking inhabitants.[9] The point is that the imagination of at least a few of Dickens's readers had a long way to go to catch up with current advances in astronomical science, in spite of what they could read in the press.

Even limiting ourselves to *Household Words* and *The Times* it is clear that there was much to read about astronomy in popular journalism. A noticeable feature is that, far from Dickens's 'death of the sun' being a cause for anxiety to the ordinary mid-Victorian, frequent reports of the sun made it almost a joke. The annular eclipse of 9 October 1847 impressed no one but journalists and astronomers, nor did the total eclipse of 28 July 1851. After bracing himself to lead off at length about its effect in *The Times*, 29 July, its writer could only pooh-pooh the terrors of the past and more backward nations, realising that Londoners went about their daily lives completely unperturbed. In *Household Words*, it seems to have slipped by unnoticed. The most striking phrase to catch our attention has to wait until an unsatisfactory essay by the literary journalist Edmund Ollier (*HW*, 23 May 1857; 15: 481–4) on 'Comets; and their Tail of Prophets'. Naturally it is not perfectly serious, though it

pleasantly looks forward to a comet due to come next June, and back at
the way that past comets were thought to foretell doom.

Its author strays into the topic of other false prophecies, such as those
who are discussing 'the extinction of the world', with a

> hypothesis . . . that the sun himself is absolutely going out, like a lamp
> that has burnt its appointed time. A gentleman, signing himself
> Helioscopus, recently wrote to *The Times* to say, that the well-known
> spots on the sun's disc are increasing in size and number. From this
> we are to infer that that robe of fire and luminosity which
> encompasses the opaque body of the sun, and which is the source of
> all the vitality of our system, is wearing out – dropping to pieces with
> celestial rottenness.

The tone is light-hearted: the comet of the coming month is to be
delivered 'by Time, like a grim bowler at an awful game of cricket, to
terminate our innings, and stump us out for ever.' Signs of panic (not
confirmed by *The Times*) are to be found only on the continent. The article
concludes, that 'the world changes, but gradually; and we have therefore
no reason to fear a sudden extinction with any comet or rival star'; nor,
one assumes, of the sun.

We might think that the idea of an apocalyptic end to the world was
an exciting subject for journalists, but not taken seriously. The article is
'unsatisfactory' because we have not traced the alleged letter from
Helioscopus between 1847 and 1857, using *The Times* indices and various
key-words. We should be glad to be shown that we have overlooked it,
because it might suggest that the death of the sun was a common enough
phrase even without taking science into account. Edmund Ollier was a
minor poet, journalist and essayist, with no special scientific knowledge.

In other words, Dickens was not particularly well informed about the
latest advances in science, and it is ludicrous to suppose that he was or
could have been. If we think this of him, we can neither have caught the
spirit in which he writes nor see his relation to his times. But, even
focused on this narrow little topic, we can see he probably shared the
general awareness of scientific change reflected in current journalism.

Yet there is finally the serious point that Dickens's 'death of the sun'
probably came from the work of Robert Pringle Nichol (1804–59), the
Glasgow Regius Professor of Astronomy, two of whose books were listed
as being in Dickens's library in 1870, *Views of the Architecture of the Heavens*
(Edinburgh, 5th edition, William Tait, 1845), and *Thoughts on Some
Important Points Relating to the System of the World* (Edinburgh, 5th edition,

William Tait, 1846). The suggestion is that Dickens's possession of these books points to an interest in Nichol's work on Dickens's part and that he almost certainly also read his *Phenomena and Order of the Solar System* (Edinburgh, 1838) and his *Contemplations on the Solar System* (3rd edition, Edinburgh, 1847).

We need to see Dickens as a reader of some popular science who had a good deal of curiosity but no expert knowledge, which can be seen in his only piece of writing on the subject, 'The Poetry of Science', in the *Examiner*, 9 December 1848. Nichol was probably suited to Dickens's tastes as an urgent populariser, in spite of his over-rhetorical style, which has perhaps resulted in historians of astronomy having little to say about him. He is noted, though, for his views on the nebular hypothesis and the birth of the solar system, looking back to the independently conceived ideas of Laplace and William Herschel. He reconsidered them in the light of observations that were being made by Lord Rosse's powerful new telescope, of which Dickens (or at least *Household Words*) was aware.[10] He was, therefore, exactly the person to reach the general reader.

Even more to the point, he was perhaps the first to put forcibly to the general reader the idea of the impermanence of the sun. As early as his *Phenomena and Order of the Solar System* he had insisted that the life of the stars was limited, explaining that the sun was a star, and adding that: 'The question is whether the Sun is now as he was and will ever be.' He directly compared the sun to the new star or supernova observed by the Danish astronomer Tycho Brahe in November 1572, which came to birth and 'apparent extinction . . . *passing through the hues of a dying conflagration*' (p. 192; emphasis in the original). He went on to repeat the idea more boldly in his *Contemplations* (1847, 3rd edition; not in the 1st or 2nd editions), making the idea of an impermanent sun even clearer. In Chapter 9, and especially the section with the running title, 'The Sun's Phosphorescence – Is this Permanent?' he put the same argument, and the statement, 'No more is light inherent in the Sun than in Tycho's vanished star . . . [and] a time may come when he shall cease to be required to shine' (p. 190). Dickens thus probably learned about the dying sun from these books.

Much more could be said about Nichol and his writing, and even what briefly follows may seem a deviation. Yet Dickens read him for his general arguments, and not for the purpose of making particular allusions. There were two notable features in what Nichol had to say. One lay in the expression of his devout reverence for God-given creation, even greater than that of most writers on popular astronomy at the time: he was deeply concerned that in studying the heavens one should still take 'into view' their 'relations . . . to the moral world' and be sure that 'the highest spirit would never exhaust the fulness of that volume which God has spread before us all' (*Views of the Architecture of the Heavens* [1836] p. 206). He repeatedly urges this and much like it, but without restraining his speculative boldness, which go well beyond the technicalities of astronomy. The second is that he was an evolutionist.

We have mentioned elsewhere Dickens's enthusiastic support for Robert Chambers' arguments in favour of evolution in his anonymous *Vestiges of the Natural History of Creation* (1844), shown in his review of Robert Hunt's *The Poetry of Science* in 1848.[11] All three were, in fact, evolutionists, though Nichol again enveloped his arguments in such elaborate prose that they are hard to follow. Yet, as early as 1846, he clearly argued in favour of evolution in his *Thoughts on Some Important Points* in saying that fossils 'recall organisations' that once occupied 'the whole world, compact and comprehensive as our own . . . descending, also, by degrees nearly imperceptible, from their ascertained loftiest point, down to the feeblest manifestation of life' (p. 220). He saw that different species had decidedly passed into one another in the past, and that this had lessons for the present: 'Strange, too, and surely not without meaning . . . the . . . interfusion in one organisation, of characters that now belong to species very far apart; for we have fish and reptile, and bird and reptile, so inextricably mingled, that it cannot often be determined on which side the preponderance lies (p. 222); and though it is hard to see progress in 'transmutations' in invertebrate species,

> one indubitable symptom of order is recognisable; for throughout the whole history of the world, vertebrate animals of *rising functions*, and a growing concentration of brain, and in due succession, come upon the scene. Fishes . . . subsequently reptiles . . . then birds, and then mammalia. . . . And the long course has terminated in the meantime with Man, the last product of this toil of Ages; – Man, who to the mind and emotions of every creature has added the power of using all, so that they connect him with the INFINITE!
>
> (p. 227)

Nichol was as convinced as Chambers that the universe was governed by laws, and that the sole difference between the 'natural' and the 'supernatural' is that we understand the one and not the other. Though he noticed 'the sagacity of Darwin' (p. 232) on geology, he was, of course, creative evolutionist long before natural selection.[12]

The point about this is the same as with Robert Chambers: if attempts are made to take into account that Dickens's conceptions may have been influenced by evolutionary ideas, we have to go back much earlier than the *Origin of Species*. This will be true even if we are simply making comparisons between Dickens and Darwin.[13] It can be seen how vigorously Dickens supported them in Chambers' book in 1848, and we now have confirmation (previously unrecognized) that he was probably well aware of them from Nichol's work at about the same time. For Dickens, Darwin was a late arrival.

What I am trying to say lies chiefly in the evidence itself, and in the fact that it is possible to unearth it from the social, personal and journalistic matrix of Dickens's life. Even that is an absurdly abstract manner of expression: i.e. in his letters, his library books and journalism, which really largely remain to be investigated.

There is a comforting circularity in many of the present arguments, because the life and writings cannot be contradictory, and they have to conform to evidence if they are to be worth study. Whether they can be critically extended into such a novel as *Bleak House* is another matter: it is possible, perhaps, if for example we were to read the novel as showing the laws of man in conflict with the laws of nature. Meanwhile we can see where the elusive phrase came from, how it got into circulation, how little anxiety his readers would really have felt, ready to accept it as a joke but well aware of the sun's impermanence. We should also grasp that, in spite of what we are sometimes told, it had no connection with the interest in thermodynamics at the time of the origin of *Bleak House*, and none with Helmholtz's lecture. Therefore Dickens's interest in popular science was little more than that of a well-read man of his time: more than used to be generally thought, but much less dramatic than sometimes recently suggested. He is a familiar figure about whom much in detail remains to be discovered.

So much is easily available, with some effort, in well-edited and well-indexed information, that should be investigated before general ideas are hopefully let loose like Miss Flite's caged birds.

Notes

1. Now in *Dickens Quarterly* (December, 1996) 3–19. I am grateful for the chance of repeating some of its points, and carrying a few a little further. But this is a continuation not just a repetition of the citations and arguments already made, though their support is needed.
2. There can be no discussion of *Household Words* (*HW*) without Anne Lorhli, *Household Words, a Weekly Journal* (Toronto: Toronto University Press, 1973), which gives the author of each article, and

an outline of his or her career. Equally necessary is the Pilgrim edition of *The Letters of Charles Dickens*, ed. Graham Storey, Kathleen Tillotson, M. House, K.J. Fielding, and others (Oxford: Clarendon Press, 1970–). From Lohrli we learn that Leigh was an ex-medical man, who had given up his former career on turning to popular journalism, and that he did not remain with *HW* after vol. 3.

3. See *The Companion to Bleak House*, ed. Susan Shatto (London: Unwin-Hyman, 1988) 25; *The Companion to Our Mutual Friend*, ed. Michael Cotsell (London: Allen & Unwin, 1986) 193.

4. The first essay, 'Origins', is in *Sex, Politics, and Science in the Nineteenth-Century Novel*, ed. Ruth B. Yeazzell (Baltimore: Johns Hopkins Press, 1986), and the second in *The Sun is God*, ed. J.B. Bullen (Oxford, 1989). The second essay has been collected in the author's *Open Fields: Science in Cultural Encounter* (Oxford: Clarendon Press, 1996), 219–41, with a silently corrected date for Helmholtz's lecture.

5. *The Catalogue of the Library of Charles Dickens*, ed. J.H. Stonehouse (London: Piccadilly Fountain Press, 1935), reprinted from Sotheran's 'Price Current of Literature'. Herschel's 1833 edition was in the library in Lardner's *Cabinet Encyclopaedia*, though I believe Dickens also possessed the 1850 edition.

6. I am nevertheless most grateful to a reply to an inquiry from Mr A.R. Macdonald of the Royal Observatory at Edinburgh, who pointed me towards J.P. Nichol, and recommended Karl Hufbauer, *Exploring the Sun, Solar Science since Galileo* (London and Baltimore: Johns Hopkins University Press, 1991), who kindly replied to an enquiry.

7. 'On the Interaction of Natural Forces', *Popular Lectures on Scientific Subjects*, second series (London: Longmans, 1893), in which he explained that the sun's heat was 'sufficient for an immeasurable time' (168), and that 'we have nothing to fear' (171).

8. J.H. Stonehouse, 93, listed only among 'Pamphlets (Various)'.

9. They converse in musical tones. Whiting (d. 1875), also wrote *Memoirs of a Stomach* (1853).

10. [Charles Thomas Hudson], 'Mr. Bubs on Planetary Disturbances', 12 April 1851, 3: 58–60, which opens, 'Although Lord Rosse's telescope will never let us put a man in the moon again, yet we may fancy one in the sun'; it is about calculating the orbit of Mars, an extraordinarily complicated piece for a popular weekly. Nichol makes acknowledgments to Lord Rosse in the preface to *Thoughts on Some Important Points in Relation to the System of the World*, p. x, and in the dedication and preface of his *The Architecture of the Heavens* (London: John W. Parker, 1850), illus. David Scott with the help of William Bell Scott.

11. We know little of Nichol in secondary literature; the *DNB* speaks of his religious beliefs as being unorthodox, alluding apparently to his evolutionary ideas. He certainly belonged to the school of 'the poetry of science'.

12. Fielding with Shu Fang Lai, 'Dickens, Science, and *The Poetry of Science*', *Dickensian* (Spring 1997). Chambers and Nichol developed

similar arguments for believing that life on earth and the universe itself had developed through evolution.

13. Plenty of comparisons have been made, most notably in *Darwin and the Novelist: Patterns of Science in Victorian Fiction* (Cambridge, MA: Harvard University Press, 1988), 'Dickens and Darwin, Science, and the Narrative Form', *Texas Studies Literature and Language* 28 (1986) 250–80. It must make a difference that we have to think of Dickens as already an evolutionist, probably of a different species from Darwin.

18

Negative Homogeneity: *Our Mutual Friend*, Richard Owen, and the 'New Worlds' of Victorian Biology

Victor Sage

Stephen Jay Gould's book, *Wonderful Life* (1989), named after a Dickensian Frank Capra movie of the 1940s, tells how later nineteenth-century natural history formed a 'Darwinian' template based on assumptions about the 'march of progress', which caused the scientists of the Smithsonian to transcribe wrongly what they found in the fossil beds of the Cambrian slate. Gould shows how Walcott and his colleagues suppressed the monstrosities and eccentricities of the creatures they were looking at – 'normalising' for example the sites of their organs – because they simply could not believe that such a purely contingent proliferation of organic differences could have existed simultaneously so near the beginning of organic life. Such a finding was simply not imaginable – it implied that radical heterogeneity of form was present at the very beginning, in some of the earliest and most 'primitive' forms of life, and that the orderly progression from the simple and homogeneous to the complex and heterogeneous presented in Victorian biological textbooks – and, indeed, in textbooks modelled on them up to the post-Second World War period – which Gould terms 'the cone of increasing diversity', was contradicted by the fossil–findings before the very eyes of these honest and dedicated orthodox Darwinian biologists. It was not, says Gould, that they faked the evidence through dishonesty – the template-theory through which they viewed the empirical evidence – which has come to be known as 'phyletic gradualism' – was so well-defined that they could not see anything which appeared inconsistent with it.

I was irresistibly reminded, when I first read Gould's fascinating account, and pored over his beautiful, and, he assures us, accurate transcriptions of these fossil forms, of Henry James's review of Dickens's *Our Mutual Friend*:

> What a world were this world if the world of *Our Mutual Friend* were an honest reflection of it! But a community of eccentrics is impossible. Rules alone are consistent with each other; exceptions are inconsistent. Society is maintained by natural sense and natural feeling. We cannot conceive a society in which these principles are not in some manner represented. Where in these pages are the depositaries of that intelligence without which the movements of life would cease. Who represents nature?[1]

James greets Dickens's book with the incredulity of a late Victorian scientist faced with the contents of the Burgess Shale – but here, in the aesthetic context, the 'template' is mimetic and the natural history analogy (what he calls elsewhere in this piece 'the habitual probable of nature', the edge, so to speak, of the template) is applied to what is seen by James as an impossibility in the representation of human society, that is, sheer difference, the blind and endless heterogeneity of character in Dickens's novel.

It is worth recalling, in this context, the language of G.H. Lewes's *Fortnightly Review* essay a few years later in 1872, which explicitly uses natural history as a reference point for its judgement of Dickens's presentation of character. Again the assumption is mimetic – Lewes's piece is the eloquent source for a common charge against Dickens's art as a novelist – the familiar contention that his characters do not 'develop' and are therefore not true to life. They are, said Lewes trenchantly, like dead, but galvanised, frogs always performing a single repeated action, not living organisms:

> It is this complexity of the organism which Dickens wholly fails to conceive: his characters have nothing fluctuating and incalculable in them, even when they embody true observations; and very often they are creations so fantastic that one is at a loss to understand how he could, without hallucination, believe them to be like reality.[2]

It is worth remarking in this context how the Lewes passage elides the biological notion of an organism with the aesthetic demand for psychological realism in character, a curiously anthropomorphic reliance on an organic metaphor of growth and development, an unselfconscious argument from nature to culture, which is all the more curious when we remember that the *Oxford English Dictionary* credits Lewes with inventing the term 'anthropomorphism'.[3]

As early as 1857, two years before the battle-lines were finally drawn up over the question of evolution by the publication of Darwin's *Origin*, Lewes's great friend, Herbert Spencer, published in the *Westminster Review* an ambitious and influential article, 'Progress: Its Law and Cause', which argues for the axiomatic law of organic growth in all fields of human culture:

> The investigations of Wolff, Goethe, and Von Baer, have established the truth that a series of changes gone through during the development of a seed into a tree, or an ovum into an animal, constitute an advance from homogeneity of structure to heterogeneity of structure. In its primary stage, every germ consists of a substance that is uniform throughout, both in texture and in chemical composition. The first step in its development is the appearance of a difference between two parts of this substance; or, as the phenomenon is described in physiological language – a differentiation. Each of these differentiated divisions presently begins itself to exhibit some contrast of parts and by and by these secondary differentiations become as definite as the individual one. This process is continuously represented – ie simultaneously going on in all parts of the growing embryo; and by endless multiplication of these differentiations there is ultimately produced that complex combination of tissues and organs constituting the adult animal or plant. This is the course of evolution followed by all organisms whatever. It is settled beyond dispute that organic progress consists in a change from the homogeneous to the heterogeneous.
>
> Now, we propose to show, that this law of organic progress is the law of all progress. Whether it be in the development of the earth, in the development of Life upon its surface, in the development of society, of Government, of manufactures; of Commerce, of Language, Literature, Science, Art, this same evolution of the simple into the complex, through a process of continuous differentiation, holds throughout.[4]

Spencer's metonymic claim that all progress works by the same organic law triumphantly carries over assumptions about biological and physiological processes into a host of other fields, including those of

Language and Art. It reminds us of the fact that fully-fledged Social Darwinism begins before Darwin.

When Spencer moves into the political and linguistic spheres, his argument begins to look not only unconvincing, but rather pompous and conservative in tone. Take language for example:

> The lowest form of language is the exclamation, by which an entire idea is vaguely conveyed through a single sound: as among the lower animals. That human language ever consisted solely of exclamations, and was strictly homogeneous in respect to its parts of speech, we have no evidence. But that language can be traced down to a form in which nouns and verbs are its only elements, is an established fact. In the gradual multiplication of parts of speech out of these primary ones – in the differentiation of verbs into active and passive, of mood, tense, person, of number and case alike – in the formation of auxiliary verbs, of adjectives, adverbs, pronouns, prepositions, articles – in the evolution of those orders, genera, species, varieties of parts of speech by which civilised races express minute modifications of meaning – we see a change from the homogeneous to the heterogeneous. And it may be remarked in passing, that it is more especially in virtue of having carried this subdivision of function to a greater effect and completeness, that the English language is superior to all others.[5]

There is more than a touch of Podsnappery about this final sentence.

Politically, as soon as he leaves the apparently firm, literal ground of natural history, Spencer's anthropomorphic discussion of the proliferation of social processes declines into a celebratory hymn to the virtues of the Division of Labour. From a Dickensian point of view, the notion of society as a ramifying organism is a nightmare;[6] indeed, from *Dombey and Son* onwards, he carries out a massive and sustained attack on the premise that adaptive specialism equals social progress: it is precisely the kind of specialisation which Spencer lists in his piece which becomes the object of Dickens's satire – the elaboration of bureaucratic divisions, the substitution of special illiterate jargons for language, the growth of legal offices, administrative departments, courts of justice, etc.[7]

Dickens anticipates and resists Spencer's biological law of progress from the homogeneous to the heterogeneous by a process of comic inversion. 'Nature' in the later Dickens tends to exist for the purposes of satire and parody of the new capitalism. To quote a famous example, the opening paragraph of *Bleak House* is an explicitly evolutionary joke about the regressive nature of the mid-Victorian society which Spencer goes on to praise as the most highly developed in the world.[8] Here the heterogeneous (modern) is systematically reduced to the homogeneous (prehistoric), its material or financial base; mud or money and, later, 'fog' and 'slime'; and, on the level of language, Dickens shows, according to Spencer's own criteria, how the language of lawyers, through specialisation, has entered into a primitive homogeneous state, which Jarndyce refers to as 'wiglomeration'. Dickens's lawyer, Mr Tangle, speaks a kind of telegraphese, a helpless series of exclamations, having apparently lost all syntax and connective tissue - the signs, according to Spencer, of linguistic evolution:

> 'In reference,' proceeds the Chancellor, still on Jarndyce and Jarndyce, 'to the young girl –'
> 'Begludship's pardon – boy,' says Mr Tangle prematurely.
> 'In reference,' proceeds the Chancellor with extra distinctness, 'to the young girl and boy, the two young people' – Mr Tangle crushed – 'whom I directed to be in attendance today and who are now in my private room, I will see them and satisfy myself as to the expediency of making the order for their residing with their uncle.'
> Mr Tangle on his legs again. 'Begludship's pardon – dead.'
> 'With their' – Chancellor looking through his double eye-glass at the papers on his desk – 'grandfather.'
> 'Begludship's pardon – victim of rash action – brains.'[9]

Or take Kenge and Carboy's crucial letter to Esther which ironically displays the same symptoms of linguistic homogeneity, the words having been so abbreviated that they form a barbarous jargon impossible to read aloud without its sinister absurdity becoming apparent:

Old Square, Lincoln's Inn.

Madam,

Jarndyce and Jarndyce.

Our c̄lt Mr Jarndyce being ābt to rēce into his house, under an Order of the C̄t of C̄hy, a Ward of the C̄t in this cause, for whom he wishes to secure an elḡble comp̄n, directs us to inform you that he will be glad of your sērcēs in the afsd capacity.

We have arrngd for your being forded, carriage free, p^r eight o'clock coach from Reading, on Monday morning next, to White Horse Cellar, Picadilly, London, where one of our clks will be waiting to convey you to our offe as above.

We are, Madam, Your obed^t Serv^{ts}

Kenge and Carboy.

Miss Esther Summerson.

Oh, never, never, never, shall I forget the emotion this letter caused in the house![10]

The sheer emotional articulacy of Esther's response here (a *true* exclamation) is ironically contrasted with the linguistic reduction of the letter, which treats her ('forded, carriage free') as a material object, not a person.

This argument about language and representation is worked out more systematically still in the first third of *Hard Times*, where Dickens deliberately pillories the primitive confusion of thought that conceives of language as a specialist set of labels. *Little Dorrit's* handling of negation and plurality in language carries the critique further.

One of Dickens's most important reference points in matters of natural history was the work of Sir Richard Owen, with whom he had a personal friendship from 1842 when they met at Drury Lane Theatre until his death in 1870. Dickens's magazines remained loyal to Owen throughout all the vicissitudes of his scientific career. As members of the Athenaeum group, the two men felt they shared a common cultural project; they both had the same low-key, but deeply felt Protestantism, and both had belonged to 'The Society for the Diffusion of Useful Knowledge'. Over a period of about 20 years, Owen's scientific papers were 'boiled' by Wills and others into popular articles. Study of these articles in *Household Words* and *All the Year Round* reveals that, in the sphere of natural history, Dickens's magazines acted a mouthpiece for the Owenite line on the question of 'the production of species'. This is no place to go into the evidence in detail on this, but the process of transmission is clearly inferable, in my view, which I have expressed elsewhere.[11]

But it is in his darkest masterpiece, *Our Mutual Friend* (1865), that Dickens's friendship with Owen is related most explicitly to this divergence on the one hand from Social Darwinism, and on the other from the aesthetic demand for character development and realism. Here the idea of the newly discovered antiquity of man, for example, and the notion of an evolutionary regression are used satirically, to expose the primitive nature of the new capitalism. In this book Dickens returns to the often hilariously destructive contrast between a society's ideas of its own newness and the prehistoric, primitive struggle into which it has actually sunk, without knowing it. The famous picture of Gaffer Hexham, in the novel's opening, is an image of an evolutionary regression, a parody of Social Darwinism:

> Allied to the bottom of the river rather than the surface, by reason of the slime and ooze with which it was covered and its sodden state, this boat and the two figures in it were obviously doing something that they often did, and were seeking what they often sought. Half savage as the man showed, with no covering on his matted head, with his brown arms bare to between the elbow and the shoulder, with the loose knot of a looser kerchief lying low on his bare breast in a wilderness of beard and whisker, with such dress as he wore seeming to be made of the mud that begrimed the boat, still there was business-like usage in his steady gaze . . .[12]

London is a dark primaeval swamp. Narrator and reader, visitors from the future, creep up on two inhabitants of the present. The movement is characteristically backwards and downwards into the geological depths: by the 1860s, the fossil record had spread considerably.[13] The boat is already sunk, and resurrected like an archaeological version of a dugout. But paradoxically, in the metaphorical system of the book, this movement backwards and downwards into the depths only reveals the surfaces of things. Dickens's narrative is full of little metaphorical touches, small moments in which a huge retrogressive tract of time is suddenly revealed. For example, as Lizzie Hexham looks dreamingly at her pictures in the fire, Charley Hexham, her brother, interjects with a quite different perspective:

> 'Yes. Then as I sit a-looking at the fire, I seem to see in the burning coal – like where that glow is now –'
> 'That's gas, that is,' said the boy, 'coming out of a bit of the forest that's been under the mud that was under the water in the days of Noah's ark. Look here! When I take the poker – so – and give it a dig –'

(44)

Lizzie's dreamy old 'pictures in the fire' motif is violated and suddenly 'modernised' – ironically, it is Bradley Headstone's 'new' education which has revealed to Charley the fact that the world of the present is built on depths and layers much older than we conventionally think. But instead of constituting it, the knowledge only parodies real development in Charley.

The same pattern of regression is discernible in the description of the Six Jolly Fellowship Porters, which is a parody of growth and development:

> The wood forming the chimney-pieces, beams, partitions, floors, and doors of the Six Jolly Fellowship-Porters seemed in its old age fraught with confused memories of its youth. In many places it had become gnarled and riven, according to the manner of old trees; knots started out of it; and here and there it seemed to twist itself into the likeness of boughs. In this state of second childhood, it had an air of being in its own way garrulous about its early life. Not without reason was it often asserted by the regular frequenters of the Porters that when the light shone full upon the grain of certain panels and particularly upon an old corner cupboard of walnut wood in the bar, you might trace little forests there, like the parent tree, in full umbrageous leaf. (79–80)

This is a world going backwards, receding into its elements. The hilarious Silas Wegg is an evolutionary nightmare of the same type, his curious anatomy an explicit parody of organic growth and development:

> Wegg was a knotty man, and a close-grained, with a face carved out of very hard material that had just as much play of expression in it as a watchman's rattle. When he laughed, certain jerks occurred in it, and the rattle sprung. Sooth to say, he was so wooden a man that he seemd to have taken his wooden leg naturally, and rather suggested to the fanciful observer that he might be expected – if his development received no untimely check – to be completely set up with a pair of wooden legs in about six months.
>
> (63)

The homogeneities of this novel are 'wood' and 'slime' (and, of course, Dust) which underlie everything built. The Dust Heaps in which Wegg hops and pokes like 'some extinct bird' are known as the Dismal Swamp. Even the bran-new Veneering's dinner-party, the epitome of surfaces and reflections, not depths, modulates from a zoological view of Podsnap at the trough, into an evolutionary joke about Mrs Podsnap:

> Reflects Podsnap: prosperous feeding, two little light-coloured wiry wings, one on either side of his bald head, looking as like his hair brushes as his hair, dissolving view of red beads on his forehead, large

allowance of crumpled shirt-collar up behind. Reflects Mrs Podsnap:
fine woman for Professor Owen, quantity of bone, neck, and nostrils
like a rocking horse, hard-features, majestic head-dress in which
Podsnap has hung golden offerings.

(25)

Such was Owen's popular reputation by the 1860s that, whether we
assume a reader who knew *Household Words* or not, the allusion
immediately turns Mrs Podsnap into Dinornis, the Moa, the giant extinct
ostrich of New Zealand, whose skeleton Owen was famous for articulating.

Articulation, of course, is a great theme in this book;[14] it is used
(amongst other things) to parody both the organic version of the body
politic and the biological metaphor of social growth and development
which had been appropriated from Darwin and Huxley by Herbert
Spencer, and which was used by Lewes and George Eliot, increasingly in
the 1860s, as the fulcrum of a new aesthetic realism. There is a touch of
affectionate parody of Owen in the figure of the taxidermist, Mr Venus,
whose card reads 'Preserver of Animals and Birds' and 'Articulator of
Human Bones'; and whose workshop in Clerkenwell is the very emblem
of Dickens's resistance to the power of the organic analogy. Venus, the
Anatomist, recycles bits: his 'museum', as the narrator calls it, is at once a
pre-Joycean microcosm of the contingent nature of reality, and an
evolutionary burial ground of extinct organs and spare parts of the
Empire's once-proud body politic:

'Oh dear me, dear me!' sighs Mr Venus, heavily, snuffing the candle,
'the world that appeared so flowery has ceased to blow! You're casting
your rye round the shop, Mr Wegg. Let me show you a light. My
working bench. A wise. Tools. Bones, warious. Preserved Indian baby.
African ditto. Bottled preparations, warious. Everything within reach
of your hand, in good preservation. The mouldy ones a'top. What's in
those hampers over there again, I don't quite remember. Say, human
warious. Cats. Articulated English baby. Dogs. Ducks. Glass eyes,
warious. Oh dear me! that's the general panoramic view.'

(25)

The picture of Owen as a cockney taxidermist was a well-known joke.
After 'hippocampus minor', a satirical pamphlet entitled 'A Report of a
Sad Case . . .' appeared in 1863, just before Dickens began work on *Our
Mutual Friend*, in which Tom Huxley, 'well known about the town in
connection with monkeys', and Dick Owen, 'in the old bone and bird-
stuffing line', are arrested for causing a disturbance. The affair is tried

before the Lord Mayor of London. Each puts the case in Dickensian cockney. Here is part of Huxley's evidence:

> Huxley was now called upon, and said as follows:
> Me and Dick is in the same line – old bones, bird skins, offal, and what not.
> The Mayor – Do you mean the marine store line?
> Huxley – No, your worship; that's Bowerbank and Woodward's line of business. Well, as I was saying, we was in the same line, and comfortable as long as Dick Owen was top sawyer, and could keep over my head, and throw his dust down in my eyes. There was only two or three in our trade, and it was not very profitable; but that was no reason why I should be called a liar by an improved gorilla, like that fellow.
> [Here the Mayor cautioned the prisoner.]
> Well, in my business I put up monkeys, and the last monkey I put up was Dick Owen's .
> [Here the Mayor declared, on the repetition of such language, he would at once commit Huxley.]
> Well, as I was saying, Owen and me is in the same trade; and we both cuts up monkeys, and I finds something in the brains of 'em. Hallo ! says I, here's a hippocampus. No, there ain't, says Owen. Look here, says I. I can't see it, says he, and he sets to werriting and haggling about it, and goes and tells everybody, as what I finds ain't there, and what he finds is, and that's what no tradesman will stand. So when we meets, we has words. He will stick to his story, your worship, he won't be right himself, nor let anybody else be right. As to this here monkey business, I can't help the brutes treading on his heels. If he was to go forward more, why you see he'd be further off from the beast; but he's one of these here standstill Tories, what they call the orthodox lot, as never moves forward . . .[15]

Owen was essentially the type who got his hands dirty. His morning postbag, with its usual quota of odd bones, chimpanzees' heads and even pieces of buried wood, sent in by missionaries, explorers and marine engineers all over world from New Zealand to Jarrow, must have frequently resembled Mr Venus's shop. It is also possible that Dickens or Forster (a key link between them) knew that he had been experimenting for years with spirit preservation.[16]

The friendship between Dickens and Owen is significant, I think, in several ways. The intellectual and social make-up of the two men was very close and conditioned the tenor of their relationship. They both thrived on popularizing ideas. One should not underestimate what Dickens's magazines, particularly in later years, did for Owen; according to Ellgard, the circulation of *All The Year Round*, at certain periods, exceeded that of *The Times*.

On the other hand, I think Owen's view of the production of species is important for Dickens. Dickens, of course, was no scientist or even naturalist, but he was trained as a professional journalist and editor, and he had both a personal and a professional interest in promoting Owen's work and reputation. This meant that he was well informed about disputes in the natural sciences; but that, in so far as he took sides, he was quite firmly on 'the wrong side' in the Darwinist dispute. This is a crude reduction, however; we have come a long way in reassessing Owen's position since William Irvine's cold war absolutism about these mid-Victorian scientific disputes. Owen has been gradually rehabilitated since the 1950s. There is now, at last, a biography, and this is what his recent biographer, Nicholas Rupke, has to say about the nature of that rehabilitation process and how it relates to contemporary debate in biology:

> The gradual rehabilitation of Owen has been facilitated by a simultaneous re-evaluation of Darwinian theory. For example, the Lyellian gradualism implicit in Darwin's theory of natural selection, and the related reliance on the imperfection of the geological record – to which Owen did not subscribe – have been set aside in the punctuated equilibrium model of the history of life. Moreover, Stephen Jay Gould and others have re-emphasised the importance of form over function in explaining organic development, and as such have restored for present-day use a central plank of Owen's epistemological platform.[17]

Certainly, Owen was a complicated eclectic; a recent writer has summed up his notoriously elusive intellectual framework as follows:

> Owen combined the attributes of an Aristotelian systematist, a Cuvierian teleologist, an Okenian idealist, and a broad Church theist.[18]

His position was theistic and transcendentalist; but it should be stressed that it was not entirely undynamic. Ellgard, who places him at the centre of a spectrum between catastrophism and natural selection, calls his position 'derivation'.[19]

Perhaps what is more important is that Owen was a comparative anatomist, not a biologist. This meant that Dickens was mainly acquainted with controversies about the production, growth and development of species, through the promotion of a structural and not a functional view of the problem – 'economy of the type, not the instrument', as one of his writers put it. His *Household Words* writers explicitly develop this point in their reviews. Owen's view of things, as Huxley complained, really excluded an account of the development of the organism. On the other hand, Owen did not follow Oken's view that animals were, as he expressed it so sublimely, 'irregular men'. As Roy Mcleod puts it:

> Owen did not subscribe to this view, in which man was morphologically the measure of all things; indeed he was quite ready to combine a 'progressionist' outlook with his idealism, and have Nature proceed not from a human referent, but from one very like a fish.[20]

In this case, the exclusive pursuit of anatomy brings with it a curious freedom from the conventionally anthropomorphic.

I think this complex of attitudes may be significant for Dickens's representation of the body, and his use of anatomical metaphors to defamiliarise. Dickens is quite obsessed by the sheerly anatomical existence of the body, whether human or animal; and at the same time increasingly resistant to the seductive anthropomorphism of those organic metaphors of growth and development which Foucault thinks of in *The Order of Things* as the nineteenth-century episteme itself.

In *Our Mutual Friend*, the cross-purposes dialogue between Eugene and Mr Boffin about the bees, for example, in which the old anthropomorphic cliché falls under a rather confusing scrutiny and is made to rebound upon itself, seems emblematic of this point:

> 'I beg your pardon,' returned Eugene, with a reluctant smile, 'but will you excuse my mentioning that I always protest against being referred to the bees?'
>
> 'Do you!' said Mr Boffin.
>
> 'I object on principle,' said Eugene, 'as a biped –'
>
> 'As a what?' asked Mr Boffin.
>
> 'As a two-footed creature; I object on principle, as a two-footed creature, to being constantly referred to insects and four-footed creatures. I object to being required to model my proceedings

according to the proceedings of the bee, or the dog, or the spider, or the camel. I fully admit that the camel, for instance, is an excessively temperate person; but he has several stomachs to entertain himself with, and I have only one. Besides, I am not fitted up with a convenient cool cellar to keep my drink in.'

'But I said, you know,' urged Mr Boffin, rather at a loss for an answer, 'the bee.'

'Exactly. And may I represent to you that it's injudicious to say the bee? For the whole case is assumed. Conceding for a moment that there is any analogy between a bee and a man in pantaloons (which I deny), and that it is settled that the man has to learn from the bee (which I also deny), the question still remains, what is he to learn? To imitate? Or to avoid? When your friends the bees worry themselves to that highly fluttered state about their sovereign, and become perfectly distracted concerning the slightest monarchical movement, are we to learn the greatness of Tuft-hunting, or the littleness of the Court Circular? I am not clear, Mr Boffin, but that the hive may be satirical.'

'Nature' in the later Dickens is used almost exclusively to parody social and political processes. It was his journalistic campaign on behalf of Owen in the sphere of natural history which helped him, in part, to escape the anthropomorphic projection involved in the cult of the organism, and to remain outside those optimistic mid-century paradigms of growth and development which are such an important common feature in the discourse of both the biology and aesthetic realism.

Notes

1.   'The Limitations of Dickens', *The Nation*, I (1865) 786–7, repr. in *The Dickens Critics*, ed. G.H. Ford and L. Lane Jr (New York: Cornell University Press, 1961) 51.
2.   'Dickens in Relation to Criticism', *Fortnightly Review* (February, 1872) 141-54, repr. in Ford and Lane, eds., 65-6.
3.   See R. Ashton, *G.H. Lewes: A Life* (Oxford: Clarendon Press, 1991) 187.
4.   'Progress; Its Law and Cause', *Westminster Review* (1857), New Series, Vol. I, 446.
5.   Ibid., 455.
6.   Spencer, ibid., 455. For a contrast see G. Levine, *Darwin and the Novelists* (London, 1988) 154, on this point, who regards *Bleak House* as 'organicist'. But he is clearly following George Eliot and imposing a version of her organicism on Dickens, which is precisely the point I am putting at issue. Cf with Levine, the account of how Dickens treats the ramifying

complexity of society in Richard C. Maxwell, 'G.W.M. Reynolds, Dickens, and *The Mysteries of London'*, *Nineteenth-Century Fiction*, 32 (1977) 188–213.

7. For detailed discussions of relations between Dickens and Science (including Darwinism), see J. Politi, *The Novel and its Presuppositions* (Amsterdam, Rhodopi, 1976); G. Beer, *Darwin's Plots* (London, Routledge & Kegan Paul, 1983); and G. Levine, *Darwin and the Novelists* (Cambridge, Mass, Harvard University Press, 1988).

8. See Politi, *The Novel*, for a discussion of 'regression' in *Bleak House*.

9. *Bleak House* (New York, Signet, 1964) 22.

10. Ibid., 42.

11. See V. Sage, 'Dickens and Professor Owen: Portrait of a Friendship', *Portraits: Cahiers du centre de recherche*, Paris-Sorbonne IV, ed. P. Arnaud (in Press).

12. *Our Mutual Friend* (Signet; New American Library), p. 16. All subsequent references to this edition.

13. In 1861, on 26 January, *All the Year Round*, Vol. II, 237, carried an article about fossil remains called 'Earliest Man', in which the writer dramatised in mock-Dickensian fashion changes of opinion in the scientific world (which is personified as a Podsnap-like character) concerning the antiquity of human fossil remains. After recent examination of specimens found in the Brixham cavern in Devon, the writer appeals to Lyell Anstey and Owen as authorities in this dispute about the antiquity of man:

> Last dying speech and confession of scientific World was published by Professors OWEN and ANSTEY and SIR CHARLES LYELL, who assisted at the mournful ceremony . . . Professor Owen says that the flint weapons found in the gravel were 'unquestionably fashioned by human hands' (alas! poor Scientific World!) and Sir Charles Lyell expresses his conviction of 'a vast lapse of ages separating the era in which the fossil implements were formed and that of the invasion of Gaul by the Romans.'
>
> Accordingly, it is no longer scientific to doubt that weapons made by the rude warriors of primeval days are to be found in the strata containing the remains of the Mammoth. That human bones have not yet been met with is no argument.

This issue of the antiquity of man continued in the early 1860s to arouse considerable interest, partly because of its relation to Darwinian claims about gaps in the fossil record; and it is not surprising that Dickens had in his library Lyell's 1863 treatise, *Geological Evidence For the Antiquity of Man*. This book was duly boiled (probably by Wills) in a piece called 'How Old Are We?' on 7 March 1863, which concludes:

> The issue of all these researches is, in the opinion now held by geologists, that although man, whose traces are found only in the post tertiary deposits, is geologically a new comer upon earth, his antiquity is, nevertheless, much greater than chronologists have hitherto supposed. (*AYR*, Vol. IX, 37)

14. See Albert D. Hutter, 'Dismemberment and Articulation', *Dickens Studies Annual*, Vol.11 (1983) 135-75.

15. *A Report of a Sad Case, recently tried before the Lord Mayor, Owen versus Huxley, in which will be found fully given the merits of the recent great Bone Case* (London, 1863), p.6. This pamphlet is to be found in the archives of the Huxley Collection, Imperial College, London. For a discussion, see Ashton, *G.H. Lewes*, 215

16. Since the 1830s in fact. Adman Desmond, *Archetypes and Ancestors: Palaeontology in Victorian London, 1850-1875* (London, Blond & Biggs, 1984), refers to the discussions in Owen's notebook (Oct-Dec 1830) BM (NH) LOC.O.O.25, for October 1830, concerning the brains of apes and men and the problems of spirit preservation.

17. N. Rupke, *Richard Owen, Victorian Naturalists* (New Haven and London, Rupke, 1994) 10.

18. Roy Mcleod, 'Evolutionism and Richard Owen', *Isis*, 56, 259–80.

19. Alvar Ellgard, *Darwin and the General Reader: The Reception of Darwin's Theory of Evolution in the British Periodical Press, 1857-1872* (Goteborg, Rupke, 1958) 30.

20. Rupke, 278. Owen's anti-anthropomorphic position was not, however, inevitable for those who believed in the 'archetype' idea, as Nicholas Rupke shows:

> Thus according to Maclise's definition, the more highly developed a skeleton is, the closer it approximates to the archetype. Accordingly, the skeletons of humans and of the higher vertebrates were thought to come nearest to the archetype, and it was on these groups that the Comparative Osteology focused.
>
> This was the opposite of Owen's definition in which the archetype bore a resemblance to the lowest vertebrate class, namely fishes.
>
> (Rupke, 190)

Part IV
Dickens and Our World

19
Translating Dickens into French

Sylvère Monod

Having published translations of 7,000–8,000 pages of Dickens, but also done similar work for several other English authors, including the Brontës, Kipling, Conrad, Shakespeare and also Peter Ackroyd, I have sometimes been asked, or asked myself, which author I had found most difficult to translate. The answer is that there are no easy authors, that translation is always both exhilarating and excruciating to its perpetrator; in the last resort, one has to admit that the author who creates the greatest difficulties for you changes all the time, for he or she is the author of the book you are presently working on. All the others can be forgotten, or even forgiven.

Instead of blowing my own trumpet, I had better tackle the more general problem of translating Dickens into French. Several branches of the question require our attention: Why do we do it? Can we do it? How do we do it?

Our reasons for undertaking this difficult task are, I take it, sufficiently obvious. No one attending an international conference on Dickens needs to be reminded that he is a very great writer, that his works deserve to be read and offer lavish rewards to their readers. We can thus take it for granted that gaining new readers for Dickens is an eminently worthwhile pursuit. And, if our target is the French reading public, the Dickens novels have to be made more accessible by translation than they are in the original. In spite of the number of pupils and students in the French schools and universities who are taught *some* English, and in spite of the constantly improving quality of that teaching, not very many French people achieve sufficient knowledge of the language to be at home with Dickens in his native idiom. Whether Dickens is or isn't one of the most difficult writers to translate, he is certainly not one of the easiest ones to read, for a foreigner. Obstacles are created by some characteristics of Dickens's way of writing English that will in due course become sources of keen delight, but begin by acting as impediments to understanding and appreciation.

The next question, after we have convinced ourselves that translations of Dickens's novels are very much needed in France, comes quite naturally: Are not the existing translations easy enough to acquire, and are they not good enough? The reply is a little more complex than the previous one. There *is* one complete Dickens in French, or at least a complete French edition of Dickens's novels and stories; it does not include the travelogues, the articles and other minor pieces called uncollected; the French edition does not include the public readings nor, of course, the correspondence. Even so, that edition, which forms part of the glamorous Bibliothèque de la Pléiade, runs to nine volumes, each of which comprises about 1,500 pages; one can contend that, although not really complete, it offers to the average or general reader all that she or he needs or wishes to know of Dickens's contribution to literature. That Pléiade series, to which I contributed translations of *Pickwick* and *Barnaby Rudge* under my predecessor Pierre Leyris's editorship, and of which I edited the last three volumes myself, has much to recommend it: for instance, it is supposed to be always kept in print; it is rather better printed than most modern French books. But those Pléiade volumes suffer from the reputation of being preposterously expensive.

In any case, the Pléiade Dickens is by no means alone in the field. But its competitors have seldom been ambitious; some of the popular paperbacks reprint, sometimes anonymously, the oldest translations. And they remain incomplete, if not haphazard. A French reader can probably find a more or less decent *David Copperfield* or *Oliver Twist*, but a *Pickwick Papers* or even a *Great Expectations* is more unlikely to crop up, and a *Bleak House* is out of the question. Thus, Dickens is not absent from the contemporary French book trade, but he is not sufficiently represented on it, either in point of quantity or of permanence.

Besides, no one is likely to claim that the existing translations are wholly satisfactory. A satisfactory translation is in any case a contradiction in terms. A translator satisfied with her or his own work would be a dangerous person. For a translation can always be improved. I once claimed that learning to translate is learning to doubt, to doubt oneself, to take leave of one's certainties about at least two languages, and one's knowledge of them, but also about the author, about meaning, about equivalences. Yet, while it is true that no translation is perfect, or ever will be, it remains necessary to rest content with a certain stage that one has reached, because the publisher's deadline is fast approaching and also because the translator's resources – linguistic, literary, imaginative, mental, nervous – have long become exhausted and she or he has become incapable of further immediate improvement. One can have to be contented without being satisfied. Contentment differs from satisfaction, especially self-satisfaction. Also, it must be said that, if all translations are thus congenitally imperfect, some are more imperfect than others. The early translations of Dickens's novels, for instance, though they sometimes possessed a contemporary style and tone that no one can recapture or recreate nowadays, suffered from massive disadvantages. Among the members of the large team recruited by Louis Hachette in the early 1850s, for instance, there were people who did not know much English, or whose French was a little shaky; Dickens was treated to a dinner with the group whom he dubbed 'My French Dressers'; he sat next to an old man who occasionally spoke to him in a strange tongue which the novelist thought must be Russian; it turned out to be the old man's attempt to speak as much English as he knew how to; therefore, at the end of the dinner, Dickens addressed his translators in an elegant little speech (we have his own word for it, if no one else's), but, wisely, he chose to speak to them in French. So, those people made mistakes of all kinds and all calibres. I have often quoted some simple examples, like the confusion between a 'direction-post' and a post-office, or between a tray and a basket, or a mangle and a kitchen-table, or 'gloomily' and 'under-handedly', or the rendering of 'Nature lived hard by' as if it meant 'Nature found it hard to live'. In addition, most nineteenth-century translators acted on principles of their own, which would be indignantly rejected by our contemporaries. I mean that a man like the famous Amédée Pichot explicitly prided himself on his offhand treatment of *David Copperfield*. Pichot must be credited with coining a brilliant title for his translation, which he called *Le Neveu de ma tante*, thus involuntarily triggering off the inspiration of a rival: Chopin's version of the first third had been entitled *David Copperfield*, but the sequel became *La Nièce du Pêcheur*. Pichot did not really like Dickens's way of writing English and telling stories. Such a key-figure in the history of Dickens translation calls for brief illustration.

When Mr Dick is seen looking up at his kite in the sky, the traditional text reads simply: 'He never looked so serene as he did then'. The Pichot variant is more elaborate: 'One would have said that his mind also rose with that paper entrusted with his complaints, and gradually, with quiet hope, approached the throne of Him who is the sovereign judge of all our deeds and all our thoughts.' Conversely, when David analyses his relationship to the adorable Miss Shepherd, he does so at some length:

'Why do I secretly give Miss Shepherd twelve Brazil nuts for a present, I wonder? They are not expressive of affection; they are difficult to pack into a parcel of any regular shape; they are hard to crack, even in room doors, and they are oily when cracked. Yet I feel they are appropriate to Miss Shepherd. Soft, seedy biscuits, also, I bestow upon Miss Shepherd; and oranges innumerable.'

Pichot may have thought Dickens was indulging himself in an undignified manner; or he may have found it difficult to render, or even to understand some particulars. In any case, his translation of the whole paragraph has been severely curtailed; it consists only of 'Que de bonbons j'offre à Miss Shepherd! que d'oranges!' (How many sweets I present to Miss Shepherd! How many oranges!) The Brazil nuts have disappeared. Yet the most amazing difference between *David Copperfield* and Pichot's *Neveu* consists in the omission of six complete chapters, all concerned with the abduction of Little Em'ly by the villainous Steerforth; obviously Pichot disapproved of the episode and refused to connive in it in any way. Such, at any rate, was his inventive but incomplete *Neveu de ma tante*.

I think that on the whole we have given up such practices. But for many decades they prevailed; and the resulting translations have been reprinted many times; some are still available in our bookshops. They may be the clearest justification of the need for new translations. Not that the new translations will be infallibly right. It was in the 1960s, I believe, that a new translation of *Our Mutual Friend* rendered 'coffee-pot' (on the breakfast table) by *boîte à café* (coffee-box, or tin)! But probably no one today would dare to do what Pichot's contemporaries did: printing side by side Dickens's address to French readers and its translation, they improved on it. While Dickens had complimented them on having bravely combated the difficulties of his text, the translation said that they had *vaincu* (vanquished) the same difficulties. There you have the whole drama of translation in a nutshell: a translator can and must combat, he can never hope to vanquish.

In any case, no justification ought to be necessary. Modern criticism by and large recognises that each new generation of readers has a right to new versions of the great classical works. It has always been the case with Homer and Sophocles, Virgil and Dante. I have just read that since the invention of printing 36 different French versions of the *Aeneid* have been published. And of course the same is true of Shakespeare, especially when the new version is intended for the stage. To a certain extent at least, it is also true of Dickens and Thackeray and George Eliot (as also, no doubt, conversely, of Balzac and Stendhal and Flaubert). If Dickens, like Shakespeare, can be called our contemporary, he will deserve that label yet more clearly if he is read by non-Anglophones in contemporary translations.[1]

Since all existing French translations of Dickens are grievously imperfect, I hope the effort to provide better ones will be recognized as a major need of the French publishing trade.

Yet, if it is undeniably true that we must go on translating Dickens into French, can we do so? Is Dickens, in fact, translatable at all? A rough-and-ready answer might be that Dickens was a fantastically creative and forceful writer, and that no one can hope to convey all of his style through a foreign translation. Anyone living much of the time on the frontier between English and French is bound to realise that those two langages are so different from each other as to be almost antagonistic to each other. Passing from one to the other, we not only do not say the same things in the same way: we do not say the same things, full stop. But that is precisely the kind of difficulty that the translator has to struggle against and if possible to overcome. A fascinating task always. And it seems to me that Dickens is more extraordinarily English in his handling of language than most of his compatriots. It would take too long fully to substantiate this statement. I shall use only one example, again one that I have employed more than once for its singular illustrative value. It could be said of Dickens, as it was said of Shakespeare, I think, that he treated the English language as if it belonged to him and not he to it. My slight, but growing, experience of translating Shakespeare has made me realise that indeed the dramatist used all the resources of an enviably flexible and even malleable tongue. Just think of the line in which it is said of a certain gory hand that it would rather 'the multitudinous seas incarnadine' than be washed by them. Like all lovers of language, of poetry and of English, I cherish that line; but I am not ready to offer a French equivalent of it; the French do not incarnadine multitudinous seas; we have no 'mers multitudineuses' to 'incarnadiner'.

There are at least two Dickens sentences that, in their different way, pose the same kind and calibre of problem to the French translator. They are to be found respectively in *Martin Chuzzlewit* and in *David Copperfield*, and there is an obvious kinship between them. Here they are, in descriptions of Mrs Gamp and Mrs Crupp. Mrs Gamp first:

> And with innumerable leers, winks, coughs, nods, smiles, and curtseys, all leading to the establishment of a mysterious and confidential understanding between herself and the bride, Mrs. Gamp, invoking a blessing upon the house, leered, winked, coughed, nodded, smiled, and curtseyed herself out of the room.

That is sufficiently intractable, no doubt; phrases like 'coughed herself out of the room' sound extremely unFrench. But in Mrs Crupp's case,

Dickens unquestionably goes one better when he writes:

> Mrs Crupp, who had been incessantly smiling to express sweet temper, and incessantly holding her head on one side, to express a general feebleness of constitution, and incessantly rubbing her hands, to express a desire to be of service to all deserving objects, gradually smiled herself, one-sided herself, and rubbed herself out of the room.

The principle is the same, but greater refinement and more esoteric manipulation are practised. This time the difficulty does not lie merely in the unusual form of a perfectly understandable phrase; there is added to that the fact that several phrases, like 'to one-side oneself' or 'to rub oneself out of a room', carry no meaning whatsoever outside of a very specific context. Dickens's English in such cases is entirely his own. We have here the illustration of his fantastically forceful treatment, or manhandling, of language. It must provide much delight to all true lovers of language, and particularly of English, with the temporary exception of his poor literary translators.

English and French, as we saw, are widely different languages. Dickens's English is highly idiosyncratic in addition, and always along the lines that characterise English and make it so nearly inaccessible to a normally constituted French mind and pen. That is the major and permanent difficulty that confronts the French translator of Charles Dickens's works. She or he will encounter many other obstacles. Not to speak of the old bugbears encountered at every stage by every translator of English into French; they are not specific to Dickens, but he does not spare us the problems of finding equivalents for *gentleman*; and the choice between *tu* and *vous* to render 'you' admits of no easy, ready-made solutions. More typical of Dickens, at least by their frequency, are the problems raised by proper names, so often evocative, or jocularly meaningful.

Then, isn't there something called Dickens's humour? And isn't humour reputedly untranslatable, especially into French, the idiom of a notoriously humourless nation. And when one has recognised the general truth of that statement, and described one or two partial exceptions, what else is there to be done? Suffice it, then, to say that among the many ways in which Dickens amuses his readers, some are more likely than others to defeat the would-be translator. Wordplay is of course unsubtle, but that does not make it plain sailing to the translator. On the contrary, in Dickens, as in Shakespeare for that matter, considerable labour and infinite ingenuity will be required to achieve what is almost bound to be in the end a disappointing result. The French translator can also feel challenged, and occasionally defeated by the cold-bloodedness of the Sam Weller stories, not to speak of the Weller spelling: 'Put it down a wee, my Lord' is a hard enough nut to crack. Obviously the Dickens novel lives most of the time in the higher spheres of humour, and where perception of character and the implied criticism, and especially self-criticism amount to an amusingly illuminating *Weltanschauung*, no harm can result from the translator's trying his or her hand at the production of a similar, if not identical, effect in French. Examples are difficult to exhibit in isolation and might sound unconvincing, where what counts is the overall impression conveyed by a paragraph, an episode or a complete character. Many of the Dickens characters are individualised by their speech; they use idiolects; just think of Mrs Gamp and try to imagine what can be done in French, or in any foreign language, with the speech of this immortal woman of whom it was well said that Gamp was her name, and Gamp her nater.

In the same way, the passages of poetical prose, where Dickens's language achieves intrinsic beauty through a kind of simplification and purity, as in the opening paragraphs of the Retrospect chapters of *David Copperfield*, are a challenge to the translator. In such cases, more than ever, what seems to be called for is a kind of recreation in the foreign language of the subtle effect produced in the original, and the recreation must be obtained according to the resources peculiar to the foreign language. Again, we have to realise that French is infinitely less flexible than English. Yet, the challenge may be faced, in so far as poetry is concerned, because we all realise that poetry, and prose poetry, *have* been produced by French writers, and so, why not?

Having reconciled ourselves to the belief that, since we must translate Dickens, we can more or less do it, we still have to define methods that will ensure, not of course complete success, but the avoidance of too blatant and scandalous failure.

There are no unfailing recipes. But there are the usual golden rules of the profession. For instance, most of us recognise that it is the translator's duty to combine ambition and humility. The ambition of doing one's best at all times, of surpassing oneself, of sparing no efforts in order to understand fully every nuance of the text, of untiringly groping for the best possible French equivalent, of consulting as many sources of information as are likely to enlighten us, books and persons, whenever we are in doubt. At the same time, one has to remain humble, not 'umble' like Uriah Heep, whose humility is affected as a disguise for his fanatical ambition and as a tool for rising in society, but genuinely humble in one's acceptance of the superior claims of the persons and things one is supposed to be serving: the author, the text, the reading public (and to a certain extent one's publisher also, who may be regarded as the founder of the feast – of the financial feast at any rate, such as it is – and who therefore has the right to impose attitudes and procedures linked to the house-style followed in the firm). The translator's humility consists in never trying to appear clever, never substituting his or her own style (if he or she happens to possess such a thing) for the author's, never attempting to correct or improve the text.

If one can strike a middle course between these two apparently conflicting claims, there remains the choice with which all translators are faced at some point in their career, between literal faithfulness and freer readability. My own practice has for many years been guided by the third golden rule of the art, which I call identity of effect. It means that a translation ought to produce on the French reader an impression as closely similar as possible to that produced on the English reader by the original text. It is one of those things that are easier said than done, but it helps in some cases. When we are tempted to be too literal in the rendering of a phrase that is intensely English in its structure, we may ask ourselves how far this is likely to strike a non-English-speaking French audience. It is not impossible to gain a little more fidelity of a different kind, at the expense of literalness; what was so eminently genuine English in Dickens's text ought to become eminently French in the translation.

Once the general rules have been assimilated by the translator, the other principles tend to be only the small change of their gold. For instance, the commonplace notion that the translation has to contain all that is in the original and nothing that is not in it. Or the idea that one should render the same word by the same word, and different words by different words. Such rules are sound, though they require to be applied with a certain amount of flexibility. Yet, when an English author uses in one paragraph many different words describing sounds or shades of light, borrowed from sequences like *shine/gleam/glimmer/glitter/glisten/shimmer/glare/flare/flash*, we are simply unable to follow suit because French lacks that variety. In that field, at least, Mr Podsnap was right to call English a 'copious' language. French is admittedly less 'copious', though it has its points, undoubtedly.

I must have appeared pessimistic about the result of the translator's efforts, and it is true that after half a century in the profession, I realise that that result can never be unquestionably good or wholly satisfactory. Yet some more optimistic observations can also be made at this point. For instance, if Dickens's translator lets the spirit of Dickens blow through her or his work and carry him or her along with it, something of the fantastic creative energy that informs and animates the great writer's prose will come through and be put across to the French reader. That creative energy is in fact so powerful that it can never be rendered in its entirety, but neither can it be entirely kept out.

Also, even when realising that there are defects in one's translations – as there are bound to be – having published them gives one the sense, the certainty, very rare in the academic and scholarly profession, of having done something real, something truly useful.

I hope I have not entirely failed to make my main point, which is that translating Dickens into French has not been pure delight all the time. It has little to do with 'cakes and ale'. It has taken me through dark periods of excruciating and hopeless struggle. Yet I am tempted to sing with Edith Piaf that 'je ne regrette rien', I regret nothing, for, now that the play is played out and I can look back serenely at my life's work, I realise that I have enjoyed an extraordinarily privileged position. It is obvious that to some extent all university professors enjoy certain great privileges, in that an enormous proportion of the work they have to do is interesting; more, I firmly believe, than must be enjoyed by members of most other professions. But a scholar whose subject happens to be Dickens is in an even more favourable position than most other denizens of the groves of Academe. Just think that one might become an expert, that many in fact do become experts, on Beowulf, or Burke, or Bagehot, or whoever; all perfectly respectable and no doubt legitimate subjects for a lifetime's dedication. I hope it isn't chauvinism or self-centredness that makes me think Dickens is a rather brighter companion than many other English writers. Nor is that the only difference between him and them. Because Dickens was my subject, I have been asked by several French publishers to work for them. Sometimes this has led to a branching out into new fields, like Thackeray, the Brontës, Kipling, Galsworthy, but Dickens was the only begetter of my career as a literary translator. If I had begun with Beowulf, Burke or Bagehot, I am by no means sure French publishers would have shown similar interest; very few French publishers know the work, or even the existence of such authors. Then, in some cases, there have been reprints of several Dickens translations. I may confess that I have made money in the Dickens industry. An academic is supposed to care little for such material rewards, but I can assure you that I never found it disagreeable or degrading to receive occasional cheques for honest work. Nor were those the only bounties that I owe to the attention attracted by Dickens: such have been invitations to talk about Dickens in some distant parts of the world. In that kind of career the choice of the right author at the outset is of paramount importance. If one *does* choose the first author. Perhaps the translator is in a way chosen, or violently attracted, by the author in question.

All of this is immensely satisfactory, but I would like to say that what counts most of all is the fact that, in spite of difficulties and ordeals, I have on the whole enjoyed myself in my career to an abnormal extent.

In short, while hoping that translations serve an author's reputation abroad, and that I have thus done a little something for Dickens, I gratefully recognise that Dickens has done much much more, has done in fact everything, for his French translator.

Note

1. At this point, I went on to illustrate the deficiencies of all French versions of Dickens by relating my adventures with David Copperfield's 'pocket nutmeg-grater'. That section of the lecture is omitted here because it has already found its way into print in Michael Hollington's 'Reflections on a pocket nutmeg-grater (after Sylvère Monod)'. See Sara Thornton, ed., *Lecture d'une œuvre: David Copperfield de Charles Dickens* (Paris: Editions du Temps, 1996).

20

Dickens and Diaspora

John O. Jordan

The opportunity – and the challenge – afforded by a volume of essays devoted to 'Dickens, Europe, and the New Worlds' lies in its invitation to consider Dickens in a global perspective. Not that Dickens's stature as a world writer has ever been seriously in doubt: the many translations of his novels into languages other than English and the acknowledged influence of his work on writers as widely situated as Dostoevsky, Galdós, Kafka and Faulkner provide ample evidence of his continuing presence as an international cultural force. One aspect of Dickens's position as a world writer that has received relatively little notice, however, is the response given to his work by writers outside of Europe and the United States, especially in what we might think of as the greater Anglophone diaspora of the former British Empire.

Recent developments in what has come to be known as post-colonial literary studies have drawn attention to the ways in which canonical British writers such as Shakespeare, Austen and Defoe participate in and even underwrite the enterprise of European colonial expansion. Rather than focus on Dickens's participation in nineteenth-century discourses of empire, however, in this essay I wish to examine a different aspect of his relation to the 'new worlds' hinted at in the title of the present volume, namely the uses made of his work by selected writers and intellectuals from the former British colonies in the period since 1945. My project thus resembles that of critics who have studied the post-colonial revisioning of canonical European texts like *Jane Eyre*, *Robinson Crusoe* and *The Tempest*. While to my knowledge there has thus far been only one attempt to rewrite an entire Dickens novel from a post-colonial perspective (*Magwitch* [1982] by the Australian writer, Michael Noonan), many writers from the former colonies have adapted pieces of Dickens or have used him as a reference point for their work. It is these allusions, references and partial appropriations that I wish to examine.

For purposes of this essay, I am interested less in questions of influence, that is of relations between individual writers, than in questions of intertextuality, of relations between texts. For this reason, I consider 'Dickens' not so much an author as a form of cultural capital exported from Britain to the world (in the form of radio scripts, films, theatrical and television adaptations, school syllabuses and curricula, as well as printed texts) and consumed, rejected, appropriated or transformed by local Anglophone elites. In what follows, I sketch the outlines of an investigation that I intend to pursue in greater detail, and I give examples of four writers from different parts of the world who engage in one way or another with the imperial legacy of Great Britain and the cultural legacy of English literature as embodied in the figure of Charles Dickens.

In the post-1945 era of British imperial decline, 'Dickens' emerged as an important vehicle for consolidating and reasserting English national identity both at home and abroad. Although excluded, except as an afterthought (and then only for his least typical novel), from F.R. Leavis's 'great tradition', Dickens retained much of the broad-based popularity in Britain that he had enjoyed during the nineteenth century. Audiences that had lived through the war were eager to renew connection with the humane, liberal traditions of the past, and Dickens provided a convenient figure around whom the project of cultural recovery could be organised. Institutions including the Arts Council and the BBC promoted Dickens in one form or another for the benefit of larger and more diverse sections of the population. The success of David Lean's two film adaptations, *Great Expectations* (1946) and *Oliver Twist* (1948), not only helped to revive the sagging British film industry after the war but confirmed Dickens's position as a sign of Englishness in the national cultural imaginary.

Eccentric characters, pubs and coaching inns, Christmas cheer, a tolerant liberal state characterised by benevolent paternalism – these qualities, or something like them, came to be associated with 'Dickens' and were subsequently reproduced and disseminated by BBC radio scripts, stage musicals (*Oliver!*), feature films and, eventually, serialised television adaptations. Something very like this trajectory with respect to the fortunes of *A Christmas Carol* has been traced by Paul Davis in his excellent book, *The Lives and Times of Ebenezer Scrooge*. Theatrical adaptations, beginning in his own time, have always been one of the principal ways in which Dickens's novels were repackaged and circulated to new audiences. More recently, with the success of Trevor Nunn's production of *Nicholas Nickleby* and the popularity of various 'Masterpiece Theatre' adaptations of his work, Dickens can be said almost to have reached the point of rivalling Shakespeare as England's national playwright.

The place of 'Dickens' in the colonies during the post-war period can be correlated, to a considerable extent, with his reputation at home. Cheap editions and popular reprints had, of course, made his novels available to generations of educated readers throughout the British Empire. To the extent that 'Dickens' was perceived somehow as representative of the English national character, his name became a token in the post-war colonialist and anti-colonialist debates. Many of these debates were staged around issues of education. Among the educated elite, reading Dickens or owning a set of his works was considered a sign, if not of allegiance to the Crown, at least of a predisposition toward metropolitan cultural values and membership in the middle class. For nationalists, on the contrary, 'Dickens' became a handy shorthand term to designate the imposition of a foreign curriculum on local populations and the implicit denigration of indigenous culture.

The Trinidadian writer Ralph de Boissière analyses the situation as follows. Local elites in Trinidad 'attached themselves to British culture without becoming cultured,' he writes.

> British education was designed to black out Negro culture and inculcate a deep sense of one's inferiority to foreign whites, with whom culture was supposed to originate. But did the middle class really absorb this British culture? Is it possible to absorb completely the culture of a country in which you have never lived? Dickens, Galsworthy, Fielding: snow, fog, springtime, white Christmases; Parliament, public school ethics, the nobility – do you *absorb* all that? it lies on you like an ill-fitting, oversize coat, a ridiculous disguise, a cast-off garment given a poor orphan.
>
> (in Sander, 5)

Although de Boissière is speaking here specifically of the pre-war period in Trinidad, his comments are applicable to other colonial contexts and to later periods as well. Moreover, his use of the ill-fitting coat as a figure for cultural assimilation anticipates similar metaphors of travesty and disguise that appear in other post-colonial writing.

At the same time that 'Dickens' figured negatively in the political culture wars of independence, 'he' retained his appeal to colonial writers as a possible model or ally in that struggle, in a way that distinguishes him, I think, from Shakespeare. Whereas post-colonial writers generally write *against* Shakespeare, and in particular, against *The Tempest*, they tend to write *with* Dickens, or at least initially so. It is surprising how many writers from the colonies mention Dickens in response to questions about how they first became interested in literature. They often cite Oliver

Twist or other figures in his books as characters with whom they identified at an early age. Writers frequently report that their parents owned a set of Dickens or that they discovered his books while they were at school. In one way or another Dickens often appears as an important figure in the accounts of how they became writers. Dickens in this sense is identified more with 'literature' than with Englishness, and if there is any hesitation or ambivalence about the original positive response to his writing on account of his identification with the imperial power, it usually comes as a second thought, after the confession of a first positive attraction has been made.

The powerful appeal of Dickens can be documented in statements by Anglophone writers from around the world. This is not necessarily to argue for his influence, but only to note how often Dickens's name appears as a positive sign in the myths of origin constructed by colonial writers. Typical, both in the enthusiasm of its response and its emphasis on early spontaneous attraction, is the following statement by Nigerian writer Wole Soyinka. 'When I was a child,' writes Soyinka,

> I *devoured* Dickens. I think there is hardly any volume of Dickens' work that I have not read. There was something that fascinated me about the kind of life he depicted and I remember that in school I read literally all Dickens' novels.
>
> (Wilkinson, 102)

Alongside the conventionally sentimental and stereotypic images of 'Dickens', other more complicated versions persisted: Dickens the social critic, driven by a strong sense of outrage at class injustice; Dickens the magical realist, haunted by scenes of violence and grotesque comedy; Dickens the verbal fantasist, creating the world out of language. In many of their thematic concerns and their formal and linguistic excessiveness, such 'other' versions of Dickens provided colonial and post-colonial writers with attractive models of resistance to dominant discourses, thereby anticipating and at times directly enabling their struggle for cultural autonomy. Despised as well as admired, at once the sign of conventional Englishness and a source of its potential deconstruction, 'Dickens' thus became a complex site of cultural conflict and negotiation for writers in different parts of the world.

Many of the intertextual references to Dickens by colonial and post-colonial writers are relatively brief, but brevity does not always mean that they are insignificant. For example, Dickens is briefly invoked twice at a crucial point toward the end of V.S. Naipaul's *A House for Mr. Biswas* (1961). A comic-pathetic figure, modelled loosely on Naipaul's own father, Biswas works as a reporter for a local Trinidadian newspaper in Port of Spain, where he achieved local celebrity for his colourful, quirky human interest stories. When his sympathetic and supportive editor, a Mr Burnett, is forced to resign, however, a new, conservative regime takes over, and Biswas is demoted. No longer a feature writer, he is assigned to cover court cases, funerals and cricket matches. Despondent, he dreams of starting his own magazine and pursuing the literary career he has long imagined for himself. At first, he reads political books, but finds that their rhetoric of misery and injustice leaves him feeling more helpless and isolated than ever. 'Then it was', the narrator continues,

> that he discovered the solace of Dickens. Without difficulty he transferred characters and settings to people and places he knew. In the grotesques of Dickens everything he feared and suffered from was ridiculed and diminished, so that his own anger, his own contempt became unnecessary, and he was given strength to bear with the most difficult part of his day: dressing in the morning, that daily affirmation of faith in oneself, which at times was for him almost like an act of sacrifice.
>
> (337–8)

Dickens not only provides 'solace' for Biswas in his position as a marginal colonial intellectual, but becomes the common ground between Biswas and his son, Anand.

> He shared his discovery with Anand; and though he abstracted some of the pleasure of Dickens by making Anand write out and learn the meanings of difficult words, he did this not out of his strictness or as part of Anand's training. He said, 'I don't want you to be like me.'
> Anand understood. Father and son, each saw the other as weak and vulnerable, and each felt a responsibility for the other, a responsibility which, in times of particular pain, was disguised by exaggerated authority on the one side, exaggerated respect on the other.
>
> (338)

Shortly thereafter, Anand records an entry in his diary in which he dutifully identifies himself with a character from Dickens: 'I feel like Oliver Twist in the workhouse' (355).

The significance of these brief Dickensian moments in the text lies in their suggestion that it is through imaginative literature of the highest order that one comes to terms with the world and eventually exercises control over it. Dickens here replaces the romantic Marie Corelli, the naive Samuel Smiles, and the stoic Marcus Aurelius as Biswas's preferred literary guide and model. Rather than a ridiculous, ill-fitting disguise (to use the metaphor invoked by de Boissière), Dickens becomes more like a protective inner garment that Biswas puts on to help shield himself from the humiliations of everyday life. The understanding that Biswas and Anand share is their common commitment to the discipline of writing as a means of coping with and transcending the pettiness of colonial society. And although Biswas never realises his dream of becoming an author, by the end of the novel Anand has won a scholarship and left Trinidad to study in England, where presumably he (like Naipaul) will pursue his own literary ambitions. Like the workhouse Oliver with whom he identifies, Anand wants 'more' than Trinidad has to offer and more than his father is ever able to achieve there. It is no surprise, therefore, that he chooses to leave for England, though his success as an exile in the land of Dickens is by no means assured as the book comes to a close.

A more extended instance of Dickensian intertextual appropriation in a post-colonial context can be found in a play, suggestively entitled *Modest Expectations*, by the Australian playwright David Allen, first performed in 1990. The play is set in the 'Iron Pot' theatre in Melbourne in 1868, so named after the prefabricated metal auditorium that Australian theatrical impresario George Coppin imported from England in 1854 to form the shell of his Olympic Theatre. The play imagines a sequence of events that might have happened if the ageing Dickens, accompanied by a lusty young Ellen Ternan, had come to Australia towards the end of his life to perform a series of dramatic readings. The action of the play follows Dickens and Ellen as they encounter first Coppin, the vulgar, good-humoured manager of the Iron Pot who has brought Dickens to Australia, and then Dickens's son Plorn (Edward Bulwer Lytton Dickens), who had actually emigrated to Australia in 1868 and was living there at the time of Dickens's supposed visit.

The Dickens of *Modest Expectations* is a snobbish, irritable, egotistical old man, full of condescension towards colonial society and at the same time threatened by its vitality. Ostensibly he and Ellen have come to Australia in order to be alone together in public, free from the prying eyes and malicious gossip that force them to conceal their relationship at home. Yet Dickens is unable to escape the past and unwilling to respond to Ellen's invitations to enjoy a more open, uninhibited sexuality. Jealous of his son and his mistress on account of their youth, at one point he deliberately humiliates Plorn for no reason other than his suspicion that Ellen may be sexually attracted to him. The Iron Pot theatre functions as a kind of nightmare memory chamber. 'There's an echo,' Dickens says early in the play. 'I can hear everything coming back at me!' (6) What 'comes back' at him in the play's second act are nightmare images from his early life, disguised as figures such as Magwitch and Micawber whom he had exiled to the colonies in his fiction. What also comes back are fears and fantasies from his present life – old age, the loss of sexual and imaginative power, and the approach of death.

The figure who presides over this theatre of humiliation – and who in the end holds out the promise of mediation and reconciliation – is Coppin. Whereas Dickens is unable to escape the past, Coppin looks with 'modest expectations' toward the future and toward his next theatrical productions. The play's crisis comes when Ellen announces her intention to leave Dickens and remain in Australia to pursue her acting career, perhaps with Coppin as her sponsor. In a key thematic speech, Ellen tells Dickens her reasons for preferring Australia to England:

> Oh, I know what England means for you. Honour, tradition, fame. All its comforts – even its own special discomforts – and of course, it's [sic] history. History means so much to you, Charles. You couldn't live without the past. But for me – well, frankly, I find it rather stifling. (54)

Tired, worn down by illness and hemmed in on every side by his Englishness, Dickens is very much an Old World figure in the play. In opposition to him stands the New World figure of Coppin, the crass, outspoken, but eternally optimistic colonial entrepreneur. In the end, however, Coppin and Dickens turn out not to be so different after all. The play's allegory of national temperaments is allowed to collapse when Coppin, in a burst of patriotic fervour, proclaims Australia to be in effect a creation of the true Dickensian spirit. 'Look at us,' he tells Dickens:

> Rich, colourful, tragic, enterprising, vigorous, corrupt, eccentric, belligerent, democratic – and full of life. Straight out of one of your three-volumed novels. If Australia hadn't existed, you would have invented us!
> (57)

What is being contested and finally affirmed here is the literary and cultural legacy of Dickens in the colonial context. Dickens the famous author returns home to England, but his spirit, embodied in Ellen, Plorn and especially Coppin, has emigrated and resettled in Australia.

A third example of Dickensian intertextuality with a post-colonial twist is the novel, *The Mutual Friend* (1978), by the contemporary American writer, Frederick Busch. An ambitious meditation on language, creativity and death that takes Dickens as its subject, *The Mutual Friend* explores the borderland between biography and fiction in ways that anticipate the fictional inter-chapters in Peter Ackroyd's massive Dickens biography of 1990. Whereas Ackroyd separates his own inventions from the body of his biographical narrative, however, Busch weaves fact and fantasy together, drawing on Edgar Johnson's biography and integrating passages from Dickens's letters and public reading texts as well as from other nineteenth-century sources.

Like *Modest Expectations*, *The Mutual Friend* focuses on the ageing Dickens and on his relationship with the people in his immediate circle, notably his manager and amanuensis, George Dolby, who accompanied Dickens on his final reading tour of America and who published his own memoir, *Charles Dickens as I Knew Him*, in 1885. The novel opens in the winter of 1899 in a London charity hospital where Dolby, dying of tuberculosis and consuming large quantities of cheap gin smuggled to him by an obliging hospital worker known as 'Moon', fills sheet after sheet of paper with reminiscences of Dickens's final years. The novel has six sections and several different narrative voices, each one introduced by Dolby from his 'coughing ward'. First Dolby speaks, then a young ex-prostitute named Barbara who once worked as a kitchen maid at Gad's Hill, then Catherine Dickens, then Dolby again, then Ellen Ternan, and finally Dickens himself. The presence of so many female voices among the narrators is an indication of Busch's awareness of the need for a feminist revision of Dickens's life and career.

Although each of the narrative voices is distinct and powerfully realised, it gradually becomes clear that all of them belong to Dolby. Dolby's is thus the voice behind the voices in much the same way that Dickens as author orchestrates the voices of all his fictional characters. There is even the suggestion that Dolby himself may somehow be an avatar of Dickens, who comes to life and speaks again in the pages produced by the dying Dolby. One of the novel's central themes is the power of language to transform and supersede reality. Dickens the man, with all his frailties and limitations, is mercilessly exposed to view, but Dickens the performer – and the words he writes – remains a vital and enduring force.

The novel takes an unexpected post-colonial turn in its closing pages when a previously unheard voice seizes control of the narrative to describe the death of Dolby. The tag phrase, 'Moon here', which Dolby had previously used to signal the presence of his supplier of illegal liquor, now assumes different meaning as the signature of this new narrator. 'Moon', we learn, is not even his real name – only a colonial imposition. A 'one-eyed nigger baby from Her Majesty's bleeding last Empire', as he ironically calls himself, Moon served formerly 'at home' (i.e. presumably in India) on the staff of 'an unimportant Major of Horse' (211) and has now taken up residence in London, where he works in the charity hospital, preferring the independence of this miserable job to the indignity of domestic service.

From his position as witness to the death of Dolby and audience to the narrated death of Dickens, Moon reflects more generally on the century's end, including the so-called 1899 'Boxer Rebellion' in China, and links these events to the historical decline of England as a world power and the 'shrinking [of] the Empire's spheres of influence' (212). As the heir to Dolby's manuscript, Moon becomes in effect his literary executor, his John Forster, as he delights in pointing out. Unwilling to be 'imprisoned by language', he vows to 'rewrite the lives old Dolby set down, his and his Chief's and my own' (219). Moon's final words – and the final words of the novel – are, 'I will make changes' (220) – changes, presumably, not just in Dolby's manuscript, but in the European literary tradition, including Dickens, to which he now stands as heir.

By turning over the novel's narration at the end to Moon, Busch suggests a parallel between the decline of the British Empire at the turn of the century and the post-Vietnam experience of America in the 1970s. Moon, he suggests, may signal the political and cultural emergence of Third World peoples not only in the colonial outposts but in the metropolitan centre as well. In specifically literary terms, Moon's announced intention to 'make changes' in the words passed down from Dickens to Dolby to himself anticipates the arrival of writers like Naipaul, Rushdie and even Busch himself, who are prepared to rewrite Dickens from the perspective of colonial and post-colonial experience. In this respect, it is interesting to note that, unlike David Allen's *Modest Expectations*, *The Mutual Friend* dispenses with generational metaphors of family and lineage that suggest the notion of cultural inheritance. For Allen, Dickens is literally and figuratively a father (i.e. source and origin); whereas Busch breaks the paternal metaphor and suggests a more radical and transformational relationship. Dickens is Dolby's 'Chief', but not Moon's.

My final example of post-colonial Dickensian intertextuality is a passage from Salman Rushdie's *The Satanic Verses* (1988). Toward the end of the novel, Rushdie's protagonist, Saladin Chamcha, attends a party on the sound stage of a London film studio where a musical adaptation of Dickens's *Our Mutual Friend* is in production. The film, entitled *Friend!*, is reported to have been a 'mammoth hit in the West End and on Broadway, in spite of the macabre nature of some of its scenes' (421). When he arrives at the party, Saladin is amazed to discover a condensed simulacrum of the novel's many London settings, jumbled together 'according to the imperatives of film' (422) without regard for logic or actual topographical proximity. The people at the party are a similarly confused and confusing mixture. 'Society grandees, fashion models, film stars, corporation bigwigs, a brace of minor royal Personages, useful politicians and suchlike riff-raff perspire and mingle in these counterfeit streets with numbers of men and women as sweat-glistened as the "real" guests and as counterfeit as the city: hired extras in period costume, as well as a selection of the movie's leading players' (422). Events at the party unfold in a dream-like sequence. As a chorus of 'bosomy ladies in mob-caps and frilly blouses, accompanied by an over-sufficiency of stovepipe-hatted gents,' breaks into song, Saladin is pushed into a fake half-timbered building identified as 'The Old Curiosity Shop', where an inebriated female member of the cast sexually propositions him, but not before delivering her own parodic rendition of Mr Podsnap's musical solo:

> *Ours is a Copious Language*
> *A Language Trying to Strangers;*
> *Ours is the Favoured Nation,*
> *Blest, and Safe from Dangers . . .*
> (423)

She continues in a similar vein, repeating the lines from Podsnap's famous speech to the foreign gentleman on the subject of Englishness. It is a raucous party, and Rushdie is having his own bit of 'ayenormaymong rich' fictional fun with it, down to the final moment when the libidinous actress bares her breast, only to reveal a map of London inscribed thereon in red and blue magic-marker.

As Steven Connor points out in an excellent discussion of this scene,

> There is both mockery and admiration in Rushdie's enjoyment of the vulgar travesty of the novel being brought about in this adaptation. As a literary novel, *The Satanic Verses* distances itself from the rank collapse of distinctions and flamboyant carelessness of the original text that is to be found on the film set; but as a novel that itself employs and closely affiliates to many of the devices and associative energies of film, the novel mirrors something of its own procedures in this episode.
> (124)

By focusing on the conspicuously counterfeit staginess of the London set, the novel not only calls attention to its own artificiality, but suggests something about the ways in which the postmodern metropolis itself has changed as a result of new technologies. Like the movie set, the London of *The Satanic Verses* is a virtual space, volatile and permeable in a way that is at times suggested in Dickens, but that postmodern fiction since Joyce has made its own special domain.

By taking London as its chief locale, Rushdie's novel places itself in the tradition of *Bleak House* and *Our Mutual Friend* which use London as a synecdoche for the nation as a whole, for Englishness. What the film set scene makes abundantly clear, however, is the way in which Englishness has become commodified and put on sale – on sale, moreover, not only to a domestic audience eager to consume its own national stereotypes but to the post-colonial visitor. Saladin returns not as an exploited victim or a naive observer, but as a cosmopolitan sophisticate, like Rushdie himself, and he is appalled at the blatancy with which England now prostitutes itself to the outsider.

It is wonderfully fitting that the climax of this passage should be a reworking of the famous encounter between Podsnap and the foreign gentleman in *Our Mutual Friend*, perhaps the most celebrated scene in all of Dickens on the theme of England and its 'others'. Rushdie invokes this scene in order to align himself ideologically with Dickens in the critique of Podsnappery – no doubt recalling Margaret Thatcher and the Falklands episode as an all too recent instance of similar cultural arrogance and chauvinism. But, as Connor rightly insists, the multiple layers of pastiche and the complex heteroglossia in Rushdie's treatment of this scene move it beyond any simple ideological satire. At a deeper level, Rushdie's revision of *Our Mutual Friend* represents an enthusiastic joining with Dickens in the celebration of carnivalesque qualities – theatricality, travesty and disguise – that the two writers have in common.

The Satanic Verses marks the conjunction of Dickens with the post-colonial and the postmodern. As such, it testifies not only to the literariness of Rushdie's imagination but to the contemporaneity of Dickens. For Rushdie, as for the other writers considered in this essay, Dickens is not simply a canonical author with a fixed position in literary history. He is also a living and ever-changing text, as important to late twentieth-century writers in the Anglophone diaspora as he has always been for those closer to the metropolitan centres. Indeed, as Rushdie's novel makes clear, Dickens is at once central and eccentric in relation to contemporary interrogations of Englishness.

The examples mentioned in this essay by no means exhaust the list of post-colonial Dickensian appropriations. What is needed, however, is not simply a multiplication of examples, but greater specificity in locating them in their historical, geographical, and cultural contexts. Further research will need to attend more closely to such differences, including differences along race and gender lines. We should not expect 'Dickens' to signify in the same way to a black, male South African writer in 1959 and to a white, female Australian writer in 1990. A more global approach to the study of Dickens's reception and impact is long overdue. Such an approach promises not only to expand our knowledge of Dickens's reputation, but to alter the ways in which his texts are read and understood. Not one Dickens, but many, should be our motto.

References

Ackroyd, Peter, *Dickens* (New York: HarperCollins, 1990).
Allen, David, *Modest Expectations: An Entertainment* (Sydney: Currency Press, 1990).
Busch, Frederick, *The Mutual Friend* (New York: Harper & Row, 1978).
Connor, Steven, *The English Novel in History 1950–1995* (London and New York: Routledge, 1996).
Davis, Paul, *The Lives and Times of Ebenezer Scrooge* (New Haven: Yale University Press, 1990).
Dolby, George, *Charles Dickens as I Knew Him* (London: Unwin, 1885).
Leavis, F.R., *The Great Tradition* (London: Chatto & Windus, 1948).
Naipaul, V.S., *A House for Mr. Biswas* (New York: McGraw-Hill, 1961).
Noonan, Michael, *Magwitch* (London and Sydney: Hodder and Stoughton, 1982).
Rushdie, Salman, *The Satanic Verses* (New York: Viking Penguin, 1989).
Sander, Reinhard W., *The Trinidad Awakening: West Indian Literature of the Nineteen-Thirties* (Westport, CT: Greenwood, 1988).
Wilkinson, Jane, *Talking with African Writers: Interviews with Poets, Playwrights, and Novelists* (London: Heinemann, 1990).

21

No, but I Saw the Film: David Lean Remakes *Oliver Twist*

Neil Forsyth

Sometimes the film *is* better than the book. This may not be true for the numerous television adaptations of Dickens, good as some of them have been,[1] nor for David Lean's 1946 *Great Expectations*, in spite of the classic status it has taken on among *literati*.[2] But arguably it is true of Lean's next film, the 1948 *Oliver Twist*. Lean was often a victim of fluctuations in audience taste, especially American. The critical and box-office failure of *Ryan's Daughter* (1970), which was judged to be completely out of touch with the new spirit of cinema and seemed a celluloid dinosaur, led to a 15-year hiatus in his career. Yet he lived long enough to enjoy renewed acclaim. He received a knighthood, an American Film Institute Life Achievement Award, and the public admiration of Spielberg and Scorsese. His final film, *A Passage to India* (1984), was hailed as the work of an old master, and when he died aged 83 in 1991, he was about to begin filming *Nostromo*. A fine new biography by Kevin Brownlow has just been published in England,[3] so it is a good time to reassess what is perhaps the best of Lean's black and white films. Not only did it establish a benchmark for adaptations of classic literature,[4] but it showed the relevance of the novel to the postwar world.

I

Dickens's novels come out of a context that already merged word and image. Indeed in their first collaboration, on *Sketches by Boz*, Cruikshank the image-maker (not merely 'illustrator') was the senior partner: the *Spectator* reviewer enthusiastically declared that 'Boz is the CRUIKSHANK of writers'.[5] Dickens himself saw their work as a shared

251

enterprise and may well have been willing to adjust his text to fit a Cruikshank etching (as Eisenstein and Prokoviev famously did for music and image in making *Alexander Nevsky*). Cruikshank later insisted the idea for *Oliver Twist* came from him, which caused ill feeling. Yet he and Dickens had much in common: they were both masters of social caricature, both adored amateur dramatics, both had an enormous vitality and both were better at villains than at the melodramatic characters the Victorians took for heroes, and especially heroines. Thackeray, himself trained as a painter, saw the likeness between them, as did other contemporaries.[6] The combination was a source of the broad appeal of this early Victorian art, and the images that have persisted in the popular mind for the story of *Oliver Twist* have remained as much those of Cruikshank as of Dickens, especially perhaps the two most famous etchings, of Oliver asking for more and Fagin in the condemned cell. It must have been hard for David Lean to exclude the latter image from his film, though he had good reasons, as we shall see. Alec Guinness's startling make-up for the Fagin role is directly based on Cruikshank. In a sense the film reasserts or remakes the image half of the Victorian collaboration.

Unfortunately, Lean's *Oliver Twist* has fallen out of favour. It is available on video and is occasionally shown in cinemathèques, or film museums, but has rarely been properly understood. There are several reasons for this. The film never achieved box-office success, partly because of the American boycott in reaction to Alec Guinness's unforgettable Fagin, which revived all the accusations of anti-Semitism that Dickens himself had undergone.[7] Though the film was a moderate success in England, it was released in the US only in 1951, and then in a sanitised version. Already the US market was crucial for the success of a film: it was perhaps still possible in those postwar years to resist Hollywood, even to envisage the growth of a separate and viable British film industry from the documentary emphasis of the war years, but this boycott was one of several signs of what was soon to happen in the 1950s – the financial collapse of British film production. The New World had already grasped the Old in its imperial embrace.

In other respects also the initial reviews and subsequent reactions were not very favourable. The film was seen as an effort to capitalise on the success of *Great Expectations* (two Oscars and three Oscar nominations) of two years before, which is certainly true. It begins even with a gratuitous storm scene, absent from the novel but imitating rather blatantly the remarkable opening sequence on the marshes of Lean's *Great Expectations*: Oliver's mother, heavily pregnant, struggles across open country towards the illusory haven of the workhouse, which is itself very

oddly located on the edge of this desolate terrain. And there are other
flaws. Near the end, the film risks losing the thread of the plot by focusing
on the death of Sykes. It introduces a vast crowd of extras to hurl their
execrations at the stranded figure on the roof, who is shot and then
hanged by his own rope.[8] It tries to keep the Oliver plot going by having
him help Sykes at gunpoint, and then briefly announces Oliver's rescue,
but doesn't show it, as the film hurries to its factitious conclusion. The
closing sequence is, even for Dickens, too sugary: it shows Oliver hand-
in-hand with Brownlow (who has now become Oliver's grandfather),
returning to their house shown in long-shot suddenly as a beautiful free-
standing Georgian mansion, despite the fact that earlier, even in the
previous shot, it is a house in a square. The final meeting with the aptly
named Mrs Bedwin, the only woman who has been kind to Oliver, or
who has been near him in bed, completes the family reunion, and Oliver
runs eagerly forward hand-in-hand with this elderly couple.[9] Finally it
forgets its major source of interest in the Fagin figure (arrested just prior
to the Sykes scene) and ignores the famous scene of Fagin in gaol.

None the less, I want to argue that the film is at least as good as the
novel. There are several reasons for this, but I shall focus on two aspects
of the film: its plot and the way it captures and enhances the bizarre
undercurrents in Dickens representations of childhood. The one is the
level of the individual sequence, even the shot, but the other requires us
to keep the whole of each, book and film, in mind. In general I want to
suggest that, except in one crucial respect, the film follows the shape of
the novel Dickens would like to have written. And so I shall be able to
answer or deal with each of the above criticisms of the film in due course.

II

There have been ten films of the novel, according to *Film Index
International*[10] (and Ana Laura Zambrano even lists 13),[11] the earliest in
1906, the most recent the 1968 Carol Reed version of the Lionel Bart
musical.[12] They include the limited but still remarkable 1922 silent
version from Blackhawk Films with Jackie Coogan, Chaplin's 'Kid', as
Oliver.[13] Rose Maylie appears in Thomas Bentley's 1912 version, but not
in James Young's 1916 Lasky Feature Play version. Here though Nancy is
married to Bill Sikes, and there is also a 'Mrs Brownlow' (but no Mrs
Bumble and so no call in Mr Bumble's indignant cry that a law that
makes a man responsible for his wife's actions must be a bachelor). The
1921 Fox Film version is 'loosely based' on the novel and set in

contemporary 1920s New York. It is also called 'The Fortunate Fugitive'. The 1922 Frank Lloyd version, the one with Coogan as Oliver, also has most of the novel's named minor characters too, including Mrs Corney, for the first time, and both Mrs and Rose Maylie. The first sound version dates from 1933. It was directed by William Cowen with 'Monogram Pictures Corporation' and is truly dreadful. If you don't believe me, read the reviews listed in *Film Index International*.[14] An amateur version by David Bradley in 1940 was the only other version that preceded Lean's in 1948. There has now also been Richard Slapsynski's Burbank Studio animation of 1982, about which the less said the better. May it die from all catalogues and all prints be swallowed in the next California earthquake. None of these versions is worth the kind of study that Lean's film richly repays.

In some ways Lean's film is an odd mixture. Silent film techniques jostle against the latest in sound technology. The music is generally a disaster: it was dubbed in at the last minute to counteract some of the more gruesome effects of the images, otherwise unsuitable for the targeted child audience (or rather their parents) and the discrepancy is nowadays simply comic. There are a couple of early intertitles, reproducing Dickens's ironic/comic narration on screen, but these are soon dropped in favour of the use of print more characteristic of sound film: especially noteworthy is the use of posters, the first announcing that Oliver is offered as an apprentice with a £5 premium, and then Brownlow's later advertisement seeking to find Oliver, which Fagin's clawed hands furtively tear off the wall.

We begin our analysis with the plot, first the novel then the film.[15] It was, we know, Dickens's first attempt at a complex plot, and though Forster remarked that *Oliver Twist* was 'simply but well constructed', most readers have agreed with Wilkie Collins, who wrote in the margin of his copy of Forster: 'Nonsense! The one defect of this marvellous book is the helplessly bad construction of the story.'[16] Angus Wilson, in his introduction to the Penguin edition, denounces 'the extreme ineptitude with which Dickens handles or botches his plot'. In particular the coincidences by which the tale advances are notorious. Let me remind you briefly: (1) Bumble arrives in London to deliver two paupers to the legal system (ch. 17), casually opens a newspaper, and the first words he reads are Brownlow's announcement requesting information about Oliver. Bumble is reintroduced with a transparent excuse, the narrator's long disquisition on the alternation of tragic and comic scenes in melodrama, and with the assurance that 'the historian' has 'good and substantial reasons for making the journey' back to Oliver's birthplace to fetch him. And indeed we do learn eventually that through his unfortunate marriage to Mrs Corney, Bumble makes an indirect contribution to the dénouement – the revelation of Oliver's mother's identity. (2) Bumble also meets Monks by chance in the pub. (3) Noah Claypole similarly goes straight to the Three Cripples pub when he in turn gets to London (ch. 42), but unlike Bumble, he makes no contribution at all to the mystery plot: he simply turns up, late in the novel, to become Fagin's spy, the cause of Nancy's death and eventually a police informer. But he never mentions Oliver or his past, and even though he actually overhears Brownlow say that 'there must be circumstances in Oliver's little history which it would be painful to drag before the public eye' (ch. 46), he does not connect this with his old enemy. Claypole merely repeats, but in a minor contrastive way, the trajectory of Oliver from Mudfog (the original serial name of his birthplace, suppressed for the publication as a book) to London and Fagin's underworld.

The reappearances of Bumble and Claypole, however, are minor coincidences. The really fantastic coincidences are the major ones out of which the mystery plot is concocted. (4) The first theft in which Oliver participates is the attempt to pick the pocket of his father's former friend, Mr Brownlow, a man who has always treasured a picture of Oliver's mother on his sitting-room wall, while (5) his first attempted larceny consists of breaking and entering the house of Oliver's aunt, the younger sister of that portrait on the wall.

If one wishes to defend these coincidences on the grounds of a dark fate hanging over the novel, as Steven Marcus famously did, one has to face the difficulty that the nightmare and the coincidences of *Oliver Twist* have little to do with each other. The two robberies are seen to be such remarkable coincidences only much later, when the history of Oliver's family is rapidly, even perfunctorily, laid before us. It might have been nightmarish if we knew that Oliver were being forced, by some dark logic, to rob his own family and their friends, but by the time we are aware of his connection with his victims, the robberies have long receded from our minds, Oliver has already been rescued, and the revelations come simply with the delight of surprise. The typically linear plot of a 'Parish Boy's Progress' towards crime and ignominy has by now been rewritten as the complex fairy tale of genteel birth reasserting its rights.

What happened, I think, is that Dickens conceived the rescue plot only after the first serial instalments had appeared in *Bentley's Miscellany* (February–May 1837).[17] Chapter 12, which appeared in August 1837, gives the first hint of the new direction the plot is to take – Brownlow's portrait. Bumble reappears in Chapter 17 (November 1837), although at this point all he can do is tell Brownlow about Oliver's early years. In order to write this instalment, Dickens had been obliged to ask the publisher for a copy of the first numbers, covering Chapters 1–8, since he had not thought to keep them by him.[18] (For later novels he began the practice of making elaborate plot notes before and after each number.) In the same instalment comes the first sign of Nancy's later development (Ch. 16), and Dickens wrote to Forster on 3 November saying that he hoped 'to do great things with Nancy. If I can only work out the idea I have formed of her, and of the female who is to contrast with her' (I, p. 328). The remark is typical for its interest in the pair of characters rather than the plot which is to bring them together.

During this period, two important events had taken place. The sudden death of Mary Hogarth had so affected Dickens that the June number failed to appear. It is in the next instalment that Oliver is first taken to Brownlow's and we see the portrait, like a mysterious vision of the dead young woman.[19] Then Dickens managed to get Bentley to accept *Oliver Twist* as one of the two novels promised under the agreement of August 1836, but the negotiations were so bitter that, according to Kathleen Tillotson, the quarrel with the publisher is the most obvious reason for the non-appearance of the October issue.[20] It is in the next instalment that Nancy begins her transformation and that the novel takes its first journey back to the workhouse for the return of Bumble. Each interruption allowed Dickens time to work out the coincidences from which the elaborate plot is built.

In February 1838, Chapters 23–25 appeared with the heading 'Book the Second', even though the initial instalment had not been introduced as 'Book the First'. It looks as if the main outlines of *Oliver Twist* as mystery novel were now fairly clear. For in this new instalment, the first of the second book, a crucial new character and episode are described. In Chapter 23 we find Mrs Corney making tea at her fireside – the romance with Bumble is beginning (made much of by Lean), while in the next chapter we hear the first report of a conversation between old Sally and Oliver's dying mother – something that the novel's first chapter, published a year before, had neither hinted at nor even allowed for. And the workhouse, in that first instalment, had a master, yes, but no matron. Mrs Corney is to play an important role as the recipient of the 'Agnes' locket, but the absence of both Mrs Corney and locket from the first year's published material suggests either that no identification of Oliver's mother was originally intended, or that Dickens had not yet thought out how to do it.

Monks, Oliver's half-brother, and his conspiracy with Fagin first appear in Chapter 26 (March 1838), but their plan to subvert the will alters, retrospectively, the overt meaning of Chapter 13 (August 1837) in which Fagin's anxiety to recapture Oliver had been caused very plausibly by his concern that Oliver would give the crime-ring away. Even now, Dickens could claim in a letter (mid-March 1838) that 'nobody can have heard what I mean to do with the different characters in the end, inasmuch as at present I don't quite know myself'.[21] Rose Maylie eventually appears the following month (ch. 28), a young girl 'so mild and gentle, so pure and beautiful, that earth seemed not her element', and who is to go through a perilous illness and, unlike Mary Hogarth, miraculously recover. But the locket itself, the main birth-token, is first mentioned only in Chapter 38, along with the business of the pawn-ticket (August 1838). And the whole mystery, with the intricate and improbable family history on which it depends, was unravelled only when the final chapters (the second part of 39–51) were published together in book form in November 1838. This section was written rapidly between August and October, the September instalment of the *Miscellany* being sacrificed for the purpose. Dickens was already publishing *Nicholas Nickleby* by then, and he also needed to upstage the increasing number of rogue versions which were capitalising on the success of *Oliver*. Only then, and all at once, did the original readers discover how Oliver was connected to all those nice people he had been forced to rob.

This evidence about the writing of the novel strongly suggests that Dickens hastily adapted what would have been a picaresque, episodic tale, like those of his favourite author Tobias Smollett, one which originated as an outgrowth of 'the Mudfog Papers' he had previously been writing for Bentley. He tried thus to turn it instead into a kind of *Tom Jones*, the novel recently given the stamp of approval by Coleridge as comparable to *Oedipus Tyrannus* and *Volpone*, with their complex plots of reversals, recognitions and rescues. The transformation required some reimagining of scenes already published, and Dickens barely managed to cover his tracks. None the less, Dickens had seen the need to plan such plots more thoroughly in advance. If Dickens had now started to write *Oliver Twist*, the locket would have been present in the first scene, the death of Oliver's mother, and so would the character, Mrs Corney, to whom Old Sally is to give it. Oliver's sinister half-brother Monks would also have been there early, and thus Dickens would have introduced the idea of the inheritance that Monks and Fagin subsequently pursue. But Dickens had already finished the novel and was onto other things: by the time he next composed such a complex plot, for *Bleak House*, he was a very different writer.

Oliver Twist, then, is a novel divided within itself: the social comment parts are superb even if limited in their relevance to the specific situation of the Victorian Poor Law, but the Maylie part of the novel is a wretched excrescence: Dickens clearly neither knew where he was going, nor knew how to swim in those emotional depths. The emotional family scenes are mostly puffery. They contain hints of what Dickens was to do with his family theme very soon, even in *Dombey and Son* and still more in *David Copperfield*, but they are still puffery. Yet most readers, I think, themselves rescue the novel, and Oliver, from all this. We repress the absurdities, and, in the memory, the book becomes a combination of the workhouse-Sowerberry sequence and the first great London novel.

III

So what do you do, then, when you make a film of the novel? One of the most serious problems with filming complex fiction is that the characters spend so much time on screen explaining the plot that there is little time for anything else: this is true of the BBC adaptation of *Great Expectations*, for example. You need to simplify, and *Oliver Twist* came ready made for simplification. Lean's first and most important change to the novel was to eliminate that whole elaborate and bogus business with the Maylies, none of whom appear in the film. Sikes and Oliver still go off on the Chertsey burglary, but the film doesn't go with them, and merely reports their success, briefly, on their return to Fagin's. In the absence of the elaborate family complications, which I defy anyone even in this distinguished Dickensian audience to remember fully, there is now no rapid unveiling of Oliver's family history at the end, indeed all we ever get is the revelation that Brownlow is Oliver's grandfather during a brief dialogue with Monks – and this comes earlier, well before the final sequence.

Secondly, the other coincidences are entirely eliminated. Monks is introduced earlier as an ally of Fagin's immediately after Oliver's arrival in London, and he now has something important to do: he becomes a silent but sinister double for Fagin, even for the *auteur* perhaps (to adopt a Bakhtinian perspective briefly), or even for the viewer as detective. He is far less of an absurd Gothic extra, and in fact it is because he goes to find out about Oliver that Bumble reappears in the film – consequence replacing coincidence. Claypole, on the other hand, disappears entirely once the Sowerberry sequence is over. No fortuitous arrival in London, no willing co-option into Fagin's gang; it is now the Artful Dodger (an excellent Anthony Newley) who becomes the (somewhat reluctant and still slightly comic) spy for the truly villainous Fagin.

Old Sally, by contrast, now dies much earlier, during the Sowerbery sequence; thus she is moved up from Chapters 23–24 to the equivalent of chapter 5. The locket is now clearly shown in close-up by Lean's camera and in the first scene already, on Oliver's dying mother's breast. Mrs Corney is already running the children's wing of the workhouse instead of the novel's Mrs Mann, so she is there to receive the locket from the dying Sally, just as Dickens (I imagine) retrospectively wished she had been. The film now tells its story visually, often with no linking dialogue, so the locket is made a key element in the filmic narration. A cut from the locket in Monk's hand to Oliver's face in a medium shot as he moves to and fro on the garden swing is enough to underline the family connection, and the scene then develops quickly to the moment when Oliver and Brownlow both look up at the picture on the wall.

In all this, the film improves on the novel. It eliminates the plot-nonsenses and focuses for the most part where the novel's main interest lies: on Oliver's helplessness, on his relations with the authorities, then with Fagin and the London boys, and then with Sikes and Nancy.[22] Indeed that, as we know, is where Dickens's own interest continued to dwell, around the murder scene and the subsequent chase and death: once he introduced it for the so-called Farewell Tour, it became his favourite public reading, an obsession that eventually killed him.[23] So if we allow for the adjustments to postwar British sensibilities, the film has the plot that Dickens would or should have written, if he had known from the beginning where he was going, and had not been distracted into romance by the death of Mary Hogarth.

IV

As it happens, though, there is another pressure at work on anyone who would make a film of this novel, since it already figured large in the history of what the French call 'le septième art'. In his famous essay on 'Dickens, Griffith and the Film Today',[24] Eisenstein discusses scenes from the book, especially the cross-cutting or 'parallel montage' between the silent Brownlow and the violent Fagin worlds, and the narrative suspense thus created while Brownlow and Grimwig play chess. At the same time Eisenstein argues that Dickens justified this technique by the very discussion of the way life alternates between comedy and tragedy which we noticed earlier as such a transparent excuse to introduce Bumble. Eisenstein is trying to show his readers how some of the basic techniques of film-making originated in D. W. Griffith's admiration for Dickens (as Griffith acknowledged). Although both Griffith and

Eisenstein were probably trying retrospectively to add some extra cultural dignity to an art form that they really both adapted from nineteenth-century melodrama, in that respect too they followed Dickens.[25] In any case Eisenstein's extended discussion makes the Brownlow/Fagin parallels obligatory for anyone making an *Oliver Twist* film and aware of the traditions of his art. And Lean's version clearly does pay homage to those great American and Russian inspirations for so much of the language of cinema, making the link between Oliver's mother and the portrait on the wall clear in visual terms without words: Oliver's eyes are simply drawn upwards to the portrait, like Brownlow's, and when the dialogue adds its comments the words simply mention lamely and self-consciously that this is a portrait.

It is important, of course, that the viewer recognise the portrait. Here, then, is the narrative explanation for that extended opening sequence in which we watch a pregnant woman struggling through a storm and suffering the pains of labour. The image of Oliver's mother needs to be well fixed in the minds of the audience, since almost all of the links between mother and son are done visually, not verbally in the film. Perhaps the opening does exploit (or simply recall) the success of Lean's earlier Dickens film, but now we see that the sequence has narrative point too.

In several other respects too the film does pay homage to Eisenstein's idea of montage,[26] which Lean uses mainly for irony. The Parish Board's pronouncement that 'this workhouse has become a regular place of entertainment for the poorer classes' is met by a decisive cut to women bent over wash tubs, while overhead a huge sign proclaims 'God is Love'. In the London streets, animals herded to market are mingled with the crush of the crowds, and then later there is more humour than irony when Fagin assures the Dodger that the spying will be 'a pleasant piece of work' and in the next shot we see him standing outside in the rain.[27]

V

Dickens's Oliver would be an unbearably angelic child but for two things. Though he is mostly a passive instrument of the narrator's power, frequently that power results in the ironies on which both the humour and the early social commentary of the novel depend. Indeed it was the connection between these that was one of Dickens's major discoveries in the writing of this novel. Lean preserves one of those early moments as an inter-title: 'Oliver cried lustily. If he could have known that he was an orphan, left to the tender mercies of churchwardens and overseers, perhaps he would have cried the louder.' But Lean drops this technique quickly, for he seems to have noticed that once the action moves out of Mudfog, the narrator's point of view moves closer to his boy hero, and he preserves this relation in the film. The film's last inter-title, in fact, is the one that announces him on the road to London. The cut from the lonely country road to the noise of the London streets is then a further example of Lean's ironic montage.

The other thing that redeems Oliver from being too angelic is the marvellous scene at the undertaker's – his sudden attack on the invidious Claypole for insulting Oliver's dead mother. The insistence on the image of that mother early on makes the film more coherent, less sentimental than the novel – it is a real woman, not motherhood in general whom we see impugned. And Lean gets a great deal more out of this scene. It further captures for the screen the weird undercurrent of childhood violence in Dickens so well described by John Carey in *The Violent Effigy*. Lean read the subtext accurately, how it takes the lid off what Dickens repressed in order to construct his sweet and innocent children, how it therefore extends and deepens the idea of moral character. Lean's sequence focuses on several moments: the extended insult, the sudden blow and Claypole's shock, the shrieks of the women, the door of the coalhole where Oliver is imprisoned, the appeal to Bumble and the beating. And in one or two shots the faces are used to express more than one emotion at once: in particular at the end of the sequence, the face of Claypole suggests his main role in the novel as Oliver's unsavoury opposite – and double. As he witnesses Oliver's punishment he manages to suggest both sadistic pleasure and then, oddly, a puzzled masochistic identification.

The darkness of the underground Sowerberry world conveys part of the meaning of the novel/film, and is picked up later in a more intense key by the Fagin house: the film is marvellous with interiors, and makes especial use of stairs, beginning here, as measures of interior space and also as metonymic signs of the labyrinth that is the world of this story.[28] That Lean is thus constructing various unifying devices for the film as a whole is clear I think also from the gratuitous dog in the Sowerberry sequence. In the book Oliver eats the scraps set by for the dog Trip, but the dog himself is absent. Lean brings him on screen, and has him eat alongside Oliver, creating a muted sympathy that points forward to the most memorable scene in the film, that other dog's yelping to escape from the room where Sikes has murdered Nancy. This links the violence of the Sowerberry sequence near the beginning with the violence of Fagin's boys and then of the Sikes–Nancy sequence. (And in view of current British troubles with mad cows, no doubt you will all have found a new implication for that famous remark of Bumble's that explains Oliver's rage to Mrs Sowerberry: 'It's not madness, Ma'am, it's meat.')

Doors have a similar function. They close Oliver in, but they can also separate the viewer from him and from the mysteries of the plot, as when the door closes and leaves us outside with the two old women in the workhouse as our on-screen stand-ins crouching at the keyhole while Mrs Corney hears the story of Oliver's birth and gets the locket.[29] Only later do we go in flashback into the room when Mrs Corney, now Mrs Bumble, tells her story to Monks.

Perhaps the main sign of Lean's sympathy with Dickens, and with the novel he found still encumbered in everything Dickens had not been able to remove, is the focus on the murder scene, to which Dickens himself constantly returned in his later public readings. We have already mentioned Sikes's dog. Lean gives him new and shifted emphasis, since he is more sympathetic than in the novel, and indeed becomes the emotional focus of the murder scene in the way that Eisenstein recommends for filmically significant objects like the famous baby-carriage in the Odessa steps sequence in *The Battleship Potemkin*. The dog's role continues as introduction to the extended hallucination that follows the murder: shots 503, 507, 511 all have close-ups on the dog as he watches Sikes's every move. Lean here exploits the cinematic indications of Dickens's writing, especially the way the sun moves across the city and lights Sikes's conscience as he thinks about the murder in flashback and in hallucination.[30] The dog even leads the pursuers to the Fagin lair to find Sikes out.

If it is not the dog's yelping and scratching desperately at the door that most people remember about the film, it is the darkness of those interiors where people are trapped in hopelessness. Especially the workhouse, of course, which had retained its position in the English popular imagination ever since 1837, and to which Lean and Bryan, the film's designer, do full justice. The scene contains one of those characteristic moments of dream-violence in which Dickens's poetic imagination revelled: in the eating scene he writes of one of the boys that 'unless he had another basin of gruel *per diem*, he was afraid he might some night happen to eat the boy who slept next him.' This is how Dickens's odd blend of nightmare fantasy and realism works, we all know. More than anywhere else, then, it is here perhaps that the film speaks its date of making, 1948. Just after the war, people thought of the Victorians, not as inhabitants of a jolly era of family values and earnestness, as some of our contemporaries now do, but as a dark period in which people were imprisoned and from which they longed to escape. The contrasting white of the Brownlow parts is all that is exempt from the low-key lighting of the whole film. Above all, the faces of Lean's workhouse children pressed against the wire fence as they hungrily watch the adult managers eating their fill not only reinvent that young Dickensian cannibal, they evoke unmistakably a connection with the recently discovered images of German concentration camps. This explains also the otherwise puzzling sound of marching feet in the workhouse that accompanies the first few minutes of Oliver's life. No wonder the sensitive reviewer of the *Los Angeles Examiner* was made decidedly uncomfortable by the experience of the film.[31] Such updated references are a necessary part of the shift from nineteenth-century page to twentieth-century screen, and make the early American reaction to Guinness's Jew (it was largely the comic parts that the sanitisers cut) especially unfortunate. It is now time to rescue the film once and for all from that rude beginning.

Notes

1.   The great television period began with Granada's *Hard Times* of 1977, followed by the BBC's *Little Dorrit* of Christine Edzard, and ended with its *Bleak House* of 1985: these serials included many filmic elements, and deliberately reflected conditions and issues in contemporary 1970s and then Thatcher's Britain, but they soon became too expensive. Channel 4's 1982 attempt to film the famous RSC *Nicholas Nickleby* was also part of this movement. See 'Who's Framing Dickens', *BBC TV*, 7 November 1994, an excellent review of TV Dickens, made to accompany their *Martin Chuzzlewit*, adapted by David Lodge, which signalled a costume drama revival, following their *Middlemarch*.

2.   Robert Giddings, Keith Selby and Chris Wensley, *Screening the Novel: The Theory and Practice of Literary Dramatization* (New York and London, 1990) 47: 'universally admitted to be a great film'. See *contra* Graham Petrie, 'Dickens, Godard and the Film Today', *Yale Review* 64 (1975) 237, and Grahame Smith, 'Dickens and Adaptation', in *Novel Images*, ed. Peter Reynolds (London: Routledge, 1993) 62.

3.   Kevin Brownlow, *David Lean* (London: Richard Cohen Books, 1996).

4.   See 'Who's Framing Dickens?'.

5.   Quoted in Richard Jenkyns, 'The Pleasures of Melodrama', *New York Review of Books* (11 July 1996) 11, a review of Robert L. Patten, *George Cruikshank's Life, Times and Art* (New Brunswick: Rutger's University Press, 1996).

6.   See Michael Hollington, 'Dickens and Cruikshank as Physiognomers in *Oliver Twist*', *Dickens Quarterly* 7 (1990). Thackeray's 'Essay on the Genius of George Cruikshank' is cited in Jenkyns, 12.

7.   A good account is in Stephen M. Silverman, *David Lean* (London: André Deutsch, 1989) 75–80. Guinness virtually invented the role, even though this was only his second film (his role as Herbert Pocket

was the first). He studied Cruikshank's illustrations, and imitated them as closely as possible, including what Harry Cohn, head of Columbia Pictures who wanted to distribute the film in America, called 'da schnozz'. This caricatural element is above all what provoked the Berlin riots and the US censorship. Lean later argued that the cutting for the American market eliminated the humour, e.g. Guinness's thieving lesson, and thus *made* it anti-Semitic.

8.   We see only the rope, not the hanging body, which would have been too gruesome for the film to receive the U certificate allowing unaccompanied children to attend. Lean limited on-screen violence to what was inescapable, and thus all the more compelling. It is a remarkable sequence partly because of this indirection. None the less the British Board of Film Censors awarded an 'A' rating, insisting that children be accompanied by adults, probably because of the famous murder of Nancy sequence.

9.   But Dickens hesitated here I think between the traditional great theme of the novel: recovery of one's parentage, one's rightful lineage as in that classic eighteenth-century model for all subsequent family fiction, *Tom Jones*, and what became the basic Dickensian theme that one's true family is not one's birth or blood family.

10.   This immensely useful CD-Rom is copyright Chadwyck-Healey France SA, contents © British Film Institute 1993–5.

11.   A.L. Zambrano, *Dickens and Film* (New York: Gordon Press, 1977) (reprint of a fine American PhD dissertation).

12.   Carol Reed had been working at J. Arthur Rank when Lean made his film, and he makes several filmic references to Lean, but does not acknowledge the debt. The musical has been a hit again recently (1995–6) in London.

13.   The 'angelic' portrait of Coogan is now available on the Internet, but beware, it is worth 5009 K just to get Coogan's picture. That means it takes forever to download.

14.   There is also a brief article by a Barry Tharaud in *Dickens Studies Newsletter* (Vol. 11), pp. 41-6 which compares this and the Lean film on the basis of what the author calls 'moral vision'. He says his class of American students hated the monogram version.

15.   Part of this analysis appeared previously in my essay 'Wonderful Chains: Dickens and Coincidence', reprinted in Michael Hollington, ed., *Charles Dickens: Critical Assessments* (Mountfield: Helm Information, 1995) 225-74.

16.   Cited by Sylvère Monod, *Dickens the Novelist* (Norman, Oklahoma: 1968) 117; cf. Arnold Kettle, *An Introduction to the English Novel* (London: Hutchinson, 1951) Vol I. 120f: 'It is generally agreed that the plots of Dickens' novels are their weakest feature', although he allows that *Oliver Twist*'s dependence on 'a number of extraordinary coincidences . . . is the least of its shortcomings.'

17.   Kathleen Tillotson in her Introduction to the Clarendon edition (Oxford, 1966, p. xv) argued that Dickens conceived the novel as early as 1833, but in fact none of her evidence indicates that the complex plot was in his mind so early. Burton M. Wheeler, 'The Text and Plan

of *Oliver Twist'*, *Dickens Studies Annual* 12 (1984), 41-61, makes a good case for the hasty reinvention of the novel as it was being published, although he does not see the importance of Mrs Corney-Bumble.

18. *The Letters of Charles Dickens*, ed. Madeleine House and Graham Story, Pilgrim edn (Oxford, 1965), I, 319.

19. Peter Ackroyd, *Dickens* (London, Minerva, 1991), 238-44, 1165.

20. Tillotson, xix-xxii; Wheeler, 46.

21. House and Story, I, 388–9.

22. I see no child abuse here, unlike Richard Delamora, 'Pure Oliver: Representation Without Agency', in John Schaad, ed., *Dickens Refigured* (Manchester: Manchester University Press, 1996) 60, though I would agree about the buried homoerotic implications. Pauline Kael noted these in her review of Lean's film, indeed she thought the film might offend homosexuals more than Jews! (cited in Silverman, 78).

23. Edgar Johnson's biography made this point in 1952, vol. II, p. 1104, but it has been disputed, e.g. by W.H. Bowen, *Charles Dickens and Family* (Cambridge: Heffers, 1956) 134–59.

24. 'Dickens, Griffith, and the Film Today', in *Film Form: Essays in Film Theory* (London: Harcourt, Brace, Jovanovich, 1949) 197–255

25. For Griffith's acknowledged debt to Dickens, see *New York Globe*, 2 May 1922, quoted in Graham Petrie's iconoclastic essay 'Dickens, Godard and the Film Today', *Yale Review* 64 (1975) 186–201. Petrie argues for an extended connection between Dickens and the visual arts rather than a specific and exclusive link between Dickens and Griffith. He begins with Cruikshank's illustrations, on which see also J. Hillis Miller, and goes on to the many theatrical adaptations of the novels, as well as Dickens's own theatre work. He thinks Lean's film of *Oliver Twist* does not do justice to the 'affinity between Oliver and Fagin' because it omits the prison-scene.

26. André Bazin succinctly defines montage as 'the creation of a sense or meaning not proper to the images themselves but derived exclusively from their juxtaposition', *What is Cinema?* 2 vols. (Berkeley: University of California Press, 1967-71) I, 25. Zambrano, 88–92, shows how Dickens anticipated the technique in various ways, juxtaposing for example Brownlow, book, handkerchief, etc., and finally in one sentence bringing all together: 'In an instant the whole mystery of the handkerchiefs, and the watches, and the jewels, and the Jew, rushed upon the boy's mind.'

27. See Alan Silver and James Ursini, *David Lean and his Films* (Los Angeles: Silman-James Press, 1992) 68–76.

28. John Bryan had won an Oscar for his sets in *Great Expectations*, but his work in *Oliver Twist* is far better. Roger Manvell observed in his review, quoted Zambrano, 299, how Lean evokes the dark atmosphere of the novel, making especial use of the great Jacob's Island set-piece in Chapter 50. Both Gustave Doré and German expressionism were important influences also on Bryan and Lean, who told an interviewer: 'The sets . . . were built in forced perspective. *Citizen Kane* did that, as did a lot of early German films. They used unreality. Today, more and more, we use reality, which is a bore', quoted in Stephen M.

Silverman, *David Lean*, 72, and rather oddly citing *Casablanca* as another influence.

29. The importance of doors in the design of the film is briefly discussed by Zambrano, 299.

30. See Zambrano, 300–2. For discussion of the relation between novel, performed readings and film in the murder scene, see Sylvia Manning, 'Murder in Three Media: Adaptations of *Oliver Twist'*, *Dickens Quarterly* (4 June 1987) 99–108. The BBC TV version of 1962, which echoed Lean in many ways, tried to outdo him by showing even more violently melodramatic murder and hanging scenes: questions were asked in Parliament and it had to be cut.

31. Quoted Zambrano, 298.

22

From Agnes Fleming to Helena Landless: Dickens, Women and (Post-) Colonialism

Patricia Plummer

INTRODUCTORY REMARKS

In recent years, challenging new readings of English literature have been provided by the fields of women's studies and post-colonial studies. They have introduced a concern with gender and race to the reading of literary texts.[1] It is the aim of this essay to cast a dual focus on feminist and post-colonial issues and, therefore, it is necessary to identify common denominators of these approaches. Both are concerned with the politics of space and the discourse of alterity. From these premises I shall concentrate on the following aspects: naming, place and the body. I want to point out developments within Dickens's writing and draw attention to the fact that neither the treatment of women in a patriarchal society, nor the oppression of the indigenous people in or from the colonies could go unnoticed. These concepts are inscribed in the texts of their time.

Whereas the image of femininity in Dickens's novels has been analysed in some recent publications,[2] his discourse on race is still a largely unmapped territory. Dickens's opinions on matters of race can hardly be quoted in detail at this point; his advocacy of the brutal treatment of rebellious African slaves by Governor Eyre during the Jamaica Insurrection of 1865 shall serve as a point of reference. Dickens strongly criticised the 'platform sympathy with the black – or the Native or the Devil – afar off, and that platform indifference to our own countrymen at enormous odds in the midst of bloodshed and savagery' that made him 'stark wild'.[3] He thus equated the African slaves in Jamaica with 'the Devil' and held *them* responsible for 'bloodshed and savagery'. Dickens also supported the cause of the Southerners during the American Civil War, because he believed the Northerners' stance against slavery to be absurd.[4] Nevertheless these strong opinions stand in a certain contrast with an underlying fascination with the racial and/or female Other as it appears in Dickens's literary texts. Such ambiguities and intersections between matters of gender and of race are of particular interest for this essay. In his recent analysis of *Colonial Desire*[5] Robert Young points out how in nineteenth-century discourse the colonial Other was treated with a mixture of desire and resistance. According to Young, the experience of London, having been not only the centre of the Empire but also the place of multiple cross-cultural encounters, of 'incongruous combinations of relationships, mentalities, genders, classes, nationalities, and ethnicities', was in part responsible for the almost obsessive way in which writers of the past have written about 'the uncertain crossing and invasion of identity'[6] which may often carry an erotic undertone.

One way of exploring the characteristic mixture between fascination and rejection of the Other in literary discourse is by paying attention to an author's use of colour symbolism, especially of the colour black. A relevant reference for this issue is Toni Morrison's study of *Playing in the Dark: Whiteness and the Literary Imagination*[7] in which she analyses American Africanism – the white Eurocentric gaze at the 'non-white, Africanlike (or Africanist) presence or persona'.[8] Morrison argues that the presence of the black population in America could not go unnoticed; even in texts that do not consciously treat the race question, images of black and white prevail.[9] Morrison has also pointed out the parallel in the critical blindness to matters of gender (the female gender, that is) and race when she observes that 'in matters of race, silence and evasion have historically ruled literary discourse'. Moreover, Morrison claims that such an attitude of 'willed scholarly indifference' is comparable with the 'centuries-long, hysterical blindness to feminist discourse and the way in which women and women's issues were read (or unread)'.[10]

It is the aim of this essay to overcome (partly) such critical blindness, to point out silences, gaps, darkness and invisibility as well as ambiguities and intersections within Dickens's discourse of alterity. The three novels selected for this purpose, namely *Oliver Twist, David Copperfield* and *Edwin Drood*, represent the early, middle and final stages of his work. Beyond their artistic value, these novels can be regarded as cultural documents, for, as Toni Morrison has argued,

> [w]riters are among the most sensitive, the most intellectually anarchic, most representative, most probing artists. The ability of writers to imagine what is not the self, to familiarize the strange and

mystify the familiar, is the test of their power. The languages they use and the social and historical context in which these languages signify are indirect and direct revelations of that power and its limitations.[11]

OLIVER TWIST

Agnes Fleming is not a very prominent figure in *Oliver Twist* although she has an important function for the plot. In spite of her significance, she is invisible during most of the novel and one looks in vain for references to this character in literary criticism. Nevertheless the action starts with her giving birth to Oliver – her own name is not mentioned yet – she dies when the baby is born, and thus leaves the story halfway through Chapter 1. What the reader knows about her at this point is summed up by the nurse: "'She was brought here last night. . . . She was found lying in the street; – she had walked some distance, for her shoes were worn to pieces; but where she came from, or where she was going to, nobody knows.'" To which the surgeon replies: "'The old story . . . no wedding-ring, I see. Ah! Good night'"(*OT*, 1,47).[12] The ring is a clue to the story of this nameless young woman. There is a place where she came from and she was on her way to an unknown destination. This indicates a potentially interesting yet silenced story.[13] The young woman herself, in addition to being invisible, is also silent. The only words she speaks are uttered almost inaudibly: "a faint voice imperfectly articulated the words, "'Let me see my child, and die'" (*OT*, 1; 46). In the course of the novel, various efforts are made by diverse characters through theft (Old Sal) and the destruction of her belongings (Monks) to erase any trace of her ever having existed. When Monks throws her trinkets and her locks of hair into the watermill, he asks Bumble what would happen to a body flung down there "'Twelve miles down the river, and cut to pieces besides'" is Bumble's answer (*OT*, 38; 342). The implied violence of this deed foreshadows the fate of Nancy and the fragmentation of her body through Sikes.

Yet despite all the destructive energies that are directed against Agnes, her story is at least partly told in the end by Monks and Brownlow and it is vital for the unravelling of Oliver's true identity. There are two striking aspects in this subplot that at first glance do not seem very cheerful. First, there is no direct authorial condemnation of Agnes. Second, despite the efforts made in the course of the action to eradicate her existence, she is always present in some way or other: apart from the above mentioned mementoes, there is her (anonymous) portrait which hangs on the wall in

Brownlow's house of which Oliver's face is 'the living copy'.[14] Her silence is reinforced by Oliver's observation that the picture seems 'as if it was alive, and wanted to speak . . . but couldn't' (*OT*, 12; 129). Thus Dickens makes ample use of the *parsprototo* principle in order to insert traces or clues to her identity into the plot. The novel begins with Agnes and it ends with her; she is there in the last words of the novel, when Dickens refers sentimentally to her as 'the ghost of Agnes' (*OT*, 53; 480). Through the character of Agnes, Dickens depicts a young woman who resists the moral constraints of her time. One may argue that she is punished in many ways for her deviant behaviour, which is certainly the case; however, there remains an ambiguity. She is not in any way presented as a negative character. Her desire for freedom is mirrored by the absence of the traditional sphere of domesticity.[15] Agnes resists these limitations and leaves the sheltered yet isolated abode. Therefore she dies; she has no body. But she does not become an angel (impossible, of course, for a 'fallen woman'), but is transformed into an invisible presence, and finally into a ghost, and a ghost that haunts. Moreover, her name is important: Agnes obviously has a religious significance and refers to *agnus (dei)* or the lamb of God. Her last name, Fleming,[16] is unusual and means 'a native or inhabitant of Flanders'.[17] The 'sinful' woman who transgresses society's conventions – in choosing a lover, in having a passionate affair, in becoming pregnant outside of wedlock – is thus displaced and identified with the Continent.[18] Dickens's choice of the name Fleming can be regarded as the earliest inscription of Otherness in his work, the earliest and possibly least conscious identification of Otherness and its equation with 'foreignness' and difference.

The fascination with the woman as Other, the desire and the fear created by it in *Oliver Twist*, that for 'moral' reasons Dickens could not develop through the character of Agnes, is personified by the two younger women, Rose and Nancy. At first glance these two are antagonists, but a closer study reveals several points they have in common, last but not least their 'sisterly' function for Oliver.[19] Nancy and Rose are thus the metaphorical daughters of Agnes. They are, of course, representations of the (pre-) Victorian stereotypes of the angel and the fallen woman, but in a sense they share Agnes's placelessness,[20] which can be read as a symbol of the absence of the restricting domestic sphere and an indication of a potentially new place/position in society. In terms of post-colonial criticism the confinement of women to the domestic sphere can also be read as a colonisation. Venturing into new places, real or metaphorical, that have hitherto been occupied and defined by men, thus becomes a movement of decolonisation.

The character in *Oliver Twist* that is most recognisably alienated is Fagin. The anti-Semitic implications of this character have, however, so far been analysed only in part.[21] It has been argued convincingly that his Jewishness is not a religious but a cultural identity. As we know, the obvious anti-Semitism of Dickens's original character treatment was not missed by his Anglo-Jewish contemporaries.[22] It is very prominent in George Cruikshank's illustrations of Fagin's exaggerated physiognomy, in his visual[23] and textual[24] depiction as a devil[25] and other details that cannot all be mentioned in this context (e.g. the anti-Semitic stereotypes of greed, conspiracy, the abduction of children). Another way in which Dickens contributes to depicting Fagin as alienated is through his references to the sphere of the supernatural[26] and to the subhuman sphere of animalism.[27] The colour black and darkness in general are very prominent in Dickens's descriptions of places and the link between blackness and evil is a connection frequently established in *Oliver Twist*: the slums are dark and squalid, their inhabitants live in 'lairs' and 'dens', and lead an almost animal life. At the centre of this chaotic sphere lies the thieves' den, which is totally black from soot and dirt. It is London's 'heart of darkness', the evil core of an anarchic counter-world of poverty and crime. And the person presiding over this world of darkness is Fagin, the Jew.

Fagin's alterity, like that of Agnes Fleming, is conveyed in terms of name. There are several theories concerning the origin of his name. It is a well-known fact that there was a friendly boy named Bob Fagin who helped the young Dickens during his spell at Warren's Blacking Factory. On the other hand, David Paroissien has argued that 'Fagin' may be a misreading of 'Feige', a derogatory Yiddish name (meaning 'cowardly') that was prominent among Jewish immigrants in England who came from Germany in the eighteenth century.[28] There are possible objections to both these explanations, neither of which seems totally convincing. First, it seems a strange twist of thought to give an *evil* fictional character the name of a *friendly* boy. Second, for Paroissien's theory (Fagin/Feige), suggestive as it is, there exists no evidence, also the point would have been lost on most of Dickens's readers who would not have understood the racist implications of the name. However, it is possible that Dickens chose the name of the helpful boy, not because of the real person, but because he may have been *Irish*.[29] Nineteenth-century depictions of and attitudes towards Irish immigrants in England provide striking examples of xenophobia: Robert Knox's *The Races of Men* (1850) is illustrated with Irish immigrants who clearly have African features in order to indicate their alleged racial inferiority.[30] For Dickens himself the Irish in London were a potentially threatening presence. Angus Wilson records an incident in the 1860s, when Dickens demanded the arrest of a young Irish girl because she had belonged to a group of young Irish who 'merry from some celebration ... shouted obscene and abusive language'.[31] Besides which, in *Oliver Twist* the first vivid impression of London is given through Oliver's eyes. When he enters the Saffron Hill area it seems to him that '[a] dirtier and more wretched place he had never seen' and he observes public-houses in which 'the lowest orders of the Irish were wrangling with might and main' (*OT*, 8; 103). Therefore, if the name Fagin was meant to evoke associations with Irish slum inhabitants, this character is marginalised in both racial and cultural terms. He is associated with two large immigrant groups, which in the context of *Oliver Twist*, are connected, directly or by implication, with poverty and crime. Being Jewish and having an Irish-sounding name is meant to identify him as an arch-villain, the ultimate outcast of society.

It can be concluded that in *Oliver Twist* Dickens is obsessed with Otherness. The characters that have appealed strongly to his readers are Nancy, woman and prostitute; Sikes, social outcast and criminal; Fagin, Jew and criminal. Therefore we can read these characters as representations or even personifications of a very troubled concept of gender, class and race. Yet Dickens's clear fascination with and his desire for the Other is mingled with fear: these three central characters are all associated with the world of crime and meet violent deaths that are described in horrible detail (in Fagin's case not the actual death is described, but we have the anticipation of his execution, which is even more vivid).

One final aspect within Dickens's discourse on Otherness in *Oliver Twist* is the issue of emigration which features more prominently in *David Copperfield*. After having informed Rose in a first meeting about Oliver and his identity – and this encounter is a highly symbolical act of female bonding: two women, socially and morally unlike, meet, without prejudice, in an empty room – Nancy meets Rose and Mr Brownlow a second time at London Bridge. During the second encounter Brownlow proposes that Nancy should escape from her old companions to 'a quiet asylum, either in England, or . . . in some foreign country' (*OT*, 46; 414). This suggestion can be read as foregrounding Dickens's subsequent interest in encouraging 'fallen girls' (for whom he would establish Urania Cottage together with Angela Burdett-Coutts within the next ten years) to emigrate to Australia. At this early point, however, Nancy rejects the possibility. She thus resists becoming an inmate of an asylum and consequently becoming institutionalised and dependent. Her choice can be read as a choice of her own free will, of preferring the open streets to the confinement of a home. Indeed in this context Nancy stresses the fact that she must return 'home' to the slums (*OT*, 46; 415). But this choice is, of course, ambiguous. From Nancy's earlier comments we have already learned that she accuses Fagin of having driven her to the 'cold, wet, dirty streets' that are her 'home' (*OT*, 16; 167). The streets do not symbolise her freedom, but they are an ambivalent image of both her destiny and her will. Nancy is in a situation of double bind, having the alternative of being an inmate in an asylum or of being a prostitute in the slums. Dickens implicitly makes a similar point here concerning the life-chances of an outcast woman, that he has made earlier in *Oliver Twist* with respect to poverty in general. In the early chapters he criticises that the Board of the Workhouse has 'established the rule, that all poor people should have the alternative . . . of being starved by a gradual process in the house, or by a quick one out of it' (*OT*, 2; 55). Nancy, the woman-as-Other, chooses the life and place (male-defined as they are) she has come from rather than the male-defined and *con*fined place, even the possible removal to a strange place, offered to her by Mr Brownlow. She will – ironically, or perhaps inevitably – meet a violent death. She will be scattered into fragments, but finally it is Nancy, or rather her phantom (real or imagined), eventually reduced synechdochically to the apparition of her eyes, that haunts Sikes the murderer, and brings about his death. She triumphs at last. The suppressed energies of the victimised women cannot be totally eradicated. The sphere of the supernatural therefore is another place reserved for characters that deviate from society's norms, another space of Otherness.

DAVID COPPERFIELD

Whereas the outcast characters Fagin, Sikes and Nancy (and the 'invisible' presence of Agnes) are of great importance for the plot of *Oliver Twist* and are proof of Dickens's barely suppressed fascination with various border-crossings in terms of crime, sexuality and ethnicity, marginalised characters command significantly less space within the literary landscape of *David Copperfield*. Nevertheless, there is the inevitable subplot that depicts fallen women, Martha and Emily, and the threat of prostitution. In addition, there is throughout the novel a fascination with transgressing gender roles. Betsey Trotwood, a female character who in comparison with other Dickensian women is unusually independent and influential, dresses in very masculine clothes. There is David, whom Steerforth endearingly calls 'Daisy'. And in the haunting childhood chapters of the novel there is the Murdstone couple: Mr Murdstone is the very personification of a threatening masculinity; his sister, Jane Murdstone, is his female counterpart who bears many masculine traits: 'and a gloomy-looking lady she was; dark, like her brother, whom she greatly resembled in face and voice; and with very heavy eyebrows, nearly meeting over her large nose, as if, being disabled by the wrongs of her sex from wearing whiskers, she had carried them to that account' (*DC*, 4; 97).[32] Brother and sister are associated with the colour black, which is clearly intended to symbolise their evil nature. Jane Murdstone's masculinity, her crossing of gender borders, her being an 'unnatural' woman, deviating from the conventional Victorian ideal of femininity, are connected with her sadism. Images that reinforce this character trait include the 'two uncomprising hard black boxes with her initials on the lids in hard brass nails' she travels with, and 'the hard steel purse' that prompts David to call her 'a metallic lady' (*DC*, 4; 97). The dark and sadistic, the 'unwomanly' woman, also features in post-colonial literature of Dickens's time. Jane Murdstone resembles the description of a sadistic female slave-owner in the contemporary slave narrative *The History of Mary Prince*: 'She was a stout tall woman with a very dark complexion, and her brows were always drawn together into a frown.'[33]

Apart from Jane Murdstone, there are other women in *David Copperfield* who deviate from conventional Victorian notions of womanhood: Rosa Dartle, Little Emily and, of course, Martha Endell, a typically Dickensian 'fallen woman'. We do not exactly 'see' Martha, as we see the initially stout and healthy Nancy in *Oliver Twist* who symbolically (and indeed quite ironically) diminishes in proportion with her growing moral awareness in the course of which she is removed from the open streets to the confinements of Sikes's close lodgings. When Martha first appears on the scene she is a shadow, a ghost that haunts Little Emily. When David meets Dan Peggotty in wintry London, Martha hovers about the streets phantom-like. Eventually David catches glimpses of her eavesdropping at the door.[34] Again, it is the image of woman-as-synechdoche that Dickens depicts here: she is merely represented as a face and a hand.[35] In a later scene, again in night-time London, David and Dan Pegotty come across Martha who is about to committ suicide in the river near a prison. The chaotic sphere of the slums where she would normally live is reduced in a nightmarish image to the waste of the big city, 'the overflowings of the polluted stream' Martha blends in with the debris, fading into it '[a]s if she were a part of the refuse it had cast out, and left to corruption and decay' (*DC*, 47; 748). This – Dickens indicates – is her place in society.

Eventually, Dickens resorts to a convenient trick by shipping the disorderly elements of fallen women and the nonconformist Micawber family off to Australia. Australia, a black continent, which from the beginning of English colonisation served as a place convicts were expelled to, qualifies as another sphere of chaos and thus corresponds with the slums of London. Dickens himself took some interest in Australia. In February 1850 he contacted Mrs Elizabeth Herbert in order to discuss the 'Family Colonisation Loan Society'. Later, he met the founder of this association, Mrs Chisholm, who became the model for Mrs Jellyby in *Bleak House*. Dickens described her in a letter to Miss Burdett-Coutts as a mother of children with dirty faces, living in a chaotic household: 'I dream of Mrs Chisholm, and her housekeeping .... The dirty faces of her children are my continual companions'.[36] In criticising Chisholm, the female philanthropist, for being an inefficient housekeeper and for neglecting her children, Dickens puts his own cause in a nutshell: as long as there are needy children in one's own home (i.e. country) one should not bother with the needy abroad. Moreover, his description of the Chisholm family is charged with a strong fear of 'contamination': it seems as if the threatening sphere of the colonies, via the children's 'dirty faces', the blackness of their indigenous people have infiltrated the sacred domestic sphere.

THE MYSTERY OF EDWIN DROOD

If Dickens symbolically purifies the plot of *David Copperfield* by shipping the chaotic characters happily off to the colonies, then the opposite is true of Dickens's last novel, *The Mystery of Edwin Drood*. The novel begins with a description of the influx of chaotic elements from the colonies. The title, *The Mystery of Edwin Drood*, sets the mode, and a strange Oriental atmosphere is evoked in the very densely constructed opening sequence with its opium-dream full of images from the *Arabian Nights*. The complex imagery of this passage contributes to a notion of instability. A contrast is established between the structure of the cathedral tower which is 'massive grey [and] square' on the one hand, and the strange '[rusty] spike' on the other. There is an intrusion of disorderly and potentially violent elements, a 'horde of Turkish robbers', which is counterposed with the Sultan's long procession that includes: '[t]en thousand scimitars', 'thrice ten thousand dancing girls', 'white elephants caparisoned in countless gorgeous colours, and infinite in number and attendants' (*ED* 1; 37).[37] On the one hand, the opening passage is characterised by binary oppositions (flashing scimitars vs. girls strewing flowers), on the other hand there is a mysterious tone, characterised by uncertainty and heightened emotions (of its 14 sentences four end with question marks and three with exclamation marks). There is ambiguity expressed in the repeated questions about the spike (which turns out to be part of the rusty bedstead in the opium den). There is violence hinted at in the images of the scimitars and the spike, as well as the overwhelming power and nightmarish quality of the sheer number of persons and animals involved in the seemingly endless procession.

When it becomes apparent that the man, who eventually turns out to be John Jasper, is awakening from an opium-induced dream, there is no relief expressed at his returning to the real world, the world of the English cathedral town, because he is actually surrounded by people from the strange Asian world of his dream: There are 'a Chinaman and a Lascar' lying on the same bed as 'a haggard woman' – another image that reinforces the intersection of alterity in terms of race and gender. *The Mystery of Edwin Drood* is a novel about the fascination with the Oriental sphere and about the fear of contamination. There is an underlying dread of how the influx of colonial subjects into the 'safe' world of imperial England will influence life. There is a tone of inevitability as well as a sense of decadence. The old world is being changed, it is not the same as it once was in the good old days glorified in *Pickwick Papers* and there is a sense of ruin and loss. Moreover, in the opening chapter there is another important clue as to the emphasis on alterity and difference in this novel. When the woman mutters something in her opium-dream that Jasper does not understand, he remarks 'Unintelligible!'. The same occurs when he shakes the Chinaman, and again when the Lascar starts having visions. This thrice-uttered 'unintelligible' with which John Jasper discards the opium-induced mutterings of the three sleepers, can be read as a comment on the Orient and the Oriental: the opium addicts are obviously lost in visions similar to those of Edwin Drood; therefore they are discarded as part of a chaotic and confusing sphere.

Into the world of the English cathedral town, there arrive two newcomers from the Asian colony of Ceylon, the twins Neville and Helena Landless whom Mr Crisparkle describes as follows:

> An unusually handsome lithe young fellow and an unusually handsome lithe girl; much alike; both very dark, and very rich in

colour; she of almost the gipsy type; something of the hunter and huntress; yet withal a certain air of being the objects of the chase, rather than the followers. Slender, supple, quick of eye and limb; half shy, half defiant; fierce of look; an indefinable kind of pause coming and going on their whole expression, both of face and form, which might be equally likened to the pause before a crouch or a bound.

(*ED*, 6; 84–5)

Their hybridity is expressed in terms of ethnic identity (their English names contrast with their dark skin and Helena's 'gipsy type' appearance) and through a series of strangely incongruous images. They are 'hunter and huntress' and, paradoxically, at the same time 'the objects of the chase'. They are thus reified and animalised. Their strangeness makes them appear 'half shy, half defiant', and their expression is of an 'indefinable' kind, just as the mutterings of the opium-dreamers in the opening sequence were 'unintelligible'. They clearly are strangers in the Old World, because when shown about Cloisterham, they 'took great delight in what he pointed out of the Cathedral and the Monastery ruin, and wondered – so his notes ran on – much as if they were beautiful barbaric captives brought from some wild tropical dominion' (*ED*, 6; 85). Crisparkle's observations contrast with and are caricatured by Mr Honeythunder, the philanthropist, who 'walked in the middle of the road, shouldering the natives out of his way', loudly explaining his absurd scheme of forcing every unemployed person in the United Kingdom to become a philanthropist. The ridicule implied by calling the English 'natives' in this context is, of course, intended to satirise Honeythunder and his preoccupation with 'natives'. This kind of satire is obviously related to Dickens's depiction of the female philanthropist Mrs Jellyby in *Bleak House* who, like her model Mrs Chisholm, fails to realise that due to her neglect her children are slowly turning into natives. On the other hand, this passage can be read in a subversive way. Neville and Helena, then, appear not so much as 'captives', and thus subalterns, from the New World of the Asian colony of Ceylon, but they become the agents of this scene. *They* are the ones who admire the relics of a partly ruined European civilisation. In calling the English 'natives' Dickens lets his readers briefly see the Old World from the New World's perspective, so that the Landless twins' arrival in England can be read as a process of decolonisation, or even a reverse colonisation.

There has been some doubt as to Neville's and Helena's ethnic background, but there is ample evidence to support the view that Dickens meant them to be of mixed Ceylonese and English extraction.

Peter Ackroyd records that when Dickens was a boy he had two schoolfellows who were 'mulattoes whose parents lived in the East Indies'.[38] In his notes for *Edwin Drood* Dickens writes: 'Neville & Helena Landless. Mixture of Oriental blood – or imperfectly acquired mixture in them. YES.'[39] In Chapter 8 Edwin Drood insults Neville for knowing better about the 'black common fellow, or a black common boaster', for having 'no doubt ... a large acquaintance that way' and for being 'no judge of white men', in response to which '[t]his insulting allusion to his dark skin infuriates Neville to . . . [a] violent degree . . . ' (*ED*, 8; 102). Also the frequent references to his 'tigerish' blood (*ED*, 8; 104), or, as Jasper puts it even more clearly, '[t]here is something of the tiger in his dark blood' (*ED*, 8; 105) seem very obvious.[40] After this passionate encounter with Edwin, Neville feels like 'a dangerous animal', he even has 'wildly passionate ideas about the river' (*ED*, 8; 103). Here we encounter another one of the many intersections between Dickens's discourses on race and gender: the 'landless' colonial subaltern is linked with the displaced femininity of Dickens's prostitutes. Neville, like Nancy when she struggles against Sikes and Fagin, becomes a wild animal; like Martha, Nancy and Little Em'ly he contemplates committing suicide by drowning himself in the river. Depicting the obviously Oriental characters of Neville and Helena as young people who have a fierce temperament and who are able to communicate through telepathy, ties in with the observations made by Edward Said in his landmark study of *Orientalism*: 'The Oriental is irrational, depraved (fallen), childlike, "different"; thus the European is rational, virtuous, mature, "normal".'[41]

Even more than her brother, Helena Landless is the Other personified, both as a person of mixed blood and as a woman who disregards fixed gender boundaries. There exists a strong contrast between Rosa Bud, the personification of excessive femininity, and her female counterpart, Helena Landless, who is unique among Dickens's female characters in that she is an androgynous and yet a positive figure. There are other female characters in his works who sport the occasional masculine feature, but these are either ridiculed, as is the case with Betsey Trotwood and her donkey-phobia in *David Copperfield*, or are depicted as threatening, as is in the case of Jane Murdstone. There is evidence of a certain preoccupation in Dickens's writing with crossing the borders of fixed gender roles which is a welcome deviation from his often stereotypical adherence to societal conventions and sentimental idealisations of womanhood. (Although some of his extremely conventional female characters have also been read as being excessive, bordering on caricature.) Yet in connection with Helena, his description of her masculine features expresses desire and is meant to imply passion and sexual availability.[42] Her masculinity is never negative. It indicates a transgression of gender boundaries, due to which Helena can be described as being an androgynous character. Such a collapsing of defined boundaries may have been possible for Dickens on account of her being black. Similar to the way in which Dickens inserted an example of female bonding through Rose and Nancy in *Oliver Twist*, Helena differs from and yet relates to Rosa. It is her contact with Helena that enables Rosa to discard her original attitude of cultural supremacy. In a scene with Edwin, whose colonial gesture is his intention to go to Egypt as an engineer and who subsequently shows a condescending attitude towards Neville, Rosa is depicted as enjoying 'Lumps-of-Delight', a Turkish sweet. Her 'putting her little pink fingers to her rosy lips, to cleanse them from the Dust of Delight that comes from the Lumps' (*ED*, 3; 58) is an image of colonial greed. At the same time she engages Edwin in a conversation on his imagined ideal fiancée, whom Rosa imagines to hate 'things' such as 'Arabs, and Turks, and Fellahs, and people' (*ED*, 3, 59). Nevertheless, when she meets Helena these binaries do not apply. The two women, although they contrast physically, are not opponents. On the contrary, the scenes in which they interact carry an almost erotic undertone. The differences collapse.

Patricia Ingham has detected 'anarchic subtexts'[43] in Dickens's writing about women, especially in his last novel. And indeed the mostly positive depiction of the Landless twins, especially of Helena, that stand out from the mystery and chaos described in *The Mystery of Edwin Drood*, has a destabilising quality. In that sense the name 'Landless' denotes the absence of a fixed place, just as their identity evades fixation with respect to race and gender. Dickens even draws attention to the fact that Neville is obviously discriminated against, and thus implicitly criticises racist prejudice (Edwin's quarrel with Neville; the townspeople's distrust of Neville after Edwin's disappearance). And, finally, he has included a very unusual woman, namely Helena. There is much dispute concerning her 'true identity' – is she a man in disguise? – but the fact that there is no such evidence from Dickens's admittedly sparse notes does not do much to support such speculations. On the contrary, Helena is one of many Dickensian females who transgress the confinements of gender roles, only that here his treatment is significantly more daring. There is no punishment. She is related to and at the same time far removed from her predecessor, Agnes Fleming.

From the very beginnings of his career, Dickens has indeed been fascinated with various versions of alterity. Although this desire is initially strongly mingled with fear, a certain development is evident: the severe punishment of deviant behaviour in *Oliver Twist* is replaced by emigration as an attempt to reinstate order in *David Copperfield*. Finally, in *The Mystery of Edwin Drood*, the marginalised characters move back to the centre. Beyond this symbolic movement from the centre to the periphery and back, there is a notion of hybridity that is linked with increasingly positive connotations. This concept is personified by female characters who deviate from traditional norms and can be regarded as searching for a new place in society. The development initiated by the journeys of Agnes Fleming and Martha Endell leads to the arrival of the Landless twins in England, which can be read as a symbolic decolonisation. It is remarkable that in the character of Helena Landless Dickens presents an unconventional and positive female character who transgresses boundaries of race and gender. Helena is a hybrid personality, she is masculine and feminine, she is white and black. Therefore she is a character who in a way foreshadows the current preoccupation with multiculturalism and the collapsing of fixed gender identities. The existence of such a character is possible within the context of Dickens's last and unfinished novel that has mystery and hence uncertainty at its core. It is this notion of instability that makes for the enduring appeal of Dickens's novels.

Notes

1. In the sense of re-reading traditional texts with an emphasis on marginality; cf. Bill Ashcroft, Gareth Griffiths and Helen Tiffin, eds, *The Empire Writes Back* (London: Methuen, 1989) 174f.
2. From Michael Slater, *Dickens and Women* (London: Dent, 1983) to Patricia Ingham, *Dickens, Women and Language* (New York: Harvester Wheatsheaf, 1992).
3. Quoted in Angus Wilson, *The World of Charles Dickens* (Harmondsworth: Penguin, 1972) 288.
4. Cf. Peter Ackroyd, *Dickens* (London: Sinclair-Stevenson, 1990) 971.
5. Robert J. C. Young, *Colonial Desire: Hybridity in Theory, Culture and Race* (London: Routledge, 1995).
6. Ibid., 2.
7. Toni Morrison, *Playing in the Dark: Whiteness and the Literary Imagination* (Cambridge, MA: Harvard University Press, 1992).
8. Ibid., 6.
9. Similar 'literary archaeology' for the context of black British culture has been achieved by the post-colonial writer and critic David Dabydeen who has literally 'excavated' the image of black people in English art and literature: e.g. David Dabydeen, ed., *The Black Presence in English Literature*

(Manchester: Manchester University Press, 1986); David Dabydeen, and Paul Edwards, eds., *Black Writers in Britain: 1760–1890* (Edinburgh: Edinburgh University Press, 1991).

10. Morrison, *Playing in the Dark*, 14.
11. Ibid., 15.
12. All chapter and page references preceded by *OT* refer to the following edition: Charles Dickens, *Oliver Twist*, ed. Peter Fairclough (Harmondsworth: Penguin, 1985).
13. For a detailed reading of Agnes Fleming's story and on female place and placelessness in Dickens's novels cf. Patricia Plummer, *Frauen ohne Raum: Entwurzelte weibliche Charaktere im Werk von Charles Dickens unter besonderer Berücksichtigung von Oliver Twist* (Mainz, Schriftenreihe des Pädagogischen Instituts, 1997).
14. *OT*, chapter 12 and George Cruikshank's illustration of 'Oliver recovering from Fever'.
15. Cf. my observations on the interrelation between Dickens's concepts of female space and the female body: Patricia Plummer, '"A home–a heart and home"': Aspekte weiblicher Raum- und Körperdarstellung bei Charles Dickens', *FrauenRäume: Dokumentation des 4. Frauentages*, ed. Der Präsident der Johannes Gutenberg-Universität (Mainz: Schriftenreihe des Pädagogischen Instituts, 1994), 77–95.
16. The only time her full name, Agnes Fleming, is mentioned, is in Dickens's list of characters.
17. *OED*, s. v. 'Fleming'.
18. Oliver's father, Edward Leeford, incidentally dies in Rome; Leeford's first wife lived in Paris; cf. chapter 49.
19. For a detailed study of these two characters cf. Simon Edwards, 'Anorexia Nervosa versus the Fleshpots of London: Rose and Nancy in *Oliver Twist*', *Dickens Studies Annual* 19 (1990) 49–64.
20. Nancy, the prostitute, is obviously an outcast and lives mostly in the streets; Rose is an orphan and like Oliver she is totally unaware of her true identity; their lack of a secure position within society is symbolised by their namelessness – Nancy does not have a family name and Rose is known only by the name of her adoptive family, as her father died 'in a strange place, in a strange name' (*OT*, 51; 462).
21. Esther L. Panitz, *The Alien in Their Midst: Images of Jews in English Literature* (London: Associated Universities Press, 1981); David Paroissien, *The Companion to Oliver Twist* (Edinburgh: Edinburgh University Press, 1992) 96–8.
22. Wilson 289.
23. Cf. Chapter 8 for Cruikshank's illustration of Fagin with the toasting-fork in his hand, roasting sausages, a caricature of the boys' souls that he has corrupted and that will thus 'roast' in hell: George Cruikshank, 'Oliver Introduced to the Respectable Old Gentleman.'
24. Fagin, like the devil in popular myth, has 'a quantity of matted red hair' (*OT*, 8; 105).
25. Cf. Lauriat Lane Jr, 'The Devil in *Oliver Twist*', *Dickensian* 52 (June 1956) 132–6; Lane does not refer to any anti-Semitic implications.
26. Cf. the mysterious apparition of Fagin and Monks at the cottage

window in Chapter 34 or such similes as when Dickens describes Fagin as looking 'less like a man, than like some hideous phantom, moist from the grave' (*OT*, 47; 416).

27. Apart from being frequently compared to a reptile, Fagin has 'fangs as should have been a dog's or rat's' (*OT*, 47: 417).

28. Paroissien, 99.

29. Dickens himself makes no reference to Bob Fagin's cultural background (cf. Forster, I, 22), but the homophonous name 'Fagan' is documented as being an Irish surname of possibly Norman origin; cf. Edward MacLysaght, *The Surnames of Ireland* (Shannon, Irish University Press, 1969) 85.

30. Cf. Young, 72–3.

31. Wilson, 288.

32. All chapter and page references preceded by *DC* refer to the following edition: Charles Dickens, *David Copperfield*, ed. Trevor Blount (Harmondsworth: Penguin, 1985).

33. Mary Prince, *The History of Mary Prince, A West Indian Slave. Related By Herself*. The Schomburg Library of Nineteenth-Century Black Women Writers (1831; New York: Oxford University Press, 1989) 6.

34. Cf. Phiz's illustration in Chapter 40 of *DC*.

35. Throughout his chance conversation with Dan Pegotty in London, David sees Martha listening at the door: 'The listening face . . . still drooped at the door, and the hands begged me – prayed me – not to cast it forth' (*DC*, 40; 651).

36. Quoted by Ackroyd, 586.

37. All chapter and page references preceded by *ED* refer to the following edition: Charles Dickens, *The Mystery of Edwin Drood*, ed. Arthur J. Cox, intro. Angus Wilson (Harmondsworth: Penguin, 1985).

38. Ackroyd, 108. He furthermore speculates: '[A]re these two raised up again in Dickens's memory as Neville and Helena Landless in *The Mystery of Edwin Drood*?'

39. W. Robertson Nicoll, *The Problem of 'Edwin Drood': A Study in the Methods of Dickens* (New York: Haskell House, 1972) 60; the complete notes are to be found on pp. 57–68.

40. After all the evidence concerning the Landless twins' racially constructed Otherness, it seems strange that Wendy S. Jacobson in her *The Companion to The Mystery of Edwin Drood* (London: Allen & Unwin, 1986) notes: 'it is mere presumption that their mother was Sinhalese, or partly so; their father's name suggests that he was English. The origin of these two remains one of the mysteries of the novel'. Jacobson has diligently included a 'Study for the head of Neville Landless, by Sir Luke Fields', in which Neville's features are strikingly oriental (Jakobson 95, plate 6; reprinted from F.G. Kitton, *Dickens and His Illustrators*, 1899).

41. Edward Said, *Orientalism* (Harmondsworth: Penguin, 1978; repr. 1995), 174.

42. Ingham, 129.

43. Ingham, 129.

23

'Doveyed Covetfilles': How Joyce Used Dickens to Put a Lot of the Old World into the New

Robert M. Polhemus

The Bible tells us we are all incest survivors, and James Joyce does the same in *Finnegans Wake*, his avant-garde, postmodernist, post-God-is-Dad, punning tower-of-Babel, tour-of-Bible, mock scripture, comic-book of first and last things and lots in between. I want to look at a short but resonant passage from the *Wake* that makes outrageous but revealing use of Dickens – and in particular I want to focus on the punny name inspired by *David Copperfield*: 'Doveyed Covetfilles'. A continual subject of the *Wake*, as of the Bible, is regeneration and revival, and Joyce, in his dream vision, is always composing and rearranging things to show how new worlds are related to old worlds, as new words are related to old words. In the following lines referring to Dickens (Thackeray appears too), the text features a prurient and hypocritical sermoniser whose libido is obviously fizzing up and bubbling over his puritanical cover of proper Victorian morality. Here the preacher is hectoring a group of pubescent, hothouse girls ready to bloom:

> 'Vanity flee and Verity fear! Diobell! Whalebones and buskbutts may hurt you (thwackaway thwuck!) but never lay bare your breast secret (dickette's place!) to joy a Jonas in the Dolphin's Barncar with your meetual fan, Doveyed Covetfilles, comepulsing paynattention spasms between the averthisement for Ulikah's wine and a pair of pulldoors of the old cupiosity shape.'
>
> (*FW*, 434.24–30)

'Doveyed Covetfilles' brings out what is latent, suppressed or sublimated in Dickens by fusing David Copperfield to his ancient and illustrious namesake, King David. I want to argue that Joyce finds, in *David Copperfield*, with its 'child-wife' theme, and in Dickens's general obsession in fiction and life with the innocent figure of the girl or child-woman as saviour, opportunities for exposing the repressed history of incestuous desire and a means of rendering, by pointing out the vital traces of Bible stories in the modern world, the continuity of literature and life generally. Dickens serves as a Victorian bridge in the history of the novel in English for Joyce to unite his imaginative, post-Freudian 'work in progress' to key patterns, moments and figures of puzzling sexual regeneration that renew and animate the Scriptures – what the *Wake* terms 'secret stripture' (*FW*, 293.F2): As David in the Old Testament is tied complexly to his problematic textual ancestry – notably, the incestuous refugee family of forebears from Sodom, Lot and his wife and daughters, Moab, the son of Lot and his daughter, their Moabite descendant, Ruth, the canonised heroine, seducer and young wife of the elderly Boaz and great-grandmother to the House of David's founder – so David Copperfield is tied to his problematic textual progeny in the *Wake*, 'Doveyed Covetfilles', and related to all the other libidinous, sublimating, creative progenitors of life, letters, history and texts in that book, including HCE, ALP, Shem the Penman, Issy the doubled daughter and would-be child-wife, and James Joyce.

In the play on Dickens, in 'Doveyed Covetfilles' and 'the old cupiosity shape', we can see the stress on the configuration that I call the Lot Complex: the suppressed, but crucial and problematic attraction, desire and relationship that have evolved in history and literature between ageing men and younger women – between, for example, fathers and daughters, male teachers and female students, atrophying potentates and trophy wives. A page later in the *Wake* after 'Doveyed Covetfilles', the ranting priestly 'father' explicitly makes the Lot connection:

> Love through the usual channels, cisternbrothelly, when properly disinfected and taken neat in the generable way upon retiring to roost in the company of a husband-in-law or other respectable relative of an apposite sex ... does a felon good ... but I cannot belabour the point too ardently (and after lessions of experience I speak from inspiration) that fetid spirits is the thief of prurities, so ... me daughter .... at 2bis Lot's Road. When parties get tight for each other they lose all respect together.
>   (*FW*, 436.14–25)

In modern times especially, a Lot complex[1] pervades representations of experience in life, language and art. As I read and reconstitute it in Victorian and modern culture, the *Lot* syndrome features the drive or compulsion to preserve, adapt and/or expropriate the traditional paternal power to sustain, regenerate, define and transmit life and civilisation – the patriarchal seed of culture in history.[2] It includes wish-fulfilling projections, unconscious desires, fears, fantasies, rationalising defence mechanisms and symbolisation of cultural and personal memories of transgressions *by both fathers and daughters – by both women and men.* I name it and define its patterns after the extraordinary Genesis account of Lot and his family: Lot, the morally equivocal, bumbling, God-fearing, tippling, faintly ridiculous patriarchal survivor of Sodom and its destruction, who had offered up his daughters to the Sodomites as a bribe to spare God's angels before those celestial messengers saved him and his girls from the city's fate; Lot's wife, who looks back and is turned to a pillar of salt; Lot's two daughters, who, thinking him the last man on earth, conspire, in the words of the Bible, to 'preserve seed of our father' (Gen. 19:32) by getting him drunk with wine to blot out the incest taboo and arouse lust in him, and then, in the dark mountain cave, lying with him to get pregnant. The incestuous issue of Lot's seed, preserved through the daughters' active agency, eventually included not only the marginal races of Moab and Ammon, Israel's neighbours and heathen foes, but also the virtuous Moabite daughter Ruth, her glorious great-grandson David, David's genealogical progeny, which could mean – depending on your faith – Jesus Christ, the Word incarnate, and thus even the Bible itself. (The early Christian scholar Origen relates a striking allegorical interpretation that reads Lot as God and his two daughters as the Old and New Testaments.[3])

What we can see figured in *Lot* are desires and projections that shake our world: the desire for immortality and faith through progeny; the desire to continue life under any conditions; the desire for sexual pleasure without guilt or responsibility; the desire of women to control the action of men to whom they traditionally have been subject, to cooperate with one another and take an active role in determining the fate and history of humanity; the desire of men to preserve themselves, to conquer time, to remain potent, to do what they always could do. *Lot* has a resonance and explanatory power for reading the history of human relationships that, especially for times and texts concerned with developing female subjectivity, the triumph of literacy, marginalised people and the nuances of social and familial power-shifts, can supplement, match and exceed that of the Oedipus myth and complex (with which it clearly has much in common). Like *Oedipus* and psychoanalysis's terminologically and conceptually impaired offshoot of *Oedipus*, the so-called Electra complex, *Lot* brings together diverse ancient legends and living impulses. *Oedipus* features patricide and the intercourse of son and mother; *Lot* features matricide – or what might more accurately be called *uxoricide*, the death of the wife (as happens at the end of *Finnegans Wake* and in *David Copperfield*) and the intercourse of father and daughter. *Lot* offers key male fantasy projections, as does *Oedipus*, but it shows these adult projections (for instance, absolute power of disposal over women; the ability to remain somehow an object of desire; continued sexual prowess and a supply of young sexual partners into old age; fulfilment through children; unlawful sexual love without sin; a successful drive to survive one's contemporaries) forming and determining the representation of the *younger* generation's voices, experience and ostensible desire, as *Oedipus* does not. It also presumes to figure crucially both rational and unconscious *female* wishes, fears and drives, as *Oedipus* arguably does not; and, unlike *Oedipus* and more powerfully and complexly than *Electra*, it stresses the arbitrary death and metamorphosis of the mother, the traumatic impact of her loss and absence, and the meaning of her replacement by the daughters. The Lot text is about the terrible sacrifices, compromises and self-deceptions necessary for survival, which the offering up of the daughters, the panic and death of the wife-mother, the stupefying of the father, his blind rut, and the desperate strategy and fertility of the daughter-wives shockingly trope.

Joyce, living in Paris, wrote punningly in *Finnegans Wake* that 'he would wipe alley english spooker, multaphoniasksically spuking, off the face of the erse' [178.6–7] and one Englishman he singled out was Dickens, or – as he called him – 'duckings' (177.35) and 'Arsdiken's' (440.1–2). What he actually did was to make pun of Dickens and use him as one of his multiphonic, metaphorical voices in his *Wake* party-line and World Wide Web reaching back to David, Lot, Edenville and various forms of 'the old cupiosty shape'.[4] Joyce ties together Dickens, David Copperfield, the saviour-girl figure of *The Old Curiosity Shop* (Little Nell) and the whole Lot theme in the Bible and in history and makes it explicitly, as Dickens did implicitly, an issue in every sense of the word.

Dickens famously called *David Copperfield* his favourite child, and *David Copperfield* presents the *issue* – 'issue' in the sense of both *produced offspring* and *central point of interest* – of child-wives. That issue is a scriptural issue. When David's immature, feckless bride Dora is unable to cope, she asks David to call her, think her, and let her *be* a 'child-wife' (543; ch. 44). When he acquiesces, the successful production of books becomes possible for him. The imaginative concept of 'child-wife' reverberates crucially in Dickens. His fiction is often moving to fuse girl and wife into child-wife, but sometimes that means that the wife is like a child in demeanour, sometimes it means that she is like a wife-mother to her child-like mate. *David Copperfield* abounds in child-wives of one kind or another – principally, David's mother, Dora, Little Em'ly, Agnes Wickfield and Annie Strong – but so does the rest of Dickens's fiction, as Little Nell, Florence Dombey, Esther Summerson and Little Dorrit, among others, attest.[5] The strange term and figure suggest desires for secure family structure, for a wedding of generations in peace and domestic harmony, for a happy and lasting childhood to counteract the traumas and defeats of early years, for male patriarchal authority unbounded by the limits of age, and for regressive cosiness and safety. They represent longings for a kind of antidote to the threat of passing time and mortality through the psychological permanence of childhood's experience, impressions and memories; they suggest too a wish for liberation from the drives and hurtful obsessions of active adult libido. They also point to the special incestuous bias of Victorian ideology and literature, a bias towards loving and adoring the family, family members and family values, but repressing sexuality for the sake of civilisation and social morality. The word 'child-wife', however, is a disturbing term, carrying complex and contradictory meanings The 'child' drains the 'wife' of its mature sexual connotation and infantilises the marital relationship, but 'wife' casts a sexual potential and a threat about the life of a child. The compound can stand as a synecdoche for that split Victorian consciousness that sought to diminish and hide the wild force of human sexuality even while finding it pervasive, looming, and often terrible.

How specifically do *Lot* and its scriptural consequences find issue in *David Copperfield*? The main traces lie in the very fact and existence of the novel's child-wives, in their sisterly scheming to serve the interests of the male hero and preserve his creative, literary seed for the future. The child-wives Dora, Agnes and Emily all conspire together, both literally and figuratively, for the good of David and his writing. These child-wives 'mother' David Copperfield's fiction, as the muse of the child-wife mothers Charles Dickens's favourite child, *David Copperfield*.

Joyce picks up on the disingenuousness of desire in the term 'child-wife' and in child-wife Dora's baby-talk name for David, 'Doady', an unconscious pun in which we might hear eerie connotations of 'Daddy' and 'daughter', a good deal of 'doting', and tabooed desire. Certainly the author of *Ulysses* did. He presumably didn't know that Dickens, according to most scholars, cast off his old wife in order to take up with a mistress, Ellen Ternan, young enough to be his daughter, but the coiner of 'Doveyed Covetfilles' wouldn't have been surprised. When Dickens, enamoured of younger women, looked at his wife, gone to fat and exhausted from ten births and years and years of near-constant pregnancy, he might well have thought of her as a Lot's-wife *'old cupiosity shape'* and listened for a tolling little (k) Nell to wring out the old so he could get the new one he wanted – in just the manner of the eponymous sleeping hero HCE, at the end of *Finnegans Wake*.

In *Ulysses* Joyce sets the middle-ageing, compromising, mind-wandering Jew, Leopold Bloom, thinking idly one morning of a Zionist project to cultivate fruit in a new-blooming Palestine:

> A cloud began to cover the sun slowly, wholly. Grey. Far.
> No, not like that. A barren land, bare waste. Vulcanic lake, the dead sea: . . . sunk deep in the earth. . . . Brimstone they called it raining down: the cities of the plain: Sodom, Gomorrah, Edom. All dead names. A dead sea in a dead land, grey and old. Old now. It bore the oldest, the first race. . . . It lay there now. Now it could bear no more. Dead: an old woman's; the grey sunken cunt of the world.
> Desolation.
> Grey horror seared his flesh. . . . Cold oils slid along his veins, chilling his blood; age crusting him with a salt cloak. Well, I am here now. . . .
> Yes, yes.
> Quick warm sunlight came running from Berkeley road, swiftly, in slim sandals, along the brightening footpath. Runs, she runs to meet me, a girl with gold hair on the wind.
>
> (*Ulysses*, 4: 218–30 [p. 50])

Through Bloom, Joyce is showing how and why, in the midst of mundane life, the sensual imagination can give form to a *Lot* complex. If we set that passage next to the parody of Dickensian sentimentality, Dickensian philo-progenitiveness (the names of some of the children here and their large number correspond to Dickens's own family), and *David Copperfield* in *Ulysses'* 'Oxen of the Sun' chapter, the Purefoy childbirth episode, which consciously lampoons the child-wives Dora and Agnes, we can see Joyce seizing on the name 'Doady' and beginning to explore the complex comic, psychological, social and scriptural possibilities that would later issue in 'Doveyed Covetfilles' and the final pages of *Finnegans Wake* (the fullest and most significant appearance of the Lot complex in modern art):

> Reverently look at her as she reclines there with the motherlight in her eyes, that longing hunger for baby fingers (a pretty sight it is to see), in the first bloom of her new motherhood, breathing a silent prayer of

thanksgiving to One above, the Universal Husband. And as her loving eyes behold her babe she wishes only one blessing more, to have her dear Doady there with her to share her joy, to lay in his arms that mite of god's clay, the fruit of their lawful embraces. He is older now (you and I may whisper it) and a trifle stooped in the shoulders . . . . O Doady, loved one of old, faithful lifemate now, it may never be again, that faroff time of the roses! With the old shake of her pretty head she recalls those days. God how beautiful now across the mist of years! But their children are grouped in her imagination about the bedside, hers and his, Charley, Mary, Alice, Frederick Albert (if he had lived), Mamy, Budgy (Victoria Frances), Tom, Violet Constance Louisa, darling little Bobsy . . . . And Doady, knock the ashes from your pipe, the seasoned briar you still fancy, when the curfew rings for you (may it be the distant day) and dout the light whereby you read in the Sacred Book for the oil too has run low and so with a tranquil heart to bed, to rest.

(Ulysses, 14.1315–41)

We can infer that Joyce, looking at that 'seasoned briar' with its 'ashes' (the ashes of Sodom?), finds 'an old cupiosity shape'. Immediately after the Dickens pastiche, there follows a Newmanesque patch of prose that connects Doady to the Biblical David and to the repressed wine-soaked, sottish, Lottish history of incestuous regeneration and desire that underlies the sacred play and psalms of David (timbrel and harp) and that haunts the dreams and texts of humanity.

There are sins or (let us call them as the world calls them) evil memories which are hidden away by man in the darkest places of the heart but they abide there and wait. He may suffer their memory to grow dim, let them be as though they had not been and all but persuade himself that they were not or at least were otherwise. Yet a chance word will call them forth suddenly and they will rise up to confront him in the most various circumstances, a vision or a dream, or while timbrel and harp soothe his senses or amid the cool silver tranquillity of the evening or at the feast, at midnight, when he is now filled with wine.

(Ulysses, 14.1344–52)

If we now return to the *Wake*'s Dickens passage and begin to interpret just a few of the countless meanings it can suggest, we can see how and why Joyce imagined Dickens *entitled* to show Lots of the past living in the present. The language of punmanship here is filled with Biblical references, Dickens references, insistent references to sexual anatomy and sexual activity – naughty bits – and typical Joycean textual and personal self-references, all of which flow together:

'Diobell!': That word includes both 'Bible' and 'devil' and connotes moral ambivalence; and, since 'dickens' means 'devil' in slang, the exclamation brings together both Dickens and Scripture in Joyce. 'Diobell' could signal a devilish Little (K)Nell who reveals the old cupiosity shape in the old curiosity shop of the world. 'Diobell' also connotes split, or doubled belles – the prurient preacher is addressing two belles, like Lot's daughters, like Dickens's serial child-wives, Dora and Agnes, or like the schizoid, split daughter figure and sexpot archetype of the *Wake*, Isobel twinned, and like the cracked Lucia Joyce.

'never lay bare your breast secret (dickette's place!) to joy a Jonas': The exclamation 'dickette's place', says that *Dickens* is just the *ticket* in getting at Joyce's point that libido throbs and shows forth in the utterances of priests, religions and public piety, that admonitions to cover up actually bring exposure by drawing attention and desire compulsively onto what is being tabooed – here rigid Victorian dress actually focuses on the *place* where (to put a fine point on it) the dick goes – that, in other words, like murder, bare breasts, *dicks*, a phallic Dickens will out. 'Jonas', Latin for Jonah, connects the passage to the Bible, but Jonas also refers to Jonas Chuzzlewit, in *Martin Chuzzlewit*, a Dickens novel Joyce knew. In it two hypocritically righteous Pecksniff sisters, Mercy and Charity, compete for Jonas's favours and even seem to grapple over him as he gropes with them in a coach, or car ride. 'Joy' and Dolphin's Barncar connect the passage to Joyce, to Ireland and to *Ulysses*, in which, for example, Lenehan remembers fondling Molly Bloom's breast in a car ride.

'your meetual fan, Doveyed Covetfilles, comepulsing paynattention spasms between the averthisement for Ulikah's wine and a pair of pulldoors of the old cupiosity shape'. This inexhaustibly suggestive prose featuring the play of Dickens's titles radiantly, if ridiculously, inscribes the historical, psychological, anatomical, linguistic and symbolic continuum between the Bible and the *Wake*, the old world and the new. In context, the puns on *Our Mutual Friend*, *David Copperfield* and *The Old Curiosity Shop* allude to the grand farce of creation, with all its pain, its dishonesty, its foolish, horrible, sweet, necessary and unwholesome sexuality and messy sublimation; and they allude also to these mutual friends and fans of erotic *filles*: David Copperfield, averting as best he can *Uriah* Heep's plot to destroy Agnes's father by plying him with wine and (like Charles Dickens) composing his serial novels in monthly spasms, so to speak, with the help of his serial child-wives; King David, later the penitential psalm-composer, who coveted and – I might add – *covered* huge numbers of young women, including the girl Abishag in his old age and, in his virility, Bathsheba, whose husband Uriah, after he gave him meat and wine, David sent to slaughter; Lot, regretful disaster survivor, who, after his daughters plied him with the wine he liked, shamefully spasmed out his regenerative seed in the pair of them; David's son, King Solomon, who had crowds of women and whose Song of Songs, referring to dove's eyes, celebrates incomparably love, sex and fertile cupiosity; Leopold Bloom, the Jew, advertisement canvasser and cuckold in *Ulysses*, whose wine-sipping releases erotic memories and who masturbates while gazing at a young woman's cupiosity shape in a pair of drawers; Bloom's sex-addled, grandfather Virag, who speaks in spasms of smutty ejaculations; James Joyce, composing *Finnegans Wake*, that collection of spasmodic attention-demanding, painful puns, amidst the notoriety of *Ulysses*, his alcoholic habits and the pulls and pressures of a schizoid daughter and an ageing mate; and last but not least, a personified phallus spouting off. This word play reveals the unfolding and persistence of the Lot complex. It illuminates Dickens anew, and it renders the longing of the Joycean speaker, the desire of the Joycean text, and the concern, conflict and unconscious of the Joycean father. It also gets at the making of texts and the phallic writing in the name of desire that describes the Scriptural text of Lot, of the Bible, of *David Copperfield* and of Joyce. Having a Dickens of a time with *Finnegans Wake* means thinking about how the idea of God, the Father, siring his divine son on a virgin daughter, how Dickens's 'Doady' and 'child-wife' inspiring David Copperfield to write, and how words such as these from the last two pages of the *Wake*, 'Yes, you're changing, sonhusband, and you're turning, I can feel you, for a daughterwife', 'Carry me along Taddy like you done through the toyfair', and 'A gull. Gulls. Far calls. Coming, far!'[6] bear on the evolving history of gender and subject of regeneration – Lots to keep in mind.

Notes

1. By the term 'complex', I mean a convergence and drastic condensation in human psychology of personal and social history, experiences, images, drives, wants and impulses which can be seen both to form and represent an integrated pattern. A 'complex', as I use and define the term, is constituted out of the interaction between members of different generations and the interpersonal relationships of childhood history and its making. As an organised and organising group of ideas, memories and fantasies of great affective force that are both conscious and

unconscious, a complex serves to structure all levels of the psyche – emotions, attitudes and adaptive behaviour.

2. For a fuller treatment of this subject, see my article, Robert M. Polhemus, 'The Lot Complex, Joyce, and the End of *Finnegans Wake*', *The Recorder: The Journal of the American Irish Historical Society*, vol. 7, no. 2 (Fall 1994) 58–77.

3. See Origen, *Homilies on Genesis and Exodus*, trans. R. E. Heine (Washington DC: The Catholic University of America Press, 1982) 120: 'But I know that some, so far as the story pertains to allegory, have referred to the person of the Lord and his daughters to the Two Testaments. But I do not know if anyone freely accepts these views who know what the Scriptures says about the Ammonites and Moabites who descend from Lot's race: (Dt. 23:3; Ex. 34:7). . . . We pass no judgment on those who have been able to perceive something more sacred from this text'.

4. I have suggested that *The Old Curiosity Shop* is the Victorian moral and aesthetic equivalent of a literary Gothic cathedral and that the figure of the child Little Nell, surrounded by a strange, complex and menacing eroticism, became a holy literary Virgin for a secularising Protestant culture that concentrated, as did the traditional Virgin of Roman Catholicism, religious feeling and faith in nurturing idealism – *Notre Jeune Fille* instead of *Notre Dame*, but sacred none the less. Nell leaves her home when sex and the moral corruption loose in the world threaten to violate and destroy her virtue. Greed and male sexual desire menace her childhood, her virginity and immaculate goodness, and she must flee into homeless wandering until she finds, in what Dickens presents as a holy, sacrificial apotheosis, her final home in the church under whose stones she is buried and of which she becomes a part. From her issues a faith that the symbolic power of her sacralised purity inspires in others, particularly sinful older men such as her weak grandfather with whom she roams around England and Dick Swiveller, who takes a poor servant-child as his ward, educates her and then in the end marries her. Nell, with her youthful promise of redemption and fresh hope for the world and the future, is brought in to revive the spiritual potency of the old, dying, patriarchal faith, impotent to command in the new world the same kind of belief and authority it once had. She seems to be conceived of as a child-bride of a failing God, a little virgin who shall lead, regenerate and redeem. Dickens's fiction intends to renew and transform supernatural faith and scriptural moral authority through faith in the child. Nell, the girl-child, preserving the seed of patriarchal morality and virtue into a new era, represents a form of the Lot complex, and Joyce seizes on 'the old cupiosity shape' to make clear the sexual sublimations of Dickens and the Victorian age.

5. Born, no doubt, out of his ambivalence and resentment towards women he had loved but deemed childish and irresponsible (Slater), such as his mother, his early sweetheart Maria Beadnell, and his wife Catherine, but also out of his gratitude for the help, love and

sweet mothering, sistering and fecund inspiration to create he got from girl-child-wife figures such as his sister Fanny, his sisters-in-law Mary and Georgina Hogarth, his own child Kate, and his putative mistress Ellen Ternan, young enough to be his daughter, his rendering of child-wives nevertheless has broad cultural significance beyond the personal.

6. 'Gulls' are 'girls' as well as 'birds' and 'Far' is the Danish word for Father.

24

Modernist Readings Mediated: Dickens and the New Worlds of Later Generations[1]

Roger D. Sell

Any grouping of human beings has its own world: a certain range of knowledge and certain modes of evaluation. Such a worldview is subject to constant modification as time rolls on. Nor can its association with the particular grouping prevent it from being adopted, to a greater or a lesser extent, by members of some other grouping. On the contrary, information, tastes, habits, modes of feeling and judgement can be transmitted from one sociocultural grouping to another, and individuals can in any case have allegiances to more than one grouping, so that they themselves are mobile between different worldviews accordingly. Dickens, though he is often described as the darling of the middle class, was not simply that, as is no less frequently recognised. Thanks to his own life-experience and his powers of empathetic imagination and mimicry, Dickens could impersonate a wide range of culturally specific humanity, and in his own lifetime he was read by readers who were already reading him in several different ways. From the start, the Dickens phenomenon involved a plurality of worlds. There was always a likelihood that his own world or worlds would not be quite the same as those of many of his readers, a likelihood which has only increased as his texts have lasted on through time.

So what did Dickens do about it? Consciously or unconsciously, he had to make a guess at the mind-set readers would bring to bear on their reading. And why was this so important? It was because, as linguists in the tradition of de Saussure point out, the relation between the two halves of a sign, the signifier and the signified, is arbitrary. The words of a language achieve nothing at all until some particular person at some particular time and place has processed and contextualised them. Today the branch of linguistics known as pragmatics confirms what traditional philologians and historical critics have said all along: that knowledge of the vocabulary and grammar used is only one of the mental reserves brought into play by readers. Readers assume that a literary text originates from somebody who wrote it in order to achieve some impact, and they try to contextualise it in such a way as to let something like that impact occur. But their success in this can hardly be total, not least because their knowledge of the state of the language used, and of much else as well, will be different from the writer's own knowledge. And even if recontextualisation were not a problem, readers' total act of understanding will always be their own, since they also bring to it types of knowledge and systems of value which the writer, especially a writer belonging to a different period or culture, could not have envisaged. Readers representing different worlds inevitably respond in different ways.

True, there are aspects of comprehension which will not much change over time, particular lines of interpretation, particular connections, particular ways of filling in gaps, to which readers of Dickens have always resorted, and always will resort in their efforts to make sense of him. Let me repeat, too, that readers accept the novels as coming from Dickens and try as best they can to recontextualize them in the way they imagine he would have expected. So much so, that they have been very interested in finding out about Dickens as a person. Biography is probably the most widely read branch of Dickens scholarship, and roughly speaking there has been one new life of Dickens for every new decade. Some of the other popular or semi-popular discussion of sociocultural minutiae which has grown up around Dickens has been channelled through *The Dickensian: A Magazine for Dickens Lovers*, published by the Dickens Fellowship since 1905. Meanwhile much other Dickens scholarship has seen the need to recreate, not so much Dickens's life and Victorian social history, as the Victorian thought-world. Harry Stone has highlighted fairytale elements in Dickens's novels,[2] and Jerome Meckier the intertextualities with the novels of Dickens's contemporaries.[3] It is one of the most important functions of Dickens scholarship to help present-day readers recreate the Victorian life-world and thought-world in order to be able to contextualise Dickens's texts in as Dickensian a way as possible.

Here, though, I am not offering a justification for narrow-minded historical purism. Even if readers' attempts to repeat Dickens's own contextualisation of his language could be successful, their different worlds also entail different ways of thinking, feeling and judging. Dickens continues to be interesting and central to our cultures, not only because of what he himself put into his texts, so to speak, but also because readers are continuing to read him according to their own lights, in ways that are typical of their own epoch. Reading is interpersonal between different individualities and is fundamentally dialogic. Dickens was himself hoping for a response. And readers can in any case not deny him a response that is their own.

New readers succeed new readers, new world succeeds new world. This has already happened several times in the reception history of Dickens, and the ways of reading of each succeeding new world never entirely die out but contribute to an ever-growing repertoire of interpretative possibilities, which can always be reactivated within some still later new readerly world. A new generation of readers will disagree with the previous generation, but often by going one stage further back to the generation before the previous generation. For the newcomer to Dickens, many interpretative options are already available, even if in the mental environment where the new reader is reading some particular option for the moment seems more dominant than others.

Psychologically speaking, different reading options are not mutually exclusive. Readers are far more flexible and imaginative than our educational institutions and the tradition of literary criticism have tended to suggest. All too often academic critics have felt obliged to be coherently monoideaistic. But not only is the process of real reading far richer and far more tentative than much published criticism. If one human being has been able to come up with a particular interpretation, then any other human being can empathetically try it on for size, without necessarily cancelling out interpretations of a completely different colour. One of the more beneficial aspects of our postmodern condition, to my mind, is that people are now altogether less ready to confer legitimacy on some single grouping's world, not only because the plurality of worlds has become so pressingly obvious, but because there is a new sense of the risk of missing out on something that might be humanly valuable. If Dickens critics and other literary critics are to keep pace with this and actually do something useful, they need to empathise with many different worlds and mediate between them – which is not the same thing as never forming an opinion of one's own. As things stand in many university departments of English at the moment, there are signs of postmodern diversity degenerating into strife. Scholars are engaged in what Gerald Graff has described as culture wars,[4] seeing themselves as the champions of just some single constituency of readers and its canon, adopting a stance of embattled sectarianism which can only aggravate the tensions which are so dangerously operative in society as a whole. But most ordinary people, including even such scholars in their less professional moments, know that the only things that really matter are peace, mutual respect, and fairness. And in ordinary reading, people are perhaps freest of all to experiment in different life- and thought-worlds.

By way of illustration, let me briefly sketch moves towards a mediation of two modernist reading habits, both of which would have come as something of a surprise to Dickens himself. In both cases I think we can trace a three-stage historical process. To begin with, there was an aspect of Dickens's texts which, though acceptable enough to many of his contemporaries, came to seem less satisfactory in the early twentieth century. This stage we can call the stage of modernist dissatisfaction. Next came the stage of modernist rehabilitation: new modernist reading habits established themselves which seemed to redeem Dickens's deficiencies as earlier perceived. Thirdly, these modernist reading habits themselves begin to come under the scrutiny of our own generation, which is more prepared to mediate between different worlds, and as a result makes a partial return to far earlier evaluations. This third stage we can call the stage of positive mediation: the stage at which evaluation is more fully informed by a flexible and even-handed attempt to empathise with differing worldviews.

One aspect of modernist dissatisfaction with Dickens's novels had to do with their structure. They came to seem too obviously constrained by the realities of serial publication, with too many loose ends, too many inconsistencies, too much random detail of every possible kind and too little unifying art. Modernist rehabilitation was here a matter of finding singleness of purpose and aesthetic design, and in this connection much attention was paid to chains of imagery and symbols. This was the reading offered by New Critical formalism, which saw Dickens's novels as symbolist aesthetic heterocosms. As late as 1963 William Axton was still writing eloquently in this mode, when he argued that the imagery of *Dombey and Son* gives it an all-embracing unity of tone.[5] In the phase of positive mediation, we will want to qualify the more extreme versions of modernist formalism by insisting on the historicity of a novel such as *Dombey and Son*, for instance in terms suggested by Bakhtin's account of heteroglossia and novelising dialogism. For us now, living as we do amidst highly volatile sociocultural processes of both assimilation and fragmentation, the field of social energies containing, say, the Toodles, Blimber, Dombey, Bagstock, Cousin Felix and Edith can hardly be refined into a static verbal icon.[6] Yet we can still grant that the New Critical approach is suggestive, and not least for the novels from *Dombey and Son* onwards, which Dickens was demonstrably trying to shape more deliberately than the earlier ones. Bakhtinian criticism is in any case no more comprehensive than any other kind of criticism, and when we weigh it against New Criticism we can find ourselves asking how to account for our sense that something in Dickens nevertheless remains beautiful. Personally, I have begun to wonder whether we could conceive of a beauty, not in the fundamentally Kantian sense of an aesthetic *tertium quid* quite distinct from the realms of reality and ethics, but as inseparable from history: a beauty from history.[7]

A second aspect of modernist dissatisfaction with Dickens fastened on his notions of gentlemanliness, which were accused of bourgeois hypocrisy. Here modernist rehabilitation took its cue from critics such as Edmund Wilson and Lionel Trilling, who tended to see human life and human nature in a pretty dim light, and great literature as fundamentally disturbing. Psychoanalytical readings of Dickens discovered psychomasochistic tensions and strongly antisocial impulses beneath genteel surfaces. As a result, Dickens came to seem authentically human in the unpleasant modernist sense. As late as 1983 I myself was seeing the most sinister and unpleasant sides of Murdstone, Rosa Dartle, Steerforth and Uriah as projections of David's own shadow self.[8] Having now, I hope, arrived at the stage of positive mediation, I still find the modernist reading very forceful, yet it coexists in my mind with a revalorisation of certain Victorian habits of thought, and a sense that the modernist prioritisation of Thanatos over Eros was in fact a dangerous distortion of human nature itself. Dickens can actually give us a new perspective on modernism, and on ourselves, who are modernism's heirs. If the 'official' Victorian persona tended to repress raw despotism, lust, greed, passion of every kind, what are we to think of an age which, understanding or misunderstanding Freud, Marx, Adler or Jung, sees such disturbing traits as quintessential and all-powerful? It is as if the Victorian shadow has become the twentieth-century persona, so that Murdstone reminds us of our own formation by the central and explicit presuppositions of our culture. By the same token, one reason why David for a time could seem so boring, dead and distant is perhaps that people *wanted* him to be that way. Was it not the possibility of Victorian virtues that the modernists relegated most firmly to the shadow? In the early twentieth century it was not difficult to find the Victorians' official view of humanity rather sanguine. Yet as the heirs of modernism, we are no closer to peace and wisdom even today. Not because the daemons are still struggling to get out. But because they got out long ago, and have created havoc ever since. Not because we have beautiful visions, like David's, which may be false. But because our visions are few and far between. There is, I think, a real chance that we shall soon be finding David Copperfield admirable. Though he remains just as evil as anybody else, his sincerity of purpose is becoming harder to dispute. His moments of generosity and tact, of spontaneous trusting loyalty, could make him, after all these years again, a not unlovable human being. And – when the last modernist taboo has finally given way – how lovable that dangerous but noble man who could create him!

The human mind can adapt to any culture, so that the most active minds of all will seem to echo the past and prophecy the future. But even the most flexible of minds has a local and temporal habitation, which really is different from the past and the future, and which actually suggests criteria by which the past and the future can be judged. On the one hand, everything a modernist reading tells us about Dickens can retain its value, rehabilitating areas of his text we might otherwise find Victorian in an unattractive way. On the other hand, if Dickens was always already a modernist, he is always still Victorian. A mediating critic cannot entertain the modernist readings without also allowing houseroom, as it were, to Dickens's own reading of modernism. Dickens can bring us some way back from aestheticism towards the real world. He can also rekindle the human desire for decency, probity, justice, pleasure.

Our minds really can work in several different ways at once. Denizens of one world, we can nevertheless enter different worlds. Readings from within different worlds still partly work, can always be recycled, and are in endless dialogue with each other. No single world can monopolise truth and wisdom.

Notes

1. The literary-theoretical framework underlying this chapter is more explicitly developed in my forthcoming *Towards a Mediating Criticism: Literary Pragmatics Humanized*. I am currently working on two further volumes, in which mediating criticism is exemplified: *Beauties from History: Literary Criticism as Mediation* and *The Pleasures and Pains of Literature: the Modernist Emphasis Mediated*. The first of these will contain a chapter on *Dombey and Son*; the second, a chapter on *David Copperfield*.
2. Harry Stone, *Dickens and the Invisible World: Fairy Tales, Fantasy and Novel-Making* (Bloomington: Indiana University Press, 1979).
3. Jerome Meckier, *Hidden Rivalries in Victorian Fiction: Dickens, Realism, and Revaluation* (Lexington: University Press of Kentucky, 1987).
4. Gerald Graff, *Beyond the Culture Wars: How Teaching the Conflicts Can Revitalize American Education* (New York: Norton, 1992).
5. William Axton, 'Tonal Unity in *Dombey and Son*', *PMLA* 78 (1963) 341–8.
6. See Roger D. Sell, 'Dickens and the New Historicism: the Polyvocal Audience and Discourse of *Dombey and Son*', in Jeremy Hawthorne, ed., *The Nineteenth-Century British Novel*, (London: Edward Arnold, 1986) 63–79.
7. There is a chapter on this idea in *The Human Faces of Literature*. Its prime exhibits are Henry Vaughan, Dickens and Frost.
8. Roger D. Sell, 'Projection Characters in *David Copperfield*', *Studia Neophilologica* 55 (1983) 19–30.

Index

Index